BY ED PARK

PERSONAL DAYS
SAME BED DIFFERENT DREAMS

SAME BED DIFFERENT DREAMS

SAME BED DIFFERENT DREAMS

A NOVEL

ED PARK

RANDOM HOUSE
NEW YORK

AME BED DIFFERENT DR
ED DIFFERENT DREAMS
IFFERENT DREAMS SAM
REAMS SAME BED DIFF
AME BED DIFFERENT DR
ED DIFFERENT DREAMS
IFFERENT DREAMS SAM
REAMS SAME BED DIFF
AME BED DIFFERENT DR
ED DIFFERENT DREAMS
IFFERENT DREAMS SAM
AME BED DIFFERENT DR
ED DIFFERENT DREAMS
IFFERENT DREAMS SAM
REAMS SAME BED DIFF
AME BED DIFFERENT DR
ED DIFFERENT DREAMS
IFFERENT DREAMS SAM

SAME
BED
DIFFERENT
DREAMS

A NOVEL

ED PARK

RANDOM HOUSE
NEW YORK

SAME BED DIFFERENT DREAMS

SAME BED DIFFERENT DREAMS SAME BED DIFFERENT DREAMS SAME BED DIFFERENT DREAMS

A NOVEL

ED PARK

RANDOM HOUSE
NEW YORK

Published in the United States by Random House, an imprint and division of Penguin Random House LLC, New York.

RANDOM HOUSE and the HOUSE colophon are registered trademarks of Penguin Random House LLC.

Photography credits can be found on page 523.

Library of Congress Cataloging-in-Publication Data
Names: Park, Ed, 1970– author.
Title: Same bed different dreams: a novel in three novels / Ed Park.
Description: First Edition. | New York: Random House, 2023
Identifiers: LCCN 2023001469 (print) |
LCCN 2023001470 (ebook) | ISBN 9780812998979 (Hardback) |
ISBN 9780812988314 (Ebook)
Subjects: LCGFT: Novels.
Classification: LCC PS3616.A7432 S36 2023 (print) |
LCC PS3616.A7432
(ebook) | DDC 813/.6—dc23/eng/20230203
LC record available at https://lccn.loc.gov/2023001469

PRINTED IN THE UNITED STATES OF AMERICA ON ACID-FREE PAPER

randomhousebooks.com

9 8 7 6 5 4 3

Book design by Elizabeth Rendfleisch

FOR MY WIFE FOR MY SONS
FOR MY PARENTS FOR MY SISTER

I was dreaming when I wrote this
Forgive me if it goes astray
—PRINCE

Contents

2333: The Scholars (2016)

WHAT IS HISTORY?

That is the question, that is the job. Might a deeper understanding of history benefit the company, or is it to be avoided at all costs? Teams are told to blue-sky it, whiteboard pros and cons. When you break the word down, what does it tell you? The Latin, from the Greek.

Three telegenic academics discuss it at an all-hands. The first speaker, an American wunderkind, sports a headset with a purple-foamed mic that resembles a levitating gumdrop on the jumbotron. "*History,*" she intones as she paces, "from the same Indo-European root that gave us *wit.*" She mimes tearing out and crumpling her notes, to signal *Enough with the old ways.* In the last decade, she says, history has toppled from the king of disciplines to a numbing data set: a litany of trackable moments, the realm of machines.

She stands at the lip of the stage. Everything you buy, view, read, and believe gets recorded. Where you drive, how you sleep. Lusts and peccadilloes. Mental lapses, steps climbed. Debits and credits, search terms and activity logs. Only by going off the grid can one enter true history. "Abolish every clock," she concludes. "Go back to Day Zero."

A concerned murmur. Is this a dig at the company and its voracious tab keeping? Or will this radical reset somehow help them do their job? The workers clap politely.

"Day Zero?" comes a coy query, from the second historian. "Hmm."

He's her former adviser. White hair, black eyebrows, with a mustache that splits the difference. Remaining seated, he offers a rambling anecdote by way of rebuttal. Early in his career, while engrossed in some eighteenth-century grain ledgers, he brooded over the meaning of history. One afternoon, sharpening a pencil, he received the answer, a metaphor that perfectly captured his calling. He wrote it down and continued his work amid those humble documents.

Four years passed, as he labored on the monograph he was sure would secure his reputation. Nearly finished, he prepared the coup de grâce: his shattering insight into the *true* nature of history. Now, alas, the full formula eluded him. After days of searching, he located the slip of paper with the aperçu at the bottom of his satchel. To his horror, a summer storm had reduced it to a blank white scrap. The more he tried recalling the words, the less sure he was about anything.

The crowd takes it all down. A cough booms through the speakers.

"My old friend asserts we should avoid metaphor when it comes to history," sniffs the third panelist, a cheeky maverick of indecipherable ethnicity, gender, and height. "Yet the nostalgic scene he presents is itself a new metaphor, as apt and useless as all others, by his own definition. What is history, you ask? A message from a genius, ruined by the rain."

For two hours, the scholars spar, drawing on video games, mirror neurons, some minor works of Poe. They speak to be quoted, and the audience sits rapt. For the most part. During the debate, someone secretly records a colleague pinching his own thighs, struggling to keep his eyes open—to no avail. Soon the man is snoring. Onstage, the first scholar booms, "What is history?" The subject wakes with a start, slurps back saliva.

The video gets forwarded, bcc'd, uploaded, liked. The self-pincher's face is only half visible, but the gist is clear. As the clip makes the rounds, viewers add captions, crude animations. It becomes a sort of folk tale, bristling with embellishment. It speaks to current events, pop culture, the environment. Versions leak outside the organization: jumping borders and slipping into foreign tongues. Spin-offs exist that

are not safe for work. This fading, drooling figure in the crowd is part of history, too, even if the official transcript omits the incident.

What is history?

At least for now, it's a three-way standoff, a memory of rain, a cure for insomnia. These possibilities are duly entered into the system.

THE SINS AUGUST THE JURY

FROM A DISTANCE, THE BLACK SMOKING station on the white pavement in front of the Admiral Yi resembled a chess piece, whether bishop or knight, I couldn't decide. The matter seemed crucial as I approached. My daughter, Story, would have an opinion, but of course she wasn't with me. She was seven, and chess figured prominently in her life. During one game, in the midst of crushing my kingside defenses, she said that the bishop was worth three points, same as a knight. (Then she put me in check.) The fact surprised me. I had reckoned bishops on par with rooks, knights a step below. Then again, the bishops were yoked to their starting colors, as though you were playing checkers. Perhaps the smoking station was just a pawn after all.

Dusk hung like velvet over West Thirty-second Street, what the sign called Korea Way, though I have never heard anyone use that name. I was in the city, on a weeknight no less, a rare event for me. My family and job were upstate in Dogskill, an hour and change via Metro-North. Not so very far; still, I didn't like visiting Manhattan. It made me miss everything too much.

My appearance was a solid for Tanner Slow: old college roommate, dispenser of numerous good deeds on my behalf, and main link to the life I'd led years ago. Tanner had worn many hats over the years. He'd been a music journalist, fired for not liking music, and briefly a literary agent—he sold my first and only book, a story collection that I couldn't bear to look at anymore. He once ran a Tucson charity that gave bikes to the homeless, and even worked at GLOAT in the aughts, hiring me during his brief tenure. But after his father the vitamin king died and left him a zillion dollars, Tanner set up

the Slow Press, devoted to his three idiosyncratic passions: political graphic novels done with woodcuts, niche cookbooks, and neglected literature in translation. Last season he'd released a revisionist account of the Haymarket Riot, a set of Malaysian curry recipes that could be done using only a rice cooker, and a collection of nature essays by "Uganda's E. B. White."

Tonight was simple. Tonight I'd meet Tanner Slow's newest author, Cho Eujin, once the enfant terrible of South Korean letters. The Slow Press had signed on to bring out his oeuvre in America, and he would be a visiting lecturer at Rue University Extension Campus that fall. Tanner swore I'd like him. I couldn't find a clear picture of Cho online, but in my mind he resembled my father, gone now over thirty years. Also slated to appear was the reclusive artist Mercy Pang, another camera avoider. My wife, Nora, was pretty sure she'd babysat for her back in the '90s, and wanted me to take a picture so she could check.

Despite the warmth of the day, I planned to lay into a tasty bowl of *seolleongtang* or *kalguksu,* down a few OBs, and say good night to one and all in my bad Korean. I'd make sure not to get roped into a karaoke situation. I was already rehearsing my exit line, the one about having to catch the train back home out of Grand Central.

Tonight would have been a rare treat—a pleasant evening with one of my oldest friends and his latest discovery—if not for all the Asian American literati who threatened to show up as well. Poets and editors and folks associated with Rue University's Wildword program. I'd mix up people's names. I'd have nothing to say to them. I was no longer in the game.

They viewed me as a traitor. My employer, GLOAT, was so vast that it almost lost definition—they all used at least a few of its many features—but in their eyes, I'd abandoned the life of the mind to service the Almighty Algorithm.

It was true that I didn't write anymore. For a while, I kept story notes, and one summer even wrestled a novel partway out of my skull. It had proved too unwieldy, even dangerous: a hydra that spoke in tongues. I mapped out the plot on yard-high Post-its, slapped them on the walls while I wrote. Nora likened it to the handiwork of a cop trying to outguess a serial killer, or maybe the other way around.

I didn't write anymore. My current fictioneering was limited to bedtime tales spun out for my daughter as a sleeping aid. They involved UFOs, her chief interest besides chess. I was good at describing alien spacecrafts zipping through the clouds and the capture of curious Earthlings with a tractor beam. Once the quarry got on board, though, I went into numbing detail about the layout of the control room, lulling Story to dreamland.

I didn't write anymore. My last jab at literary journalism had been years ago, for the late lamented *Lament,* which had since gone from elegant bimonthly to wisp of a quarterly to dysfunctional website, before disappearing completely. "Clean Sheets" was a jeu d'esprit about the titles I'd salvaged, to Nora's dismay, from the basement laundry rooms of apartments where we used to live. The essay posited that these castoff libraries—self-help tomes, mouse-munched thrillers, hiking guides in foreign languages—told a building's secret history. It was my love letter to the city; right before it came out, we moved to Dogskill. When the issue arrived, I put it directly into the recycling bin. On Friday morning I wheeled the bin to the curb, where at 9:13 a truck with a robot arm held it aloft, turned it over to release the empty bottles and printed matter, then replaced it before driving off: the quintessential suburban port de bras.

I didn't write anymore. My book of short stories, *Pretenders,* had come out a lifetime ago, before I met Nora, who was not yet a nail salon mogul; before Story opened a new chapter in my life; back when I was still ready to take on the world. Now all I did was work at GLOAT. I was a Rung 10. Like other company veterans, I'd bounced around various projects, not all of them slam dunks. I learned to own my failures: a key tenet of GLOAT's corporate culture. After a while they started to seem like successes.

In my spare time, I lost at chess to Story, which made me proud, and walked our dog, Sprout, which calmed me down. I cleaned my inbox assiduously. Once a week I skimmed and deleted messages from GLOAT's Korean culture listserv that I couldn't escape. Even the company's touted spam filters failed. Every so often I'd wade into a debate. Hot topics included the impossible reunification of North and South Korea, whether Japan owed reparations for World War II, and the genius of *hangul,* the Korean alphabet. (Word that a remote Indonesian tribe had chosen *hangul* over Roman letters

as its mode of writing had recently sent the forum into ecstasy.) Sometimes I wondered what my parents would have said about such peninsular matters. Maybe my interest in the forum was a way of keeping them alive. In dreams, oddly, they spoke to me in Korean. They'd stuck to English while alive.

Up close the bishop was fuming. Where was the phantom smoker? Instinctively I scrabbled in my satchel for a loose cigarette. I barely smoked anymore, a pack a month. But even that was too much for Nora, who'd seen all the men in her family, down there in Argentina, and some of the women, most of them up in Canada now, succumb to diseases of the lung. I puffed outside, on the trail that wound behind Westgate, our development, and kept flasks of Scope like I was having an affair with the tobacco industry. Still Nora would tell me I smelled like death. I had to set a good example for Story.

A face in the window of the Admiral Yi put a stop to these thoughts: *my face*, looking uncertain, then relaxing into a hangdog grin. *Pas mal,* I thought. At least I'd lost some pounds, after taking on weight with Story's advent. The secret: a few extra cigarettes. Further inspection of my middle-aged visage gave me vertigo, the pavement turning to sand beneath my shoes. Blood rushed away from my head, and I felt ten thousand brain cells evaporate by the second. I used to faint a lot, waking to worried voices on a nurse's cot or a park bench or in a friend's car. Now on Korea Way I reached out to steady myself, touching the strange glass before me. It was of variable thickness, optics changing with the slightest shift of perspective. I looked dark, then pale as milk. Adding to the confusion, oddly shaped regions lit up with video streams of Korean news, music videos, dramas. These miniature people had gleaming white skin, tinted hair, chins so chiseled they could double as can openers. In a generation, the whole race would be carved to perfection. Was this a form of self-hatred, to think of them as an army of attractive robots? I missed the homelier Koreans of my youth. Which is to say, I missed my mom and dad.

The cigarette dwindled. Life was short. Our dog, Sprout, was sick with Dorchester syndrome. The vet said three months, tops. How would Story take it? How would I? Our ailing mutt was exhibiting all the symptoms: chasing his tail, walking backward, bumping into things. I got one of those fancy GLOAT collars, which tracked his vitals, reporting anomalies to the vet. Sprout developed the classic Dorchester symptom of "archiving," in which he eviscerated a book or magazine, then hid sections around the house or buried them in the backyard. The habit was distinct from the age-old practice of bone interment. The vet advised keeping our bedroom doors locked, our bottom shelves free of first editions.

Lately Sprout looked part beagle, part hairbrush. He wasn't especially adorable, or even what might be termed "fun," but he'd been with me forever—like Pretenders, he predated my time with Nora. I told him a lot. He was my four-footed pal, or at least my furry psychoanalyst. And he let me smoke without judgment. So what if he lunched on the printed word? Lately I wondered if my nicotine habit had made him ill. The vet said no, that Dorchester's was congenital. He had likely expressed symptoms for years, only I'd been too blind to notice. Still, every time Sprout licked my hand, I thought: This is my fault.

The high-tech window of the Admiral Yi held a scattering of video screens. On the biggest oblong, a row of airtight vixens shimmied. Their hair color drew from every slice of the spectrum except black. I was pretty sure it was D5, a K-pop outfit that Story followed, or else Reality, a rival group. The word "Ah!" kept blinking on various surfaces—a street sign, a lollipop, someone's pleathered butt—in English and hangul: 아! AH! (ah!) 아! In the lower-right corner, a variety-show host in blue-rimmed glasses chortled at his guests' outrageous statements. On yet another screenlet, a Korean soap unfolded, Doctor Loves a Doctor, which Nora and I had wolfed down earlier that year. I could even identify the scene: Joonie, the country's first female brain surgeon, was agonizing over whether to accept an offer at a more prestigious hospital, which would take her away from her secret crush on a manly nurse named K.T., who was actually from three years in the future, or something like that.

Amid these foreign illuminations was my real face, longer than I recalled, as though warped by a fun-house mirror. Distinguished, cerebral; a man of letters. For a moment I could picture myself in one of those tall black hats Korean men wore in the nineteenth century. Then my face coughed into a fist—but *I* was still smoking, cigarette between lips. I discerned a wash of stubble in my reflection; but *my* chin was freshly shaved. I watched in astonishment as the face turned away, dissolving into the depths of the Admiral Yi.

It was with considerable unease, then, that I opened the stout wooden door and followed that phantom inside.

THE ADMIRAL YI WAS two years old, but this was my first visit. In keeping with the name, a maritime theme ran through it, though its application was haphazard, anachronistic: a tiller here, skeins of netting there, and too many rubber crustaceans. I spotted a poster for the film version of *Moby Dick*, another for *Jason and the Argonauts.* The air was clammy by design, recessed misters spritzing. Everywhere I looked were portraits of the titular hero, next to scrolls of calligraphy that may or may not have related his deeds.

Admiral Yi was a legendary naval commander, the most famous figure in Korean history. He repelled a Japanese invasion back in the sixteenth century, using armored "turtle boats" called *kobukson*. They had enormous shell tops that protected the crew while they fired the cannons that lined the sides. The prows featured fearsome reptilian heads spouting smoke, baleful flames flickering in the eyes. The tale involved some heroic ratio, doubtless inflated, like thirty *kobukson* fending off an invading force of three hundred warships, the admiral using his intimate knowledge of tidal peculiarities to his advantage. It was enough to keep the Japanese at bay for a few more centuries.

The hostess greeted me in Korean.

"I'm with the Slow party," I replied, charmlessly steering our interaction into English. "I think there's a private room?"

"S . . . roe-uh?" She gave it three syllables.

"It's a large party under the name Tanner Slow. S-L-O-W."

I took a menu, which doubled as a pamphlet modestly titled *Admiral Yi: The Greatest Naval Genius in the World.*

"Ess . . . err . . . Oh, Mr. *Slow!*" She beamed, rattled off something in Korean that I didn't catch. I heard the word for "author," and for a second I thought she meant me. But of course she meant Tanner Slow's latest literary find: Cho Eujin, the so-called Scourge of Seoul. She took out a sleek Korean paperback and showed me his autograph, freshly affixed to the flyleaf.

"*Architect and Dictator*," she said, with touching precision. "I'm biggest fan."

As she led me back, I passed portholes cut in the walls: cunning video screens that showed turquoise waves splashing against the side. My phone throbbed with a message from Dr. Ubu, my supervisor at GLOAT. I silenced it. We turned a corner and there they were.

"THE MAN OF THE HOUR," said Monk Zingapan, as I made my way to the one empty chair. He sounded baked, but then he always did. "You're late, dickweed."

"It's eight," I said amiably, then noticed that the guests were well into their main courses. How had I gotten the time wrong? It didn't matter. I was happy to be there. I loved the smell of the meat cooking, the hit of garlic, the notes of beer and egg and rice.

Two long tables had been set up end to end, with a shorter one jutting out where they intersected. They were heaped with *banchan* dishes: four kinds of kimchi, five kinds of greens, the brown gelatinous acorn slabs known as *muk*, potato salad, grilled mackerels, wedges of *pajeon*, dense dark beans that I didn't know the name of, on and on. We rarely had Korean food up in Dogskill, so far from civilization. How I missed it! I wanted to pour it all into my mouth, one morsel after another, followed by *bulgogi* wrapped in lettuce leaves and slathered with *ssamjang*, and a bowl of *jjajangmyeon* for good measure, but Monk felt the need to keep talking.

"Didn't you see my text? We started an *hour* ago." His amazing old face, with its ten million creases and skin tags, hardened into a mask of outrage. Then he relaxed and gave me a fist bump, which became a clumsy play for

my balls, which meant he was drunk. "Mr. Soon Sheen here needs an en-graved invitation," Monk brayed. "He lives in his country manor up there in Fishkill and never checks his messages."

"Dogskill," I corrected.

"I didn't ask what you did for lunch."

"Kill is Dutch for 'creek.'"

"You pedantic gook." He reeked of soju.

"You gook has-been."

"The gook, the thief, his wife, and her lover."

"I think you mean 'your mother.'"

"Too many gooks spoil the plot."

We used to argue over the etymology of that slur. Monk, originally from Manila, said it dated from the Spanish-American War, a corruption of some Filipino phrase; I had read that it was a relic from the Korean War, a misun-derstanding or perversion of the word for *country.* We were both trying to take ownership, as they would say at GLOAT.

"C'mere, grasshopper," he cough-cackled, arms wide. "Bring it in."

We hugged. He looked like Yoda's older brother, with the hairiness of an Ewok, but then he'd always looked like that. Monk had held some vaporous editorial role at an overstuffed arts and culture rag called the *N.Y. Whip,* where I worked on the IT end of things, way back in my twenties. It was my first real job in the city. The *Whip* was in decline, everyone told me, though people had been saying that for years. Nothing was ever as good as it had been. The fat, lemon-colored broadside, virtually impossible to read on the subway without triggering a border skirmish, was subsidized by voluminous ads for risqué chat lines and affordable futons.

Monk had been at the *Whip* since its late '70s heyday. A decade later, he began *Manila Wafers,* an immense poem cycle about . . . it was unclear. Cer-tainly his heritage played a role. Life in the Coast Guard. A doomed romance, a child he never knew. (Or maybe *he* was the child?) Portions appeared in the *Whip* as column filler. The manuscript ultimately ran a thousand pages, albeit some with only a few words scattered like birdfeed or even just an inverted question mark. Every year, he submitted it for dozens of prizes, and in 1999, *Manila Wafers* beat out sixty other entries to win the Peter Dong

Award for Distinguished Pan-Asiatic Writing, named after a Rue trustee who'd given several buttloads of cash toward the notion of a Shanghai satellite campus. Dong in hand, Monk Zingapan made the jump—spryly, for a sexagenarian—from the fading realm of alternative newspaperdom to the marginally less moribund world of academia. Now he headed the Wildword creative writing program at Rue University Extension Campus, what he called the Harvard of West Twenty-seventh Street. Matte-covered journals from Brooklyn to Berkeley tirelessly brought out his work.

I took my seat. At ten o'clock was Yuka Tsujimoto, award-winning playwright, resplendent in her trademark gilt fez. She sported a necklace that looked like one of those sleep pillows you wear on an airplane, and a sort of asymmetric denim romper. She had tenure at Rue and could wear anything she damn well pleased. Alarmingly, I'd known Yuka more than half my life, since we were both twenty and on the Penumbra College Advisory Board on Asian-American Life, or PCABAAL. We had dated, stayed frenemies. Yuka was pointedly avoiding me, perhaps still sore from the time Nora and I left one of her plays early, a six-hour reimagining of *The Taming of the Shrew* set in feudal Japan. Reviewers called it her best yet, but audiences never warmed to the wordless adaptation, done in the style of Noh drama and featuring actual shrews.

I could see Tanner Slow at the end of the table, head bent in conversation. He was roughly six foot, five thousand inches. Visible even from this distance were large tracts of poorly integrated sunscreen that enhanced his ghostly pallor. He was religious about sunscreen, applying it even in the depths of winter. His hair looked different, like he'd lost some on top but gained follicles on the sides. He was talking to a serious-looking Korean in a dark suit and blood-red tie.

Closer to me, lean, handsome Padraig Kong, his striped silk shirt open at the collar, was sitting next to a thin, extraordinarily pretty woman resembling my long-lost cousin Gemma.

"What I really want is *meeoguk*," he announced. "Do you think they have *meeoguk*? If someone opened a *meeoguk* place, they'd make a killing."

Padraig appeared determined to repeat *meeoguk* as many times as possible, a display of his forays into Korean cuisine. Even over the course of

Tanner walked over with the man he was talking to—who was, I now realized with a start, the one I'd observed through the glass. The man I took for some stubbled version of me.

"Meet Echo," Tanner said, patting the man's shoulder and mine.

"Echo?" I stood up and shook his friend's hand. Then I bowed. Then he bowed, amused, and gave me the once-over as I did the same. He was older, with streaks of gray in his still thriving head of hair. Something more than a five o'clock shadow lent extra drama to his face. Large eyes nested in wrinkles. There was something ruined about his mouth, maybe the ghost of a harelip or residue of a grimace from angrier days. In that light he looked like a Korean Bogart. He wore a kind of poetic suit assembled from thirty different kinds of silk, with subtle beltings and folds that might have been pockets. It looked simple and complicated, very humble and very expensive all at once.

"As you know, the Slow Press is proud to be publishing all the works to date, and many works to come"—Tanner rapped the table for luck—"of the great Cho Eujin, under a *new* name: Echo."

"Echo, echo, echo . . ." Monk added, for effect. No one laughed. He had likely pulled the same gag earlier in the evening.

I gave a low whistle. "Just one name."

"Yes."

"Power move."

"We took the *E* from 'Eujin' and connected it with the 'Cho,'" Tanner explained.

"You'll save a lot on printing costs, throwing out four letters," Monk grunted. He'd moonlighted as production manager when *The New York Whip* was renamed *N.Y. Whip,* later extracting the periods for even greater savings.

"I think this is going to do the trick, honest to God," Tanner said. "We hired some marketing ninjas." He nodded in Loa Ding's direction.

"The mononym route has risks, but can lead to great success," she said.

"Worst fortune cookie ever," Monk laughed. Loa gave him the finger.

"I am like Madonna," said Echo, in surprisingly fluent English.

"I wonder what's a literary equivalent," Tanner mused.

"Rumi," Loa Ding said. "Echo is going to be the next *Rumi.*"

Echo arched an eyebrow. "Who-me?"

I liked this guy, and hoped I would like his actual writing. I'd accumulated a dozen works on Korean history and politics since college but had barely read any fiction. Not a lot had been translated, and the titles I'd managed to find—at places like Koryo Books, just up the block from the Admiral Yi—had struck me as clunky on the sentence level, overly rustic, or both. Also, the names blurred together, even for me. Korean names, with their three rigid, often interchangeable syllables, would always be hard for the anglophone reader to tell apart. In this way, at least, "Echo" would stand out.

"And as you can see, some of our old, ah, friends on the Wildword faculty at Rue U. Extension are here in full force," said Tanner. "They're getting acquainted with Echo, who's teaching there in the fall."

A server passed our private room, tray loaded with cups of persimmon punch. Tanner snagged one on the fly. He brought me face-to-face with Echo again.

"This is my dearest pal, the one and only Soon Sheen, who is Korean, pardon me, Korean *American*. He's one of our great unsung writers." I could tell Tanner believed every word. "He wrote a *brilliant* thing not long ago about books you find in *laundry rooms*. Do you have those in Korea?"

The author smiled politely.

"A lot of New Yorkers have to do their *laundry* in the basements of their *buildings*," Tanner continued, "and they leave *books* there for other people to *read*. Of course, in this country, laundro*mats* are, ah, associated with Asian immigrants—ADC, if you will—so the piece was working on multiple *levels*."

Tanner's faith was touching. He seemed to recall every paragraph I'd ever put out into the world, conveniently ignoring the fact that I no longer wrote. It should also be noted that the last time Tanner did his own laundry was perhaps never. Even in our Penumbra College days, he'd have it done by a service called W&C, which I later learned stood for Whites and Coloreds.

"We'll hit a bookstore tomorrow," Tanner said. "Or tonight! I want to get you Soon's first one, *Pretenders*." He turned to me: "Can you recall, did we ever sell the Korean rights?"

"We did not." *Pretenders* was a rarefied creation, unavailable outside the U.S. and more often than not unavailable inside the U.S. as well. I might as well have written it with a twig on the surface of a puddle.

Tanner didn't miss a beat. "In any case, you *must* read it. And I have to tell *you*, Soon Sheen, that Echo is the most *fantastic* Korean writer you've never heard of. A situation that is going to change, and change soon." He winked. "Pun not intended."

"Ha."

"Now, I'm not supposed to say this, but a source tells me Echo's on the secret long list for the . . . you know."

"Eh?"

"The Big N."

"I don't know what that is."

"The Nobel Prize."

Echo shook his head humbly, just as Loa Ding collared him for a word.

"Hope I didn't jinx it," Tanner said, rapping the table three times. "The Slow Press is kicking things off next month with one of his best: *The Sins*."

I blinked. That had been the working title of a project of mine, many years ago. Something I'd never finished. "What's it about?"

"It's, ah, hard to say."

"My kind of book." Much as I admired Tanner and the Slow Press, my old friend had a track record of putting out books that were the written equivalent of chloroform.

"That's the spirit. You won't know what hit you. He calls it a novel in three novels. Brilliant, right?"

I didn't mention that the advance copy was in my bag. I'd had it for a month or so, without cracking it open, or even registering the title—*my* title. *The Sins!* Of course, Tanner had no clue that I'd tried to write a book with the same handle, but I felt irritated all the same.

"Think of a cross between H. P. Lovecraft and, ah, L. P. Hartley," he said, then sighed. "Nobody reads L. P. Hartley anymore." Sixty percent of that sentence was a template he used regularly, in the past filling it with such names as Karel Čapek, Mary Butts, B. S. Johnson, Amos Tutuola, and others known only to a dwindling cognoscenti.

"Loa Ding says I can't use that comparison," he griped, "unless I want *negative* sales."

"Probably true."

"Anyway, what I like about Echo's new name is that it feels contemporary, but also carries with it an *echo of the past.*"

"Echo, echo, echo," came Monk's joke, which was getting funny again.

"Because he's not just, ah, charging forward with the art form. He's also got all of modern Korean history swirling inside him."

"It's like having dizzies," the novelist said. *Disease.* "A dizzies from which there is no cure."

"Not that he's trapped in the past. He worked in computers for a long time. It gave him a real perspective on technology."

"It gave me carpal tunnel," he said, massaging a wrist.

"They call Echo the Scourge of Seoul. His feuds are legendary—and so, too, his love affairs. But he's a real sweetheart, as you can see."

"I come to America, and I behave," Echo said with a wink. "But not for long."

"You should have my buddy Monk take you out on the town." I indicated the head of Rue's Wildword program, who was trying to pick up a waitress, in both senses of the phrase.

Tanner Slow shut down that avenue of talk. "*Thankfully,* we have his wonderful translator and aide-de-camp, Daisy Oh, all the way from Seoul as well, to keep our man in line."

I hadn't noticed Daisy before, but now she was right in front of me. Barrettes fortified her short hair. Thick cat's-eye glasses balanced on a wide, freckled nose. Her lips were askew, giving her a skeptical look, as though Tanner had bungled the intro. Her necklace was strung with trinkets, each a Korean signifier: a celadon pitcher, a yin-yang pendant, an old broken coin, even one of Admiral Yi's *kobukson* shrunk to the size of a peanut. As with Echo, I liked her at once, if for different, even opposing reasons.

DAISY WAS QUIET AT FIRST, looking right into my eyes. That wasn't what Asians did, at least not those of my generation and Nora's. Here was the new breed. I held her gaze for two seconds, then looked away as I always did.

"Mr. *Soon Sheen.*" Her voice was both dead and alive. "I've wanted to meet you since forever."

Proclaiming herself a superfan, Daisy brought up *Pretenders,* not to mention stray bits of Sheenian paper-blackening I barely recalled. Some pieces, such as my 1995 pull-no-punches reappraisal of T. S. Kim's 1985 novel *Man in Korean Costume,* in the pages of the defunct *NY Whip,* had never appeared online. It was pre-Y2K, practically pre-internet. How had she seen it? There was no digital archive. Back then, you either read something or you missed it forever.

She slapped my back. "Dude, I've read your book five times."

"No way." I burst into what Nora called NAL, Nervous Asian Laughter. NAL wasn't solely a symptom of anxiety or embarrassment. It could be triggered by surprise, pride, lust—by almost anything save actual humor.

"*Pretenders,* man. The last line gave me the chills."

Did Daisy mean the last line of the story "Pretenders" or the last line of the last story in the book *Pretenders*? It had been so long since I'd thought of my book that I couldn't recall either passage.

"Your stuff is on the same wavelength as Echo's," Daisy said.

This was flattery with an aim, I knew. Still, it felt nice to be praised for a change. At GLOAT, my value corresponded to how fully my identity was subsumed by the team's. At home, it wasn't clear I had much value at all.

"Echo, Echo," she said, testing the name. "Hope it sticks. Have you read *The Sins* yet?"

I shook my head. "Is it about the seven deadly sins?"

"Hardly. It's a novel in three novels."

"Everyone keeps saying that."

"One of the novels is a locked-room mystery, where the victim gets killed through his computer."

"Gnarly." Gnarly?

"Echo's the real deal. Colorful life, too. Tragically orphaned in the Korean War. Found in a ditch in his dead mother's arms, trying to suckle. Can you imagine? Wrote raunchy poems during the Park Chung Hee regime. He had a column in a left-wing paper in the seventies attacking his fellow travelers, then moved to a right-wing rag and did the same to them. Drank. Got a hundred girls pregnant. Lampooned the lit world. The Scourge of Seoul. His first novel was *The Architect and the Dictator,* which won all the awards before it

was banned. The awards were withdrawn. It became popular in North Korea, sold on the black market. There was a rumor that he died while working on the follow-up, rubbed out for political reasons. But he's still around, as you can see."

Looking at Echo, creator of important work, I plunged into glum remembrance of my own *Pretenders,* which Tanner had touted as "Alice Munro meets H. H. Munro." A debut story collection, barely distinguishable from the six other debut story collections that launched the same day. It's bad taste to say ". . . and that day was 9/11," but that day *was* 9/11. It was hard not to see that as a sign.

"*The Sins* is good," she said, "but his *next* book is the one I'm stoked for. Coming out in December. Or March. Or never. He has a bad case of gums."

"Gums?"

Daisy looked shocked. "You forgot?"

"Huh?"

"GUMS! From your *Lament* piece about Robert Musil—you know, Great Unfinishable Masterpiece Syndrome?"

"Right, right." I had coined countless acronyms in my time.

"He keeps adding, subtracting, recasting. He loses whole sections for months at a time. A Korean journal published a chapter, and readers went nuts. In a bad way."

"Like fistfights breaking out after *The Rite of Spring.* But why did people hate it?"

"It wasn't hatred but something more primal. A fear of going insane. Echo called *Same Bed* the hidden history of Korea. People didn't recognize their country."

"A little *too* hidden."

"Now Echo says he wants to publish the whole thing only in the U.S.— translated. A big middle finger to Korea. Like Thomas Bernhard refusing to let his books come out in Germany."

"Austria."

"What?"

"His native country—he hated it. But he was fine with his books appearing elsewhere."

Daisy took out her phone to fact-check. If she was looking on GLOAT for answers, she was reading text I'd written, circa 2008.

"What a coup for the Slow Press," I said. "An Echo original."

"The contract is a nightmare. Tanner's wary of committing, since it might never be finished."

"Good old GUMS." I emitted some NAL. "What's the book called?"

Daisy set down her phone and put her hands together as if praying. "*Same Bed, Different Dreams.*" Her palms opened like a book. "We might lose the comma."

"What does the Scourge of Seoul think about the title?"

She peered at the man of the hour. "Echo's super mellow when you get to know him. He's not this, like, sex addict with steam coming out of his ears. Well, not usually. He can't stand most other authors."

"Wonder how he feels about T. S. Kim."

"Probably hates him, just like you. Your article tore Kim a new one."

I let out some NAL. In truth, I felt bad about that review-slash-jeremiad. I hadn't exactly *read* Kim's work. It was a book a lot of people liked, a perennial sentimental favorite from the '80s. But the opening bugged me: a shameless exoticizing of Korea (or, as it's called in the book, *Corée*). T. S. Kim's inspiration was a Rubens sketch depicting a man he saw in Antwerp, clad in a voluminous robe. In the novel, he's a Korean slave, brought to Rome in 1607, who turns out to be a concubine pregnant with King Seonjo's child.

Years later, Nora read *Man in Korean Costume* for her book club and told me to give it another go. After finishing, I could see the appeal. But it was too late for a *re*-reappraisal. The book already felt like a relic. I thought about my old copy. Maybe it was moldering in the laundry room of my former building on West Eighty-third Street. Maybe Sprout, gripped with Dorchester's syndrome, had turned it into confetti, somewhere in the basement of the Dogskill house.

I said, "It's really not bad, when you take a step back."

"Yeah, he does his own thing. Like with point of view."

"Right." Point of view?

"And how it goes back and forth in time."

"Yeah, totally . . ." I said, between bursts of NAL.

"It's kind of *pandering* though, you know?"

Daisy told me she was just in New York for the summer, subletting in DUMBO. She normally divided her time between Seoul and London.

"Ah, my wife loves London." That was a reflex on my part. When meeting a woman, I had a habit of mentioning Nora, *my wife,* as if to put up a force field behind which nothing untoward could happen. Maybe because I didn't wear a wedding ring. I wasn't even attracted to Daisy. Or did mentioning Nora mean that some part of me was?

The reason I didn't wear a wedding ring was because I lacked the appropriate finger on my left hand. A gap I tried to conceal. In photos, my hands stayed behind my back.

"Ah, got yourself a wife then, guv'nor."

"She lived there for her junior year abroad," I lied. Nora had never set foot in London; nor had she expressed any desire to do so. I was just making things up, making things worse.

"Wot does Mrs. Sheen do?" Daisy said, continuing with the Cockney.

"Nora kept her name: You."

"Me?"

"I mean that's her maiden name: You."

"What a total feminist."

"She owns a chain of highly regarded nail salons," I said, as though saying Nora had written a string of well-reviewed novels.

That changed Daisy's tune. "Daily Divas? *That* Nora You?"

I blushed with pride. Nora's literal handiwork had recently been celebrated in a slew of fashion mags and K-beauty sites.

"I have a nail fetish." Daisy splayed her digits. The nails on her left hand spelled her name, from pinkie to thumb, in a shiny manual-typewriter font on a matte cream background. "In case I forget who I am."

I envisioned her sending secret messages by drumming her fingers to spell out words, though it would be practical only if you were talking about days, a dais, the id, or being sad. The nails of her right hand bore intricate ocean scenes in the mode of Japanese *ukiyo-e,* a tradition that some members of GLOAT's /koreana listserv claimed had been stolen from Korea. A vocal faction insisted that anything quintessentially Japanese, from sushi to

ritual suicide, actually hailed from Korea. Some took it further, asserting that swaths of *Chinese* culture had likely originated in Korea—indeed, asserting that a chunk of Manchuria had once fallen within the bounds of an ancient Korean empire.

"I got them done in Tokyo last week. I was at a translation conference."

"You only live twice."

Eventually she returned to her seat. The server had prepared a plate of rice and *kalbi* and *pajeon* for me. I put my face directly over it, let the steam invade my pores. I heard Loa Ding calling me: "Footnote . . ." Only then did I see that her T-shirt said *New York Review of Boobs*. I heard Monk reminiscing about our time together at the Union Square offices of the *Whip*. "The bad old days," he laughed. He was getting the facts wrong, as usual, including the location, and ascribing to me all sorts of lewd acts that, in fact, he had committed.

"Did you happen to catch Mercy Pang?" Tanner Slow asked distractedly.

"I'm not sure. I thought I saw her talking with Monk." It was hard to remember someone who's never been photographed. "Is she on the slim side, normal-looking?"

"She *was* here," he said, perplexed, indicating an empty seat at the south end of the table, what could conceivably be seen as the place of honor. "She'll be back."

"I don't know her, but I'm a big fan of her work," I said. That was an overstatement. I'd recently come across an old magazine profile while waiting at the vet's office. Mercy, I'd learned, was an artist who never gave interviews or posed for photographs. A native New Yorker, she traveled the world creating temporary "collaborations." At first she used only vegetation, rocks, bits of trash found on-site. Viewers—those in the know—were welcome to alter the work by adding sticks, removing leaves, kicking everything over. The collaborations were never definitively finished, only abandoned. Sometimes she wouldn't even tell people where the art was or what she had done. She herself wanted to disappear. Mercy Pang also worked in cities, her arrangements barely distinguishable from the usual urban detritus. For a year, she snuck antique typewriters into chain décor stores, to see what people

would peck out in an idle moment. At the end of each week, she'd gather all the paper and assemble a grand, disjointed narrative. Most of it was unspeakably filthy. The line "Is this working?" appeared repeatedly, gaining in poignance. The Slow Press had brought out the project in facsimile as a limited-edition art book, a thousand individual sheets.

The profile said her collaborations had infiltrated the online world as well, though their extent and nature were not known. It was unclear whether Mercy even considered her output art. Her work could be seen as a commentary on income inequality, environmental degradation, and other contemporary woes. The profile suggested that Mercy's *actual* project was to generate a body of criticism. The article itself was thus part of her art.

"Is Mercy Pang teaching at Rue as well?"

"She's artist in residence, which means you, ah, get to do your art, but you don't have to teach, or even set foot on campus. Most artists do a show, but they waived that requirement. It was the only way she'd accept."

TRADING PLACES WITH TANNER now was the lovely woman who resembled my long-lost cousin Gemma. Her hair was magic: silver, black, and violet all at once, shimmering as if each strand had been attended to separately. She was humming and looking askance.

"Why did she just call you 'Footnote'?" she asked, pointing.

"Who, Loa?" I didn't want to get into it. "Must have thought I was someone else."

"She *definitely* said 'Footnote' and you *definitely* responded."

I stammered through my NAL. She winked a smoky eye. She really did resemble Gemma.

"Wait," I said. "Way-hey-hate."

"Sup, cuz?"

"Gemma!"

"*Soon dubu jigae,*" she said, poking me with each word. "*Soon dubu jigae!*"

It was the pun I most objected to, so much that a whiff of that spicy soup made me recoil. But Gemma could call me anything she wanted. She was

my late mother's kid sister's only child. It was a wonder I could even recognize her. She had come to the States in utero, her parents attending a PhD program in the Midwest. When my folks died, I had just started at boarding school in Nebraska, and her family made the trip to comfort me the best they could. Gemma was tiny. I became a regular guest during winter recess and spent parts of two summers with them. But we lost touch after I went to college at Penumbra and they moved to Germany.

The last time I saw Gemma in person, she was finishing up junior year at an international high school in the UAE. At least in theory. Spring break had arrived and she was breezing through New York, staying at a hostel with a pack of scruffy schoolmates, each with their own ornate origin story. Since then, she'd surfaced on my screen semiannually: GLOAT's algorithm, attuned to my family tree, served up paparazzi shots of Gemma at fundraisers and gallery openings. But we hadn't been in touch.

"Will you autograph my book so I can sell it in twenty years and retire?" She took out a copy of *Pretenders* and unsheathed a lavender Uni-ball. The book had a Strand sticker on it, $4.98. I loved that she hadn't even bothered to peel it off. I smoothed back the title page.

"Oh," I said. It seemed I'd already inscribed the book many years earlier—to Loa Ding, now a few feet away. I felt a pang seeing my clean sincere hand: "Warm best, Soon Sheen."

I drew two thick lines through the old words, turned April 6, 2002, into August 2, 2016, and swiftly obliterated Loa's name with two yin-yang symbols. I wrote, "Dearest Gemma, I have no idea what you are doing here. Love, your cuz, Soon." I drew a little bowl of my namesake stew, heat lines waving, and wrote *soon dubu jigae* in Korean characters. Then I drew a body underneath, so that the bowl was the head. I added sneakers.

"Okay, Picasso. We get the idea."

"This will make it go up in value," I said dubiously. I kept adding things—horse, bird, carrot—till Gemma pulled it away.

She squeezed my cheeks. "Did you gain weight?"

"A lot, when Story was born. But then I lost most of it."

Gemma looked unconvinced. "Anyway."

"Anyway. *You* look amazing."

"I just did a cleanse," she said, as if that explained it.

"What are you doing in New York? And how did you know I'd be *here*?"

"What?"

"At this party. Isn't that why you brought my book?"

"Aha, this is famous Soon!" interrupted a deep if wobbly voice. It was the man in the dark suit: Korean, taller than me, and so muscular it looked like parts were inflated. Rings glinted on his fingers, and small sober collegiate crests decorated his tie. "Gemma always she mention you, famous famous."

"Not *that* famous."

"Famous!"

Gemma said, "Soon, this is my husband, Hans."

"Hans?"

"Handsome," he said.

He proffered his business card, left hand supporting right forearm, as though the limb might otherwise crash to the floor. I accepted in reverse, right hand touching left forearm. That was probably wrong. There were grades of Korean punctilio I could never fathom, even after watching sixteen hours of *Doctor Loves a Doctor*.

Gemma's husband's name was Hans Um. His card told me in three languages that he was South Korea's consul general, based in New York.

"It's nice to meet you," I said.

"We are ond," he said.

"Ond?"

"*Honored.* Hans went to school in Germany," Gemma said, as if that explained everything.

Hans put a hand on his wife's bare shoulder. He looked coarse, whereas she was creaseless, as though he'd been expressly built to absorb any misfortune headed her way. The short hair was silver at the sides.

"Did you get hitched in Germany?" I asked.

"Geneva," said Gemma. "It was a small ceremony."

"But you live here now?" I asked. Was this a power marriage, arranged by parents?

"We just moved a month ago to Park Avenue," said Gemma, as plainly as if she resided on 123 Main Street in Averageville, Wisconsin.

Monk Zingapan was back from making his rounds. "Soon, your cousin should be a model."

"Technically, I still am," Gemma said matter-of-factly. "I'm too lazy, though."

"They give you drugs, it's all good," Monk said, unnecessarily doing the universal sign for snorting coke.

Hans wagged a finger. "No dope for Gemma," he said, dragging her away.

"KARAOKE TIME?" I HEARD Tanner Slow say. He loved karaoke, despite his poor singing voice. His go-to was "Turn the Page," a sly nod to the publishers' art. "A little *noraebang* action?"

"Not tonight," said Yuka and Loa, a touch too quickly. Yuka, I knew, used to favor "Turning Japanese," while publicity-savvy Loa crooned "Everybody Was Kung-Fu Fighting" in front of that *Harvard Business Review* reporter, predicting that the anecdote would appear in the profile's lede.

"I would, but I gotta get up early," said Monk. "Not really. I just don't wanna."

"*Noraebang* gives me hives," said Daisy with a shiver.

Tanner Slow was crestfallen, but he rallied. "Well, let's stick around for a while here, then."

I was levitating a little. I studied the restaurant's minimalist logo on the napkin: Admiral Yi or maybe Captain Ahab, clutching a sword or harpoon. The debonair Padraig Kong came by with a beer for me. Few men could pull off wearing what appeared to be a vintage woman's scarf at the height of summer, but Padraig did it with style. I wondered if I'd ever seen him without a neck covering. Maybe he was a vampire, hiding the fang holes. It would explain his persistent, much publicized youth. In his lapel was a grapefruit-shaped button for AAWCWA.

"Cheers," I said, clinking his bottle. "To Awkward."

"To Awkward. And to writing! How *is* the writing going, old man?"

I focused on draining my beer. The label said REGAL LAGER.

"What's it been, two years since *Pretenders*?"

He could multiply that estimate by seven. Padraig was exactly twelve years younger than me—we shared a birthday—and he had once told me that reading *Pretenders* opened a door in his mind. It was a kind thing to say. I tried to remember that when he got on my nerves.

"I don't write anymore."

"I thought you were working on a novel about the Korean War."

"That's not me."

"Or wait—the comfort women?"

"Nope."

"The North Korean thingie?"

"Sorry." It was clear he'd confused me with another, more prolific writer of Korean extraction. Maybe T. S. Kim was coming out with a follow-up to his hit, decades later. Padraig switched tacks.

"Do you still use a typewriter?"

"I don't write anymore."

The typewriter had been the problem. The computer I used for *Pretenders* had been malfunctioning daily, so I dusted off the Shalimar—a rare electric prototype, never commercially available. (I'd picked it up off the sidewalk outside my first New York rental, along with other debris from the breakup of a couple down the hall.) My story took place in the early '80s, so it seemed fitting to revert to an older form of word-processing technology. I would be like those historical novelists who limit their vocabulary to the dictionaries of the era.

In two weeks, I cranked out seventy vivid pages. It was pure fiction, I told myself: the fable-like story of a utopia, set on a chain of tiny islands called the Sins. Except it wasn't just fiction. The two main characters were named after my parents. It was a way to bring them back, some twenty years after they were torn out of my life, though I didn't realize it at first. Then the pages vanished, as though a fierce wind had whisked them away.

This was back in New York, in a firetrap called the Sans-Souci, where robberies happened on a monthly basis. But why would someone break in and take only a manuscript? (I cringed at another possibility: that in a fit of adrenalized spring cleaning, I had mistakenly tossed the folder where I kept the pages.) I had no backup. Once those words were gone, they refused to

come back. For a while I tried again on my computer, in files with no-nonsense names like "4-03 summary draft 2.2." But the spell was broken. I didn't write anymore.

Padraig continued his interrogation: "But when you *do* write ..."

"I use a computer."

"Spoken like a true GLOAT-acrat."

I knew people who religiously opposed GLOAT, railing against its reach. Its presence was more ubiquitous than most of them imagined. It claimed to foster connection and information, but instead led users to create echo chambers. It profited off services that they didn't know it owned, from meme factories and food delivery to a furniture barter site and a popular "alternative" horoscope newsletter. A growing range of smart devices had layers of GLOAT technology within: "handless" electric shavers, self-measuring rice cookers, home-security drones. Sprout's dog collar didn't just collect data on his health but knew our house's layout, collected the shopping habits of our neighbors. No one could stay completely pure.

"Can you, ah, slip me some Gloatables?"

"That's a hard no."

Gloatables were a form of virtual currency that could be used within the GLOAT ecosystem. You could convert real-world currency into this e-moolah, at rates that fluctuated by the millisecond; also, vigorous GLOAT activity could send a stream of Gloatables into your virtual coffer. They were like stocks, but also weren't. I had trouble wrapping my head around the concept, let alone how to cash in, but then you could say the concept of money itself isn't terribly natural to begin with. The rumor was that GLOAT chose its Dogskill site to grab rights to a rare mineral that fueled its cryptocash. Could that even be true? It sounded like a digital-age legend, spun to explain the deep rumblings, the fleet of trucks entering the compound on weekends.

I added, "They seal that stuff up pretty tight."

Padraig polished off his beer and got to the point. "That girl you were talking to is hot."

"Gemma? She's my cousin."

"Wait, *what*? You don't look anything alike." He kept staring and sighing. Then he said, "I've always been a big believer in laughs."

"Oh?" I said, perplexed.

"You know, LAFS—love at first sight. From your *Lament* piece about the death of the rom-com."

My prose was proving popular tonight. But I didn't like where this was going. Padraig was practically panting.

"I'm going to ask her to the Hamptons next week."

"Her husband's sitting right there."

"Aw, fuck me," Padraig groaned. "The consult, counsel, consulate, whatever he's called?"

"Yes."

"That ape in the bad suit?" He groaned again. "Fuck me."

"Please stop saying that."

"I'll do ya," offered Monk Zingapan, weaving by. He mimed something unspeakable, then flopped on top of Yuka and Loa.

Padraig shifted to face me, a shoulder blocking out Monk's collapse. "Soon, what am I going to do about her? I mean, this is love. This is *real*."

"You probably proposed to the waitress, too."

"I could see myself growing old with her. Gemma, not the waitress." He looked around. "Do you think I have a chance?"

"How should I know?"

Tanner Slow tapped my arm. "I need to, ah, steal you."

"To be continued," Padraig said optimistically, as my tall friend pulled me over to the chair between him and Echo.

"Come, come," Tanner said. "We want to play a game."

"A game?"

"A Korean drinking game. And Mr. Um will translate."

"Hans?" Gemma's husband was rubbing his face with a handkerchief.

"Mr. Um is the South Korean consul general here in New York. He was extremely helpful in bringing Echo over for this visit."

"But his English isn't that strong."

"Well, he insists, and we should keep him happy. He's paying for the spread."

"Okay. What's the game?" I sat down at one of the corners formed where the smaller table bisected the longer one. Two places to my right

was Daisy, one to my right was Echo, Tanner was on my left, and Hans and Yuka sat across. Then Tanner switched with Daisy, Hans with Gemma, and Yuka with the woman I'd pegged as Mercy Pang. New conversations started, the chatter rising like locust song, until Echo hit a soju bottle with a chopstick.

"Let's drink!" he said. "Enough talk!"

"A man after my own heart," said Yuka Tsujimoto, glass raised. "Here's to Echo."

"Echo, echo, echo," Monk said.

"Echo saying, Let's dispense of talking, let's drink of some beer," Hans announced. "My job here is translate, making a guests feeling *most* welcome."

"Echo's English is good," I said politely. "Also, isn't Daisy his translator?"

"No, no. Daisy *book* translator." He poked a thumb at his meaty chest. "Mr. Um is here to *talking* translate personnel."

"So how do we play?" Tanner asked his author.

Echo reached over to Daisy and delicately lifted one of the amulets on her necklace.

"Do you know," he said, "the story of *juryungu*?"

"We don't know!" Tanner said.

"Yeah, tell us," Monk slurred. "Tell us who Shoe Wrong Q was!"

"Not person," he said. "Game."

"Ah," Padraig said.

Loa, I noticed, was taking a video with her watch, one of GLOAT's newer models. Daisy glared at her, but she kept going.

"In the area where I grew up, called Cheorwon, many many many *many* years ago, the nobles, the high-ups, yes, the *yangban,* played this drinking game with a dice."

"*CHULL-wan,*" Hans Um said, improvising a map in the air to show the relative location of the province in question. It wasn't clear whether he meant to indicate the extreme south or the far north or the west or, for that matter, the east. It was possible he was outlining a shapely if swaybacked woman. "You do this dice with rolling, lots of rolls."

Daisy unhooked the clasp of the necklace. It took only a second, but the way she and Echo didn't look at each other told me they were sleeping together.

"The *juryungu*," Echo said, holding up the object. "Unusual, *neh*? Only found in Korea. Fourteen sides, but not equal. See? Some square, some triangle."

"Fourteen pieces," Hans mumble-translated. "Square, try anger."

"Fourteen *faces,* not pieces," Gemma patiently corrected her husband. "*Triangles.*"

"I know, I know!" he said, annoyed.

"We can call it the Jury," Echo said, passing the die to me.

The deep brown color of the wood put me in mind of a hunk of *jangjorim,* the boiled beef my mother used to make, and I had to resist the impulse to take a bite. It had the dimensions of a squash ball, with faint incisions in Chinese on each side. I touched the many facets: six squares, eight triangles. The distribution couldn't be equal; surely the die landed on the latter shape more than the former.

Though it was only a replica, the Jury felt like a connection to some time-shrouded Korea. I'd put away three beers, a bottle of soju, and countless bowls of *makgeolli.* I was in the mood to be transported. I passed it to Tanner, who rolled it to Loa Ding.

"Woah, dodecahedron," Padraig said when it got to him.

"Dodecahedrons have twelve sides," Daisy corrected, touching that spot on her necklace where the charm had once hung. "What we have here is a *cuboctahedron.*"

Echo clapped his hands. "So now we start, *neh*? When you roll, you get an instruction."

"You do rolling," Hans said. "Then it tell *you* what to do."

Padraig blew on the Jury. "Luck be a lady!"

He looked at Gemma, who turned away. She was blushing. He shook the die in his fist and sent it ricocheting among the *banchan* dishes. Loa Ding kept shooting video with her GLOAT watch. I could see her lips move as she murmured her own narration.

The Jury landed close to Hans. "What does it say?" Echo asked.

The consul general put on a pair of reading glasses and stared hard at the thing. "I don't know," he said. "It's Chinese."

"Yes, of course it's Chinese." Echo looked annoyed. "*Hangul* hadn't been invented yet."

"I can't read it," Hans said. "I lose all my Chinese since life in Germany."

He handed it back to Echo, who said, "This means 'Dance without a tune.'"

"Do I take a drink?" Padraig asked eagerly.

"No, not this time. You just dance. Without music."

Padraig got up. At his full height, he was nearly as tall as Hans. He did a foolish thing and went to where Gemma was sitting, bowed deeply, and offered his hand.

"What?" she said.

"May I have this dance?"

"I can't."

"But it's part of the game," Padraig pleaded. "We can't be rude to our guest of honor."

She looked at Hans, who clapped lustily even as his huge hands longed to twist Padraig's neck. Gemma slipped off her heels. All of us drummed on the table as Padraig pulled Gemma in, dipped her, spun her out despite the close quarters. They froze, mouths an inch apart.

"Okay, good job!" Echo said. I took a picture of him holding the Jury with his fingertips, as though handling a precious gem. "Now who rolls? You, cute Japanese girl."

He put the Jury in front of Yuka Tsujimoto, my old flame. She blushed and let it fly. Loa deciphered the Chinese: "Drink three glasses of wine."

"That's it?" You could tell Yuka wanted to do something more creative than get blasted.

"Yes," Hans said. "You can do with soju."

"Yu-ka, Yu-ka!" chanted Loa.

Yuka downed three small cups with comic flair, shaking her head to convey the impact of the alcohol.

"Now who?" Echo said, lording over the scene.

It went on like this for some time—rolling, dancing, drinking, singing, drinking some more, singly and communally. Several results called for others to abuse the roller's nose or otherwise mount a physical attack. I could see Tanner positioning himself in case this got out of hand. Monk Zingapan studied the die intently for what seemed like ten minutes, as though he'd seen it before. At last he rolled, and received the directive to improvise some poetry—perfect for him—but I recognized the lines as a canto from his award-winning *Manila Wafers*. Did most poets know their own stuff by heart? At one point in his interminable recital, I looked at Daisy, who mimed falling asleep. I spit out the beer I was drinking, partly from laughter and partly because someone had stubbed out an illicit cigarette in it. There was lipstick on the rim. I was getting soused; I *was* soused. Little warning bells, muffled alarms, were going off somewhere. Loa kept recording it all with her massive wristwatch, the latest GLOAT model.

The *juryungu* was getting a lot of play. There were too many people in the room. Loa Ding, commanded to hook someone's arm and drink, linked a long tan limb with the waitress. Yuka looked cross. Even in my haze I could see Padraig directing electric glances at Gemma. Was she looking back? I felt a pang of sympathy for Hans, then a pang for Padraig's future face upon meeting his fist. In any case, I was powerless to stop what had been set in motion. Echo rolled next. The Jury told him to "ask anyone to sing." He chose Daisy, who belted out a verse of something in Korean. I could make out a word here and there: *good, love, office.* Echo seemed to know the tune, keeping time with a chopstick.

When Daisy finished, Tanner Slow said, "Give it to Soon."

"Give it to *Tanner*," I protested, my words emerging three seconds after I formed them. All the alcohol was hitting at once. A chant rose: *Soon, Soon, Soon.* The painted screen by the wall seemed to accordion. Echo pressed the Jury into my palm. I looked at Gemma, who was looking at the ceiling, instead of at Padraig's hand on her knee. Hans was smiling at his beer, face like an heirloom tomato. I puffed on the die. The room spun as the Jury tumbled out of my hand, looping among cups and dishes till it stopped at Daisy's metal rice bowl.

"What's it say?"

"Hold on," she said, lifting it to the light. " 'Reveal secret things.' Fess up, Soon Sheen."

The table moved, or the things on the table moved. I felt my eyeballs trade sockets. From somewhere came an eruption of NAL that I traced back to me. "Fess . . . ?"

"You're supposed to *reveal secret things.*"

"Something embarrassing," Loa Ding added. "Something *scandalous.*"

The floor buckled under my chair. I gripped the edge of the table.

"We will be judges," said Echo. "If not secret enough, you have to give another one."

"We will insist!" Hans declared.

"Can't I just have a drink? Sing a song?"

"No, it's trial by Jury," Tanner said.

"It's only a game," Echo said cheerfully. "A game cannot kill you."

"A game can kill you!" Hans restated sloppily.

"Fine." I gulped down my drink and poured another. "Let me think."

IT WAS LATE WHEN we left. As I stepped outside, the cool night air snapped the world into focus. Summer rain had washed the city, and big puddles surrounded the Admiral Yi. I checked my watch and hefted my satchel. The train would be leaving soon. I did an Irish goodbye, my specialty. After a few steps I thought of going back, but I just stood in the shadows and watched the party dissipate. I saw Padraig, scarf trailing picturesquely, murmur something to Gemma, mouth close to her ear. I saw Monk Zingapan balance a water bottle on his nose, finding some success until he ran into a hydrant. I saw a happy Tanner Slow waltzing with a figure—Mercy? I lifted my phone to take a picture for Nora. I saw Hans slapping his cheeks to wake himself up, as his driver opened the door to the black Hyundai Genesis. Echo walked with Daisy Oh, one arm low around her hip. I saw Yuka with a cigarette in her lips, frisking for matches. Daisy drew out an antique lighter so big it looked like a small flask. Yuka cupped a hand but no flame emerged.

Work texts swam to the surface of my phone, courtesy of Dr. Ubu, my tireless supervisor. There was a mandatory online workplace sensitivity

training module due at midnight. I hit Delete, thought better of it, reclaimed it from the electronic trash. Then came a reminder to "gloat" about the evening. Posting my whereabouts on GLOAT had become second nature over the years. In a way it was part of my job, even as a Rung 10 employee. I had a facility with puns, glib pop culture nods. Yet I hesitated. After clicking my avatar (a photo of me asleep at one of Story's chess tournaments), I pulled up the photo I had taken of Echo, then tried encapsulating the evening: *He's a Seoul man: Snacks & revelry with Echo, Korean novelist & great guy.* The tone was off. I tried again: *Korea opportunity: Food and revelry with Echo, the Scourge of Seoul—novelist (and a great guy)* . . . The words felt false. Although the Slow Press would appreciate the advance publicity, I suspected Echo himself didn't care. I let the cursor gobble it up.

I flagged a cab to Grand Central and hustled onto the train right as the conductor stuck his head out to scan the platform. The dozen other passengers were already asleep or listening to music. The train rumbled out of the depths. It shot up to 125th Street. Three people got on. The doors closed again. I would be cast out of the city soon. Pieces of the night came back to me. I checked my phone for the shot of Mercy, but it was too dark to make anything out—in fact, it was pretty clearly a picture of the pavement.

My mind fixated on the game at the Admiral Yi: What had I said when the Jury told me to "reveal secret things"? I remembered time stopping as I spoke. The looks on their faces. Appalled? Amused? My exact words had slipped away. At some point, Daisy patted my arm, as Monk or Yuka rubbed my shoulders. Trying to comfort me—or hold me back?

I felt my face flush, embarrassment taking hold on the capillary level. To put my mind off it, I rummaged through email. I clicked through to the required GLOAT employee course on racial sensitivity. Similar quizzes popped up every few months; the system nagged you if you didn't complete them. I hit Start and swept through the slides. It was true-or-false at first, each query appearing against a well-lit tableau of office life. But my thoughts were elsewhere. The battery was dying.

Ghost lights floated over empty platforms. The sky looked softer outside the city. I fished out the advance copy of *The Sins,* Echo's book. This version was strictly utilitarian, far from the finished product. Title and au-

thor didn't appear on the cover, and in lieu of a photo and bio was a gray box captioned with pure *lorem ipsum.* No wonder I hadn't registered it before.

Only this wasn't *The Sins* at all, but the *other* Echo book that Daisy told me about: *Same Bed, Different Dreams.* The one Tanner meant to publish next spring or never. The one Daisy said wasn't quite finished. How did it get in my bag?

I started to read, and the world tumbled away—the train, the sleepy towns, the meal, and my mortification. *Same Bed* appeared to be a series of five communal dreams. Contrary to the title, the tone wasn't outwardly surreal or wafty, indeed it could get so soberly factual as to appear omniscient. Daisy Oh had said that some Koreans had gone mad after just a taste; had she herself suffered adverse effects? Even in translation, and despite its modest, unready physical appearance, the book drew me in, made me question which things were real and which invented.

Time grew elastic as I reread passages. Halfway through Dream One, between Cortlandt and Peekskill, I realized the train had stopped. A track issue. My brain was broken, too. I kept going, eyes gasping, as line by line Echo's world replaced my own. At some point, the engine started up again. When the conductor called my stop, I rose as though hypnotized and read-walked out the door, under the station lights, a hand on the rail when I came to the steps. The air was still humid here. I sat in my car with the light from my phone and the sound of my breath. I finished Dream One as the battery died. Then I drove home in silence with the windows down and the rain about to start.

SAME BED, DIFFERENT DREAMS

BEING A TRUE ACCOUNT OF THE KOREAN PROVISIONAL GOVERNMENT

DREAM ONE

1905–1937

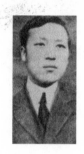

1. Metamorphoses

Suh Jae-p'il becomes Philip Jaisohn. Yi Sung-man becomes Syngman Rhee. Ahn Jung-geun becomes Thomas Ahn. Yi III becomes Earl Lee. Pak Yong-man becomes Youngman Park. Yi Myongbok becomes King Kojong.

Architect Kim Hye-gyung becomes poet Yi Sang. Kim Jung-shik becomes Kim Sowol. And Kim Song-ju becomes Kim Il Sung. These are some members of the Korean Provisional Government.

The KPG is established in 1919 in Shanghai, China. From its foreign headquarters, this government-in-exile works to free the Korean Peninsula from the crushing embrace of Japan, which took over the country in 1910. The body dissolves in the late 1940s, sometime between the end of World War II (when Japan's defeat by the Allies means a briefly liberated Korea) and the start of the Korean War.

This is what the scholars say, anyway. That the KPG *failed*. Failed because it didn't stop the Americans and Soviets from drawing a line at the 38th parallel, staking out their new zones of power. Failed because its own violent infighting paved the way for the division of Korea into North and South. Most unforgivably, it failed to prevent the Korean War in 1950—a conflict that remains unresolved to this day.

2. The Real Cause

But the KPG lives on—working behind the scenes, laying the groundwork. As long as the country is split in two, its people divided, the Korean Provisional Government will be the sole sovereign body acting on behalf of *all* Koreans.

When the two halves finally reunite—when that day comes, whatever the public explanation, it will have come about through the unstinting efforts of the KPG.

3. To Our Critics

Though the KPG is originally based in Shanghai, its members are spread across the globe. Syngman Rhee, in Hawaiian exile for decades, gets elected as its first president in absentia.

It's said that the Korean Provisional Government is more a state of mind than an actual governing body. That the KPG is impotent, holding no official power, and that it has trouble reaching consensus on even the most basic matters because its officers are spread across the globe. (Indeed, some haven't attended a single meeting.) That its proclamations have *hurt* the Korean cause, over the years; that its members have shown a damning lack of unity by their constant backstabbing. That its main accomplishment is fundraising for an impossible dream, and what is there to show for all the money?

There will be things to show soon. Do not despair.

4. Q&A

Q: But wait. Thomas Ahn (mentioned above) was executed in 1910, nearly a decade before the founding of the KPG. How can *he* be a part of the organization?
A: Ahn and several other men and women who died before the group's formation are considered *anticipatory* members of the Korean Provisional Government.

Keep in mind: some of its members are secret. As the Korean Provisional Government already functions as a secret

society of sorts, its "secret" members can be so sub rosa that the *regular* secret members are unaware of them. Sometimes even the secret-secret members don't know they're members.

Incidentally, some of the secret-secret members of the Korean Provisional Government *aren't even Korean*.

Here's another question: What is history?

5. Twelve Lines

It's unclear whether Kim Sowol (né Kim Jung-shik), one of the two poets in the KPG, knows he's a member. His lyrics are limpid, but his mind is hard to decipher. He's still in his teens when he writes "Azaleas." To this day, its dozen lines constitute the most famous poem in Korea—North *and* South.

Twelve lines—about one for every year and a half he's lived. Not a bad rate, for immortality.

6. The Path

The shamans of old Korea held both male and female selves, and thanks to "Azaleas," Kim Sowol is sometimes called the shaman of the Korean Provisional Government: a young man wresting out of his own soul or some *spiritus coreanus* the emotions of a woman saying a wordless goodbye to her lover, a man who will never return.

Even if I die, I won't shed a tear, she promises—or threatens. (The Korean word for *tears* is literally *eye water*. When you cry, you spill eye water.)

From Medicine Mountain, in Yongbyon Province, she has come with an armful of azalea blossoms, which she sprinkles on the ground for her lover to tread as he leaves. It's a beautiful scene. But the more you try to picture it, the less real it becomes. A path of flowers, electrically pink, leading where, for how long? The poem feels like a hallucination, a deathbed vision: *Something is leaving, something is leaving forever . . .*

7. Red Dirt

A memory. As a child, Kim Sowol travels with his family, from the far north down to the capital to see King Kojong's procession. It is a three-day journey. Every soul in Seoul turns out to watch the ministers in their finery, the soldiers in their polished armor. Running down the center of the road is a stripe of bright red dirt, which has been laid down over the course of a week. This ensures that the king's feet will not touch a single pebble on which his subjects have trod. There is literally no common ground.

Kim, age four, watches servants carefully scoop red earth out of baskets, pouring the grains evenly. The edges are exact, as if cut from paper. Years later, this is all he recalls: not King Kojong, the last real Korean monarch. Just that thickening crimson stripe, like flowers, like blood.

Some of the KPG's more literary members suggest that the lover in "Azaleas," the one leaving, represents Korea herself. Kim Sowol takes his own life on Christmas Eve 1934, at the age of thirty-two, while Korea is still firmly under Japanese rule.

8. Medicine Mountain

Shamans can predict the future. Kim Sowol's prophecy is that the location of Medicine Mountain, in Yongbyon, is the same place where, seventy years later, North Korea will develop its nuclear weapons program, the one poised to kick off the end of the world. That is, if it hasn't done so already. (We don't know when in time you are reading these words.)

9. The Queen and the Rebel

The *official* roster of the KPG at its inception is all male, but in fact many women fill the ranks. Some are anticipatory or *posthumous* members, whose contributions are recognized and embraced only later. One is Queen Min, the wife of King

Kojong—smart and strong-willed where he is timid. An American friend describes her as having "an interesting face and a well-shaped head." One night in 1895, Japanese thugs savage the queen in her palace. They cut off the well-shaped head, burn the body to ashes. The outrage goes unpunished. King Kojong mourns by wearing white and speaking in one-word sentences. He does this for three years. A transcript of his day might look like this: *No. Yes. Who? No. No. No.*

Another key figure is You Guan Soon. On the morning of March 1, 1919—a glorious date to which we shall return—the young Miss You hides copies of the new Korean declaration of independence in her sleeves. At precisely 2:00 P.M., You and her classmates pull out the documents as though performing a magic trick, pass them to the crowd.

At a later demonstration, her parents are killed. The Japanese jail her. Guards rip out fingernails, pluck out teeth, break every bone in her seventeen-year-old body. You does not repent. A year later she is tortured to death, cut into pieces. As with Queen Min, the body must be violated, erased so that no trace remains.

You Guan Soon is a *secret foundational member* of the Korean Provisional Government.

10. The Festering Stream

In 1919, the Korean Provisional Government pledges to rescue Korea, but is it worth rescuing? Up till the late 1800s—before Japan really starts putting its claws into her—Korea has its face turned away from the world: the Hermit Kingdom. (When an American trading ship enters the country without permission, the Koreans set it aflame.) Its current monarchy has ruled for four hundred years. Its history stretches back millennia.

Many live in wretched conditions, though, as her upper crust sits idle. The British-born travel writer Isabella Bird, in

Korea and Her Neighbours, is struck by the squalor, such as the wide conduit in Seoul "along which a dark-coloured festering stream slowly drags its malodorous length, among manure and refuse heaps which cover up most of what was once its shingly bed." (This is from a *sympathetic* Westerner.) Things are as stagnant as that old drainage ditch. Jack London, reporting in 1904, finds its people lazy: "The Korean is the perfect type of inefficiency—of utter worthlessness."

Some Koreans have sounded the alarm: the old ways cannot hold. Change comes from abroad. Many in the KPG have embraced Christianity. For others, Japan is a model of progress. It has taken the world's pulse, caught the tempo of this new mechanical dance. Japan is the only modern country in all the East. China is a sick man with long, matted hair. Maybe it's Japan that will rescue Korea, after all.

11. Yi Kwangsu, the Exile

Yi Kwangsu is Korea's first modern writer—and a charter member of the Korean Provisional Government. The bright young patriot wants to move his nation forward. He attends high school in Japan, where he swims in a new world of stimuli, even as he chafes at the race hatred. He casts off Confucian morality, reads Lord Byron, loses himself in sensory pleasures. But he bristles when he hears his classmates call Seoul by a new name, "Keijo."

On January 21, 1919, Emperor Kojong drops dead—as does his maid, a sign that they were likely poisoned. This is too much for Yi, studying at Waseda University in Tokyo. By February 8, he has drafted Korea's declaration of independence, and he helps translate it into English.

12. The Twenty Million

March 3, 1919, is the day that Koreans plan to mourn the death of Kojong, their last king. But a whisper plot tells them to come

out two days earlier and turn their mass gathering into a protest of the Japanese occupation. Printers surreptitiously carve woodblocks with the declaration of independence, the letters etched backward. Pressed in ink, they make the right impression. The document has thirty-three signatories, a number chosen to represent every year of Christ's earthly life.

On March 1, then, at two in the afternoon, tens of thousands of broadsides are in the hands of the people. Speakers all over the country, in small towns and big cities, read Yi Kwangsu's words aloud: "We make this proclamation, having back of us a history of forty-three centuries and 20,000,000 united, loyal people."

The words are desperate, proud, at times poetic. Most important, they are spoken.

Insects stifled by their foe, the snows of winter,
are also awakened at this time of year by spring breezes.

Koreans are the insects. Japan is the snow.

13. Na Ungyu, the Locust

On March 1, in Seoul, then, the sixteen-year-old mosquito You Guan Soon marches with her parents, shouting, *Mansei!* May Korea live ten thousand years!

On March 1, then, in the small town of Hwajiri, a seventeen-year-old locust named Na Ungyu takes to the streets, hopping with excitement from place to place. He leaps to those sections of the crowd where passions burn hottest. In his head he cuts from one subject to the next: an annoyed policeman's twitching lip, a housewife chasing a chicken, a flood of children waving flags. His thumbs and index fingers make a frame. He cuts again: a fellow in a black cap holding up his hands in the same way. Na puts his arms at his side, and the stranger does as well. The man has a scribble of a mustache, just like him. And a slit across his neck.

Who are you?

The stranger's lips move, too, and Na sees he's staring into a big mirror, propped against the wall. The glass is mottled, cracked across the middle. He laughs—*both* of them laugh.

14. The Jerusalem of the East

The police are furious. They missed the signs that the gathering would happen two days *before* March 3. Now, on March 1, after the declaration of independence is read in public up and down the peninsula, they fill the jails or deal justice on the spot. According to the first report in *The New York Times*, appearing nine days later: "The gendarmes arrested a number of students of the Ping Yang Theological School . . . stripped them, and tied them to wooden crosses, exclaiming that as their Father had borne the cross, they, too, should have the privilege of bearing it."

Ping Yang is later known as Pyongyang, the future capital of North Korea, where religion is outlawed. In those days, though, it is reputed to be the most Christian city in all of Asia.

15. The Invisible Movie

To the south, in Seoul, Chungpa Han takes up the cry of "Mansei!" Just back from studying in Japan, he mixes with the crowd. His excitement turns to terror when he sees a policeman stab a marcher in the hand. Then he feels something—a hook around his neck. They take him to jail.

Na Ungyu is quicker. The Locust flees Hwajiri and heads to the hills, makes it north across the Tumen River, separating Korea from China. For two years, the Locust jumps about the map. He hides in Manchuria and Siberia for a time, finally returning to Korea in 1921. Deprived of moving pictures for so long, he takes up residence inside the movie houses of Seoul, feasts on silver light. Often he spots a boy named Shin. The two form a fragile fraternity of *ciné* freaks.

The local fare is scant; most of the movies are Japanese, American, French. Even the bad ones are transporting. One of the worst is about a Chinese named Chang who goes to England to spread the teachings of the Buddha. It's a British or American movie; the Oriental is clearly played by a white man. In the film, Chang meets a poor girl whose father beats her. They are not lovers, but the father suspects that they are. On her deathbed, the waif "smiles" by propping up the corners of her lips with her fingers. Afterward, Shin catches Na's eye and does the finger-smile gesture. They double over. Even funnier is the fact that Shin is a girl, and a pretty one at that. (She has to dress like a boy, she explains, as no theater would let her in alone.) Both Na and Shin prefer the long French serials that unfold like dreams, in which masked burglars race along rooftops and villains fill parlors with clouds of poison gas.

One evening, Na waits with Shin for a streetcar after a long day at the movies, dreaming of a kiss. There's a tap on his shoulder: the police want a word. As soon as they are out of Shin's sight, an officer clubs Na in the stomach, while another jams a bucket onto his head. The Locust, caught at last! The murky charges have to do with his role in the March 1 Movement. *What role?* he wonders. They say he made a movie and must relinquish the film.

A movie! If only. Na explains that he was just a kid then—no money, camera, film. The Locust cackles as they lead him away, elated by his sudden fame.

16. Other Things

Shanghai, 1919. At the dawn of the Korean Provisional Government, modern-minded Yi Kwangsu arrives from Japan. He publishes the *Independence Monitor*, a newspaper for the Korean diaspora, out of the KPG office. His wife is a physician, trained in Western methods. Yi writes at a white-hot pace, his technique sparked by Japanese and European models.

His most ambitious novel, *The Soil,* is serialized from 1932 to 1933. It stretches to five hundred pages in book form. In an afterword, Yi confesses: *I am ashamed that I didn't reflect more and write better. I wrote the novel in brief moments of spare time while working and doing other things. But I wrote what was truly in my heart.*

The following year, his son Pong-a dies at age six. *Now there is no way that I can see you except in a dream,* writes a grieving Yi. *Maybe it, too, is a dream that you came and went.*

Maybe it, too, is a dream that I am writing this, he writes. *Who knows?*

17. The Human Fly

During his three years in jail, Na Ungyu's prized possession is a hand mirror, of German make, into which he directs every wink, glare, moue, and hiss. Na's last name is the same as the word for "I," so when he says the syllable out loud into the glass, he could be anyone. His face is elastic. The other prisoners think he's nuts, but soon enough, they are acting in the full-blown dramas he writes. With a chunk of coal, he marks the floor, indicating imaginary furniture, forest, stream.

One night, the warden ushers the prisoners to the mess hall. They chuckle nervously, the laughter of the damned: they are going to be shot. It was only a matter of time, after all. Two guards wheel in a hulking instrument of death, draped in thick black cloth. Na feels faint. One guard pins a bedsheet to the wall, to protect it from the splatter of blood. Another extinguishes the lamps. Some prisoners weep. Then the machine is uncovered, and after a minute of clatter a death ray leaps out. The sheet goes white.

They're being treated to a movie. A movie from America.

A man as pale as Na is about to be hanged, the noose visible in the foreground. The jailhouse audience gasps. Then the camera pulls back. The pale man with the enormous eye-

glasses isn't about to meet his maker but, rather, is off to seek his fortune in the big city. The noose is a sort of loop to which the conductor attaches a ticket. Everyone hoots with relief— the prisoners, the warden, the guards. They call him "Mr. Glass." One of the guards interprets the title cards, though he doesn't translate fast enough.

Na doesn't care. The whole thing is magic. Movies are *always* an improvement on reality.

In the city, Mr. Glass gets a job at a big department store, trying to earn enough to marry his hometown sweetheart. His roommate, meanwhile, makes money by performing death-defying stunts in public as the Human Fly. (America is a strange place indeed.) One day, as the Fly prepares to climb the side of the building where Mr. Glass works, he gets in trouble with the cops. They mistake Mr. Glass for the perpetrator—and the fun begins. The police give chase, and *he* climbs up the side of a building to escape. As he goes higher, a crowd gathers below, gasping at every near slip. So does the audience in that prison theater. They shout in a kind of ecstatic distress, replicating the sound that the crowd in the film would make.

Every time Na thinks Mr. Glass will plummet to his death, some neat coincidence or bit of cunning lets him mount one more story. At a certain point, a window opens as he climbs past, knocking him off the bricks. Desperately, he clutches at the hands of a big clock fixed to the side of the building. The entire face falls forward, its hands bending with his weight. Time is melting. The prisoners are *screaming*. Na can't bear it. He covers his eyes, then peers between the cracks of his fingers. The sequence barely lasts a minute, or it goes on forever.

18. Arirang

Free at last, Na Ungyu finds work as an actor. He gets cast as salt-of-the-earth types: the farmer with a blade of grass between his teeth, the potato vendor rattling an abacus. Even-

tually he has the cash to make *Arirang*, the first modern Korean movie. Or is it *post*-modern? (We never know the difference.) It's about a young man (played by Na) who gets three years in jail for being in the March 1 uprisings (just like Na). Then he goes insane.

Na Ungyu is a member of the Korean Provisional Government. He dies in 1937 of tuberculosis.

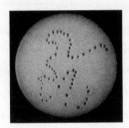

19. Collaboration

In 1937, three years after the death of his son Pong-a, novelist Yi Kwangsu is jailed by the Japanese. By the decade's end, Yi, whose words defined the March 1 Movement, has given up on the dream of a free Korea. Now in his mid-forties, he abandons the KPG. (At least he *thinks* he does; membership in our little racket is for life.) Collaboration with Japan is the only way for his country to survive.

Yi's decision to side with the occupier mars his literary reputation. Future accounts of the March 1 Movement often omit his authorship of its declaration of independence. In 1945, after Japan's surrender in World War II, Korea is free—free to fracture along political lines. The government in the South jails Yi, accusing him of past collaboration; five years later, the *North* Koreans kidnap him, and lock him up for the same reason. (The Japanese had wound up banning Yi's books anyway—and thrown him in jail for good measure.) Forsaken by every audience, he dies in a North Korean prison in 1950 at age fifty-eight. As with Na Ungyu, the cause is tuberculosis.

20. The Spirit of Syngman Rhee

Syngman Rhee is born in 1875, the only son of an only son of an only son of an only son of an only son of an only son. Somewhere in his lineage was a prince, but any such glory is long gone. At nineteen, Rhee enrolls at Pai Jai, a new school in Seoul run by American Methodists, and starts putting out a newspaper. One of his teachers is Dr. Philip Jaisohn, a Korean expatriate with a Westernized name. Jaisohn has returned from Pennsylvania, having fled the country a decade ago in the aftermath of a botched coup. Jaisohn publishes a paper himself, *The Independent,* with the motto "Korea for the Koreans." He starts a debate society to discuss the pressing matters of the day. Back then, in the 1890s, Korean lacks the vocabulary for certain concepts. They enter a new realm, mint words that made no sense just a day earlier.

The debate society is called the Yes or No Club. Their sentences move fast, against a background of no movement at all. Their calls for change appear in *The Independent.* In 1896, Korea is still a sovereign nation, but the Japanese maintain a presence in Seoul. Pressured by the Japanese, King Kojong orders the club to disperse. Philip Jaisohn goes back to Philadelphia. Some members quit in exchange for plum government posts, while others end up in jail, guests of King Kojong. Syngman Rhee is in the latter camp. He spends seven months in solitary confinement. Guards flay his fingers, plunge bamboo wedges under his nails. And that's *before* the trial, where the judge hands down a three-year sentence, later extended by four.

Doomed, Rhee writes a book called *The Spirit of Independence.* When his youthful cellmate, Youngman Park, is released, he takes the text with him to California. Park prints up a few hundred copies, some of which get smuggled back into Korea. People conceal it from the police by ripping the book apart and hiding chapters around the house. But few readers can

remember where all the chapters are, which means the book is often encountered out of order.

More important than the book's contents is the fact of its existence: that it has been composed in extremis, cut up, and concealed. Told in the form of hectoring sermons, *The Spirit of Independence* becomes one of the secret bibles of the KPG.

Syngman Rhee lacked a library in jail, and his attempt to tell the history of Korea—and the world—is rambling and often inaccurate. It's possible no one has successfully read all of *The Spirit of Independence,* even in its undissected state. This too gives it power.

21. Youngman Park, the Smuggler

Six years younger than Syngman Rhee, Park views his cellmate as an older brother. For the rest of his life he tirelessly scares up money for Rhee, who he believes will save the country. In those early years of the twentieth century, Park defends Rhee from naysayers, even as his friend treats him shabbily.

Youngman Park hates the old ways of Korea as much as he chafes at Japan. He wants to abolish his country's monarchy and rigid Confucian belief system. Korea must modernize or die! He is a man of action. Frustrated that foreign countries are not lifting a finger to save his homeland, Park builds up an army of exiles, founding the Korean Military Academy near Hastings, Nebraska, in 1910. Someday, he swears, he will lead them back into Asia and force Japan to withdraw.

Syngman Rhee strongly opposes the idea of armed tactics, and though Park never says a word against his "big brother," the rift never heals. In 1928, after adventures in San Francisco and Siberia, Youngman Park is assassinated in Beijing. The Korean Military Academy in Nebraska is shuttered—at least it seems to be.

22. Princeton Arirang

Syngman Rhee's exile begins soon after he is freed from prison in 1904. He studies in the United States, at George Washington University (1906), Harvard (1908), and Princeton (1910). In five years, he completes a course of advanced study that would normally take at least twelve—a *total mystery*, as his most astringent biographer will note, for someone who never finished middle school. (And all done in a foreign language, to boot.)

Rhee is older than most of his fellow students by a decade. When he's not in class, he gives public lectures on the situation at home. There's so much ground to cover—does any Westerner even know where Korea is? A decade earlier, the travel writer Isabella Bird had noted with amusement that even her "educated, and, in some cases, intelligent" friends couldn't for the life of them guess the location within two thousand miles. Some placed it in Greece; others thought that, like The Hague or the Bronx, it was called "*the* Korea."

The curious crowds that Syngman Rhee used to attract eventually wane. The typical American at this point in history has a positive view of the Japanese and is skeptical of Rhee's condemnation of them as power-hungry barbarians.

Syngman is thirty-three when he arrives at Princeton. He finds lodging at the Calvin Club, among seminarians, though he is a student of political science. He befriends Woodrow Wilson, the school's president, enough to get invited to weekend hootenannies chez W. In the parlor at Prospect House, the future president of the United States pounds the piano, while the future president of the KPG stands stiffly, mouthing the words to songs he doesn't know.

Every time he tries to talk to one of Wilson's daughters, his tongue confuses *r*'s for *l*'s, *she* for *he*. Better not to talk so much. Better not to accept these invitations at all. Jessie, the middle

girl, is a decade younger, so lovely he immediately looks away when she catches his eye.

These evenings are intolerable. Who are these people, and why is he among them? (What a nice carpet.) He feels like a fool—*pabo gatchi.* Then he thinks of his cell inside the rice warehouse, the nightly visits from the rats. He thinks of the heavy wooden cangue they put around his head by day, and often leave on at night.

The evenings in Princeton, Syngman decides, are more than tolerable.

"You'd think with his name, he'd be able to—as it were—*sing*?" a student whispers to another.

Syngman Rhee hears this, so when it's his turn, he trots out "Arirang," the quintessential Korean folk song. Wilson makes space for him at the piano bench. Rhee doesn't know how to play, but he presses some promising black-key clusters in a lilting rhythm. Flames of pain shoot up his fingers. He sings louder, swaying above the keys. He stops before spilling eye water. No one knows the song, of course. It makes no difference when he ends.

"That is my homeland song," he says.

"What does 'Arirang' mean?" asks Jessie.

"Old Korean word," he says. He wishes he had a better answer. "*Arirang* is a sound, an emotion. Nobody knows what it means."

"I see your country's problem right there!" says someone else—a student or Wilson?

"It's a song about leaving," says Syngman, with a meaningful look that lands not on Jessie but on Margaret, the eldest daughter. He coughs. "Leaving behind a place or person you love."

"*You* have come a long way, Sigmund," Wilson says, sipping his Scotch.

Syngman needs to correct him, but in the end he just sighs.

Speech #7 comes to his lips, about the plight of his homeland in general, swiftly moving into an account of his political awakening. Getting thrown into jail—thick cangue around his head—Japan this, Japan that!

He cuts the lecture short, instead dusting off Speech #3: the tale of Dangun, mythical founder of Korea. He doesn't take it seriously. He's a Christian through and through, except on lonesome nights when he lies in bed as though in a crypt and feels the spirit of Dangun right in his heart.

"It is very much like a Bible story," he assures them. He speaks slowly, eyes closed. "Two thousand years before our Savior Jesus Christ, there is a god who allows his only son to visit Earth. He teaches mankind the harmony, and the science, and the art."

"In *the* Korea?" sneers a fellow student.

"Yes, in the north, near where I was born. One day, lady tiger and lady bear come to visit this son-of-god from above." He stoops, giving a rough imitation of the beasts. Woodrow grins with approval. "They are tired of the animal life. They see how the mankind has prospered under his guidance, and they want to become people."

"Humanity is rather overrated," says Jessie Wilson.

"This son of the god tells the two animals they must stay in the cave for one hundred days, eating the garlic."

Jessie wrinkles her nose. Wilson slaps his knee. Syngman thinks of his time in jail, more than twenty-three hundred days. Did he become something else—a god? Or an animal?

The room waits for him to finish.

"After a hundred days, they will become the human. But the lady tiger, she find the cave too dull. She jump out after just the two days. The she-bear eating the garlic, she stays deep inside the cave. She keeps a faith. After day twenty-one, the son-of-god enters and turns her into human woman." He feels lightheaded. "They make love. She gives birth to *Dangun*, who

founds the first Korean kingdom. Naturally, I do not believe in these stories, but 'there you have it, boys.'"

Wilson paws the keyboard and launches into "The Preacher and the Bear." The guests guffaw. Everyone knows it but Syngman. There are roughly two thousand verses. Wilson adds witty flourishes with his right hand. Somewhere around verse six hundred, Jessie gives Rhee a consoling look, but she doesn't come over. He sits on the sofa alone till it's time to leave.

23. Legends and Lore

This origin myth, by the way, is recorded in a medieval book called the *Samguk Yusa*, written in 1281 by a Buddhist monk named Ilyon. The title means something like *the stories left out of the official history of the Three Kingdoms*. Over many years, in between the writing of many other books, Ilyon set down folk tales and true accounts from earlier eras, not so much weaving them together as offering a procession of curiosities. Here are well-known myths and colorful Buddhist legends, vivid sketches of long-forgotten royals that read like parables. The *Samguk Yusa* is packed with lusty songs and weird visions, prophecies and transformations. Above a battlefield, the clouds are shaped like swords and spears. A woman, ravished nightly by an unseen intruder, pins a purple ribbon to his coat, so that she might identify him when the sun is out. The next day, she spots a strip of purple moving on the ground—stuck to an earthworm.

24. The Wonders

Such metamorphoses were Ilyon's stock-in-trade. Rejecting the stuffy format of official chronicles, he was free to include whatever struck his fancy. This makes the *Samguk Yusa*—another translation might be "miscellaneous legends"—a work of wild history. Its two main parts, called *Wonders*, are divided into dozens of brief entries, some just a paragraph long. (We like to translate *Wonders* as *Dreams*.)

The book lacks all proportion. The heroic, the whimsical, and the grotesque all get equal billing. The sum of what we learn about the reign of King Kyongmyong (917–24), for instance, is that one day in February of 920 C.E., dogs in a mural leapt out, took a turn in the courtyard, sending papers into disarray and gnawing on furniture, before hopping back into place. The only thing relayed about one of his predecessors, King Hungdok, is that he took pity on a pet parrot who was mourning his female companion. The king put a mirror in front of the bird, who recovered, only to hit the glass when he went in for a kiss. The bird died of grief, and the king wrote a poem about this—a poem, Ilyon tells us, that is lost.

Every page of the *Samguk Yusa* holds strange, even thrilling things, yet it defies easy reading. Its devotees are like birds who flit from branch to branch, going where impulse takes them. In this fashion, the *Samguk Yusa* remains unread yet alluring: What if the key to it all is hidden in some heretofore undiscovered passage, three-quarters of the way through? Thus the words become eternal, a book for all time. It's another secret bible of the Korean Provisional Government.

25. A Letter from Wilson

In 1910, Syngman Rhee earns his doctorate. He badgers Woodrow Wilson for a letter of recommendation, at last obtaining one of those all-purpose endorsements that academics are obliged to manufacture:

> Mr. Syngman RHEE is a graduate student in Princeton University and has commended himself to us by every evidence of ability and high character. He is singularly conversant not only with existing conditions in his own country, Korea, but also with the general standing of affairs in the East, and has been unusually successful in presenting those conditions to general audiences. He is a strong man of patriotic feeling and of great enthusiasm for his people

and should prove very useful to them. It gives me pleasure to recommend him strongly to those who wish to learn directly of the interests which should be studied and conserved in the great East.

Eight years later, Wilson—now president not of Princeton but of the entire nation—delivers his Fourteen Points, a path to ending the Great War. Syngman Rhee's heart drops when he sees no mention of his homeland. Then he reads between the lines. When Wilson calls for the independence of a country as small as Montenegro, for example, or for the adjustment of all colonial claims according to the wishes of the governed population, it is a clear sign that his former professor has taken Korea's plight to heart. Rhee dictates an ecstatic letter to his old teacher, saying that he trusts that the new "League of Nations" Wilson proposes will surely recognize Korea's situation. Things are about to change.

Wilson never replies. The next year, the newly formed KPG sends a delegate to the Paris Peace Conference. He is turned away.

26. The Strange

We turn at last to Kim Hye-gyung, born in 1910, the same year Korea becomes Japan's colony. At age two, he is adopted by his father's older brother, who has no children of his own. Hye-gyung studies engineering at a premier school, one set up by the Japanese. Virtually everyone else there is the son of a foreign bureaucrat or businessman. The boy becomes fluent in Japanese, makes many Japanese friends.

With the tuition my parents paid, he later recalls, *I only learned words they don't understand.*

Kim Hye-gyung finds work as an architect for the colonial government. Under the name Yi Sang, he composes hundreds of poems. The early ones are written in Japanese and appear in a magazine promoting modern architecture in Korea, or

"Chosen," as the occupiers call it. One poem asks, "Did the straight line murder the circle?"

His pen name, Yi Sang, means *strange*—Koreans say *yisanghae!* when something bizarre comes up. *Yisanghae!* is an understatement when it comes to his work, which he packs with eerie repetitions, non sequiturs, even shapes and numbers. Some of his poems can't even be read aloud—they go beyond language.

Yi Sang. The Strange of the Korea.

27. The Diagnosis

Like the American horror author H. P. Lovecraft, Yi Sang publishes chiefly in periodicals, achieving literary sainthood after death. Both die in 1937, a month apart.

Many of Yi Sang's pieces are horror stories, too. They're full of skeletons and dolls, dismembered limbs and weird transformations. Yi Sang frets that his reflection in the mirror is out to get him. He enters dreams, only to be handed a death sentence. Because Yi Sang has contracted TB, every syllable seems infected. The body is confusion. *I wrote my own obituary in my autobiography,* he writes. *My lung had appendicitis,* he writes. He writes that he suffers from insomnia *and* narcolepsy. The world is a hospital to Yi Sang. His poems read like short, scared gasps, with bloody riddles in the phlegm.

All the nutrition I get is through my nose.

Resting at a hot spring, he falls for a *kisaeng* named Gum, who seduces him with a song of Yongbyon—a sweet variation on Kim Sowol's "Azaleas." (A *kisaeng* is a sort of cultured prostitute, like a geisha, but with a bit more dancing.) He doesn't pay for her company. He accepts her line of work with equanimity, even introducing other guests at the spa to her.

It's unclear whether he and Gum officially marry, but back in Seoul they live together scandalously. In his most famous

story, "Wings," the narrator is like a child, forbidden by his wife to enter her room at night. What's she up to in there? He knows and doesn't know, like a detective who deliberately misfiles the clues that could solve the case. With coins from his wife, he kills time at a teahouse until the coast is clear, not wanting to run into any of her clients. In real life, Yi Sang and Gum open a teahouse together called Swallow. Its street number is 69. All the furniture is tiny, as though built for children. The only art on the walls is a picture of himself.

I am wasting away.

In photos, his hair is fiercely unkempt, as though sprouting a wing. His hair is a quotation of Rimbaud's hair.

Yi Sang's strangest poem, "Diagnosis," is mostly numbers. They run backward in a grid, each one turned on its axis. It's supposed to represent the patient's face:

```
·  0  ℮  8  �RED  ∂  ƺ  Ⴤ  Ɛ  ς  I
0  ·  ℮  8  ↥  ∂  ƺ  Ⴤ  Ɛ  ς  I
0  ℮  ·  8  ↥  ∂  ƺ  Ⴤ  Ɛ  ς  I
0  ℮  8  ·  ↥  ∂  ƺ  Ⴤ  Ɛ  ς  I
0  ℮  8  ↥  ·  ∂  ƺ  Ⴤ  Ɛ  ς  I
0  ℮  8  ↥  ∂  ·  ƺ  Ⴤ  Ɛ  ς  I
0  ℮  8  ↥  ∂  ƺ  ·  Ⴤ  Ɛ  ς  I
0  ℮  8  ↥  ∂  ƺ  Ⴤ  ·  Ɛ  ς  I
0  ℮  8  ↥  ∂  ƺ  Ⴤ  Ɛ  ·  ς  I
0  ℮  8  ↥  ∂  ƺ  Ⴤ  Ɛ  ς  ·  I
0  ℮  8  ↥  ∂  ƺ  Ⴤ  Ɛ  ς  I  ·
```

It's signed by the physician on call, "Yi Sang." The ailing poet has become his own doctor.

Dots run diagonally through the array of numbers, tracing a sick person's declining life force. The patient might be Korea or snoozy hidebound poetry—or Yi Sang himself. The tubercular oddball. The Strange of the Korea.

28. Upswing

But! Since each number is printed backward, perhaps we're seeing it from the wrong side of the mirror. Viewed the *other* way, the patient's condition is on the upswing. He writes somewhere that TB destroyed his body even as he experienced an artistic rebirth—the ability to write lines that will never die. The trick, then, is to get to the other side.

29. I'm Scared

In 1934, the fifteenth year of the KPG, a newspaper runs some of Yi Sang's poetry under the title "Crow's-Eye View." The response is violent. Readers single out the non-poem "Diagnosis." They accuse him of insanity, of driving *them* insane. The feedback is so hostile that Yi Sang withdraws the rest of his poems. Only half of the thirty poems are ever seen. Even in its incomplete form, "Crow's-Eye View" is one of the secret bibles (and weapons) of the Korean Provisional Government.

The first poem sets the tone, plunging us into a menacing landscape right from the start: *The 1st child says I'm scared.* Except the words all run together: *The1stchildsaysI'mscared.* The kid's frightened out of its wits. The line repeats, everything jammed together, going from the 1st child to the 13th. You imagine each one coming to a horrible end.

The poem is too scared to take a breath. For Yi Sang, breathing is life and breathing is death. You have to get all the words out at once, and then you can die.

30. Twice Thirteen

By 1936, Yi Sang and the *kisaeng* Gum are no longer together. He marries his best friend's sister, Pyun, but he keeps writing stories like "Wings," which appear to be about Gum. They fight. Later that year, he abruptly takes off for Japan—alone. In some ways, this isn't so strange. He used to be employed by the Japanese government. Not only did he often write in Japanese,

he was drawn to the literary culture, the avant-gardes bor-
rowed from Europe. But things go wrong. The whole city stinks
of gasoline. It is twenty times more modern than Seoul—or
"Keijo," as the colonizers call it—but he hates it. He speaks perfect Japanese. He doesn't appear to resent the Japanese; nor is
he enamored of their "advanced" thinking, the way Philip
Jaisohn and Yi Kwangsu sometimes were.

Tokyo doesn't know what to make of Yi Sang and assumes
he has ulterior motives. The secret police arrest him for illegiti-
mate thoughts. (Even his indifference is provocative.) They point
to "Crow's-Eye View" from two years ago and say: *Please explain.*
Why is a poem dedicated to a "fat triangle"? Why is the word
sCANDAL written in English, with *most* of the letters capitalized? What's the deal with "Diagnosis"—the backward numbers, the dots?

> **POLICE:** Isn't it true you published a similar poem in 1931, in
>   Japanese, only with the numbers printed normally?
> **YI SANG:** [*Nods.*]
> **POLICE:** Why?
> **YI SANG:** [*Shrugs.*] Did the straight line . . . murder the circle?

They lock him away. His TB worsens. Those dots on that
grid lead down, down, a staircase to the grave. He can't find a
way to the other side of the paper. Yi Sang, the Strange, is
released from prison only to stagger into a Tokyo hospital,
where he dies a few weeks later.

The catch is that the authorities were correct to suspect Yi
Sang, even though they couldn't put their finger on his crime.
He *did* have ulterior motives. He wanted to pierce the heart of
Japan. *That's* why he went to Tokyo. He needed to get close
enough to stab it with incantations. He had other, more potent
poems, never published—thousands of works that no sane

mind could contemplate. The Japanese destroy his papers without even a glance.

But not all of them. Before his capture, he mailed a large packet home to Pyun, his wife-in-name-at-least.

Yi Sang dies at twenty-six (twice thirteen), an undercover operative for the Korean Provisional Government.

31. In the Vault

Most of the Korean movies from the '20s and '30s exist only in written accounts or scripts. During World War II, the Japanese melted down every reel they could find to extract the silver, and *Arirang* is no exception. Is it still called alchemy when *art* is turned into a precious metal?

Some argue that it's the absence of the movie that has fueled its legend: the public can't see it—therefore it *must* be great.

That might be so, but we can tell you: we've seen *Arirang*, and it's as astonishing as the old accounts say. Na portrays insanity so acutely that you think *he* must have lost his mind as well. The street scenes show a bustling Seoul, crowds from every walk of life. We glimpse that noxious conduit of filth, which so transfixed Isabella Bird and other foreigners, the sludge moving like the back of a serpent. Shin, Na's friend from their moviegoing days, plays his sister, her hair grown out. She fends off a rapist—a neighbor who has thrown in his lot with the Japanese. And the Locust himself glows and flickers: a piece of light.

32. The Interlude

We see something the experts don't know about: an interlude absent from the surviving script of *Arirang*. Fleeing from a cop, our hero starts climbing the outside of the Government-General Building, a sprawling, sinister mass that has just gone up in

downtown Seoul. Did Na use the actual structure, or is it trick camerawork? No matter. We feel the pull of vertigo, cringe every time his hand claws at empty air. He wears a straw boater and huge spectacles.

The interlude lasts twenty seconds, a flurry of cuts until Na reaches the roof. Our hero gets snagged by a Japanese flag being run up the pole by an oblivious soldier. His glasses and hat fall off. Suddenly he's back on the ground, looking much as he did before scaling the wall. *It was all in his head.* Now the police are charging down the road. *That's* not in his head. He does a double take, pushes up his glasses, and *runs.*

33. The End

Thus ends Dream One of the Korean Provisional Government.

2333: Extradition to Gambrinus (1966)

THE WAY IT USED TO BE, Parker Jotter came home early every Wednesday to Oak Street from his appliance store on Michigan, fried up a brick of Spam with toast, then tapped into the Freak. Short for the *frequency,* it was a quality within him, activated by props and ritual. Parker would set his Zippo atop a radio tuned to static, then sit at the Shalimar, his homemade electrically assisted typewriter with the self-reversing spools (patent pending). A faint signal blossomed behind his ears, like the thrum of the world's smallest tuning fork. The Freak coaxed him to write three chapters of his new book at one go, the Shalimar burning like a hot plate. A kind of self-hypnosis. The rest of the week, he let his brain rest.

In the early days, back from the war in Korea, Parker couldn't tell when the Freak was coming. There was a rumbling only he could hear, like that of the F-86 Sabre he'd flown over MiG Alley. Words in his head. Strange names. It felt scary at first, till the tumble of syllables resolved into a planet, a weapon, an alien species.

Now he was more in control. Across four Wednesdays, the Freak peaked as the project came to fruition. He would then mail the pages to his Boston publisher, a man named D. M. Zephyr, and wait. He didn't see his words again until a parcel of books arrived. Parker stocked them on a small wire rack by the register of his store, Jot Electronix, with a card that said MEET THE AUTHOR—IF YOU DARE! Curious customers

bought copies, though rarely commented on the outré contents. (Parker Jotter called the frequency the Freak because he felt like one.)

The previous installment, *2333: The Louse,* had sold well, thanks to the spacefaring nudist splashed on the cover. Now the pressure was on, and the Freak was AWOL. Maybe it was Parker's fault. He'd slept poorly, woken by his wife's three A.M. muttering. Parker used to love hearing Flora talk in her sleep, but lately she spoke of the sky going red, rivers of filth.

Or maybe the Freak was on the fritz because of his late arrival to the garret. Heading home earlier that afternoon, he glumly pondered the ledgers of Jot Electronix. Buffalo had changed so much in the past few years, and he was worried. It seemed like yesterday that the city had started clearing a swath for the Kensington Expressway, so people could get to the airport faster or home to the suburbs more easily. Which people? He remembered driving on part of what used to be Humboldt on a spring day five years ago, wind making music with the leaves. Returning a month later, he saw that every tree was gone, the white stumps like a row of buttons. Houses came down. Then the digging began, snapping the spine of the city.

Now the Kensington was basically done. He couldn't see it from the store, but he sensed it on his walks: an impassable border cutting off the city from itself, a scar teeming with cars. He imagined Buffalo becoming a miniature Korea, bisected by a DMZ.

As he walked home that Wednesday, gusts of organ music drew him into a church. A midweek wedding. He stood in back as the sound swirled. Six guests were scattered on the pews. The hunched organist threw back her head, possessed. Parker sat down. The groom turned: a saffron face with oblique eyes. Parker's blood froze. An ambush by his former captors? He instinctively touched the lighter in his pocket, then ran before the bridal veil was lifted.

TODAY, PARKER PACED and swore. Pitched crumpled pages at the waste bin. He leaned out the window, brooding like a gargoyle, while

inside the garret the Shalimar hummed in expectation. The air smelled like rain. Crows crowded a distant steeple, perched on the crucifix even as the bells struck four. Was that the church he'd stopped in? Hard to say. On Sycamore Street, the gaunt paperboy started his rounds. A misnomer: the messenger looked as old as Parker. Drawn face, ash white. Tweed cap, rain or shine. A mythic being, tirelessly dipping into his ragged copious sack to pull out bundles of black and white. His pace never slackened as he fired with accuracy at porches and driveways, now sideways like a discus thrower, now overhand like Jack Kemp drilling the pigskin at the Rockpile. The late edition landed with a *thwap*. Enough. The afternoon wouldn't last forever, and Parker still had to locate the Freak.

Just then two angels ran headlong down Oak, as if late to meet the future. (As he wrote in his first book, *2333*, "Life is a time machine that only goes in one direction.") The smaller one lost a wing, asked her friend to stop. The voice was that of his seven-year-old, Tina. His angel.

"Tina!" cried the gargoyle to his daughter, but she didn't hear.

She caught up with her friend, collapsing in giggles, and Parker savored the rare sound. For the last year, her mother had been flailing. Flora spent most of her time at "church," the basement of a house on Vulcan Street, with a group of weirdos who believed that the world would end in 1967. Just months away, if the apocalypse began on January first. In any case, they should have built a bigger cushion, made doomsday fall in 1970. A nice round number. There were complex mathematical reasons, he gathered, why it *had* to be 1967. But here they all were, already in October '66, and the world had the pesky habit of existing.

The Divine Precepts, as Flora called them, met just a few doors down from the house where he and Flora had lived briefly after his return from Korea. An ever-shifting number of DPs had made it their residence, sleeping in narrow bunk beds, cooking communal meals. Flora went three nights a week now, to discuss the latest portents in their favor: a plane crash that left thirty-three dead (thirty-three being

the final age of Jesus), a hit song that repeated *fire* thirteen times. Ronald Wilson Reagan, the actor running for governor in California, carried the number of the beast: six letters in his first, middle, and last names. To the Divine Precepts, everything was a sign.

Parker had spied on them one night in March. The group consisted of foreign students with watery eyes, two Teutonic blondes who spoke as though hypnotized, and several worn-down types, likely common drifters attracted by the food. He would have liked to give the ringleader, Miss C., a good talking-to, but she was in her private bedroom, indisposed. What bothered him most was seeing Flora cleaning up. He'd never known her to wear an apron. Would this be her role in their utopian scheme—to scour and dust? At last he barged in, saying she was needed at home. Flora stared daggers as they drove. *We all take turns,* she said.

Parker could handle Flora, just about. But her behavior scared Tina, who later told him her secret rule of survival: keep one room away from her mother at all times.

It was unclear to Parker Jotter whether D. M. Zephyr, his editor, actually finished reading any of his books; after all, he joked that the goal of Neutron Books was quantity over quality. As far as Parker knew, Zephyr never changed a syllable of his work. The only real surprise had come at the beginning. In 1957, Neutron printed his maiden effort, 2333, in the same volume as another debut: Kim Tollson's Priest from the Stars. Threw him for a loop. These double features were called Take 2s, ideal for the reader on a budget. Each volume had two front covers. You could start with 2333, then flip it over for the second feature.

In Miss Tollson's book, a fist-sized meteorite lands in a midwestern town. A microscopic alien burrows into the brain of a preacher, who leads his flock into a life of crime. Parker couldn't finish the thing, which was made into a rather shocking movie. Now Kim Tollson was Neutron's main attraction, while Parker Jotter fretted that his well had run dry.

How had things gone so wrong? Parker had returned from Korea in the fall of '53, after months of aerial glory and a year as a prisoner of war. Highs and lows. In Buffalo, Flora eyed him warily, suspicious that he'd been replaced by a robot.

"Would a robot do . . . this?" He did a mad jig, kicking like a Cossack till Flora snorted. She finally relaxed. She no longer maintained that Parker was a robot, though it was unclear how he had become her *husband*. She even worked with him at the store half the week, made high-quality small talk with the customers. Jot Electronix was three cramped aisles' worth of new appliances, old typewriters, questionable television sets, and her husband's own "ungodly" books about alien takeovers and other blasphemies. She didn't dare read them, but at least within the store she had a sense of humor. If a customer asked if that copy of *2333: Escape from Tyosen!* by the register was on sale, Flora announced on the intercom, "We found another sucker!"

When Flora got pregnant, things started to slip. Odd phrases snagged in her mind. She accused Parker of being an actor, paid by the military to pretend to be her husband, so that she would safely deliver the baby to term. Then the "authorities"—variously American, Korean, or Russian—would take her child for "experiments."

"Would an actor do—this?" Parker flapped his lips like an outboard motor.

Another Floral snort. That was something. Tina was born healthy in the heart of a January squall, 1959. By summer, though, Flora had grown convinced that her *real* baby had been snatched at the hospital. The replicas, she insisted, were getting better every year.

PARKER STARTED TYPING again. Halfway down the page, he noticed that the date at the top was wrong: 10/5/56 instead of 10/5/66. A bit of time travel on a Wednesday afternoon.

What if he could get the last decade *back*? What would he do over? Maybe he would have left Flora. But then there would be no Tina. Sure, he could have gotten hitched again, become a father, but that child

wouldn't be Tina. Well, maybe this hypothetical kid would have other qualities, which Parker would love. . . . Or what if—what if there *already* was some ghostly version of himself, leading another life, yearning for *this* existence, the one he actually had? Some version still locked in that cold Korean cell, memorizing sentences in a tongue he didn't understand . . .

That was how the Freak worked sometimes: you started floating away from reality.

THE SERIES BEGAN with *2333*, a space opera that concludes with a twist: the massive starship exploring the edge of the universe is in fact the uneasy dream of an average soldier, dog tag #2333, wounded on a battlefront on present-day Earth. Creating a vast story in his mind is his desperate attempt at survival—in spirit, if not body. On the last page, he shuts his eyes, to continue the interior interstellar voyage.

Parker Jotter had been one of a handful of Black men in an integrated squadron, and his time as a fighter pilot lent verisimilitude to the scenes of deep-space combat that erupted every couple chapters. He had asked Neutron Books to send copies of *2333* to his favorite s-f authors: Robert A. Heinlein, Arthur C. Clarke, Isaac Asimov. Days began with a glimmer of hope, which was extinguished upon opening the mailbox. After six weeks passed without a word, Parker vowed never to read them again. He asked that the sequel, *2333: Escape from Tyosen!*, be sent to Clifford D. Simak, Gordon R. Dickson, and Brian W. Aldiss. These writers also failed to respond. Maybe the "race" aspects were too controversial: Tyosen's Lost Tribes (the O'rë and F'falo) wage endless war but also interbreed like crazy. Or maybe these authors didn't trust someone without an initial in his name.

In this latest book, the sixth in the series, rogue explorer Greena Hymns studies the denizens of the rainy moon Allîhs. They were aquatic, tentacled beings—the opposite of the winged creatures that ruled her home planet, Tyosen. Though their worlds whirled at opposite ends of the galaxy, the events of one directly affected the other.

(The physics—or "fyzx," as he called it throughout the series—wasn't terribly well thought out yet.) In *2333: Escape from Tyosen!* (1959), an apple dropped from a tree in Tyosen; now, on Allîhs, a sea-spud *rises* from the ocean floor, in cosmic counterpoint.

But if the planets were linked, shouldn't the apple fall *again,* as the aqua-tater rises, and so on, on Tyosen and Allîhs, falling and rising . . . everything in a sort of intergalactic yin-yang? As the irrepressible D. M. Zephyr once wrote him, "Don't overthink it, man!"

Parker reread his story. But without the Freak, he couldn't continue. Every phrase rang false. He typed up a fresh outline, then grabbed it from the Shalimar. Crumpled. Threw it behind him.

"Ow."

"Tina?"

"Hi, Pops." She was chomping loganberry bubble gum. "Writing another amazing book?"

"Naturally," he said, with a snooty British accent.

"Is it *funny*?"

"Not particularly."

She picked up the crumpled ball, which had landed by the window. "Why not?"

He shrugged. "I'm not feeling that funny these days."

"Is it part of your series?"

"Naturally."

"Am I in it?" She unfolded the paper.

"Ah, don't read that. It's garbage."

She blew a bubble. "What's an 'eddy'?"

"A small whirlpool."

"What's 'fyzx'?"

"Too complicated."

"What's 'warlock'?"

"A male witch."

Tina looked up from the page. "So it ends with . . . a mirror? You mean, all these people have never seen themselves before?"

"Not once." It sounded stupider when someone else said it.

"Pops."

He sensed she was going to mock him. That seven-year-old sarcasm. "Yes?"

"Do you ever think," Tina said, shutting the window, "there's someone on the other side of the mirror?"

"The other side?"

She blew a deep red bubble, which paled as it swelled, until she chomped it back to its primordial state. "Like when you're looking at yourself, brushing your teeth . . . what if someone's on the other side? And she's in a room that looks like *your* room. Well, anyway. I used to think there was another me there. Not anymore!"

That phrase *used to* broke his heart. Already she had a past. "Was she nice, the other you?"

"Don't know. But her name was *also* Tina. She looked exactly like me except she was always happy. She had friends who— Pops, why are you crying?"

THE MAGAZINE *GRAVITIES* called *2333* "a dose of rigorous storytelling," and *Analog* noted its "fly-by-the-seat-of-your-pants plot." (Parker wasn't sure these were compliments per se, but he would take them.) Local papers—the *Buffalo Evening News* and the *Courier-Express*—ignored it, though a *Courier* reporter who knew Flora's family interviewed him for a feature that didn't pan out. It lost in the Best First Novel category for three separate s-f prizes. Parker Jotter made up business cards that said "Award-Losing Author."

The sequel, *2333: Escape from Tyosen!,* was embraced by the fan magazines, which Neutron's clipping service monitored. The warmest praise appeared in *Lost Cause,* a mimeographed affair out of Atlanta. In his column, Mr. H. E. Woods deemed the growing series "the best science fiction I've read in years." The words went to Parker's head. He was more than "rigorous"; he was the *best.*

The publication's name stopped Parker short, as did its headquarters in the South. Was it a racist deal? Nothing in the contents bore this

out, but the unease sparked his third novel, the unpopular *2333: Extradition to Gambrinus.* The main character, Sal Hermes, is a science-fiction writer who happens to be Black. Fired from his day job at a bottle factory, he takes up gambling, a pursuit in which he shows a singular lack of talent. Bookies are getting mad. Out of the blue, a telegram arrives from a wealthy eccentric, Linus K. Mig, inviting him to stay at his residence so he can "finish his next masterpiece in peace."

Sal accepts. On the three-day train trip, he imagines what his benefactor is like. Sal assumes Linus is white; does Linus know that his favorite author is Black? Upon reaching the estate, a former plantation, Sal's sole interaction is with Rongo, the Polynesian butler. Each room in Sal's suite is grander than his apartment. Reference works and his own obscure oeuvre (hand-bound in leather) line the shelves. Delicious meals arrive in clamped salvers. Afternoons, he walks to the dock and feeds the turtles.

Linus, Rongo says, considers Sal's books a quote vision of humanity in the cosmos so precious and underline enthralling unquote that he is intent on taking care of him for as long as the author wishes, even quote till the end of time itself unquote. Sal drools, envisions a trilogy of trilogies. No more soul-crushing jobs. No more hiding from bookies and their thugs.

Though Linus is rather fragile at the moment (Rongo says), he is delighted that Hermes has arrived, and looks forward to meeting someday. Sal embarks on his project using a brand-new typewriter—a Shalimar that works like a dream. Swiftly finishing his first book, Sal Hermes gives the pages to Rongo. The butler returns the next day with an ecstatic letter from Linus. Further funds have landed in Sal's account. He bulks up on a diet of chops and pastries.

Sal Hermes is summoned to the main house. Rongo warns him that Linus has a phobia: he doesn't like watching people eat. It is indeed the case that Linus sits facing the wall, in a high-backed chair. Sal can't see his patron's face, but has a splendid time nevertheless. In the months that follow, the dinner invitations become more frequent, and soon he is eating in the main house weekly, feeding Linus tantalizing snippets of

the plot for Book 2. They converse on art, philosophy, history—the kind of intellectual stimulation that Sal has always craved.

In nine months, he finishes the first trilogy, comprising *A Single Atom, Second Earth,* and *Three on Saturn.* Rongo puts each book in a custom pine box. Sal is keen to get it out in the real world, but Rongo reminds him that by contract, his benefactor will handle all such matters.

"Linus thinks the trio might benefit from being bound together as a single book—a novel in three novels, as it were."

"Wonderful idea!" Sal agrees.

Rongo signs him up for a second trilogy to be composed on the premises. More dinners follow, Linus facing the wall. Sal Hermes basks in his praise but frets over the publication plans.

"It's *science fiction,*" Linus drawls. "It'll keep!"

They debate "art for art's sake." Does a book—or a painting or a play—have value mainly as a reflection of its time or as an expression of the artist's singular vision, untouched by social reality? Sal takes the latter position, while Linus plays devil's advocate and pokes holes in his defense. It's all in good fun, but later as Sal Hermes finishes *Four Rockets* and starts *Playboy of Universe Five,* one exchange gives him pause.

LINUS: You would be satisfied, then, to pen a book *exactly* matching what's in your head—the perfect execution of your vision—that only ten people ever read?

SAL: Oh, naturally. Only ten people have read my books anyway, I believe.

LINUS: [*Laughter.*] And I'm one of them!

One evening, Hermes leaves his quarters and slips into the main house. Carefully he enters Linus Mig's reading parlor, with its sumptuous settees and floor-to-ceiling bookcases. He knows that his own new works likely still sit in the handmade boxes Rongo carried to his—*their*—employer. A shard of moonlight helps him find the way. With clammy hands he takes *A Single Atom* from the shelf. Why is it so light? He opens the box. A cloud rises in the lunar light. There's a terrible taste

in his mouth. Frantically he opens *Second Earth* and *Three on Saturn*. All contain only ashes.

"Art for art's sake," says Rongo, standing at the threshold with a lantern.

For a week, Sal Hermes is a quivering wreck. Could he have imagined it? By the terms of his contract, he is slated to start his next book in just a few days. Perhaps the work will take his mind off the bad joke that the rich man has played on him. But no ideas arrive. The plots he had devised mean nothing now, for the first three books are no more. He can never reconstruct them.

Instead, he takes down a random volume of the *Encyclopaedia Britannica* and types its contents on the Shalimar. Fear and anger subside; he is an efficient machine. When he finishes, Rongo whisks away the impressive stacks of pages. That night, he breaks into the main house to confront Linus K. Mig. (Rongo should have inspected his suitcase, all those months ago, for the pistol.)

Parker's title *2333: Extradition to Gambrinus* refers to the volume of the *Britannica* that Sal Hermes copies out. (Oddly, Neutron published the novel without the final page. An accident?) D. M. Zephyr telegrammed: NEVER AGAIN. After that, it was back to space opera and planetary invasion for Parker Jotter. No more playing with the color line. Message received.

SATURDAY THE MERCURY fell, the day ten degrees colder than expected. On his way to work, Parker Jotter wondered if he should turn back for a warmer coat. Every block, he stopped to consider this. Home? Onward? In the end, he pushed on. He'd ring Flora, ask her to bring it when she came in at one. *If* she came in. Knowing her lately, she would have Tina walk it over alone.

A car full of DPs had dropped her off after midnight. What a bunch of charmers. He'd watched from the garret. The back-seat passenger looked familiar. White and skeletal, the grim specimen stared straight ahead, tweed cap in lap. The driver was a short woman. The shadow of

the rearview mirror fell across her face, hiding her eyes from the porch light. . . . The Divine Precepts were pathetic, believing the world would end in '67. But what would Flora do when it *didn't*?

Last week, Parker had found a DP tract in Flora's nightstand: *The New Message,* a palm-sized volume in blue leatherette. Every other word was capitalized: *Mankind, God, Truth. Messiah* and *World to Come.* The translator had a shaky grasp of punctuation, tenses, and spelling. Parker suspected that Flora went to DP meetings to have all this cryptic wisdom explained in person.

Tucked among the pages were several one-line classified ads, cut out of the *Criterion,* the newspaper Flora used to work for. Each had a question and one of the old-fashioned telephone exchanges, from before all of Buffalo fell under the area code 716. A number she must have called, at a low moment.

WHY the rapid increase of anxiety today? BA 4-4300

WHY the rising rate of suicide in Buffalo? BA 4-4300

WHO can stop the decay of values? BA 4-4300

WHERE can you find the key to perfection? BA 4-4300

More alarming was the back cover, which had a mailing address for global headquarters. Meaning the Divine Precepts weren't local crackpots, but an international entity. That house on Vulcan Street was an American outpost for a Tokyo church . . . which turned out to be a Japanese outpost of a *Korean* church. It was a monster in hiding, sliding its tentacles through holes in the world, one of them oozing out through the surface right here in Buffalo . . .

He thought of the bridegroom whose wedding he'd stumbled into. The Yellow Peril, grinning behind a Christian mask.

FOURTEEN YEARS EARLIER, heading for Korea, he heard all the reports of its bone-breaking winter but figured that being from Buf-

falo made him impervious. First night there, he took off his uniform and saw a rust tinge on the collar: the cloth had frozen into a blade, dug into his neck. It got worse. By the time the squadron flew missions up in MiG Alley, hard by the border with China, he'd stopped thinking of temperature as a quality that applied to human experience.

On dawn patrol, he spotted a strange aircraft, a huge disk peaking at the center like a coolie hat. The *fyzx* was all screwy, like it was rewriting the air as it moved. Within him, time and space. For a moment the immense pavilion flew directly below the Sabre, as if inviting him to dock. That's when he sensed the Freak for the first time: a new frequency, as much in his bones as his ears. A message, not in words but pulses, pauses, intimations . . .

Then the ship sank into a cloudbank. Parker tried to follow, but his trusty Sabre stopped responding. Said *We're not doing this, no sir, not today.* The sky turned upside down. He flailed at the controls. The cockpit held together long enough for him to see that the rest of the plane was gone.

"Flora," he said, falling with the snow.

Next thing he knew, he was in a cell with a captured ROK soldier, Ko Pan-gu. Ko had seen ghastly things, which he related in broken English. He was grateful for the Americans, hated the Russians, didn't trust the Chinese. . . . The next day he'd reverse it, despising the U.S., giving the others the benefit of the doubt.

How was it, Ko demanded, that these nations had fought against Japan just a few years ago and were now pitted against each other, taking Korea apart in the process?

Parker would shrug and say, "Beats me, champ."

"Shrimp between whales, eh?" Ko cackled, flicking a Zippo. "Korea—she is shrimp."

He also said, "Same bed, different dreams. Korea—she is bed."

He claimed "Ko Pan-gu" was an alias, that he would never reveal his real name, suggesting he was of sufficient rank or pedigree that their captors might use him as a bargaining chip. The guards pressured all the

prisoners to go red: denounce the South, fight for the North. Parker saw other South Korean POWs break, but not Ko.

One Sunday, the guards informed Ko that they had captured his family. Each week thereafter, they described the tortures they'd inflicted, saying they would stop only when he revealed his real name. Parker told his cellmate it was all lies, but Ko was shattered. He refused to eat, sat in the corner with his lighter, put a palm over the flame. Every day he brought flesh closer to fire. Then one morning he got hold of a broken bayonet and cut his throat out.

That night, Parker couldn't sleep. The filthy pillow felt strange. His fingers found a slit. Inside, Ko Pan-gu had left a parting gift: his beloved Zippo, engraved with his initials in English.

K

P

G

Presently, Parker's own reeducation commenced. For ten hours a day, his captors repeated phrases in Korean, turning his brain to putty, so they could remold it. To keep his spirit intact, he focused on the Zippo in his pocket.

A year after P. G. Ko shuffled off the mortal coil, the prison camp was liberated, and—following a spell at an American hospital in Japan—Parker Jotter shuffled off to Buffalo.

BUSINESS AT JOT Electronix was brisk that Monday. The cold snap got people thinking about what they didn't have. He moved six space heaters, six snowblowers, two electric blankets, a sewing machine. They sold out of jumper cables. At five, a shadow fell across the counter.

"We're just about done today," he said, "so if you know what you'd like—"

Parker Jotter was surprised to see his old cellmate Ko Pan-gu, alive

again and with hair parted smartly, holding a gray felt hat to his chest as if about to break out into song.

Parker stared. What was he doing, back from the dead?

"Excuse . . ." Ko fumbled for the word. "Brenda."

"Uh . . ."

"Excuse!" His old cellmate fished a slip of paper from his pocket that read: *Osterizer.*

"A man who knows what he wants," Parker said, coming around the counter to take him down the second aisle. "An Oster *blender.* We have that, sure. There we are."

The man received the blender with a small dip of the head.

"Big celebration coming up?" Parker asked.

"Ah, ha-ha." His laugh was nervous but the smile was genuine. "Wipe, birthday!"

It took a second for Parker to hear *wife.* He rang up the sale, then plucked a copy of *2333: The Louse* from the wire rack. An underrated title. He pressed a rubber stamp into a blue ink pad, marked the top edge with the store's logo, then tossed it into the bag.

"Compliments of the house."

"Thank you!"

"I wrote it."

The man flipped to the back, scanned the description intently. "I will read."

He studied the stamp, a letter hidden in a plug:

"Don't let the wife read it." Parker winked. "Gets a little racy in spots."

Only while walking home, the wind sending leaves into space-time eddies about his feet, did it dawn on Parker who his customer was. Not

Ko from the camp, of course. (Ko was taller, not to mention dead.) His last customer of the day was the same man he'd seen getting married. Of course. A newlywed, buying a blender for his new home. He was like a space explorer: crossing vast distances, living among strangers, stumbling through the language.

Parker cursed his own cunning. Why had he sold him a used blender, one he knew would break in a few months? He thought of the meals the wife would make, the life they were starting. What a bastard he could be.

"Good luck," he said to no one.

ON WEDNESDAY, THE Freak returned, stronger than ever. The latest *2333* chronicle was coming together. Though good old Greena Hymns had forged a temporary truce between warring clans on Tyosen, other worlds like Allîhs were splintering into factions. Her only hope was to locate the Tan Gun, a mythical weapon mentioned in passing two books ago. Parker was plotting the climax when Tina swooped in.

"I lied," his daughter said. "Her name wasn't Tina."

"Whose name?"

"My friend in the mirror world. She *said* her name was Tina. But I knew that her real name was Anti."

"Auntie, like an aunt?"

"*Anti,* like opposite." They must have learned it at school. "Also my name, jumbled up."

Tina sounded tough, a regular Greena Hymns. Balls of paper from last week still clogged the basket. She tried to juggle with them. "Were you fighting with Momma last night? She was home so late."

So Tina had been up, listening to them hiss like alley cats. "Maybe a little."

A paper ball bounced off the Shalimar.

"Sorry, baby."

"Pops, are we moving?"

"No."

"She keeps saying *next year.* How we'll be in a different place—how we have to get ready."

Parker had a vision of that infernal coolie hat hovering over Vulcan Street, Flora levitating into the cold Buffalonian sky, as if sucked up by a giant Electrolux. Which was crazier: Believing you saw a UFO in the war, or that Armageddon was nigh? He explained the DP's muddled belief system as best he could to Tina, careful not to make it sound insane. Which wasn't easy. He told her that the world wasn't *really* going to end. That when they made it to 1968, Flora—everything—would return to normal.

"But what if she doesn't?"

"Then we'll just have to see."

She snapped her fingers twice, fast. "I know. Put it in your book—the end of the world! Then Momma can read it, and if you write it good enough, she'll believe it."

Parker nodded, buoyed by her excitement, though he wasn't sure how that would work.

"Or write about it *almost* happening." Tina tossed paper balls at the window, the wastebasket, his head. "Then, at the last second, somebody figures how to stop it."

"One problem," he said. "Your mother doesn't read."

"She's always reading."

"The Bible, sure." *And those strange DP pamphlets,* he thought. "But not my books."

Tina looked baffled. "Even though they're all for her?"

"They are?" He had dedicated the first one, *2333,* to Flora, but not the rest.

"The title of your *series.*" She picked up a falling-apart copy of *2333: The Louse.* "It's Mom's birthday."

Parker Jotter stared as though he'd never seen it before in his life, as though the name on the cover wasn't his. With a pencil, Tina added slashes: 2/3/33.

A shiver went through him. He had picked "2333" on a whim. Zephyr liked its futuristic quality, and told him to showcase the num-

ber in each subsequent book: as a year, a satellite model, a crucial page of an immense cursed manuscript. Occasionally, fans wrote to ask what it "meant," and he spun fanciful answers. But now he knew the Freak had led him to it, all those years ago. February 3, 1933, was Flora's birthday.

How had he not seen it? In a way, all the books were secretly about her. And now he had to write one more, to save Flora from falling off the brink.

"I'll do it," Parker Jotter said, flicking the Zippo. "I'll write about the end of the world."

THE BLACK SATCHEL

FOR THE REST OF THE SUMMER, that evening at the Admiral Yi wobbled as if seen through a rain-glazed pane, a dream in which people from disparate chapters of my past appeared alongside new faces: Monk Zingapan and Cousin Gemma, Echo and Daisy Oh. Even Mercy Pang, phantom artist, belonged. These figures suggested an optimistic moral: nothing is lost; everything connects. It was food for thought while brushing my teeth, sweeping the garage, driving to my job up the mountain at GLOAT. Then the weird finale would swim to mind: *reveal secret things.*

The night was missing a paragraph or a page. What had I *actually* said, there at the end? I wanted to call Tanner but was too mortified. I could hear the Jury bouncing around, that weird little die with so many sides it looked like a ball. Searching the archives of GLOAT's /koreana forum turned up an English version of the drinking game's fourteen commands. Under the title "The Jury," the uncredited translator had modernized the list, and put it in sonnet form to boot.

Drink up *tonight,* old pal, and laugh out loud!
A dozen friends will bonk you on the *schnozz*
Ask anyone to sing—they won't be proud;
Now sing yourself, then drain without a pause!
Behold the moon and name it in your tune!
Howe'er your pals transgress, you must stay calm
Though feathers peg your face, just act immune

Dream up a bawdy poem or a psalm
No *karaoke* blares, but you must groove!
Imbibe while on a buddy's arm you latch.
A glass of wine, two *more,* the truth will prove
Two cups to lips, now send 'em down the hatch!
End your solo singing with a boom
Your true confession now must fill the room . . .

Whoever posted the poem, six years ago, did so anonymously. It might not even have been their translation, but one pulled from some forgotten book. A few directives rang a bell: Monk unleashing a bawdy couplet, Padraig and Gemma's twirl on the cramped floor. At one point, Loa Ding tormented Tanner Slow with a feather from a boa. But my own confession was beyond recall. Had I spoken too bluntly of Padraig's memoirs, Yuka's plays? *That* would explain their frosty silence.

YUKA TSUJIMOTO'S RECENT PLAYS really *were* the worst, though. Back in our Penumbra College days, she'd put on inspired productions—twisted fables set in a treacherous mindscape I'd dubbed Yukaland. Things in Yukaland had a tenuous connection with the real world. Language came out wrong, reversed; characters might be dressed to look like clumps of seaweed or giant paper clips. (Tanner Slow, in the *Penumbra Pennant,* described one of her works as having "no plot, theme, catchy lines, or even *people.*") Audiences were sparse, but I couldn't get enough.

Had we truly "dated"? I was more like an unpaid intern who occasionally got to see the boss naked. She enlisted me as combination lighting assistant, ticket taker, poster designer, and gofer. I lugged equipment, xeroxed flyers, and folded seats while she tested monologues, mapping out the dappled meadows of Yukaland. For most of that year I was her servant, and her comments frequently suggested that she felt this was the natural order of things. Which is to say, the idea of a Korean doing the bidding of a Japanese taskmaster comported with her notion that hers was the superior race. She

knew the Korean word *pali,* "faster," which she'd bark out in jest as I col-lected props after the show. Was it a kink? No, maybe, I don't know.

Right out of Penumbra, Yuka won the Peter Dong Fellowship for Drama-tists of the Diaspora. Her sense of purpose changed. She would now write on Issues with a capital *I,* namely those involving the lives of Asian Ameri-cans (I was still getting used to that term). It was a task for which her par-ticular talents were ill-suited, and her plays sagged under the weight of her thesis. Audiences stayed away, until she had the idea of rewriting works from the Western canon "to explore the Other from within," as she put it in an interview.

By then, Yuka and I had split. We didn't talk for years. Eventually, Tanner, who produced some of her work, brokered a détente, and Yuka invited Nora and me to her premieres. Though Nora reliably conked out ten minutes in, we always went, bouquet in hand.

Interactions since our Dogskill exile had been few. Now, just a few days after the Admiral Yi dinner, Yuka called while I was at work.

"I just wanted to say sorry."

Every word sounded artificial, as though ready to shrug off its definition. For a moment I thought she had fed me a line that *I* should say.

"I'm sorry for how I treated you," she said.

"Why? When?"

"Oh, *you* know," she said dramatically. "All the times I treated you as a second-class citizen. It wasn't *conscious,* Soon. But now I see we got off on the wrong foot."

That was a strange way to put it, as though we'd known each other for only a few days, rather than decades.

"I'm really, really sorry." In a shaky voice, she told me about her last few weeks. *The Bing Cherry Orchard* had flopped. A little high, she'd taken to the comments section of a chatty theater blog. She'd griped that the current culture was so debased that she would no longer write for the stage. It was appalling that critics failed to grasp how her drama reimagined Chekhov to honor the forgotten Chinese American stone-fruit pioneer. Now everyone hated her.

On top of that, there was the visit to her father. He had not been well for a while; even back when Yuka and I were in college, his health had been a concern. He suffered from a mystery ailment, with symptoms both physical and mental, one miraculously disappearing only to be replaced by another equally idiopathic. Periodically he would gather the brood—Yuka and her two far-flung sisters—to his room at an assisted-care facility in Santa Ana, where he would look surprised, even annoyed, at their presence, having forgotten that he had hailed them to begin with. Eventually he'd cheer up, regale them with elaborate stories about their childhood and memories of growing up in Japan after the war, no doubt fictionalized.

This time, however, her father delivered a bombshell: he wasn't Japanese, or at least not the way Yuka and her sisters had understood it. In fact, he was Korean. Born in 1928, he had been conscripted into the Japanese army at fourteen, and later lived in Tokyo, where he formally took on a Japanese name to avoid discrimination. Yuka's dad had buried this secret so deep that a decade could pass in which he didn't think of it once. Her sisters, to a degree deracinated already, both having shown a certain independence of mind by marrying white guys they met in law school, shrugged. But for Yuka, who felt everything in her core, it was life-changing. What did it mean to be Korean rather than Japanese?

"How did this all come up?" I asked.

"He was watching *The Chosen,* one of those Korean soaps you and Nora love."

"Haven't seen it."

"It's set in the forties, and there's a character that's basically my dad: a Japanese doctor who hides the fact that he's Korean." She paused. "The actor even *looks* a little like a younger him."

I had met Yuka's father, Sho, just once, at our Penumbra graduation. He was charming, friendlier than I'd expected, given Yuka's typical tone of complaint regarding her upbringing.

"What happens in the show?"

"The guy—the Japanese guy who's really Korean—gets recruited as a Korean spy."

"To spy on Korea?"

"I think maybe. Yes."

"For the Japanese?"

"Unclear. It's possible. Or for a kind of secret society? I can't remember. I only caught one episode. There's, like, thirteen discs."

Secret society? The pages of *Same Bed, Different Dreams* flashed in my mind. I wanted to ask if the character had been spying for the Korean Provisional Government.

"I had a crazy thought," Yuka said. "Want to hear it?"

I did and I didn't. "Sure."

"We might be related. *What if?*" She warmed to her subject. "My dad's last name, in Korean, was Lee. But his mother's maiden name was *Shin.* Which is the same as Sheen, right?"

"Yes," I said.

"I mean, what are the odds? If I were writing this for the stage, we would find out we were related *while* we were together, our parents would go nuts, we would elope . . ."

"Just please don't turn this into a play."

"Don't worry," she said, which had the opposite effect.

Yuka hung up before I could ask what I'd said at the dinner. Had my "true confession" provoked her to tell me a secret of her own? Aspects of that evening were sliding out of reach. At least I had Echo's book to assure me the night had really happened. But then, to my alarm, I didn't. *Same Bed, Different Dreams* was nowhere to be found.

OUR HOUSE WAS NEAT, thanks to Nora's natural tendencies, a weekly cleaning service, and a fleet of GLOAT micro-Zambonis that rumbled out of their docking stations to vacuum and spray twice a day, to our dog's delight. (Was Sprout controlling them, via his fancy GLOAT collar?) But books went missing on a regular basis. I suspected Nora was winnowing, transplanting raggedy volumes to benches in the landscaped octagon near the Dogskill branch of Daily Divas.

Where had I put Echo's book? I had a clear memory of removing it from my satchel when I got home. But it wasn't in any of the usual places: on my

desk in the loft, or my nightstand, or the living-room end table where the kitschy princess phone sat. It wasn't by the door, or in the closet, or in the upstairs bathroom. The more I searched, the more I wanted to read it. I tried picturing it. The humble cover and indifferent print job just made it more alluring. In the house were hundreds of books I'd been meaning to get to— but only one title would do.

"Come on out," I whispered dementedly. "Come to Papa."

I did another sweep, even going into the basement, which I hadn't visited in weeks. I pretended to be a robot, eyes methodically scanning the three metal bookcases, the ziggurats of opaque storage bins. The cold concrete floor penetrated my socks. As I started up the stairs, the answer came to me: it must still be in my satchel. I hadn't taken it out after all! I dashed upstairs, slid across the foyer to the closet, and took the bag off the peg. It felt dismayingly light, and before I opened it, I knew there was no book inside. I gazed at the void, put the satchel back, and went to bed.

LOOKING FOR *Same Bed* again a few nights later, I peeked into Story's room. She was absorbed in her tablet, playing a game that reflected off her blue-light glasses. Theme music leaked from the pink headphones: a K-pop song.

"Is this D5?" I asked, lifting the cup off one ear.

She shook her head without breaking her gaze. "It's Reality."

"What's the difference?" I joked.

"Min and Jackie got kicked out of D5 and joined Reality," Story said, with a note of exasperation. She had kidsplained the drama to me before. Reality had been a second-tier, five-member boy band; adding the pair of ex-D5 singers caused friction, and three of the founding Reality performers departed. If my math was right, it was now a co-ed four-person enterprise.

The headphones were off, but she was still playing.

"What did I say about no devices on school nights?"

"Soon, you literally work for a tech company."

She called me by my first name, a sign of weak parenting. What was I doing wrong? Time to put a foot down.

"Who said it was okay to download a new game?" I asked. No answer. "Story, put the tablet down."

I didn't love it when Story went into an electronic zombie trance. Which was hypocritical. How many hours a day did I peer into screens of various sizes, for work, play, news, nothing? I even did it in my dreams.

"Hi," she said a minute later, as though I'd just walked in.

"You're too close to the screen. Bad for your eyes."

"That's racist."

"Not when I say it. Sit up straight. You'll turn into a hunchback."

Times change, but certain phrases live on. My mother used to prophesy my future hunchbackdom, critiquing my posture as I watched TV. If only she could see me now, diminished after years in front of my office computer.

I choked back a tear.

"What's the game, anyway?" I asked.

"Hegemon," Story said. "It's for school."

Story attended Measures, located a few towns south. Her school was the second in a chain of for-profit institutions that would cover the globe. (GLOAT had recently bought the chain, or maybe even started it.) It drew pedagogical inspiration from Scandinavia, Italy, China, and, it seemed, colonial America, if the emphasis on churning butter was any sign. But it also looked to the future: once a week, kids test-drove a batch of video games, as GLOAT researchers gazed at them behind one-way glass. I called it the Arcades Project.

"What about your chess drills?" I asked. Coach Dmitri had inculcated in his students the idea that chess was not only the king of games but the noblest activity in recorded history. All else was mere recreation. A heavy lesson, but one that seven-year-olds took in stride.

Story made a distracted hand gesture, possibly with Sicilian roots. I peered at the action onscreen. The austere graphics were a throwback: thin, bright green vector forms against depthless black. A dime-sized spaceship floated upward, en route to a planet. Story steered it with a tap. Occasionally it absorbed a glowing blue triangle, some sort of fuel boost, or swerved to avoid nuggets of space junk. Story alternately shook her fist in triumph or let out a grunt.

As soon as the spacecraft landed, the scale shifted abruptly. The graphics deepened. A voice boomed, "Dreams are your only reality" as a figure in red combat armor stepped out of the ship: Story's white-haired female avatar, an arsenal strapped to her frame. You could see the shadows in the folds of her clothes. A lizard with about a dozen legs charged at her, only to bow its neck and allow her to mount.

The pair made for the horizon, where a giant spider lay in ambush. The word "FIGHT!" exploded across the screen. The constant action made me jumpy, but Story was in control. Her eyes narrowed. With practiced swipes, she made her character leap and roll, stab and blast. In the corner of the screen were some inscrutable figures.

KNO 60 **POW** 77
GRI 43 **AGI** 13
ESP 92 **CHA** 55

"What's K-N-O?" I asked her.

"Knowledge."

"And POW is . . . prisoner of war?"

"No. That's just power." She explained how everyone's avatar had six attributes. The others were grit, agility, ESP, and charisma (which she pronounced *cha*-risma). You could gain or lose points in these categories, depending on how you handled certain situations.

As she talked, I felt close to cracking the code. Hegemon's traits—knowledge, power, grit, and so on—all sounded familiar. I had the sudden memory of a role-playing game I experienced exactly once in boarding school, a D&D knockoff set in outer space. Glorious Legends? Gamma Lizards? There were five of us; I was in tenth grade. A kid in my dorm had found the game behind his dresser, residue from a past student. Part of the fun was trying to figure out how to play. We were soldiers, mutants, cyborgs, looking for a rogue computer bent on destroying the planet. Something like that. I remembered that the box had a velvet bag filled with gemstones that turned out to be dice with eight, twelve, twenty sides. I remembered the lurid cover painting: a mountain with its top blown off, androids with proton guns. I

even remembered the artist's enticing signature in scarlet: *Euphrates.* The session lasted hours, and it was understood that we would play again some-time. But then finals week came, and the kid—whose name was the one thing I couldn't recall—switched schools before spring semester.

Story's tablet was a next-gen GLOAT model, a device even I hadn't seen before. On the back was a peach-colored decal with a doodle of a flying saucer hovering over cacti, under the words "I Want to Believe." An ani-mated sequence loaded onscreen. Approaching her white-haired avatar was a feral squirreloid brandishing a harpoon. Story readied her carbine. The figure raised a paw, spun around, trudged away.

"What's the goal?"

"You have to find pieces of this thing called the Tan Gun. The ultimate weapon. The first one to put it together wins fifty thousand Gloatables and gets to rule the planet."

"How many pieces do you need?"

"Eighteen. I have three so far."

"Not bad. Who are you up against?"

"There's, like, a hundred players now. I mean, a hundred thousand."

She toggled to the high-score board, pointed at her initials: SOS. She ranked in the low 400s.

"Is it like chess?" I asked, hoping for an educational angle.

"Sure, sure," Story said, as the squirrel turned around and charged. She rolled a grenade underneath it, walked away as it exploded. "Just like chess."

FIXING A SANDWICH BEFORE work on Monday, I decided I would read the next chunk of Echo's unpublished book—Dream Two—at the lone picnic table at work, in the little scrap of nature out back called Little Eden. You needed a key to get there. Only a few Rung 10s still had the key. (For some reason, I had two.)

I craved a place to wrap my head around Dream One. Its thirty-three short blasts of history had soothed me that night on the train, even as they'd disoriented me. Dream One was fiction, of course—part of a novel—but some of it plugged into my ragged knowledge of Korean history. Were Echo's

micro-essays based on actual accounts? I couldn't recall ever reading about the Korean Provisional Government, though maybe I had, years ago. Poking around online, I learned that it was a figurehead group, more symbolic than effective. Had the KPG wielded real power, as Dream One suggested? Were all these politicians and poets and martyrs really members? I reminded myself it was fiction.

Other things perplexed me. Echo mixed verb tenses vigorously, sometimes in the same sentence. Was this a flaw or a tactic of Daisy Oh's? Also, in rendering names into English, she employed two different systems, the McCune-Reischauer and a more modern one, though for transnational figures like Syngman Rhee (whom I'd heard of) and Philip Jaisohn (whom I hadn't), she used spellings coined by Western media of the time or by the people themselves. And there were names she appeared to anglicize incorrectly, but that must have sounded right to her ear. Had Echo okayed Daisy's haphazard approach? I considered dropping her a line, praising the work and asking for clarification, but I thought it better to read the whole thing first.

GLOAT had offices all over the world, but its headquarters—which I'd dubbed the Asterisk—were here, on a mountain in the Hudson Valley. Some days, the air was so fresh, the vista so clear, that you could imagine yourself far from Dogskill. I used to eat lunch and read at the table daily, weather permitting. It was rejuvenating to be outside the confines of the office, soaking up the sun. I'd block out time on my public-facing calendar, labeling my noonday slot BOOK. Then things got too busy.

All of us at GLOAT posted even our most mundane activities, a running commentary that enhanced our so-so lives and, indirectly, our market share. But Little Eden, attained through a door disguised as a vending machine, was a tech-free zone. Not only did the internet not work here, but devices would go weirdly haywire. (One coworker said her laptop sent out all the messages in her drafts folder.) In five years, people joked, Little Eden would be the last acre on earth to stay untagged. I liked it as a shield against the prods and asks of my supervisor, Dr. Ubu.

The clock said ten to nine. I had to find Echo's book and go.

"Babe?" I called to Nora.

The syllable echoed. It leaked into the basement and up to the loft, reaching her meditation nook, Sprout's sad bed.

"Doll?" I said, a little louder. "Have you seen my book?"

I walked upstairs, a finger in the groove of the wainscoting, scooping out a soft gray fin of dust. I headed back down.

"Babe?"

"Babe?" echoed Story, seated at my laptop.

"What are you doing on my computer?"

"Playing Hegemon."

"Again?" I heard Sprout yip from his post by the front window. "I thought Mom was taking you to school."

"Chill, Soon," she said. "We're leaving in fifteen minutes."

I tried petting the dog en route to the kitchen, but he rolled away, at impressive speed. He stood up only after putting a few yards between us. He was getting weirder by the day.

"Something else," Nora was saying. She was doing lunges on the deck, her phone on a low glass table. I looked past her, at the strip of forest behind the house. Rain had polished the leaves, and the grass below glistened.

"Something else," Nora repeated, still not seeing me.

"Mom," Story said. Nora held up a finger, keeping us both at bay.

"Something else," Nora said in a firm voice, no accent. "Speak to a representative."

"Your mother is a corporation," I said to Story as I put my sandwich in a bag.

We stared at Nora You, LLC. It was a bit of an accident that she owned a string of beauty centers—Nora, who as a girl despised fashion and showered, as she put it, fortnightly. She grew up in Manhattan with her artist mom, her tycoon father having fled the country to evade tax-evasion charges. As a socially minded Barnard sophomore, she went undercover in the hopes of getting the city's Asian manicurists to unionize. Instead, the boss hired her as a marketer/translator, and a year after graduating, Nora found herself the owner of two nail salons, on the Upper West and Upper East Sides. Talk of a union vanished. Then she became driven to deliver premium spa services at low prices.

More branches opened in the outer boroughs, then the burbs. Nora blended her own artisanal nail polish, in thirty hues and counting, and was an early importer of high-end Korean cosmetics, with their odd names and surreal ingredients: masks marinated in snail spit, moisturizing mitts packed with royal jelly. She was always hashing out details with suppliers, talking next steps while attacking the spin bike. The touchscreen offered real-world scenery to pedal through, but Nora was glued to her phone, earpiece in. That was where everything happened. Story and I were the wallpaper. Nora was on it all the time, but so was the rest of the world.

PULLING OUT OF THE driveway, resigned to missing out on Dream Two for another day, I caught Sprout loping by the bushes. His jaw looked weird, as though insufficiently pixelated or built with papier-mâché. The dirt on his chest was like a coating of cinnamon. I lowered the window. He opened his mouth so wide that his eyes closed. He gagged and hacked, gave up a bolus. I stopped the car.

"Eating the newspaper again, huh?"

I took it for another symptom of his Dorchester syndrome. Poor Sprout turned around, and around again, nipping at his tail. I got out and put him in a gentle headlock, scratched his ears, and peeled the damp wads from his muzzle. A gust blew leaves off the Japanese maple. That's when I saw it: under a bush was a scrap of paper, of the same gray stock used for the cover of *Same Bed, Different Dreams.*

"Bad boy," I scolded, then felt guilty. "What did you do to my book?"

He coughed and whimpered.

"I'm not angry," I said unconvincingly. I was late for work. "Gotta go."

All day I thought about Dream Two. I went out to Little Eden and basked in the unwiredness, free from all communication. I had to clear my head. I could take only so much anonymity, though. After five minutes, I rushed back inside to sit at my computer and write to my old friend Tanner Slow, asking for another copy of *Same Bed, Different Dreams.*

"I'm slightly obsessed!"

The out-of-office reply came at me so fast it seemed to bend time. He

was on a deviceless retreat for the next month. Next, I searched for Daisy Oh, the translator, but she didn't have any sort of digital shingle out. Then I tried to find Echo, the author himself, but aside from a brief author profile on the Slow Press site, he'd left no trace, at least not in English. There was no photo. His profile didn't mention *Same Bed,* touting only *The Sins,* the first of Echo's books on the Slow Press slate. The title surprised me again. No one knew I had wanted to call my second book *The Sins*—not Tanner, and certainly not Echo. It was just a coincidence.

LATELY MY JOB INVOLVED maximizing S-D points. The abbreviation stood for Sex-Death, a term that had been around since GLOAT's early days. Nobody seemed to know what it meant. In terms of my job, though, it meant supervising mini-trends that would allow us to reap just a little more information on anyone who participated. An innocuous "challenge" would emerge from my team: draw a mustache on a picture of your celebrity crush, say, or name the best chase scene from an '80s movie. You couldn't help but gloat about your results. An addictive word game let us guess your education level, down to the GPA; a prompt to post a fun photo of your grandma extended GLOAT's reach into your past, filling out the family tree it was already working on. Even *quitting* a challenge spoke volumes. In this way, we fleshed out the S-D profiles of millions.

The S-D data helped GLOAT better direct ads from its sponsors, but there was something else to it. Even old salts like me could only guess the larger purpose. As GLOAT's profile of every person, place, thing, and emotion got more granular, every connection and reaction became more predictable. (A few weeks ago, when Story asked how we knew we weren't just living in a dream, I unhelpfully replied, "Maybe we are!") The company knew what you were likely to do at any hour on any given day. It knew your mood and your blood sugar level. It could probably predict the day you would die.

That afternoon at the Asterisk, around the time I should have been basking in the sun with Echo's book, Dr. Ubu called, asking what I thought of the latest challenge.

I reread what she'd sent yesterday: *You're in charge of inventing a cocktail at a family reunion. What do you name it? (Nonalcoholic is an option!)*

"It's perfect," I told my supervisor. "Let's run it up the flagpole."

She asked what I would name my drink.

I thought about it a second, then said, "Same Bed, Different Dreams."

WHEN I GOT HOME, Nora was holding my trusty satchel.

"Whose is this? Sprout's been dragging it around the house."

I thought it was mine—the one I'd brought to New York a few weeks back—but I could see that this one was cheaper and newer. The corners were more defined, and the material was stiffer. My strap had a worn spot, whereas this one was intact. The lining had two dividers instead of one. Inside, there was no name tag or business card to identify the rightful owner.

"Look what it says on the strap!" Story said.

Embroidered in gold thread was the word ASS, part of a brand name, perhaps.

"Weird," I said. "It's a mystery."

Clearly, the bags had gotten mixed up in the coatroom at the Admiral Yi. Whose did I have? Most likely Daisy's—had she meant for me to have it? That would explain why an early copy of her *Same Bed* translation was inside. But why not just give it to me, in the open?

"The mystery of *ass*," Story giggled. Sprout dashed up and down the stairs.

"Go to your room," Nora ordered.

"I thought you liked that satchel," said Nora, meaning the one I'd lost. She'd given it to me as an anniversary gift two years ago.

"I did!" I said. "I mean—I *do*."

"We should maybe talk about your drinking."

"Keep your voice down."

"Does Soon have a drinking problem?" Story chirped from her room.

"Quiet," I said. Then, softly to Nora: "I had too much, one night. A dumb mistake. But you know me. I go weeks without touching a drop."

"We both know that's not true."

Nora went upstairs without another word. I stepped outside. It was later than I thought, the sky a knockout purple. A clean moon hung near that mountain where I spent my days tricking people into divulging their likes, dislikes, habits, fears. Harvesting histories. Building up their S-D profiles for God knows what.

I could hear Sprout scratching at the door from the inside. I let him join me.

"Hey now," I said, kneading his forehead. His tongue lolled and his eyes narrowed in bliss. This surge of happiness instantly shot up my arm and into my heart. Dogs were the best. I thought how nice it was that Sprout didn't care about Echo or the KPG or S-D data, my drinking or non-drinking.

With my other hand, I wiggled a few fingers under his collar and scratched. *Woof.* The sound startled me. I couldn't recall the last time he had barked so loudly. He wriggled out of my grasp and raced to the far edge of the neighbors' backyard. I jogged to catch up. Sprout trudged among the trees, then swiveled and pointed his nose at a patch of crabgrass. He started to dig, and soon I was dodging clods and pulling out damp clumps of paper. The green LED dot on his GLOAT collar waxed and waned. Sprout's breathing thickened as he reached his quarry: a lump of paper.

He'd been archiving again. I recovered about fifty filthy rain-warped pages, laid them out in the garage. I brought the hair dryer from the bathroom and got to work. Sprout cowered, ashamed, but I wasn't upset. I was excited to be reunited with Echo's book, even just a part of it. I gave my sick pal a hug. Then I made a 1.33-Gloatable e-payment to a Dorchester's syndrome charity. I didn't know if that was a lot or a little. Later, after Story and Nora went to bed, I drew a bath and entered Dream Two.

DREAM TWO
1901–1909

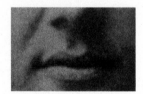

Korea has already been judged impotent and unworthy to be trusted with the management either of her own internal affairs or of her relations to other nations in the Far East and in the world at large. Japan has been judged to be the most favorably situated and, for the protection of her own interests, best entitled to undertake and carry through the reform and reconstitution of Korea. Japan also will in the future be judged, by the judgment of the civilized world and by the verdict of history, according to the way in which she fulfils her duties, and accomplishes her task, in Korea.

—George Trumbull Ladd, "The Solution of the Problem"

1. Multiple Choice

What is history?

    (a) a vital lesson

    (b) amusement for the idle

    (c) the sum of symbols

    (d) a record of pain

This is the second dream of the Korean Provisional Government.

2. Into the Pan

August 28, 1901. A young man tubercular arrives in Buffalo from Cleveland. It's his second visit to the Pan-American Exposition, a glorious world within a world: 350 fevered acres of lights and canals and majestic plaster castles and prize livestock and midway barkers and soft drinks and belly dancers and dairy goods and pergolas and incubated mewling newborns and Esquimaux melting in their furs.

This time, he rents the room above Nowak's saloon, giving his name as Friedrich Nieman—that is, *Fred Nobody*. Fred's real name is Leon, but he hates it. He hates his last name even more, a snake's nest of sibilants. Better to be Nieman and become Nobody.

3. Anniversary

What is history? Scholars insist that dates matter. Only then can you see the patterns, trace the flow. It is three years to the day since Fred Nieman left the Newburg Wire Mill. He quit for his health, but he coughs even more now. The worst eruptions bring up blood, strange formations, liverish chunks that wriggle for a time on the pavement.

He steps into the dream city, the taste of iron in his mouth.

4. Leaving Ohio

September 1, 1901, Canton, Ohio. Ida McKinley looks for her pocket diary. Most of the early pages are blank, but the upcoming trip, the prospect of the Pan, coaxes her pen a few inches. *I wish we were not going away from home My precious and I had a very delightful ride to-day.*

5. Meditation on Dust

September heat. Fred Nobody sits in his room above Nowak's saloon as dust swarms in the light. If each mote is a human soul, could all the people in the world be contained in his quarters? All the people since time began, rich and poor alike, the Slav and the Hindoo and the Hottentot—all souls dead or alive?

A tortoiseshell cat cuts through the invisible millions. Nobody pets her from head to tail. The cat closes her eyes in ecstasy. He coughs, for two minutes straight. The gray visitor curls into him as he spits into a cup. He strokes the fur one way, then the other.

6. Nobody

After Leon is fired from the mill, he grows a mustache. He waits a month before going back, applying for work under the name "Fred C. Nieman." The mill hires him again. (The mustache—nature's costume.) Leon does more detailed work, with a finer

title but for the same pay. (There should be a word for this.) He quits, having proved his point, which is that factories don't want to hire *people*. They want a set of hands, a pair of eyes.

His father (a Pole from Prussia) doesn't agree with this worldview, especially when his son moves back to the farm. There, Leon acts like a man of leisure. He shoots rabbits with his Iver Johnson pistol (or doesn't), pets the dog (or ignores it), reads late into the night while eating loaves and fishes. He cooks the fish in the kitchen and carries it on hunks of bread down the hall to his room. Eats in small bites, so he doesn't cough. He keeps vampire's hours: stays up till dawn, sleeps till noon, when his stepmother raps on his door. Curses in Polish till she leaves.

It is freeing, this life of Nobody. Once you stop dwelling on your own small history, you can grasp the workings of the world. He frequently has strong thoughts like these that would shock anyone who knew him. It would shock most of his former workers (the dopes) at the wire mill. It would shock his seven brothers (the morons) and his father (the Prussian Pole, or is it the Russian prole) and his god-awful stepmother. Only his dead mother would understand.

7. Red Emma
While *Nobody* floats in realms of gilded thought, *Leon* is stuck in a rage: at his mother for dying, at his father for remarrying, at his stepmother for everything. He curses his youngest brother, whose sin was being born (killing their mother in the

process), his old foreman, most of all his own body for being so sick. And he *is* sick, he is certain, because of the metal air in the factory, the twelve-hour days where you feel like you're eating a pencil.

During his worst coughing fits, Leon tries to count to ten between eruptions. He can barely make it to three. Then he reaches six. Nine. One. A doctor named Rosewater gives him potassium iodide and sulfuric strychnine. His condition flares and wanes. *In hospitals, only the rich get better,* he writes. But in the hospital of life, anyone with a willing mind can locate the underlying causes of misery.

Thus, the lectures. He will improve his mentality. This year Leon has visited Cleveland to hear speakers illuminate the workings of society. He gives his name not as Leon but as Fred Nieman, Frederick C. Nieman, F. C. Nieman.

In Cleveland, he listens spellbound to Emma Goldman. "Red Emma," the papers call her, though she's neither Communist nor socialist but something else: anarchist! With her pince-nez she resembles a small, clean old man, barely clearing the podium, but she is the most appealing woman he's ever seen. Light glints off the lenses, mesmerizing as she talks, her voice like an auctioneer's. He seeks her after the conference ends. A spark of pure understanding bridges their souls. He asks what books one must read but is too dazed to note her reply.

Two months later, he travels to Chicago to see Red Emma speak again. He understands anarchy abstractly, but what would it mean in reality? She's as electric as before but has to stop every few minutes to address the praise and tirades from the audience. A man with a bulldog face asks if the country needs to experience socialism before arriving at anarchism. Nobody came with a question, too, but he doesn't care now. He just wants to speak with her again, away from these people.

He studies a crack in the ceiling, imagines the hall caving in. Her lecture is over at last. As soon as Red Emma vanishes

behind the blue curtains at the back of the stage, Nobody bolts up the aisle, hacking, and out the front doors. He runs west past three storefronts until he spots an alley, where he figures the rear of the hall might be. Presently they are face-to-face, two people at the center of a maze. Street noises fade as Red Emma lifts a hand. She pushes a strand of hair from his eyes and says, "Nobody . . . Nobody, my boy . . ."

His face burns. *She remembers him.* Knows his name, and—naturally—gets the joke within the name. *Nieman, Nobody.* His innermost being.

"I have been wondering," he says stiffly. "Does anarchy mean anyone can do *anything*?"

"Insofar as both parties consent," she says in a judge's voice, drawing his mouth to hers. Those small hard lips blossom as her fingers outline the figure in his trousers. She comes up for air, laughing, just as the police walk by.

8. Syllabus

At home in Ohio a week later, Nobody writes to Emma Goldman, care of the magazine *Free Society.* He is sorry to be so empty-headed, but which books should he read? Jack London, Oscar Wilde? He includes a scrap of wire from the mill, looped into a flower. Weeks pass with no response. He's convinced his stepmother has stolen Red Emma's letters and burned them. Which is giving her too much credit. She has stopped thinking about her stepson entirely.

Nobody thinks of Emma touching his hair. He thinks about this frequently. She is just a few years older but she called him *my boy.* In these daydreams he is not the Polack but instead the *beautiful chap* with the *golden hair.* He comes to as the coughing—*ach, ach*—returns.

At last, a parcel: *The Conquest of Bread* and *The Diary of a Nobody.* The first is impenetrable (he was hoping for a cookbook), but *The Diary of a Nobody* is eye-opening: a British com-

edy about a bourgeois banker named Mr. Pooter. What is Emma trying to say?

9. The Preview

September 1, 1901. The *Buffalo Morning Express* reminds its readers that President William McKinley will visit the Pan in a few days' time. It lists the foreign princelings expected to be present. The Duke of Arcos. A Japanese, Marquis Ito, en route to New Haven, to accept laurels at Yale. Assorted Turks. Who are these glittering entities from overseas? Nobody envisions capes and scepters, vests thick with medals for bleeding the masses dry. He tosses the paper in disgust.

10. Ida Writes

September 4, Ida McKinley writes in her diary: *Left Canton for Buffalo to visit the Fair. Stopped at John Milburn's house Sarah Duncan and Mary Barber came out with us.*

11. Geronimo

Nobody enters the fairgrounds at dusk, just as the outlines of the buildings light up. More bulbs glow as it gets darker. The walls shimmer in their different colors like a rainbow.

The Electric Tower. Nobody takes in the tracery, holds his breath. (If he doesn't breathe, he doesn't cough.) For a moment he imagines this is heaven. But it's just plaster and light. In a

few weeks, they will break down the unreal city, and in a year few will recall quite where the buildings stood. (Nobody coughs.) He walks in the cooling night, reads the handbills. Premiering at the Pan: a Japanese has invented a powdered coffee. (Bitter but good.)

Nobody passes through a pair of obelisks, gets disoriented in the Beautiful Orient. Nothing is real. Back on the midway, spielers tout the rides. Trip to the Moon. Darkness and Dawn. Glowing in the twilight is an immense white head, thirty feet high, eyes closed in mysterious slumber. It's as though she's been buried up to her neck. He walks through the door in her throat into darkness. This place is called Dreamland. He's startled by the eminently presentable fellow who recoils at the sight of him—his own reflection. A labyrinth of mirrors. A woman hurries past, vanishes to the left. By a trick of the light, all he sees is white: white ankles and dress, long white hair. But the way she moved—could it be . . . ?

"Emma," he whispers. Like a fool he follows the phantom. Like a fool he exits alone.

12. The Canals of Buffalo

A gondolier lets him ride for a penny. Someday, soon enough, even these canals will vanish . . . His whole chest relaxes. Coughless as the night swallows him whole. (This dream city.) Whenever they pass another boat, Nobody peers, as if by some miracle his Emma will be on board.

In his wallet is a souvenir from his first visit to the Pan, over the summer: the king of hearts. Nobody had stood in line to see Geronimo, that old Apache, sign playing cards for a quarter. No message, just his name in capitals. Some people wanted more. They'd whoop it up, try to pluck the buttons from his coat. Geronimo wouldn't say boo. Dark eyes dead to the world.

Tonight, by the light of the Electric Tower, Geronimo is pissing off the side of a gondola. (Nobody rubs his eyes.) Imagine

your whole race wiped off the face of the earth. You'd piss from a boat, too. On the floor is a cardboard tube that turns out to be a kaleidoscope. Nobody puts it to his eye and sees the Pan's colored lights cut up by bits of glass, resolved into a meaningless spray. Dizzy, but he can't stop.

At Nowak's saloon, the electric shapes of the Pan still dance in his eyes. The tortoiseshell cat leaves its prints across the sawdust floor. Fred Nobody asks for a glass of milk to take upstairs. He speaks in broken Polish, and the bartender says something clever and just as broken. (They sound like men speaking in code.) Fred makes a laughing face without an accompanying laugh. He says in English that Nowak was his mother's name. *Was?* the barkeep asks. She died, Nobody says. The barkeep pours him a glass of something clear and strong. *Did she have people here?* Meaning Buffalo. Nobody shakes his head. Only me, now. In his room he chomps five Uneeda Biscuits, washes the mash down with the milk. He reads *The Diary of a Nobody* in bed. Pretends the cat he pets is Emma.

13. The Sights
September 5, Buffalo. Ida McKinley's diary: *We visited the sights of interest to-day. My Dear seemed to enjoy visiting very much. Mr. Milburn is very pleasant his wife away.*

14. Ohio Life
Nobody ventures out before noon, kaleidoscope in hand. He takes a streetcar to the fairgrounds, gets swept up in a crowd bound for the Esplanade. All these Mr. Pooters with their civic pride and mustache wax. Their wives flutter "Pan" fans, showing North and South America as sylphs, hands clasped over Mexico.

Silk parasols clog walkways, as a hundred unseen trumpets sound. Fat old President McKinley is here today to give a fat old speech. The buildings look spun from colored sand, more

insubstantial in the daylight than in the dark. The Electric Tower is dead in the punishing sun. Close up, the dark bulbs look like diagrams of sooty tubercules. A military band blasts a medley of anthems, ushering one foreign dignitary after another. Everyone's head is about to explode.

In this world you are born either high or low, he thinks. You are Somebody—or Nobody! He passes the "natives" in the Philippine Village display, paddling their canoes, and the bored, bearded man in white clothes and a tall black hat who stands in for Old Corea, and the grinning actors along the Streets of Mexico. He thinks of how far from home they are.

Someone should ship Fred Nobody halfway across the world, set up a sideshow for Australian gawkers called Ohio Life. Watch him: *Fry up fish!—Scratch a cat behind the ears!—Spit into a cup!* His life would be rich with meaning, if only someone noticed.

15. The Period of Exclusiveness

Nobody surveys the scene through his magic tube. Why do some people get so much in this life, others so little? Who is born a prince, and who a carnival freak? (McKinley already has a *mountain* named after him.) There he sits, in the presidential chariot, holding his wife's hand as though it were a bird's nest. (Ida was an invalid, they said.) Both from Ohio, just like Nobody. Hoofbeats, the turning of wheels. Nobody fights off a coughing fit, as the family next to him glares. (He'd love to get *them* sick, is the truth.) The procession stops and the mighty descend. Ida slips and McKinley steadies her. The whole world quiets as he reads his speech. The sun bouncing off his monocle makes him look like a Cyclops. McKinley's voice starts small but spreads like summer thunder. Nobody picks apart each line in his mind, looking for a clue.

"Isolation is no longer possible or desirable," the Cyclops says. "God and man have linked the nations together."

The Pan-fans flutter, setting North and South America in rapid motion. The crowd feels different now, charged. It's a storm about to break. Nobody picks up on the energy. What would Red Emma say, if she could hear the old Cyclops speak? (He coughs, coughs.)

"Shh," scolds a portly Pooter. Nobody would like to pick him up by the suspenders and throw him into the canal. There is a boy looking through the wrong end of a tube like his, fancier. Scenes from the midway decorate the sides: the giant stone face in front of Dreamland, the delicate minarets and the massive Aerio Cycle. Around the middle it says: **KALEIDO-PAN GAMES**.

"The period of exclusiveness," McKinley says, "is *past*."

The president is talking about the Philippine Islands. He does not *say* he is talking about the Philippines, people are not fully *aware* that he is talking about the Philippines, but the old Cyclops most assuredly *is* talking about the Philippines. If they walked five minutes, they could enter the Pan's Philippine Village. Smiling men in straw hats sit on the dirt floor, weaving—what, exactly? Day after day, the work remains no closer to being finished. (Do they pick it apart every evening so that they can start anew at dawn?)

America fought the Spanish not to liberate the Filipino but to rule him. Fred Nobody learned this from reading *Free Society*. (A cartoon of that walrus Taft, appointed to pacify the dark ones.) Today every presidential proclamation brings cheers.

The heat and the crowd have purified things. All is clear. There is no Leon anymore—no Friedrich Nieman, even. Only Nobody.

That night, Nobody lays out his best clothes. He has a dozen handkerchiefs—he is always coughing up the secrets of his lungs—but seeks one in particular. Faint stains resemble an archipelago in a musty atlas. Pressing it to his face, he catches

Red Emma's scent. In a flash he recalls how it fell from her hand as she took off his belt in that room in Chicago.

In the washroom down the hall he scrubs the cloth with a hunk of soap that looks like a caveman's dagger and drapes it on the sill to dry. The cat watches with approval.

16. The Temple of Music

September 6. Nobody shaves slowly, parts his hair with a metal comb. He puts on a brown suit, drinks milk at the saloon like some weird cowboy. Then it's off to the Pan. The Expo map has been folded so often it's torn into six pieces, and sometimes he forgets how the rectangles are supposed to be arranged. Nobody uses the Electric Tower as a point of reference. Everything is grander than grand. Mirror Lake is—there. The Court of Fountains is—there. Across from the pergola is the Ethnology Building, meaning the Temple of Music is—

Already people have lined up to greet the Cyclops. For hours, the queue winds slowly through the stifling heat. Vendors sell refreshments to those held captive in line. Finally, at four o'clock, Nobody enters the Temple of Music, swooning at the pipe organ's blare, loud enough to crush bone. Twenty minutes later, a Pooterish official takes down his name and shuts the door, to the protest of those outside. The walls are rose, nearly scarlet where shadows have started to creep.

McKinley stands at the front.

Nobody's teeth rattle from the organ's wail. (The buildup in his lungs is coming loose.) In his coat pocket, swaddled in the kerchief, is his trusty Iver Johnson. He sticks his hand in and blindly reworks the cloth to cover everything up to the wrist. A few guests take note of the lumpy bandage, murmur in sympathy. Nobody will play their object of pity. He flutters his lashes shamelessly. Here is a humble laborer with a bandaged mitt, an American mangled in the course of an honest day's work, yet

dressed in his finest, to pay respect to the most powerful man in the land.

17. The Cyclops

You need a biscuit, Nobody thinks, clamping down on his nerves. The music is a devilment, like a symphony in metal.

"Mister Frederick Nieman of Cleveland," announces Mr. Pooter. "Come on, let's move along."

It takes a few seconds for Nobody—Leon—*Fred*—to realize he's being called.

"A pleasure, friend," says the Great American Cyclops. "We Ohio boys need to stick together, eh?"

Reaching to shake Nobody's right hand, the president sees the bandage and kindly extends his left hand instead.

An insane chord, two loud coughs, a cloud of smoke, and history looks different. The Cyclops pats his side as if searching for his watch, reclining to the ground by degrees. (Nobody stares at his own murdering unraveling hand.) There are two holes in the handkerchief, already slipping off the gun. There are two holes in the president's shirt. McKinley is led to a chair, as every burly man for a mile around tackles Nobody. The first hit is so hard that the *beautiful chap with the golden hair* floats in the air for a moment, his eyes filled with the rose tint of the vast curved ceiling or his own blood.

"Don't let them hurt him," the Cyclops says, as his monocle slides from his face at last to crack on the temple floor.

18. The Missing Word

September 6: *Went to visit Niagara Falls this morning My Dearest was receiving in a public hall on our return when he was shot by a —— I am feeling very badly.*

The dash is for *anarchist,* the word Ida McKinley doesn't know or knows but doesn't want to say.

19. Last Words

Before his execution a month and a half later, Fred Nobody says, "I am not sorry for my crime. I am sorry I could not see my father." Then electricity makes a fairground of his body.

Frederick C. Nieman (né Leon F. Czolgosz, a.k.a. Fred Nobody) is an *anticipatory* member of the Korean Provisional Government.

20. Circles and Lines

Weju, Korea, by the Chinese border, 1904. A reporter for the *San Francisco Examiner*, calling himself "Chaney," tramps through town on a rental horse, so slowly that it seems to kick up a cloud of dust and then lose itself inside. The trees have all been cut down along this road. His guide said it was to flush out the tigers. The tigers were almost all dead now, too.

There's something funny with the horse's right leg, a hitch, or maybe this is how all the Korean horses strut.

The word for horse is *mal*. Same as the word for *language*.

There are twenty-four letters in this alphabet, which combine in clusters of two or three or four. Circles and lines. On the steamer from Japan, Chaney learned the sound each shape made. By the time the ship docked in Pusan, he could write his name. Circles and lines. Chaney passed a few days in Seoul, staying at Sontag's Hotel. With the help of Stevens, a high-strung American, he attached himself to a Japanese regiment. The leader blinked about a hundred times while reading the letter of introduction, looked Chaney over with panic and lust, then allowed him to tag along. Chaney drank with a Canadian newsman, McKenzie, and by night's end, he was the employer of a Japanese translator and a Korean coolie-guide. He had also become a veritable ranch owner, shelling out for his gammy-legged horse, a second steed for the interpreter, and a sensible pony for the guide.

Circles and lines, circles and lines.

Even on a malingering *mal,* he's a day ahead of the army on their drive north, and half a day ahead of his translator and manservant on their respective steeds. The goal is to spend some time alone here, in the dusty town of Weju, to see what he can see. After securing a cot at a glorified hut, the American rolls a cigarette and goes out in the gloaming to fix his horse's lameness.

Men puff their long pipes and stare at his skin, bright as a fish. One seems interested in his cigarette. The reporter rolls a fresh one, offers it, but the man has already disappeared.

His guide told him that the Japanese brought tobacco to Korea. The difference between the two races is extreme. Koreans are lazy and timid, stuck in the eighteenth, if not the sixteenth century. They cower inside mud-walled homes and head for higher ground at the first agitation, valuables strapped on backs. Meanwhile, the Japs make hay of the Russians, on sea and land.

One of these Korean mice has approached his fire. *Migook?*

"American, yes." Chaney puts out a hand. The man is his height.

The Korean stares blankly at the wiggling digits. *Eerim,* he asks: Name?

"Ah, I'm Jack." Going with his real name.

"Jeck?" White pipe smoke curls in the dusk.

"Jack." He finds a twig and makes eight strokes in the dirt.

"Juck?"

He scumbles the dust and attempts his real last name, his byline at the paper.

"London," he says.

The Korean scrutinizes the fresh markings. "Loon Dune?"

"*London,*" says the American, rubbing out the letters to try again. "Like London, England."

"Ron Ton."

"No, dammit—*London.*"

They titter like schoolgirls and wave him away.

"Horse," the reporter says, with a note of desperation. "Foot." He draws a horseshoe in the dust, points to the bum hoof. He mimics a hammer pounding a new spike. He points to the horse, who rolls its huge eyes as if mortified by the proceedings.

One Korean grasps the gist and points at the animal, while another shakes his head at the impossibility of procuring a horseshoe anytime that evening or the following day or in all times to come.

"*Upso, upso.*"

That word drives the American mad. *Have not got.* Every other word during his sojourn here has been *upso.* We don't have a nail, a horseshoe, a knife. We don't have meat, wine, rice, paper. *Upso.* We don't have it—and never will!

Upso, upso, the others concur.

21. The Tall Ghosts

The American takes out a postcard showing Sontag's, his hotel in Seoul. The German proprietress told him about her friend, the late queen of Korea, the one with the well-shaped head. The one murdered in a Japanese raid.

He writes a note to Fred McKenzie, the Canadian, who might still be there.

SONTAG HOTEL Seoul Korea.   J. BOHER Proprietor.

Shake a stick at them as they stand chattering about your camp-fire,
& the gloom of the landscape will be filled with tall, flitting ghosts,
bounding like deer, w/ great springy strides which one cannot but envy.
They have splendid vigor & fine bodies, but they are accustomed to
being beaten and robbed w/o protest or resistance by every chance
foreigner who enters their country.

Yours, Jack London

22. Physical Culture

October 1904, Edinburgh. The intrepid travel writer Isabella Lucy Bird Bishop dies at age seventy-four. In *Korea and Her Neighbours* (1897) she notes that Koreans have "good physiques."

"The Koreans are certainly a handsome race," she writes.

For this line alone, she is the first non-Korean unanimously and posthumously inducted into the Korean Provisional Government.

23. A Letter from Hawaii

June 1905, Honolulu. Earth the color of a robin's breast. Leaves the size of arms.

At thirty, Syngman Rhee still has nightmares, even under the tropical sun. The Koreans of Hawaii are mostly farmers, a little less poor than they were at home. In one speech, he describes what he endured in jail, lifts up his scarred hands. Afterward, a listener named Chang praises him. They are the same age, and both hail from the north of Korea, but the dialects are like different languages. Chang, who makes a dollar and a quarter a day, doesn't dare shake the great man's hand. He bows as Syngman Rhee passes, trembles in his presence.

Secretary of War William Howard Taft stops at Hawaii en route to Tokyo. Hundreds of Koreans greet him, plead the case for their homeland's independence. Taft is poorly disposed by the voyage, with barely the strength to groan. Nevertheless,

before he sails for Japan, he writes a letter of introduction for Syngman Rhee and a friend from his Pai Jai School days, Reverend P. K. Yoon. The two have been selected to represent the cause of a free Korea. (Yoon has promised the governor that he will convert every Korean on Hawaii to the Methodist faith, in exchange for this audience with Taft.) Giddy with hope, the pair drafts a letter to President Theodore Roosevelt, who was sworn in after McKinley succumbed to his wounds.

They address TR as "Your Excellency" and patiently explain why America's latest treaty with Japan has proven so objectionable. Its noble purpose (they write, disingenuously) was to preserve Korean independence by allowing Japan to protect it from Russian designs. Japan would help modernize Korea in exchange for using the country as a base for its army.

Alas, to the Koreans' dismay, Japanese nationals have run roughshod over them, *forcibly obtaining all the special privileges and concessions from our Government, so that to-day they practically own everything that is worth having in Korea.*

Syngman's fingers cramp. Only a year ago he was still behind prison walls. His torturers paid special attention to his hands. Pastor Yoon takes up the pen. "We are now afraid that she will not keep her promise of preserving our independence as a nation," he writes of Japan, "nor assisting us in reforming internal administration."

Syngman dictates: *We know that the people of America love fair play and advocate justice towards all men. We also know that your Excellency is the ardent exponent of a square deal between individuals as well as nations . . .*

They sign it, "Very respectfully, Your obedient servants . . ."

24. Oyster Bay

July 5, 1905, Hawaii. Inwhan Chang and two thousand others have handed over a third of their pay to send Syngman Rhee to the mainland as the voice of Korea. Rhee and P. K. Yoon set

sail at last. From California they travel first to Washington, then Philadelphia, where Syngman's old teacher Philip Jaisohn polishes their letter with his editor's pencil; then they stop briefly in New York, where they rent silk hats, before heading to the Octagon Hotel in Oyster Bay, Long Island. Without any official standing, they fear there will be no meeting with Roosevelt. Meanwhile, they see Japanese delegates on their way to lavish events at his "summer White House," Sagamore Hill.

Taft's letter helps. TR agrees to see the Koreans. He weighs two hundred pounds and shows every ounce, dressed for the hunt. The president is all pep. He cheerfully crushes their hands and shouts, *Bully!* It's as though nothing could delight him more than a pair of Hawaiian tramps turning up at his home, as though he relishes this impromptu meeting and can't wait to see what other marvels the day has in store. He thinks P. K. Yoon's name is *Picayune*. He notes their hats and says, *Proper toppers!*

Roosevelt tells the envoys he'll do *everything he can* for their cause. All they need to do is have the letter go through the Korean legation in Washington, and thence to the State Department. Everything will be taken care of. *Bureaucracy—but there you have it.*

Though the meeting is brief—five thousand miles for five minutes—the Koreans leave walking on air. They ebulliently overpay their bill at the Octagon and head for D.C. Pastor Yoon had feared that TR might have heard lies about their country from his friend Durham Stevens, Japan's mole and mouthpiece in Seoul. Or else that TR's Harvard chum Kaneko Kentaro had poisoned the president's opinion. But clearly Mr. Roosevelt is his own man. There is nothing to fear!

25. Prizes

Later, legends grow around Syngman Rhee. He is nine feet tall. He is so fluent in English that he can write a sentence with two hands, each pen starting at one end and meeting in the middle.

But this is a dire time, back in D.C. Even if Syngman could write beautifully with the pen gripped in his teeth, it wouldn't matter. He has a sinking feeling as they approach the doors of the legation on Logan Circle. Minister Kim made himself unavailable on the first leg of their trip; now he tells them what they already know: only the government in Korea can authorize such a letter—something that will never happen, as Japan already holds the legation in its grip.

It's one of many outrages that necessitate the birth of the Korean Provisional Government. Another is that Taft, days after the warm Hawaiian welcome back in June, assures Tokyo that the United States will leave Korea alone. Japan may do with Korea as it wishes. In September 1905, the Treaty of Portsmouth seals Korea's fate. Roosevelt brokers a peace between Russia and Japan that acknowledges the latter's claims on Korea. By the end of the year, Korea is Japan's protectorate. The next year, TR wins the Nobel Peace Prize.

26. The Worst Parts

George Trumbull Ladd, professor of philosophy and psychology at Yale, visits Japan twice in the 1890s, lecturing on education. He becomes an informal adviser to Ito Hirobumi, Japan's first (and fifth, and seventh, and tenth) prime minister. When Ladd returns in 1906, Ito is resident-general of the newly annexed Korea. It's said Marquis Ito has such a deep desire to do something good for the territory that he has adopted a girl from among the natives. What compassion!

Ladd receives the Order of the Rising Sun (third class) for his service, though his utility as an educator is dubious. Enough Japanese have absorbed wisdom overseas that his insights are hardly new; indeed, Ito himself studied in Europe in his twenties and again in his forties. Instead, the Yale man is just one of several American writers used as a public relations screen. This credulous son of Ohio, descended from *Mayflower* stock, will

return to America and tout Japan's efforts on behalf of backward Korea.

Ladd and his wife spend two months in that benighted country. The professor lodges elaborate complaints about the dull landscape, the stupid people, their wandering minds akin to the rambling wall that weaves through the capital, lacking all purpose. The Korean king looks like an attractive young woman but for the hopeless teeth. Ladd is a former pastor but nonetheless disdains the American missionaries, who take up the natives' cause against the occupation—against *progress.* Ladd knows all too well the wish to save souls. But this urge has blinded his God-fearing countrymen as to what Korea really needs.

Everything is an exercise in exasperation. The guides take him through the *worst* parts of Korea, "proving" the superiority of Japan. It's an easy sell. How can you ignore what's right before your eyes?

27. The Unwritten History

Back in the United States in 1907, George Trumbull Ladd finishes his account of that peculiar peninsula. The following year, Charles Scribner's Sons publishes *In Korea with Marquis Ito.* "Of no other civilized country than Korea is the truth of the cynical saying more obvious that much of what has been written as history is lies, and that most of real history is unwritten," Ladd states in the preface, before admitting he has been unable to finish any of the various books about Korea.

"Can Korea—such a people, with such rulers—be reformed and redeemed?" Ladd ponders. "Can her rulers be made to rule at least in some semblance of righteousness . . . ? Can the people learn to prize order, to obey law, and to respect human rights? Probably, yes; but certainly never without help from the outside."

28. The Adviser

March 24, 1908, San Francisco. Durham Stevens, Third Class of the Order of the Rising Sun, arrives at the Fairmont Hotel on Mason Street. Fresh flags whip overhead. He has been in America only a few hours, his body's clock at odds with the time around him. The ground shifts, like a floating dock a hundred miles long.

It's his first vacation in a decade. Stevens washes up, reads a brochure as he changes for a late dinner with an Oberlin pal he hasn't seen in decades. The hotel is a year old, built by McKim, Mead and White. Did the architect Stanford White live to see it? Stevens had read about his death, and the scandalous trial in New York. His sisters sent him only the most sensational items.

He tries to recall details as he puts a medal around his neck, red with golden rays. A bit of flash, why not? The ribbon is the same white as his shirtfront.

Stanford White was shot by a man named Snow. No— a man named Ice. No: *Thaw!*

Stevens chuckles as he leaves the room. His mind is all brambles today. Downstairs, to his dismay, four Koreans call his name. Three of them sit in the lobby like steamed Buddhas, and one of them, who for some reason keeps saying the word "early," stands and stomps his foot. At least their hair is cleanly trimmed. They look almost Japanese in their Western clothes.

Since the 1880s, Durham Stevens has worked for the Japanese government. He received his medal from Emperor Meiji, and the Koreans are now glaring at it. For the past four years, he has been Japan's adviser to the "Korean emperor at Söul," as *The New York Times* puts it. A fiction. There is no Korean empire. In time, there will be no Korea at all.

29. Same Bed

"Japan is doing in Korea and for the Koreans what the United States is doing in the Philippines for the Filipinos," Stevens has told the papers. Modernizing—moral uplift—basic hygiene: Who could object? This is the trend of things. The most forward-thinking Koreans knew this.

The year before, that Yale man, Ladd, had accompanied Mr. Ito Hirobumi, the resident-general, on a visit to Korea and could hardly stomach the utter degeneration. What lack of vigor! What stupid faces! Ladd saved special venom for the winding stream cutting through Seoul, into which people threw their garbage—into which the citizenry openly loosed their bowels! (Even the Korea-loving Isabella Bird couldn't mask her revulsion.) In Seoul, Durham Stevens spent as much time as possible in the comfort of Frau Sontag's hotel.

His friend Count Mutsu, gone now almost a decade, told him what the Koreans believed: that their country was but a prawn caught between clashing whales: Russia, Japan, China. The deposed emperor, Kojong, whined that Korea was a small bed into which bigger countries were trying to fit. Something like that. Stevens just wants to get to Atlantic City, where his sisters spend their summers. Cover his feet in cold water. Forget the endless metaphors of the Orient.

30. Syllables

Mind drifts. In Korea, he found it amusing how they couldn't manage the diphthong and fricative in his name, two syllables becoming four: *Suh-tee-bun-suh.* An inefficiency typical of the race.

Mind drifts. Harry Thaw shot Stanford White. Durham's middle name is White. Koreans stretch it into *Wah-ee-tuh.* . . . Enough. Dinner awaits.

31. Porridge Eyes

Hours later, dyspeptic from sauces and starches, Durham Stevens returns to the Fairmont, where a welcoming party has gathered. It is all rather shouty. He listens for a mystified minute as one of the six Koreans, clutching a newspaper in his fist, repeats the word "early."

Slow down, he wants to say. *Take a long breath.* "Who *are* you?"

"Early!" the man keeps exclaiming, until it's clear that it's his name: Earl Lee.

Other guests are staring. Stevens suggests they all repair to a room off the lobby.

Earl's as tall as Stevens. Who is this importunate man? What does he want? Earl Lee reads the diplomat's quotes back to him from the evening edition, as though listing the contents of a garbage pail, a diet of worms. What if this man trails him across the country? Then it will be Earl Lee to bed, Earl Lee to rise.

These are unnatural Koreans, situated too far from home. They have darkened from their time working sugar in Hawaii. The Koreans in *Korea* accept their fate, in his experience. Many of the brightest young men sincerely look to Japan for guidance—they hold the Japanese in awe for beating the Russians. (Hell, *Stevens* holds them in awe for beating the Russians.) If the natives grumble, it rarely rises to the level of outright conflict. Strong words with nothing behind them.

Yet here in the United States, the exiles are free to reach the most ludicrous conclusions. *Dementia Americana* might be the term for it.

The medal feels heavy around his neck.

Another Korean scans the column and sputters, "Do you believe that Koreans are *unable* to *govern* themselves?"

Un-ay-burr to *gub-uh-lun.*

"You must understand, this is a time for guidance," Stevens replies. Especially, he thinks, after Marquis Ito forced Kojong to abdicate. Now Kojong's half-wit son sits on the throne.

"A lie," spits Earl Lee.

It is decidedly *not* a lie, but Durham Stevens bites his tongue. He knows what's coming next. The old saw about how Korea had been *gub-uh-ning* itself just fine for five hundred years (a lie), how it had been around for millennia before that (another lie). Inevitably one of these men would compare the vast historical age of Korea to America's century and a half, and didn't you know that all Japanese culture originally came from Korea?

And, indeed, this information is conveyed to him, there in the lobby of the Fairmont, as though off a script, by a chorus of Koreans stepping on each other's lines. Doesn't *Suh-tee-bun-suh* know that the Japanese are *killing* the Koreans? Replacing the officials in the government? Making schoolchildren bow eastward, to Tokyo?

The cheek. It's *Stevens* who has been in "their" godforsaken country, coming up on five years. Five years he'll never get back. Even here, his movements are not his own. This vacation is not about sisters in Atlantic City or the string of public lectures he's arranged, on the subject of subject nations. In Washington, there is talk of ending the flow of Japanese into Hawaii, where they work the sugar fields. His job is to end this talk of ending.

"I fear you've been away from home too long," Durham Stevens tells Earl. "You have no earthly notion of what is taking place."

"Our families send letters."

"Don't believe everything you read," he says with a wink. He spots the billiard table at the other end of the room, covered by a sheet. If only he can make his way there, take up a cue for

defense. He thinks of the dim Soonjong, the new Korean emperor installed by Ito, whose sole talent is apparently snooker. One Sunday, the usually languid royal taught him, with great enthusiasm, the rules of Russian pyramid, using a different set of balls, which had been presented by Ambassador Waeber. ("Bigger balls!" the man-child marveled. "Hit harder— *bigger balls!*")

Durham Stevens smirks and takes a step backward.

"What is funny?" Earl grunts. "Where you go?"

He stops in midstride. "You're dreaming if you think that Korea can rule herself now."

At this, a bigger Korean stands up, shouting, *"Porridge Eyes!"*

"Eh?" *Apologize.* Stevens shakes his head and through the open doorway frantically signals the staff, who all appear to be reading their own palms for fortunes. "Certainly not."

Then the Koreans are upon him, four of them swinging their chairs. He fends them off with his own, in the manner of a lion tamer, as he attempts to maneuver back into the lobby.

Porridge Eyes! Porridge Eyes!

It is all too absurd: busted rattan everywhere, bellboys dodging behind columns, a confused couple from Akron trying to disappear into the newspaper rack. Stevens shoves Earl Lee into a planter just as his largest opponent slips on a sliver of wood. Then he hurls his chair into two others, blocking them barely long enough to run up the stairs. The desk clerk finally blows his whistle as a doorman hails the police.

Safe in his room, he throws water on his face and stares at the mirror. A bruise on his forehead throbs, but that's not what fascinates him. He looks different. Every part of his body is shrinking, save for his head. In another year he will resemble an Oriental sage, his white eyebrows long and soft like dove feathers. He moves up close, an inch from the glass.

"Porridge eyes," he says.

32. The Medal

The next morning, Stevens rides the hotel omnibus to the Ferry Building, for a quick trip across the bay to Oakland, where he will catch a train east. The maître d' arranged it the night before, so that he can elude the mad Koreans, who no doubt hope for round two at the San Francisco station. But what if they are *here*? What if the Koreans have a spy at the hotel? He makes a solemn promise that upon boarding the train, he will set up a row of cocktails and drink till Atlantic City.

The horses clop through steaming streets. Stevens can smell the water. Gulls circle with malign precision. Their number seems to grow with each rotation. He mourns his medal, missing after the evening's melee. Maybe the Koreans made off with it.

33. Dangerous Toys

At half past nine, Chun and Chang chomp Uneeda Biscuits as they wait by the Ferry Building. A foghorn moans. Chang studies the wrapper. The slogan reads, "Energy is well-nourished muscles plus well-nourished nerves."

"What is 'nourished'?"

Chun shrugs. He was at the Fairmont last night, catching Stevens behind the knees with a pool cue before he was thrown out. Today he's brought a toy gun that looks like a real gun, which he thinks will scare Stevens into repenting. Inwhan Chang, conversely, has a real gun that looks like a toy gun, which will do whatever else is necessary. Chang covers it with a handkerchief, the way McKinley's shooter did. The cloth makes his hand look extravagantly damaged, as though trod on by an elephant in a cartoon.

Even with a mustache—nature's costume—Chang looks like a twelve-year-old. Chun is about the same age but looks like he could be his father. The odd couple first crossed paths in Hawaii, working for pennies while fleeing the Japanese. The

two met again only last week, here in San Francisco. They belong to rival Korean organizations, united this week for the sole purpose of confronting this devil Stevens.

A horse pulling a green-and-gold wagon arrives and unloads six passengers for the ferry. Each one stumbles on the last step. It takes Chun and Chang a few seconds to pick out their man. Chun shouts, "Mister *Suh-tee-bun-suh.*"

Stevens turns as Chun closes the distance. The Korean clubs him on the cheek with the grip of his real-looking fake gun. Stevens lashes back, slamming a heel into the Korean's ankle while gripping his shirt.

"Enough," grunts Stevens. The two are tangled. His medal tumbles from a coat pocket. "Enough!"

Meanwhile, Chang lifts up his fake-looking real gun and circles, trying to get a clear shot. The handkerchief throws off his aim, and the first bullet hits Chun in the chest. The gulls on the ground rise at the sound, cawing in distress, then settle ten yards to the left in the same positions, as though the ground has simply shifted beneath them.

"*Inama!*" Chun groans, annoyed, as the blood pours out.

"*Mianhae!*" Chang apologizes.

Stevens jams an elbow into Chun's ribs and claws at the black hair, saying, "I—want—my—*medal.*"

Chun's blood is everywhere. Stevens looks up just in time to see a grimy handkerchief falling from Chun's partner's real gun. Chang pumps two shots into Durham White Stevens. Without a word, Stevens rolls next to Chun on the pavement. Their fingers nearly touch. His *porridge eyes* spot the cloth on the street, a few feet from his head, like a flag of surrender. Then they look up to the white sky full of gulls.

34. What Chang

Stevens and Chun are both admitted to Lane Hospital. Once Stevens learns this, he demands a transfer. His new doctors at

the San Francisco Harbor Hospital expect a full recovery. The shooting makes the front page of papers all across the country. "Mr. Stevens is a man of fine physique," notes *The New York Times*, calling him "the American dictator of the Hermit Kingdom."

The *San Francisco Chronicle* gives the name of the shooter, Inwhan Chang, as "What Chang."

What Chang is unrepentant: "Yes, me shoot him. Me sorry? No. Him no good. Him help Japan."

35. Helpless

From his hospital bed, Stevens jokes to the press that this is a swell start to his vacation. A reporter sniffs for a link between the local Korean "tongs" and conspirators in the Korean court. Stevens scoffs; the Koreans can barely manage anything at home, let alone trigger such intrigues abroad.

"I consider it merely the work of fanatical students who may be classed as anarchists," he says. It has nothing to do with real politics.

"I *would* like my damn medal," he tells a nurse, who doesn't understand.

Meanwhile, Chun survives Chang's errant shots and is released. Only "What" Chang, dispenser of real bullets from the fake-looking gun, will stand trial.

Chun, twenty-five, tells the papers: "I came to America as a student, but have no money. Since I left, the condition of Korea became worse. Japan thinks might is right. My brothers and relatives have been killed by the Japanese, but I have no power to do anything here, and so I have always had to stand around helpless."

36. The National Character

While Stevens clings to life at Harbor Hospital, George Trumbull Ladd writes a furious letter to *The New York Times*, saying that

Chang's crime reveals the *true* nature of Koreans: quick to anger, slow to reason. Throughout their ignominious history, he claims, Koreans have resolved things not by informed debate but by simply killing the opposition. Even those who support Korean independence, he writes, should "take some pains to clear their skirts of the taint of sympathy" for the "young ruffians in San Francisco." The missive is headlined: KOREANS A BLOODY RACE.

Durham White Stevens succumbs to his wounds the day Ladd's letter appears.

37. Oddjob in the Afterlife

A half century later, in Ian Fleming's spy novel *Goldfinger*, the titular criminal mastermind employs a fearsome bodyguard named Oddjob. Auric Goldfinger explains to British secret agent James Bond why he prefers Koreans: "They are the cruelest, most ruthless people in the world."

Oddjob is musclebound and mute; only Goldfinger can understand him. He wields a razor-brimmed bowler, which he flings like a lethal Frisbee. Goldfinger plies his retinue of Korean henchmen with London prostitutes: "The women are not much to look at, but they are white and that is all the Koreans ask—to submit the white race to the grossest indignities."

In the hit 1964 movie, Harold Sakata plays the hulking Oddjob to Sean Connery's suave Bond. In his most memorable scene, Oddjob decapitates a garden statue with his bowler. A Hawaii-born pro wrestler and an Olympic medalist of Japanese descent, Sakata later appears as Oddjob in commercials for a cough syrup. He has the film character's trademark mustache, black suit, and hat. And, like Oddjob, he doesn't speak: he's completely overcome by his cough.

In one commercial, a pleasant walk home turns into a hacking fit. His limbs thrash in frustration, destroying scenery. He knocks over a fire hydrant, and water shoots up like Old Faith-

ful. His wife is at home, watching through the front window. She rushes to get the syrup but can't open the door fast enough. Oddjob's meaty fist busts through a panel to grab the elixir. Relief.

"Extra Strength Formula 44," declaims the voice-over, in deep accentless American English. "To help control a cough—before it goes on a rampage."

Harold Sakata is a member of the Korean Provisional Government.

38. The Club

Vladivostock, March 1908. Thomas Ahn and seven other examples of the cruelest, most ruthless people in the world meet in the cellar of a noodle shop. They are Christians. Two are former teachers in the chain of Catholic schools Thomas started, back in Korea. One is a woman, Bae, who works in the shop. The youngest is eighteen, the oldest forty-nine. After sober speeches about their ailing motherland, the eight rebels scheme how to save her.

Thomas Ahn grinds an inkstone and loads his brush. On a fresh scroll, he writes fifteen reasons why Ito Hirobumi must die. For all his crimes against the Korean people. For murders high and low. For the burning of textbooks. For the changing of names. For the indignities heaped on the former king, Kojong . . .

His brush is a blur. Afterward, Thomas's friend—they call him Fatty—takes off his oilskin coat and spreads it over the table. At the edge he places a stack of clean handkerchiefs, a bottle of vodka. Then he brings out a cleaver.

"To the Cut Finger Club," Thomas says.

They understand at once. The oldest—they call him "Harabaji," or Grandpa—goes first, gripping the cleaver and bringing it down at the last knuckle of his *petit doigt*. The tip bounces away like a misthrown die. Blood oozes from the

stump. Thomas Ahn is next. Gritting his teeth, he lops off his *annulaire*.

The others follow, with similar resolve. Bae loses hers without a wince. Fatty blanches, however, and asks someone else to do the deed. He unleashes a curse as the blood spurts. In the end, no one backs out. Eight morsels of bone and flesh lie scattered across the table and floor. Harabaji brings out the scroll with its list of grievances.

"To the Cut Finger Club," Fatty says, as they press their amputated fingers to the paper. Here in this port city at the southeastern tip of the Russian Empire, they sign in blood the death warrant of Ito Hirobumi, architect of their sorrows.

39. The Wolf

TO TRY KOREAN ASSASSIN reads an ambiguous headline in *The New York Times* on July 27, 1908, as though offering readers an alternate identity, a costume, a disguise. Inwhan Chang, a.k.a. What Chang, is to be sentenced for the killing of Durham White Stevens. Korean groups in San Francisco scare up funds to bring Syngman Rhee, now studying at Harvard, out to the trial, hoping he will serve as interpreter. His upbringing and education and silver tongue would do much for Chang's cause. Once in San Francisco, however, Syngman sniffs that translation is no job for a gentleman. Some of the Koreans now want to kill *him*.

Next to the piece is an article about a timber wolf in the Central Park Zoo, grown "lank and lean" after the death of his mate. The beast hails from the forests of British Columbia, where he led a pack until trappers sold him to the zoo.

His "mournful howling" so disturbs the other animals that an East Side matron asks the zookeeper what might relieve the beast's misery. "All that can save him now is freedom," he replies. The next day, she arranges to buy the wolf and return him to the spruce forests of Canada. The wolf's name is White Fang, after a novel by Jack London.

40. The Trial

One of the men who confronted Durham Stevens at the Fairmont Hotel explains things to the irate crowd outside the courthouse: *We Korean residents in San Francisco* [jeers] *who escaped
from Japan's barbarous rule* [loud protest] *knew that hundreds and
thousands of Koreans have been persecuted by Japanese military
and police forces* [boos] *because they have advocated freedom and
liberty as you Americans did during the Independence War against
Great Britain.*

Someone yells for the yellow devils to be lynched. Another
man, confused as to the nationality on display, calls the Korean
a *dirty Jap.*

41. Code Name What

On Christmas Eve 1908, the court finds Inwhan Chang guilty of
murder in the second degree. The following autumn, *The New
York Times* notes that he has been put to death, but this is not
so. Chang serves ten years of a twenty-five-year sentence, during which he is made an agent of the Korean Provisional
Government—code name "What." After his release, What settles in Korea. He meets two fellow KPG members: the suicidal
poet Kim Sowol and the tubercular filmmaker Na Ungyu. (What
plays the "dream" policeman in Na's great lost film *Arirang*.)

Alas, the Japanese suspect him of involvement in the KPG
and depatriate him in 1927. A pious Christian, originally from
the God-fearing city of Pyongyang, Inwhan Chang returns to
San Francisco, where he dies by his own hand in 1930.

42. Thorns in the Mouth

October 16, 1909, Harbin, China. Thomas Ahn dreams in French.
The son of a general, Thomas learned the language from their
priest, a Frenchman who hid the Ahn family from the Japanese
when the occasion demanded. Thomas has been a Catholic
since age sixteen, almost half his life. He sells scrolls of his

calligraphy—Confucian sayings, some invented, some adapted from Jesus Christ, his Savior.

Unless reading every day, thorns grow in the mouth.

The money goes to ammunition. He is a crack shot, once sniping a rabbit on the other side of his house by sighting it through the doorway and an open window.

43. Cathedral Dream

In one dream, he enters the Cathédrale Notre-Dame. It's empty save for a hooded figure under the rose window. Even at this distance Thomas understands that the person is standing over a coffin. Already, Thomas knows that the man standing there is Ito Hirobumi.

He touches the cold gun inside his coat. His fingers trace the initials tangled on the handle: FN. Fabrique Nationale, a Belgian model. He charges, and the figure flees. Thomas steps on his robe. The hood falls just enough to reveal that the figure is indeed the dread Ito. Thomas Ahn trembles. Who is inside the casket, then? Thomas thinks he knows, knows, too, that it would be better not to look, but he cannot stop until he sees that the dead man's face is his.

The Notre-Dame of dreams crumbles, delivers Thomas Ahn into a cool, smooth sarcophagus. A towel folded over the edge bears raised letters:

Харбин

He touches each one until he comes to, in the bathtub of a two-room suite at a Russian hotel in Harbin, China. The tub was never filled. He's completely dry, intact, alive.

Alive! Awake! Thomas hoists himself out. The stump of his *annulaire* burns and itches. He has scratched it savagely while

asleep, and now cleans his bloody fingernails over the sink. Cold water is colder here.

44. The Telegram

October 16, 1909, Kyoto. Everything is how it should be. Sun slants across a well-appointed desk. Aroma of peeled fruit and strong tea. Newspapers in three languages, freshly ironed.

The wallpaper of flowing vines soothes him, a near copy of the pattern decorating his old suite at the Sontag Hotel in Seoul. The only thing amiss is a telegram delivered overnight. The cipher is in English. Ito Hirobumi stares at it so long he might lose his mind.

> H G H A R O R A T B N E I D L N

The vines on the wall form a net. The eye follows one stalk as it goes over, under, over another, a vegetable web copied from some hoary British hunting lodge or Bavarian coffee-house. *Hgharorat Bneidln.* The name of a secret agent?

Durham Stevens, the American, was the one who'd told Ito of the Korean king's subterfuge two years ago—sending secret letters to the heads of Europe, pleading intervention. Ito said nothing at first. He let black rumors infect the palace guard, as fresh spies moved among cooks and concubines. Arbitrary new routines threw King Kojong into such a state that when Ito ordered him to give up the throne, he was helpless to resist. His son Soonjong was nothing but a simpleminded snooker fiend. Stevens used to say the dynasty was ending not with a riot but with a spinning bank shot, yellow ball dropped softly into side pocket.

45. Holding the Rabbit

And yet. In the months since giving up his post as resident-general, Ito has urged caution. Korea cannot easily be turned

into a colony, as his more belligerent countrymen desire. Korea is no Taiwan, which China ceded with a shrug. Taiwan is shaped like a sweet potato, there for the picking. Korea resembles a rabbit held by the ears, waiting for a chance to skip away.

The conditions are not right. Too much tension and mistrust. But in a decade, even the most reluctant Korean won't be able to deny the improvements. Already, *Homo coreanus* is aware of how much more rice his land is yielding—even after the best bushels are sent to Japan. He benefits from modern construction methods, the movement of the mail. Faster travel on better trains, from Pyongyang down to Pusan.

Or, rather, *Heijo* to *Fusan*. Seoul, which the natives also call Kyongsong, is *Keijo*. All the cities will be Japanized soon. Next, all the people will be renamed. Korea will be known as *Chosen* in every atlas. Then will come the process of *amalgamation*. As Ito told that stuffed shirt Ladd, *In less than a hundred years, the average inhabitant of Chosen will not know whether his great-grandparents were Korean, Japanese, or a mixture of the two.* All will be Japan in the end.

46. To Harbin

Hgharorat Bneidln. A man's name? A weird curse? Spooked, Ito can't focus on his agenda. In an hour, he embarks for Harbin, China, where he will discuss the Korean Question, the Manchurian Question, the Chinese Question, and the Russian Question—first with the Chinese, and then with Kokovsoff, the Russian minister. All of these have to do with the Railroad Question. Which has to do with the Japan Question. Or does he have it the wrong way round? He will collect facts and opinions. Shake hands. Commit to nothing. Come home.

He used to take pleasure in the game. Now he feels his head turning to paste. *Hgharorat! Hgharorat Bneidln! HGHARO!*

47. The Prince

Harbin is a city of layers, not always visible. Now run largely by the Japanese, it was built up by the Russians in China, for workers on the Chinese Eastern Railway, which is a Russian line. It makes more sense when you get there. A city without passports for a minister without portfolio.

Ito stands at the head of the Privy Council since resigning his Korea post a few months ago. This means he has the emperor's ear, but in truth he is being shown the door. Power lies elsewhere in the body he once led. The Imperial Army would prefer that he disappear—or even die. The army believes it *is* Japan.

They call him *Prince* Ito now, a title that signifies decline. Sounds better, means less.

48. Eventual Life

On Prince Ito's desk in Tokyo: a stack of books to bring on the trip, or to leave behind for the maid to throw out. Horace Underwood's *The Call of Korea* states that the country is about as large as New York and Pennsylvania combined, which makes it bigger than Great Britain, half the size of Germany. Underwood, a missionary, has lived in Korea for decades, and speaks out against Japan of late. But the Christians want dominion, too. Underwood and his Presbyterians have won converts throughout the country. How are these Americans any different from the Japanese? The arrogance of the West.

IV. *Best Points of Attack.*
1. What strategic points in Korea have been laid siege to by missions?
2. What new strategic points should be besieged?
3. How can the land be taken?
4. What would be the effect on China and Japan if Korea became a Christian nation?
5. What has been the attitude of the various classes in Korea?
6. How does the distribution of the people affect the work?

Next, he picks up *In Korea with Marquis Ito,* by George Trumbull Ladd. Strange to see his name on the cover. Ladd is a preacher, philosopher, professor, sap. The inscription is florid, indeed a trifle indiscreet. It came out a year ago, though it only reached him recently. The tops of the pages are still uncut. A playing card—Ladd's?—is wedged inside as a bookmark. Ito has hesitated to read this volume. At his age, he opens books with no illusion of reaching the end. He mounts an attack on the first few pages. In the preface, Professor Ladd says of Ito that "one of the greatest statesmen of the Orient is giving— with all his mind and heart—the later years of his eventual life."

What does that mean—*eventual* life? A cosmic irritation grips him. (Not to mention: *one* of?) Ito skips to the end. With a letter opener, he slices free the still-joined pages of the last chapter, "The Solution of the Problem."

> As to the destiny of considerable numbers of the lower orders of the people, that is perhaps unavoidably true which has been said of the Korean farmers: "A large percentage of them are past all hope of salvation."

The blade slices a knuckle. He brings his hand up to lap the blood. Warm taste of steel.

> The professional robbers and beggars, the riotous "pedlers," the seditious among the disbanded troops or the "tiger hunters," the wild and savage inhabitants of the mountainous regions, the people who live by thieving, counterfeiting, soothsaying, divining, and other illicit ways, will have to submit, reform, or be exterminated. Doubtless, many of them will prefer to be exterminated . . .

Ito grabs the dustbin to vomit his perfect breakfast. Did Ladd come to these thoughts himself? Or did *he* direct this line of logic?

To reciprocate for his visits to Japan, Ladd brought Ito to America in 1901. They made it all the way east to New York, thence Connecticut, where Yale—Ladd's school—fêted him and bestowed an honorary degree. The trip took place a week after his sixtieth birthday. The original plan had been for a late-summer arrival, stopping for the Pan-American Exposition at Buffalo, but official matters kept him in Tokyo. By the time he docked in America, a pall was hanging over the "Pan" after McKinley's shooting. The papers related how the anarchist, Leon F. Czolgosz, had covered his gun with a handkerchief. Ito read that the F. did not stand for anything, that Czolgosz just liked how it sounded. He saw a photo of a bright old man who was actually Emma Goldman, wanted in connection with the crime. He saw a photo of Roosevelt emerging from a mansion in Buffalo, magnificently somber and newly the president of the United States.

The world has spun eight times round the sun. Earlier this year, the same month Ito relinquished his post, Roosevelt stepped down to make way for Taft. Dim men often follow the great ones, but that is how it goes.

49. The Design

In comes Morita, secretary of the something or other. He will accompany Ito on the trip, first to Mukden and then Harbin—when it is safe.

"There are designs on Your Excellency's life!" Morita says. He has a touch of the hysteric and wants to postpone.

Ito motions him to sit. He had almost succeeded in forgetting the baffling telegram, that mad scramble of letters. Now it's back in his head, and he has the sudden desire to belch out the cluster of nonsense at prim little Morita: *HGHARO!*

Instead of roaring, he says: "I would feel neglected if there *weren't* designs on my life."

"Do not joke!" Morita wails.

A year ago, Korean saboteurs derailed a train bound for Keijo from Fusan. Ito had been on a later train; the only people hurt in the smashup were a dozen passengers, a member of the rail crew, and two of the plotters. One ran away—police believed she was a woman, based on the slender footprints in the snow. The other killed himself while under arrest. He had no papers. He was a perfectly anonymous man, save for the fact that the top joint of his left ring finger was missing.

A year ago, too, Durham Stevens was shot in America by a Korean named Chang. He had a cloth over his gun, just like the man who killed McKinley.

50. Fatty's Fate

HGHARO . . . Is this about someone named H. G. Haro? He knows no such person. Ito cracks open the drawer as Morita prattles about moving the meeting from Harbin to Vladivostock (which actually lies *east* of Harbin) or, indeed, to a ship off the southern coast of Korea. Morita wears some of his wife's makeup across his cheeks.

Ito wonders if the train incident last year was caused not by Korean terrorists but by the faction at home in Japan that wants him gone. A cutthroat going by H. G. Haro?

Eventual life.

"Several conspirators have been uncovered in Harbin," Morita says.

"New ones?"

Morita reads from the police report. One of their own agents, known as Fatty, infiltrated the Cut Finger Club a year ago. He has been in Vladivostock, unable to establish clear communication until a week ago. According to Fatty, the Cut Fingers started out small, but each member pledged to recruit five other "patriots"—starting a new five-fingered "hand." They

were devoted to the dismantling of Japanese rule, beginning with the death of Prince Ito.

"Top of the list, eh? I'm flattered."

Morita's eyes glance at the curtains, as if expecting random Koreans to leap out. "It is not known how many members exist at present. Likely scores. The report states that the leader, Thomas Ahn, knows Your Excellency will be in Harbin. He has taken rooms at the Grand Hotel."

"Ah."

"No—*Ahn*." Morita mops his brow. "He is an excellent marksman."

"Can Mr. Thomas Ahn shoot me from his hotel window?" he asks sarcastically.

"Do not joke!"

"So this Mr. Thomas"—*Doe-mas*—"will approach me on the platform, eh? And shoot me with his four-fingered hand hidden under cloth? The latest fashion in assassinations, I hear."

"Please!"

"In Harbin it is already winter," Ito says softly. "Too cold for such fevered plots."

Prince Ito, head of the Privy Council and former resident-general of all Korean lands, is gripped with a thought. He dismisses Morita, says he will see him aboard the steamer at Hiroshima. From the drawer he abstracts the cryptic message from earlier, and with the tip of the letter opener he trims away the rest of the telegram to leave a strip of paper.

The Lover's Cipher. Ito spreads his left hand on the table, wraps the strip of letters around his little finger.

H G H A R O R A T B N E I D L N

Blood thuds in his ears as the gibberish resolves. Every third letter forms its own word.

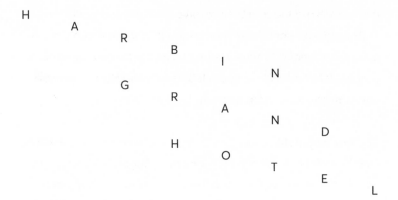

51. Native Amusements

October 23, 1909, Harbin. For dinner, Thomas Ahn tries a fantastical dish downstairs called beef Stroganoff, which practically paralyzes him. He prays for a while in his room, mostly about his stomach, then walks outside to digest. Vladivostock was frigid, but Harbin is ten times worse. He trudges a few blocks, toes frozen solid, then surrenders to a building marked ILLUZION.

It's impossibly warm. A movie is already playing. Nearly every seat is filled, a hundred in all. He finds a spot in the balcony. He's never been inside a picture house before. The screen says NATIVE AMUSEMENTS IN MOMBASA. Africans in white clothes sit on benches that spin up in a circle like a miniature Ferris wheel. Then a stout white man in a pith helmet reviews a tribe of warriors. They raise their shields and spears, then approach the audience. Thomas's finger stump throbs as he tries to make sense of the exotic scenes. The last one goes on forever. The same white man now perches on the shoulders of a native crossing a stream. More Africans follow, hefting cases and boxes above the waterline. Where are they heading? They march off the screen and out of his life.

ILLUZION. The flickering ghosts make him dizzy, but he stays through the last show, a quick clever comedy: *Les Joyeux Microbes*. A doctor with a microscope inspects a sick man and declares he's full of germs. The microbes are cartoons, specks

that dance around and then resolve into people—politician, mother-in-law, chauffeur. Thomas laughs, at ease with the language, his second tongue. He laughs as the patient exclaims, *Que je suis malade!* Walking back to the Grand Hotel, Thomas's hands tingle, covered in Assassin Germs.

52. Taro Tsujimoto

October 26, 1909. Even in his room, nine-fingered Thomas shivers. He wears one of Fatty's jackets, insulated with two other coats of decreasing size. On his head is a hat bought off a Mongol. The walls might as well be ice.

He checked in as a Japanese. Now he has to keep up the *illuzion* with the hotel staff. *Arigato* this and *sayonara* that. He signed in as Taro Tsujimoto, using one of the bland aliases favored by the Cut Finger Club. Whenever the bell captain— a Russian—calls out, "Tsujimoto-san!," Thomas cheerfully barks a few unintelligible syllables, like some damned judo instructor.

Thomas regards his breakfast with suspicion. He restricts himself to nibbling a crust of bread. Timetables in several tongues are spread out before him. Harbin is China, but also somehow or even *mostly* Russia.

There's a patch of light at the threshold: an envelope. Inside, he finds not a bill, but a playing card. The king of hearts. Someone has written one word in English, near the monarch's stubby sword: *Geronimo.*

Today must be the day. Thomas gets ready. Ito's train will stop at the station in two and a half hours. The Russian delegate will board for a brief reception. Then both parties will disembark and move to a room inside the station.

From his vantage at the Grand Hotel, the Harbin terminal looks like the skull of some nightmare leviathan, beached and stripped of flesh. He breathes on the pane and writes his Korean name in the fog. Then he dresses: collar perfect, hothouse boutonniere. He has less than an hour, but the station is

close by. He tucks the Fabrique Nationale in his right pocket, then switches it to his left. He will shoot with his maimed left hand, to punctuate his contempt.

Which member of the Cut Finger Club sent the card? It doesn't resemble Fatty's handwriting. The old man, Harabaji? The letters are very neat but possibly written by a foreigner. Downstairs, he is about to query the desk clerk about the envelope's provenance, then stops. Maybe it's all a trap.

On the back, printed in a box amid the woven blue design, is the name of the manufacturer: **KALEIDO-PAN GAMES** .

Ohio Goat Sigh Moss! hails the maître d'hôtel.

Thomas Ahn, né Ahn Jung-geun, reminds himself that for the purposes of today, he is Taro Tsujimoto.

Ohio Goat Sigh Moss! Taro replies brightly.

The man bows and hands him a large lunch pail. *Bento!*

Ah, bento! He tips his hat. *Arigato, arigato!* He discreetly crosses himself as he exits.

At the station a lame panhandler lays out a line of patter, first in Chinese, then in a high, singsong Japanese. The words break Thomas's concentration. He doesn't know how to reply—which language, what to say. Something about Harbin mixes him up. He's a Korean Catholic who's taken up residence in Vladivostock, masquerading as a Japanese businessman named Taro Tsujimoto, on the loose in a Russian-Jewish city in China. With his good hand, he flips a coin into the cup.

Standing behind a newspaper kiosk, Thomas secures the handkerchief around his left hand. He empties the lunch box

and places the Fabrique Nationale inside. He comes around the other side to give the wrapped food to the panhandler.

The cold minutes pass, his face like a mask. A crowd gathers to greet the diplomats. It is a Russian and Japanese affair, hardly any Chinese. Strange to think that less than five years ago, they were bent on slaughtering one another wherever they met. That is what passes for civilization.

His ruined finger throbs. He pictures Assassin Germs, wearing bandit eye masks, covering his stump.

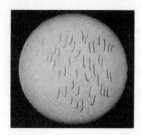

53. The Convention

Hg . . . hgh . . . HGHARO!

An hour from Harbin Station, Prince Ito sneezes, so violently it wakes him from his nap. He sees Morita dealing a hand to his wife and two other spouses. They rise from their seats for half a second, like marionettes, and bow Ito's way. The waiter brings a small brandy, bows as he sets it down. Another pale puppet.

George Ladd's book never fails to put Ito to sleep. He can recommend it wholeheartedly as a soporific. Right now, it looks like a roof blown off a dollhouse that has landed on his chest. He picks it up, but the bookmark has slipped out. He jumps to the appendixes, where Ladd has faithfully reproduced the convention of 1907. These points had been agreed to by King— that is, Emperor—Kojong *with a view to the early attainment of the prosperity and strength of Korea . . . the speedy promotion of the welfare of the Korean people. . . .* Sometime around then, Ito

recalls, the late queen's nephew committed suicide, crying that there was no hope left.

"One can't feel guilty about such things," Durham Stevens had told Ito. "He would have done himself in anyway."

"I don't feel guilty," Ito said.

54. The Slope

Yesterday's meetings with the Chinese at Mukden ended in pleasant vagaries. Prince Ito had known before leaving Japan that it would be so. Better than unpleasant vagaries, always a possibility when it came to China. What he would discuss with Kokovsoff, in one hour's time, was less clear. Some *resolution* was needed, yet the Russian Question hinged on the Chinese Question, which all came back to the Railroad Question. The Railroad Question actually hinged on the Korean Question. Did the Russians, after all this time, have designs on Korea? He remembers what the impertinent Kojong had muttered: "Same bed, different dreams." He was always saying that.

"Same bed, *same* dreams," Ito would always correct him.

Hgharo! At sixty-eight, he is too old for the game, the questions. He is no longer prime minister of Japan, visiting Berlin to learn from its great minds, hammering out his country's new constitution. He is on the downward slope. There is no doubting.

> ARTICLE I.—*The Government of Korea shall follow the direction of the Resident-General in connection with the reform of the administration.*

Still, how could Ito not feel pride? Japan, a modest string of islands, had brought two enormous countries to heel inside a decade. No wonder the Imperial Army was calling for more. Not just the army but the people. He understands this. First take Korea outright. Next, eat around the edges of China. Win over what Russia cannot hold. Then, inevitably, all of Manchuria

will be for the Japanese, and Harbin itself, and the Koreans now bred for labor . . .

Yet Ito disagrees that Korea should be part of Japan. For some unfathomable reason, he loves the land (which Ladd found so insipid), its climate (which Stevens despised), and even the food, all roots and pickles. . . . It was said that Ito Hirobumi looked more himself in Korea, even in the heat of summer, whereas in Japan, hemmed in by formalities, his skin looked slack, his hair fell out in clumps. . . . *Eventual life* . . .

> *ARTICLE IV.—No appointment or dismissal of Korean officials of the higher grade shall be made without the consent of the Resident-General.*

Another cloying brandy arrives, its surface dimpled from the rumbling of the wheels. In his forties, well before he put his stamp on Korea, Ito had adopted a Korean, a headstrong girl who had fled to Japan after the execution of her father by some faction of the Korean court. She had taken the name Sadako. Heaven knew what her real one was.

He was prime minister then. Acting foolish. Did Sadako understand what their "adoption" agreement was? (Did he?) Their arrangement was not spoken of by the other ministers, or spoken of *too* firmly as an *adoption*, nothing more. Cartoons ran in the opposition papers, puzzling if you were not in the know, cutting if you had heard of Ito's predilections.

Sadako must be forty now. He has not seen her in years. The final time, in Seoul, the nosy Durham Stevens had caught them in a fond embrace. A minor embarrassment that by no means required Ito to send Stevens back to America for a vacation. America, where the Korean exiles—so patriotic, so bloodthirsty—could get a clean shot.

> *ARTICLE VI.—The Government of Korea shall not engage any foreigner without the consent of the Resident-General.*

The train slows under a cold sky of folded silk. The wives resume their card game, each pink finger controlled with invisible string.

55. The Lunch Box

The beggar shakes his bowl of coins, the clatter breaking Thomas Ahn's concentration. Just as he's about to scold the panhandler, the sound is lost in a bigger sound. Prince Ito's train pulls in, smoke white as snow. Its sides are deep red, polished like the world's biggest ruby. The train stops, and all on the platform applaud. The Russians step aboard for their meeting.

Thomas—or Taro Tsujimoto—resembles the other Japanese well-wishers gathered on the platform, save for one thing: the Fabrique Nationale, the gun in his left hand, cloaked by a handkerchief. After an eternity, Prince Ito steps off the train, with a thick coat and a beautiful hat. He lifts his walking stick to greet the crowd. His attention gets diverted by a lunch box tumbling to the ground. He looks up. A figure approaches, raising a slender arm, hand in a cloud. *Eventual life.*

56. Another Gun

Thomas Ahn shoots, then wonders: Was it *Ito* who sent him the card, indicating that today was the day? It makes no sense. Unless . . . Does Prince Ito *want* to be killed, by Thomas's Korean hand, on this cold day in Harbin? What mad trick is this?

Ito's last words reach his killer. *Pabo gatchi.* Sputtering in Korean, his tone that of a father to a child. *Like a fool.* Policemen wrestle Thomas to the ground. Amid the struggle he spies a boy tossing a gun onto the tracks. The boy's hand is visible for a second—a hand that's missing something. A boy from the Cut Finger Club? No—not a boy but a *woman.*

Bae. Of course! Thomas cackles as his face gets punched in. He wriggles under a pile of shouting men as he spots her

walking away. *Bae* was the one who slipped him the card. He was never alone. She was there in the hotel, and there in the theater, and here at the station disguised (now he sees it) as a panhandler. She was there all along, an angel of vengeance, making sure he didn't miss.

Kicked in the ribs, slugged in the head, Thomas Ahn, a.k.a. Taro Tsujimoto, is about to disappear, to turn into Nobody.

57. Knowledge, Life, and Reality

A year after publishing his love letter to Marquis Ito, George Trumbull Ladd smoothly produces another book, with the modest title *Knowledge, Life, and Reality*. When he dies a decade later, his ashes are divided between Yokohama and New Haven.

The murder of Ito in Harbin in 1909 does nothing to reverse the Japanese domination of Korea. Instead, it has the opposite effect: five months after Thomas Ahn is executed, Japan formally annexes Korea.

58. The Future

October 26, 1909, New York City. Syngman Rhee, now attending Princeton, is visiting a friend in Manhattan when word of Ito's death hits the papers. Syngman curses. Killing *Ito*, after the murder of Durham Stevens? Nothing good can come of it. These idiot peasant patriots.

Appended to the article is a note: *The news of Prince Ito's assassination reached New York at 3 o'clock this morning. Tokio time*

is fourteen hours faster than New York time, which explains the possibility of printing news of the tragedy, which occurred on Tuesday afternoon, in a New York newspaper on Tuesday morning.

Syngman Rhee writes to Philip Jaisohn: *Is Korea in the future or in the past?*

59. Exit

So ends Dream Two of the Korean Provisional Government.

2333: Harmony Holdings (1977)

CLARA EUPHRATES AND MONK ZINGAPAN MET at a marathon poetry reading on New Year's Eve 1975, in a gallery downtown with no art on the peeling walls, unless the walls themselves were the art. With her angular bob and terrifying eyeshadow, Monk mistook her for a punk designer he'd read about in *The New York Whip*. A chick from Taiwan. Clara mistook him for Sirhan Sirhan. Other poets kept getting called up before them, armed with interminable cantos. At half past one, Monk gave up. He trudged east as the snow thickened, erasing the lights of the Twin Towers to the south. He hoped Clara would follow.

She tracked his solitary footprints to a diner. Over hours-old coffee, she read her poems. She'd composed them by twisting the television dial and transcribing what she heard. Monk caught snatches of *Barney Miller* and *The Dating Game*. Her father was a boisterous Korean transplant who got his start in wigs and now had tendrils everywhere—textiles, insurance, toys. Like him, she wanted to sell things and make money. One day she'd crack the code, write a poem as popular as TV.

Monk was the opposite. He buried things under wanton wordplay. The verses in his pocket were from "The Newt Salad," a stanza-by-stanza anagram of Eliot's "The Waste Land." Clara had never heard anything like it. Her mind was perfectly blown. She learned that he'd begun it while stationed in Vietnam, that he now juggled odd jobs, had no fixed address. They ate pie à la mode. Clara took him to Euphrates Towers on

West Ninetieth. (Upon buying it five years ago, her father had expanded his surname, Yew, to match the name on the north façade, and pestered her to do the same.) The faint white letters still advertised:

EUPHRATES TOWERS
Living Pleasures.
Single—Double Rooms.

A fourth line was too faded to read. Though it was four in the morning, Clara talked to the night manager, who gave Monk the keys to a single, up in Tower A. There was no bed, but the heat worked.

A week later, Monk had a new job at Euphrates Industries, offices conveniently located on the tenth floor. He wrote ad copy for a few months, touting the Euphrates Erasable Ballpoint, the Euphrates 2-in-1 Toupee. Then he moved to the firm's new game division, run by Clara. Their debut, Valet Battle, was a card competition in which you parked and retrieved as many cars as possible. The inspiration had come from Monk's old job at a midtown lot. Speed was key, but go too fast and you risked denting a Jaguar. (Lose two turns.) A two-player match took fifteen minutes, the sweet spot that made players reshuffle, deal again.

Clara's trippy lid art showed an attendant juggling keys as his legs pinwheeled. To the left, an irate plutocrat shook a fist as his shapely date clutched her mink. Every card bore Clara's flights of automotive fancy. They looked less like drivable vehicles, more like desserts, sex organs, spaceships. Clara's secret was that she'd never driven in her life.

Monk and Clara won Best New Talent at the 1976 Diversions gala, held by the magazine of the same name at a hotel in Fort Lee. Sales spiked. *Newsweek* wrote it up. Mr. Euphrates had Clara and Monk develop a deluxe edition. They added a board, toy cash, a spinner, and tally sheets. Production costs ballooned, and playing time stretched to an hour. *Diversions* gave it two chess pieces out of five. Stores only wanted the original. But Clara's father didn't hold it against them. The other parts of Euphrates Industries were having a very good year.

. . .

WHILE VALET BATTLE 2 languished in the warehouse, Mr. Euphrates received a request from someone called the Dowager. She wanted to commission a game based on *2333*, the old series by a science-fiction writer named Parker Jotter. ("The what by who?" he said.) Clara and Monk would write the rules and do the art, then hand it over to the Dowager, who would handle the rest. Was such an arrangement possible? She needed product in six months. Pinned to the back was a check.

Mr. Euphrates wasn't familiar with the funder. Calls went to a service and were never returned. Even stranger, the address on the stationery said Euphrates Towers, without a room number. Meaning one of his tenants *was* the Dowager. Who could it be? Norberto at the front desk gave his default shrug. Denise, his secretary, pored over rent records to root out the source, but nothing stood out. He studied the check. It was an unwholesome amount of money, a truly filthy sum. The signature was a terse mountain range. Friday morning, Denise made the deposit at the Chemical Bank. It cleared Tuesday, and on Thursday a tightly wrapped parcel arrived at Euphrates Industries, containing well-thumbed copies of Jotter's five books and a brief letter. The game, it said, must evoke the flavor of *2333*. Rather than focus on winners and losers, it should resemble a free-flowing serial adventure, in which the bizarre aliens and technology found in Parker Jotter's works became like toys in a sandbox, to which players would bring their own imagination. Mr. Euphrates found the request insane, but it gratified Clara. According to the letter, the company had been chosen on the basis of Valet Battle II. What others saw as flawed, the Dowager found sublime.

CLARA READ ALL of the *2333* series in a weekend, a whopping seven hundred and seventy-seven pages. The books were only loosely related, and she would have liked to bend Parker Jotter's ear, ask how it all hung

together. But the author had been silent for over a decade, was perhaps deceased. The publisher, Neutron Books, had no knowledge of his circumstances. Clara found the novels gripping all the same. She doodled space stations big as cities, a horde of buglike robots. Over and over, she drew portraits of Greena Hymns, briefly introduced as a bionic servant girl in the first volume. By the series' end, Greena commanded the Galactic Legions, an order of interstellar knights.

Science fiction wasn't Monk's bag. ("First off, what kind of name is *Greena?*") He skimmed the first three books. It would have been one thing to design a standard war game based on the interdimensional battle between the F'falo and O'rë tribes. But he struggled to turn Jotter's work into the sort of never-ending experience their funder desired.

"What's the goal?" he sputtered to Clara. "What are the players supposed to *do?*"

"It's a fantasy. A game. Matter of fact, it's what's known in the trade as a fantasy game."

"*Space* fantasy, more like. A space-fantasy role-playing game, with bug-eyed monsters and UFOs instead of dungeons and dragons."

"Don't say those words."

"Which?"

"The ones starting with the fourth letter of the alphabet."

Although Galactic Legions unfolded in the far future rather than the mythical past, some at Euphrates Industries feared legal action from the creators of Dungeons & Dragons, out in Wisconsin. In a few years, D&D had gone beyond its core audience of Tolkien fans, college students, and stoned medievalists to become a sensation. You shed your humdrum life and became a hero—fighting man, magic user, thief. (You could play an elf or a dwarf, if humanity had started to grate.) All you needed was some weird-looking dice. Who wouldn't want to live in a world filled with wandering monsters and enchanted potions?

Monk, for one, didn't see the appeal. "It's just a bunch of people talking."

"It's storytelling."

"I thought we were in the game business."

"Stories are games," Clara said.

"*Games* are games."

Clara wore him down, and soon he threw himself into the design. As in D&D, dice were key, shaping everything from the speed of a F'falo stealth cruiser to the number of tentacles found on the astral squids of Allîhs. He collected fugitive Yahtzee cubes, plus a slew of the peculiar new polyhedra: four-sided pyramids, jewel-like dodecahedrons, milky twenty-siders that were nearly spheres. He also whittled his own ten-sided dice out of soap, modeling clay, cedar, and other promising materials—a useful way of generating percentages. The facets ran from 0 to 9. You rolled a dark die for tens, a paler die for ones, to get a range from 1 to 100—or, rather, 01 to 00.

Making new worlds out of numbers proved irresistible. Monk filled notebooks with dozens of charts. Clara teased him for stage-managing the climate on Planet Tyosen, in a meticulously grim chart.

BAD WEATHER	
Roll	**Conditions**
01–09	Mild, some sun, no breeze
10–15	Mild, cloudy, light breeze
16–30	Cold, some sun, no breeze
31–45	Cold, cloudy, cold rain
46–70	Bitter cold, no clouds, windy
71–80	Bitter cold, snow squalls, windy
81–95	Bitter cold, blizzard (visibility reduced to 1–6 meters, ground vehicles immobilized)
96–00	Bitter cold, *severe* blizzard (visibility <1 meter, all vehicles immobilized; 1 in 6 chance of frostbite, +1 for each additional 5 minutes outside of a heated structure/vehicle)

Gazing out the office window, Clara would declare, "Mild, some sun, no breeze" or "Bitter cold, snow squalls, windy." But in the end, she agreed that "Bad Weather" should stay. It helped tell the story by grounding it in reality.

His own life felt like a game. Monk pondered the uniqueness of his

situation. What were the odds of being born outside Manila in 1945, to a family of six? Of doing two tours in Vietnam? Of meeting Clara at a gallery, of living in Euphrates Towers? Who rolled *his* dice?

Even the day's smallest decisions could be the result of cosmic coin flips: bus/subway, coffee/tea. A pair of his handmade decimal dice lived in his pocket, onyx and gold, tips smooth with use like the worn teeth of some ancient forest critter. If the radio said a 60 percent chance of rain, a roll of 01 to 60 would bring showers; 61 and up, it would stay dry.

Weirdly, the dice were always right.

Every day, Monk set up his own modest odds. A 15 percent chance of finding a fiver on the street, a 13 percent chance of scoring on singles night, a 10 percent chance of losing his mind. It made him feel alive. It made him trust the dice.

CLARA AND MONK had a rough version of Galactic Legions ready in six weeks. Her cover painting showed Greena Hymns and her henchmen on the roof of a building, high above a decaying city, gazing across a river of fire at a herd of mutant scorpions. The building looked like Euphrates Towers, shattered and abandoned, and the river was more or less the Hudson. (It stood to reason that the real horrors lay in New Jersey.) Her signature blazed in red across the scorched façade.

Playtesting was rocky. The rules were so dense that even Clara and Monk got confused. The game proved unpopular with multiple demographics. A trio of D&D aficionados, recruited from a midtown hobby store, kvetched about its unrealistic combat rules; volunteers from an old folks' home left in tears after just twenty minutes.

Fast Eddie, the resident computer whiz at Euphrates Industries, told them he could streamline things, cook up a program that reduced all the complex dice rolls to a single command. The math would be invisible. Clara and Monk were skeptical. They thought it took the spirit out of the whole thing. But they let him give it a shot.

Fast Eddie had started at the company just a few months before

Monk. He liked to say he was in "systems," implying a grasp of the inner workings not only of Euphrates Industries but the world itself. Politics, money, culture: all of it fell under his purview. His office was the world at large. He did his best thinking at the track in Yonkers. He lived on a houseboat. He knew karate and had seen flying saucers on three separate occasions. He rode his bike to stamp conventions in neighboring states. He read four newspapers a day and was teaching himself Aramaic. His favorite book was *A Million Random Digits with 100,000 Normal Deviates,* which was just page after page of numbers. Some were long and some were short. Some were negative and some had decimals. He called it the literature of the future.

One afternoon, at an automat on Seventy-second, Fast Eddie watched as a co-ed high school debate team eyed the cheapest eats behind glass. He treated them to roast-beef sandwiches, then hired them to type Monk's rules into the hulking Gambit 2000. The file headings began with GAL-LEGS. The teens now puffed stogies, just like him. On the rare days when Fast Eddie graced the tenth floor, he kept one eye on their progress, another on the *Daily Racing Form.*

On a rainy Friday in April, the phone trilled in Monk's room. He picked up on the fifth or fiftieth ring. It was Clara. It was always Clara. The Dowager, whoever that was, had been itching for news on Galactic Legions. The letters still came from within Euphrates Towers.

"I'm calling in sick today," Monk mumbled. He was nestled in the threadbare armchair where he'd dozed off the night before, reading Parker Jotter's *2333: Return to Tyosen!* The book was from 1963, but it was science fiction, so it hadn't dated much. It was just as bad or good as the day it came out. The least believable part was that everyone used the metric system.

"I called you," Clara clarified. She was in the office, six floors up. "Hot date last night?"

"Yeah, with our good friend Parker Jotter," he grumbled.

Return to Tyosen! was Book 5 in the *2333* series—the last thing Jotter

published. A fleet of enlightened beings zip through hyperspace in queer "semi-conical" spaceships, bound for a planet they created millennia ago. Tyosen has descended into appalling chaos. The world is so riven that even its colors have separated—top half a red desert, bottom a blue-white tundra.

The book had started slow, then got exciting. After that, it was hard to say. Pages had detached, and some scenes appeared in the wrong order, which he detected too late. In one case, toward the end, the assassin Komiko himself gets assassinated, after a long trek from Tyosen's wintry hemisphere to its sultry side. His spirit imparts to his followers a riddle: *Did the straight line kill the circle?* To which one of them answers, *Dreams are the only reality.* It took five minutes before Monk grasped that the reply actually came from earlier in the book—the tail end of a speech that the heroine Greena Hymns used to rally her troops, back in chapter 3.

"Just come up," Clara said. "You can look at what Fast Eddie's done with our rules. He almost has the whole thing in his computer now. It's like magic—press a button, boom."

"You're even talking like him."

Monk distrusted computers, but the clutter of Galactic Legions was too much. Drifts of drafts and endless hex maps covered his desk. Once everything was on the Gambit 2000, he could throw it all out. Clear his mind, move on with his life.

"Dad's been asking why you're never in," she added.

"Is he at the office?"

"Not at this *precise* moment, but he swung by last week. Twice. I said you were sick. He said who gets sick in April. I said in your native Manila that's what happens, everything's reversed."

Monk wasn't too worried. Mr. Euphrates had been distracted lately, spending a lot of time at a new church in midtown, even during the week. He'd invited Monk, who was running out of excuses. "What time is it?"

"Half past."

"Half past what?"

But Clara had hung up. Monk found clean socks. It took forever to undo the seven locks. These included two dead bolts, three chains, an iron rod running through four rings set in the door (its tip buried in a divot on the crumbling threshold), and a metal plank, spanning the entrance and supported like a ceremonial sword by a brace of U's. He imagined the security increasing piecemeal over the years, each new lock spurred by a gruesome stabbing, a holdup gone awry.

As he turned the dead bolts, a familiar voice warbled: "Another day, another dollar."

Tonawanda Ted held the *Times* in his hands. His corduroy suit was two decades out of style and counting. He allegedly roomed above or below but roamed the halls round the clock. He referred to himself as the Mayor of Euphrates Towers, though no one else did.

"Another day, another dollar," Monk echoed, planting a thumb on the elevator call button.

The little man glanced up knowingly. "Ah, so you toil for our landlord and Savior."

"That's right." Monk was sure he'd mentioned the fact before.

"Send my regards." Tonawanda Ted gave a neat bow. "You don't look like the typical Euphrates bean counter."

"I'm in games."

He cupped a hand by his ear. "Gains?"

"Games. Like checkers, chess, Monopoly."

"Ah." Tonawanda Ted stroked his chin. Monk braced himself for some well-oiled anecdote. "He's making games now, eh?"

"Valet Battle is our big one," Monk said, trying to impress. "It won an award."

The old man clapped his hands in recognition. "Yes!"

Monk felt a wave of warmth for Tonawanda Ted. "You've heard of it?"

His face lit up. "No!"

The elevator doors opened and Monk practically dove inside. A

mystery woman clutched a small paper bag. Steam coated her sun-glasses. The button for 10 was already lit. Her blouse was wet from rain. Practically see-through. The door closed.

"You dog." She hit his leg with her umbrella. "You were looking." It was Clara, back from the Health Nuts store with lunch. "You were looking."

"False."

"Perv." She shoved playfully, let a hand linger. "Or can I still not touch?"

He had declared a vow of chastity early in their collaboration, which made her dub him Monk, which stuck. They needed to keep things professional. Clara, he knew, was engaged to an important business associate of her father's. Juan Yang was heir to a leather fortune and lived in Argentina. Clara had seen one blurry picture. She laughed off the arrangement, but Monk knew Mr. Euphrates would have his head if their path to the altar was interrupted.

Suite 1000 was thick with cigarette smoke. Denise, filling in at reception, waved to Monk without looking up from the phone, her Pall Mall nearly scorching the huge portrait of Mr. Euphrates behind her. Clara had painted it last year. Her father posed before a vertiginous bookcase, looking homicidal in a navy double-breasted. She'd messed up the eyes, redoing them so much that the daubs flashed urgently when they caught the light just right.

The office clattered with activity. A team of accountants tapped adding machines and calculators. One old salt even slapped an abacus. Someone had the radio on. In the corner by the Telex and the Mr. Coffee, Fast Eddie leaned back in his chair, puffing a gordito as he manhandled a keyboard. Amber characters glowed on the Gambit 2000, which rested atop his copy of *A Million Random Digits*.

Monk's phone rang just as he reached his desk. It was Denise, who he could see through the nicotine fog.

"You have playtesting now. They've been waiting an hour."

He poured himself a cup of coffee and entered the conference room, the only smoke-free section in the office. Seated around the wood-grain

table were three boys and two girls. They had name tags, bangs, scraped elbows. Monk took a seat opposite Clara.

"What is this, day care?"

"These are our very special volunteers," she said cheerfully.

"Galactic Legions isn't a kids' game," he sputtered. "How old are they?"

"I'm nine," said Malcolm.

"I'm twelve," said Pablo, looking out from spectacles so thick they nearly bent time.

"I'm eight," said Melanie, the girl to his right.

Monk signaled time-out.

"How many of you know why you're here this morning?" Clara kicked him, flashed her watch. "Uh, afternoon?"

Denise had maneuvered the Gambit 2000 onto a cart and was rolling it into the conference room, careful to keep the long tan cord connected to the hard disk by Fast Eddie's desk.

"Anyone?" he snapped.

Pablo looked ready to cry. "Are we in trouble?"

"Don't be silly," Monk said. Time to regroup, put them at ease. "We're going to play a—well, it's more a cartoon than a game. A story that we all tell."

The children were silent.

"It takes place in outer space."

No one said a word. Clara came to the rescue.

"Now, I want you to do something for me," she said. "It's so simple but *very* important. Ready? Close your eyes."

She took out a pile of business cards. On the backs, she had sketched things found in Parker Jotter's pages: a meteor shower, a UFO with extendable claws. She slapped him away.

"Shh," she said to the kids. "Melanie, I said everyone. Pablo, you too. That's great. I'm doing it as well. Darkness. The darkness of outer space. Good."

Clara shuffled the cards as she cast her spell. Monk felt queasy, as though falling in love or something.

"Imagine we're all on a huge rocket. We've left home, but we're not scared. We're moving so fast, ten times faster than an airplane. Already the moon looks as small as a pea. We're passing Mars, Jupiter. Picking up speed. Neptune is just a dot now." She turned over a card. "There's a bright pink cloud that's bigger than anything you've ever seen."

Monk pictured Clara on the night they met. The diner and the poems and the snow. This somehow led to a daydream in which they'd gotten hitched and had five children. Three boys, two girls.

"Behind the cloud is a black hole. A rip in space. But we aren't afraid." She reshuffled, drew a new card. "We get pulled in. Our space-ship travels for twenty years, but for us, it seems like twenty minutes. That's how black holes work."

Monk tried to engage his dream-children. "We're in a galaxy where no one from Earth has ever been. Ahead is Planet Tyosen."

"Weird name," Jenny said approvingly.

"The top half is red sand, the bottom is all snow."

Denise put a pair of Monk-made decimal dice before each kid. Clara explained that once they stepped out of the rocket, she would become the Space Master, guiding them through their adventure. Each of them would change into a brand-new character, with special talents. Hadn't they ever dreamt of being someone else? Everyone agreed that they had. (Even Monk found himself nodding.) The dice rolling com-menced. Each result measured a key trait: grit, ESP, agility, and so on. Denise entered it all into the Gambit 2000.

To come up with their DPCs, or Defining Physical Characteristics, the children rolled more dice, consulted various charts. The weirder the outcome, the giddier they became. Jenny was a blue, pig-eared biped, Melanie had six arms, and Pablo turned into a ball of hyperintelligent light. They drew portraits with colored pencils. Oliver's was particu-larly good, like Charlie Brown with antennae.

As Denise typed, the Gambit 2000 made a rude noise. The screen was packed with numbers, which blinked ominously as they marched across the glass. The grunts got louder. Fast Eddie rushed in. Digits froze, then reversed as though spun on an axis.

In a panic, Denise hailed Fast Eddie. "Did we lose everything?"

"Happens all the time," he said. He switched off the computer, counted to five in his head, and turned it back on. After ten tense seconds, the machine gave a reassuring rumble. The game data returned to the screen line by line, a little sheepishly.

"Boom!" He patted the unit. "Mind if I join?"

FOR THE NEXT two hours, Clara led the kids through a series of improvised escapades. Though it was warm on the tenth floor, they shivered as she described the ice forests of Tyosen. Monk rifled through the Galactic Legions folder whenever a specific chart was needed, but Fast Eddie found it quicker with his keyboard. During lulls, Clara would flip over a business card to look at a new sketch—a shortcut into Jotter's imagination that helped her shape the story. Thus it was that the adventurers found a crystal statue of a bear, which (flip) turned out to be a time machine, with which they went ten years into the future, where (flip) they fought a pack of cyber-wolves.

Denise and Fast Eddie took on bit parts as needed: glum arms dealer, rogue astronomer. Monk played the assassin Komiko, hit with a germ-coated dagger. As he went into his death throes, he thundered, "Dreams are the only reality!" The kids loved it. They loved *him*. Could he ever be a father, raise a couple of little ones? That was madness. But for once he could see the appeal.

Clara flipped a card showing her favorite character, the resilient Greena Hymns. In a gravelly voice, she warned the children that the ice was cracking. Flip. A huge claw rose from the depths. Flip. The kids had *one weapon left*, a long shot. The talons got closer. Everyone rolled their dice at the same time, a beautiful sound.

WHEN IT WAS all over, Denise sent the kids home with a dollar apiece. Fast Eddie buzzed with excitement; the Gambit 2000 had held up in the heat of battle. Even Monk was won over. The rest of the office emp-

tied out early. It was Friday. Mr. Euphrates had never shown up. It rained again, lavishly.

Clara and Monk called the elevator. She was going home. Her family kept an apartment on the penthouse level but also had places throughout the neighborhood. Clara usually stayed in her studio off Amsterdam in the Eighties. Monk, too, had been inspired. He had a shopping bag with five manila folders stuffed with his rules and her drawings. It was the only full copy of the work in progress, apart from the version on the computer, which didn't have the art. The end was in sight.

"The kids were in heaven," he said. The elevator stopped at seven, but no one got on.

"The cards helped. Why didn't we think of that before?"

"You know why. Valet Battle II. We wanted to avoid cards after that fiasco."

"Anyway, it was fun," Monk said. The doors closed again. He felt the atmosphere change.

"I know what else could be fun." Clara tugged his sleeve. "A reward for our hard work."

The floor sank. There was a 30 percent chance that the vow of chastity was in jeopardy. He felt the dice in his front pocket.

"Very hard work," she said.

"Stop that," Monk said, as the door slid open on four. "This is me."

But Clara stepped out first. She wasn't headed to Amsterdam. Not just yet. The odds hovered at 60. They were at the door. If only he could roll the dice and see.

"Sounds like it's raining again," she said, "and I forgot my umbrella."

The seduction was interrupted by footsteps in the stairwell. The shadow of a hat brim appeared, grotesquely huge, followed by the diminutive Tonawanda Ted.

"Ah, the happy couple!"

"We're not, uh, together," Monk clarified.

The Mayor of Euphrates Towers ignored the objection. "Terrific weekend plans?"

"Work, work, work," Monk said, holding up the bag with Galactic Legions. He took out his keys.

Tonawanda Ted winked at Clara. "I told your boyfriend this afternoon that I'm not one for games. But I'm sure this new one he's got cooking will be out of this world."

"We'll give you a copy," she said sweetly.

"Good night," Monk said. He shut the door and immediately did up the locks.

"I thought all Filipinos were friendly," Clara said. "It's us Koreans who get moody."

"Shh." Monk peered out the peephole till he was sure Tonawanda Ted had gone.

"She looked familiar." Clara snapped her fingers three times but it was no use.

"She?" They were still in the dark.

"That nice old lady in the hall."

"Lady?" Monk burst out laughing. "He's a man. Tonawanda Ted."

"No, no. She told me her name once. I was at Health Nuts, and she needed help scooping the sunflower seeds."

"That," Monk said, "was a man named Tonawanda Ted, in a corduroy suit and ridiculous hat."

"No, no. It's just her style. Don't be so close-minded." She lit a cigarette. "For a while she used to hang around the tenth floor, by the office. She wanted me to call her *halmoni*."

"Harmony?"

"*Halmoni*. Korean for *grandmother*."

"She's Korean?" Monk had always been so keen to get away that he'd never noticed.

"Shh," Clara said. "We Koreans aren't so terrible."

The odds jumped to 85. He fumbled for the light. Pages that had fallen out of *Escape from Tyosen!* littered the floor. Clara picked one up and read aloud, a ponderous scene in which Greena Hymns flees Tyosen, as the war still rages.

"Huh," she said, flipping it over. "Never noticed this before."

Monk went to look. The final page. On the other side was a single line: "To be concluded in Book 6, **THE TAN GUN**."

"Guess we'll never know what it was," Clara said.

"Maybe we can invent it ourselves," Monk said. "In our game, I mean."

"Maybe," she said, switching on the radio.

The static blended with the downpour outside. She picked up news and weather. Rain, heavy at times. Jackknifed tractor trailer. She kept turning, stopped at a flourish of harps.

"Our song," she said.

Clara looked weary, even sad as she hummed along. Was it that the game was almost done? He recognized the tune at last. It had been on the jukebox in December, when they went for drinks with Denise and Fast Eddie and others from the office. A de facto Christmas party. An hour in, Mr. Euphrates had set up a tab, kissed everyone on the forehead like some haunted potentate, and left for church. At midnight, Monk and Clara had clutched each other, trying not to laugh as they swayed to a song about barefoot lovers on a beach. Now in his room, in the building her father owned, she drew him closer. She knew all the words.

A BLADE OF sun cut the door in half. From his bed, Monk saw the metal plank dangling from its thick cord on the jamb. The chains were off, too. Clara. Had she left at night, alone? He rang her number. No answer. There was a 75 percent chance that Clara had made it home okay. The dark die came up 7. His heart went double-time. The pale one resolved into a 3. He had to stop tempting fate.

Just then an envelope slid under the door, stamped with a sigil: an *E* made of vines. Note from Clara, explaining all? Early paycheck? No: telegram from the boss.

BRAVO ON FINISHING GAL LEGS EXCLAMATION POINT THE DOWAGER
REQUESTS A MEETING AT EIGHT PM UNIT EIGHT ONE FIVE EUPHRA-
TES TOWER B PERIOD BRING GAME WITH YOU NATURALLY CHEERS E

Monk felt proud to be entrusted with the handover. The Dowager could do with it what she wished. Maybe she was backing a movie based on Jotter's books, and Galactic Legions was part of the marketing plan. Or maybe she meant to turn it into a computer game. Since the beginning, Monk and Clara had known they were only hired guns, a step in the process.

That was the deal. So why was he suddenly reluctant to let the game go?

He tried Clara again. They were a team, after all, and should visit their client together. Things had gotten out of control last night. But the vow would be reinstated. Clara would marry Juan Yang, of Buenos Aires. That was that.

He went outside to clear his head. At Chock Full o' Nuts, he had coffee and a cream-cheese sandwich. Someone had left the paper on the counter, and he did the crossword as he ate. He was rusty. When he was deep in his own poetry—polishing stanzas of "The Newt Salad"—his synapses were drenched in language, but his time at Euphrates Industries had dried them out. He put the puzzle aside, having made inroads only along the lower-right quadrant. Heading back, he spotted a small figure walking with his nose in a book, cloth grocery bag hanging from an elbow. It was Tonawanda Ted. Monk almost said hello but didn't.

At seven he brushed his teeth. He dusted off the suit Mr. Euphrates had bought him for the Diversions gala. A vision in lightweight plaid. He looked like he insured golf courses.

The Dowager's apartment was in the other tower. Holding Galactic Legions in an accordion file, Monk went to the lobby and crossed the cool, barren passageway to Tower B's elevator bank. Everything was so much tidier here. Reflections of the chandeliers swam in the mosaic floor. An attendant in a clean shirt held the gate open.

"Floor?"

"Eight. It's Clive, isn't it?"

"No, sir. I'm David." He closed the gate and pushed the lever. "Clive left last year."

"Aren't you Norberto's cousin?"

"Clive was his nephew. I'm not related."

"Are you positive?"

"Quite. I'm nobody." Monk gripped the bulky file and stared through the gate at the floors going by. David released the lever and the car stopped perfectly on eight. Monk had an idea.

"What do you know about the Dowager?"

He pulled open the gate. "That a movie?"

"No, it's—never mind."

The corridor had four units on each side. The carpet was free of mystery stains, and the chandelier shone serenely, unlike the choppy fluorescents in Tower A. The door to 815 was ajar. The front room was bare, save for a ziggurat of packing boxes, marked with the name of the moving company, HARMONY. Had this been her home or a temporary office? The windows were closed, and the cabinets were open and bare. He heard footsteps but couldn't tell where they were coming from. In Galactic Legions, a player in such straits would declare that he was checking for traps. If he had a high ESP score and rolled a 45 or below with the decimal dice, he'd sense that something was amiss. He'd jump away before the trapdoor was sprung, hold his breath as sleeping gas filled the air.

CLASHING CHURCH BELLS woke Monk up the next morning. He was still in Apartment 815, curled in a square of sunlight. No trace of the Dowager. The accordion file was missing. The big boxes that said HARMONY were gone. He took the stairs down and returned to his room, in ramshackle Tower A. When he called Clara this time, someone picked up.

"*Yobosehyo?*" A man's voice.

Monk hit the plunger and tried again.

"*¿Sí?*" Different language, same voice. The man put his hand over the mouthpiece. Clara was saying something in Korean. "It's just a wrong number," she said in English.

"*Nooguya?*" the man growled at him. "Hey? *¿Quién habla?*"

Monk slipped the receiver back onto the cradle. It could only be one person: Juan Yang, fiancé. Maybe he had surprised her with a visit the other night, found the pied-à-terre empty. And waited, furious. Monk saw his career at Euphrates Industries drawing rapidly to a close.

CLARA WASN'T AT work on Monday. Denise said she was traveling. No idea where, or for how long. All too convenient, but Monk didn't press. He said nothing about the accidental call with Juan Yang. Instead, he told her about bringing Galactic Legions to the Dowager in Apartment 815, Tower B. He showed her the telegram from Mr. Euphrates, in the envelope with the stylized *E*.

"That's not his," she said. "Too fussy."

So it was a setup. The Dowager had known when Mr. Euphrates would be out of town. She had somehow learned that playtesting had gone well. Had the Dowager known about him and Clara—that she'd spent the night? His head was swimming.

"I know I've checked 815 before," Denise said, "but let's take a look."

They went to the storage alcove behind the Japanese screen. She opened a file cabinet and walked her fingers over the tabs until she found the folder marked 815B.

"Just as I thought," she said, fishing out a lease agreement. "No one's lived there for years."

The last tenant had been installed in 1953, then turned out in '73, a year after Mr. Euphrates (né Yew) took over. Monk inspected the carbon, signed by Theo DeGraw.

"It's been empty for four years, then?"

"Lots of rooms like that in Tower B. The units are nicer, so rents are higher. No one wants that right now. These things are cyclical. You just have to wait it out."

He tuned out the lecture on Manhattan real estate. How had the Dowager operated undetected out of Euphrates Towers itself? Maybe she had found a vacant room just that week and paid David the elevator

man to "send" a telegram right back into the building. His brain tingled with paranoia. He gripped the metal drawer to steady himself. If only Clara were here. She'd get to the bottom of it. But he couldn't risk another call. Sitting at his desk, he had an unwelcome vision of her showing up at the office with an outraged Juan.

Monk walked up Riverside. The storm had littered the path with puddles. Clouds looked clearer in the water than they did in the sky, as though purified by the leftover rain. He and Clara sometimes slipped out here during the workday for lunch. He'd have a sandwich and she'd munch her seeds and sprouts. The memory crushed him. Maybe he would confront Juan, tell him what happened the other night, in his room with the seven locks.

A huge puddle spanned the path near 106th. Pedestrians had to move one at a time across a thin isthmus. He paused midway, as if waiting for a dice roll to advance to the next space. A cyclist on a rusty three-speed cut through the water, drenching his leg.

"Monk!" It was the cyclist, clad in man-made fibers. "You okay?"

"Fast Eddie?"

"Finally taking my advice. Letting the city be your idea furnace." He noticed Monk's distraught state. "Is it about Clara? Denise told me she left for Cape Cod with her beau."

Monk wanted to puke. "What for?"

"The wedding!"

"Oh." A lump formed in his throat.

"Do you figure it's a shotgun thing?"

"How? I thought Juan lived in Argentina."

"He was here two months ago, but who knows."

Monk staggered to a bench by a bronze Civil War cannon aimed at New Jersey.

"I went to see the Dowager," he said, changing the subject.

"Our mystery funder, eh?" Fast Eddie rubbed his eyes. "Mr. E. wanted to go door-to-door, sniff out every tenant. I told him it was a bad idea."

"She lives in Tower B, Apartment 815." Monk shuddered. "Or *did*."

"Tell it from the beginning, yeah?" Fast Eddie said, like some gum-shoe in an orange tracksuit. "Go ahead. Let's map out what we know."

It all started with the Dowager hiring them late last fall. Clara and Monk finished Galactic Legions in record time, and spent months testing. Finally, after the first successful session, Monk was summoned by the Dowager (impersonating Mr. Euphrates by telegram). Clara was incommunicado, so Monk went solo to her hidden lair in Tower B. The front room was empty. He went in, got knocked out, woke up the next day alone. Also, Denise had found documents showing that 815B had last been occupied by one Theo DeGraw, long gone.

Fast Eddie whistled morosely, pondering scenarios. Maybe the Dowager actually lived in a *different* room in Euphrates Towers and had lured Monk into a unit she knew was vacant. Maybe she was CIA or FBI and this was all a cover for something *else*. (Seeing webs of con-spiracy everywhere, Fast Eddie's mind generally leapt to the CIA or FBI.)

"It's the only copy of the game," Monk moaned. "How could I be so stupid?"

"You're forgetting something." Fast Eddie grinned. "We've got it on the old Gambit 2000."

"But that's just a computer program. No offense."

"Forget it. Let's assume the right people picked up the game, yeah? No third party. No CIA. A straight-up deal. The Dowager is hiding something from us. So she waits till the boss is away, gets you alone, takes the product she's purchased, and boom: she disappears."

"That makes it sound like a drug deal gone bad."

Fast Eddie checked his watch and mounted his Schwinn. "Every-thing will work out," he assured Monk. "And with that, I'm off to the races. Meant literally. There's a trifecta that has my name on it."

AT A CUBAN-CHINESE on Broadway, Monk lunched on a roasted half chicken and fried plantains, washed down with a bottle of Coke. The calories sharpened his mind. He scrawled on the place mat a maze of

names, some from Euphrates Towers, others from *2333*. Greena Hymns and Clara Euphrates, the Dowager and the Tan Gun. Fast Eddie and Denise. Did he trust Norberto? What about this Clive, or was it David, character, whom he had never seen before? Mumbling, Monk mapped the path from his room in Tower A to Tower B's 815. Down four floors, across, then up eight. It looked like a J.

J as in Parker Jotter? Or Juan Yang?

Monk wasn't making sense, seeing links that weren't there. He had another Coke and considered. Why not let things be? Galactic Legions had been a job, nothing more. It didn't matter who the Dowager was, or why she wanted the game. He and Clara would move on to the next project, a new chapter.

Except now Juan Yang was on the scene. The story of Clara and Monk was over.

Monk leaned back, stared at his handiwork. Pulled apart words, shuffled letters. He circled "the Dowager" and "Theo DeGraw," the two names connected to Apartment 815. And froze. *The letters.* Their names had the same letters. *Theo DeGraw* was *the Dowager.* A man, not a woman.

Or a woman—pretending to be a man? Was Theo short for Theodora? Monk walked home in a daze. Euphrates Towers came into view. He had never seen it look so glorious. For once, all the painted words on the north façade were legible. The light had to hit just right. *Living Pleasures.* Under that: *Single—Double Rooms.* The last line, invisible to him till now, was two words long: *Permanent. Transient.*

THE SINS SEPTEMBER THE LOUSE

"WE HAVE TO TELL HER."

"I know, I know."

"Now is better than later."

"Is it though."

"We'll deliver the news together."

"On the count of three. I can just picture."

"The deal was always the two of us together, in her room, on a weekend night right before bed, with her favorite snack, which we let her eat, or not eat, depending on what she feels comfortable with. We grant the one-time provision that she doesn't have to brush her teeth if she doesn't want to."

"I thought it was 'floss.' "

"We abolish limits on screen time for a period not in excess of forty-eight hours."

"Let's do it next week."

"You said that a year ago."

"How is this still a thing."

Nora and I were interchangeable in this dialogue, a feature of our periodic mutual insomnias. When and how to tell Story she was adopted? The conversation had begun even before we'd picked her up, an elf with wild blond hair; she was almost eight now. Were we horrible people? What was our problem?

We had not been prepared for parenthood. We had gone through years

of failure and heartbreak, trying to conceive. We'd binged reality shows featuring teen moms, knocked up after a single night of passion. ("Lucky bitches," Nora would mutter. "Ungrateful lucky *bitches.*") After myriad procedures, Nora said: No more. We opted to adopt. We threw our CV's and innermost thoughts into a new GLOAT engine that matched potential parents with the right agency and child. All of it felt impossible, if not insane. A week after the agency greenlit our application, we were summoned to a hospital waiting room in Astoria, Queens.

"That was fast," Nora said, taking off her coat.

We had expected a more protracted process—a frazzled voyage through twenty time zones, misunderstandings at the border—not a seven-minute cab ride with the stoplights in our favor. (We were living in Astoria that year, while our Manhattan apartment was being treated for slime mold.) The hospital gave us pillows and water and Wi-Fi, as though our comfort was key to the baby's smooth delivery. Nora watched knitting videos on her phone, while I paced the atrium, my phone clocking the steps. A Mylar balloon kissed the ceiling, drifting in the ventilated air.

Nora hadn't checked a box for ethnic preference, figuring it would increase our chances of a match. We expected our shade or darker. We had to reread the message informing us that our new baby would be white.

"White's good," I said to Nora then.

"What do you mean?"

"I just meant white was a neutral color."

But did I? Was it? Would she have certain invisible advantages over us, which would complicate our lives? Would she feel as though she'd gotten a raw deal, forced to live with parents who looked nothing like her? There was no way of knowing. Nora said that she herself was darker than her mother, Clara, that this had been an unspoken source of friction.

At 3:46 A.M., we met our daughter, swaddled in a soft striped blanket. She wasn't just white but bright white.

"I'm going to need sunglasses," Nora blurted, crying as she took the baby up in her first embrace.

We named her Astoria, our queen of Queens, and called her Story for short.

.   .   .

"DO YOU THINK SHE'S figured it out?" Nora said in bed. Everything was quiet: our house, the street, the world.

"Definitely."

"That hardly gets us off the hook."

"She's a smart girl."

" 'Beyond gifted.' " Nora was quoting the Measures report card. "Do you know what she said the other day? She told me she knew what dreams are."

"What did she say?"

"Everything that's not online."

"Whoa."

"She takes after you. Don't cry."

"I'm not crying."

"Don't cry, or I'll cry."

Our breaths came out shattered and we just lay there awhile, holding each other. I was crushing her arm a little. She went into the bathroom to fill her water bottle in the dark. She was the most hydrated person I knew. They say people are 70 percent water, but Nora must have been pushing 95.

"Story probably guessed the truth years ago," Nora said when she came back. "But why doesn't she say anything?"

"You're putting this on her."

"That's not what I meant."

"Let's not argue."

"This isn't arguing," Nora said. "It's parenting."

"Hold on while I stitch that on a sampler and sell it online."

"I want one that says 'Dreams Are Everything That's Not Online.' "

I liked that. I could probably sell some to my GLOAT colleagues. I could see it being big. Maybe Dr. Ubu would approve it as a new, counterintuitive motto for our sleep-aid products.

"Not to change the subject," Nora said, "but I let her download another game."

"That's fine," I said. "We agreed it was okay as long as there's no violence."

"It's robots shooting other robots. She said it was for school."

"I think it's called Hegemon," I said. "You don't think she's angry, do you?"

"Story doesn't get angry except when she loses at chess," Nora said. "And I wouldn't call that anger. I would reframe it as productive rage."

The word *rage* simmered unpleasantly, stirring up the assorted assassins from Dream Two. Long ago, I had learned about President McKinley getting shot in Buffalo—part of my hometown's lore—but I had never come across the killer's alias, Fred Nobody. "What" Chang and Chun were also new to me, as was their victim, Durham Stevens. Equally unfamiliar was Thomas Ahn, who'd plugged Ito Hirobumi full of lead at the Harbin train station. Was Echo making them out to be doomed heroes or disturbed zealots? Maybe both or neither. I thought of the question posed in both Dreams: *What is history?* And I thought of Thomas Ahn, who had nine fingers, just like me.

"Last week, Story commented on my hair," Nora said. "She was asking when *her* hair would turn black."

"Oh no."

"She said she wanted black hair, brown eyes."

"Like us."

"Like us."

"The other day, she asked if I was growing a mustache."

"Please tell me you're not."

I was and I wasn't. A search for *Thomas Ahn+assassin+Korea* on GLOAT had returned a bouquet of dead links, plus one that rerouted me to results under his Korean name. Thomas glowered from a half dozen sepia photos. Some showed the shortened finger, but what intrigued me was the fin de siècle facial hair, foliage fit for a psychopath or a hero. I had begun not shaving. An experiment. It might take a while.

Nora sat up, looking at the door. "What's that?"

"What?"

"*Whir, whir.*"

I couldn't hear anything. "Garage door?"

"No, it's like a *whir, whir, click.*"

I held my breath. I could hear Sprout in the loft, wheezing through a dream of pork chops and belly rubs and well-masticated novels in translation. Just before I let myself inhale, I detected a mechanical sound beyond the dog noise. *Whir. Click.*

"Is it the thing, the Tolga?"

Tolga—more properly, TOLGA—was a Talk-Out-Loud Guidance Asset. It was a three-inch-high silver pyramid with a blue light at the apex and a British accent. When we first got it, Nora kept almost throwing it away. GLOAT was developing Tolga to take over the world, and as usual I was a test driver. It couldn't do much except tell us the weather and make a rude burping noise without warning. But Tolga wasn't making any sounds now.

"Must be the 3D printer," Nora said, sipping her water. "Story's been sending game pieces to it before she goes to bed, since it takes forever."

"Chess pieces?"

"She said 'game.' She hides them in her desk. She told me not to look."

It was all coming together. Most mornings, I'd see Story open the printer cabinet and gently chip away at the base with a small spatula, freeing her creations. They probably had something to do with Hegemon. I thought about her virtual game world, everyone searching for the parts of the Tan Gun, the weapon that would make them supreme ruler. Then what—game over? *Whir. Whir. Click.*

"Is it educational?" Nora asked.

"Supposedly."

Then I felt something warm and silky making its slow, soft journey down my chest. But Nora was facing away from me in the ink-black room. We weren't touching. In the silence I could hear the humming from the other room, the 3D printer weaving Story's enigmatic game pieces.

"Ah," I said. "Oh?"

"Hi," Nora said, looking over her shoulder in what I took to be oblique foreplay. "Do you like it?"

"I think so. What *is* it?"

The mystery sensation now felt different: stretched thin, smooth yet clingy. It kept moving, massaging as it went.

"A new T-O-Y."

"How does it W-O-R-K?" We were spelling things out the way we used to do, before Story could read, when we wanted certain pieces of information to elude her.

"Don't T-H-I-N-K about it."

"O-K."

I put my hands in her hair as the device changed shape again, purring as it burrowed between us.

"It's called the Louse," she said.

There was some grappling. The Louse started moving in a different way. Nora and I were connected yet apart.

"Do you like?"

"Smiles slowly." Sometimes we spoke as though reading closed-captioned stage directions from our favorite new K-drama, *Oh! My Jeju*, about people who think they're on the paradisaical Jeju Island, off the coast of South Korea, but are actually on an island off the coast of *North* Korea of roughly the same dimensions.

"How about," she said, clicking a small remote on her wrist, "this?"

"Sighs happily."

Click. "And now?"

"Gasps audibly," I said.

The shape kept changing. The Louse seemed to gain mass as it made circling motions, humming gently.

"Clucks faintly," I said. I closed my eyes, or they were already closed. Time was melting away.

"Do you like the Louse?"

"Nods vigorously."

"Say it."

"I like the Louse."

"Say that you love it."

"I love the Louse."

"Louder." She put her hand on my mouth, rubbing the stubble above my lip.

"I love the Louse." I breathed through her fingers. "But what is it?"

"A shipment arrived at the store a while back." Breath. "These plain

cardboard boxes that came with an order of snail masks. I had no idea what they were. I kept throwing them out." Breath. "Then Keiko told me what they were for."

Keiko was Daily Divas' senior aesthetician, a sage woman in her seventies. She had an institutional memory of Daily Divas, from when it was Lush Ladies in the '80s, and spent most of her non-work hours online, researching conspiracy theories. Her latest fixation was that the K-pop group Reality was completely computer-generated. Then again, she was what was known as a 5iver, a die-hard fan of the defunct group D5.

"The neat thing," she huffed, "is that soon you'll be able to program them."

"How so?"

"You upload a profile, which other people can download onto their Louse."

"And then their Louse can . . . imitate you?"

"And vice versa."

"Anonymously?"

"For now. That's the Louse business model."

The name tugged at something from long ago. A book I read as a kid, when my parents were still alive. The main character was called the Louse. An outcast living by his wits who swept floors at an old appliance store. Something like that. He turned out to be a computer genius and came to rule the known universe using just three primitive commands. It was the kind of adolescent power fantasy I enjoyed for a while. I'd long forgotten the title, let alone what happened at the end.

Now I pondered whether GLOAT had some stake in the Louse. Did it feed into the S-D profiles, the Sex-Death data on our users that Dr. Ubu was constantly goading me to uncover? I imagined the Louse sending this rich vein of S-D dirt to a cloud somewhere, filling it up. The Louse twitched, and my thoughts turned helplessly to . . . *Mercy Pang*? Did the Louse somehow know I liked conceptual art? Mercy's face escaped me; even when I saw her at the Admiral Yi last month, she had been rigorously nondescript. But I could feel her aura as the Louse kicked into overdrive. Maybe Nora was thinking of someone else, too. Our Lice spun tandem fantasies, heating up.

I could picture them exploding: the bed set ablaze, our strange demise the talk of the town.

"Grunts savagely," Nora said.

"Pants heavily," I added. "Playful scream."

"Playful scream," she echoed.

"Intense scream," I said. I half-expected Dr. Ubu to interrupt, question my Mercy fixation. "Falls away," I said.

"Sighing."

Blobs of dawn stained the ceiling, dripped down the wall like glaze.

2333: Man in Korean Costume (1985-1980)

FROM THE OFFICE OF D. M. ZEPHYR
CANTICLE PUBLICATIONS

Ms. Tina J. Pang
160 W. 95th St., #33
New York, NY 10025

August 12, 1985

Dear Tina (if I may),

This letter's been a long time coming. It must be five years since I read about your father in the paper, and how that monster, Joseph Christopher, tried to rip out his <u>heart</u>. I read how they dubbed Christopher the ".22-Caliber Killer" & jailed him for shooting all those men. How he was never tied 100% to the stabbings. But didn't the police find the knife in his hunting cabin? I heard he threw nothing away.

That's my reputation, too, around the office. (Bad segue—I'm not a writer.) I've got matchbooks from the Nixon administration, letterhead older than my secretary. (I swear I'm coming to the point.) Last week, I moved to a room down the hall & Canticle's office manager read me the riot act. While I was chucking out a pile of unsolicited manuscripts,

a big unopened envelope caught my eye. Mailed from "ECMC" in Buffalo, postmarked 2/10/81 & forwarded from the office of my ex-employer, Neutron Books.

I guess I ignored it back then; probably the institutional address made me think it came from a correctional facility. (We publish religious magazines, so a <u>lot</u> of prisoners send us their stories.) My jaw dropped when I opened it. Inside was a notebook, a diary of Parker's hospital stay after the attack. (He appears to have torn out some pages, judging by the thinness, gaps between entries, & bits of paper still caught on the rings.) Why had he sent it to <u>me</u>, up in Boston, after 10+ years of silence? The diary mentioned your married name & that you were (probably) in New York, so yesterday I looked up your current address at the library. They have the Manhattan White Pages there, in a box near the encyclopedias.

Tina! You have no idea who I am! Somebody from your dad's past, yes... I got to know Parker in 1954, when I was a junior editor at Neutron Books here in Boston. I published all five of his "2333" novels, from the action-packed debut (which made his name) to the thought experiment that is <u>Extradition to Gambrinus</u> (which everyone hated). We rubbed along, though we never met. Alas, when Auroch Bros. bought Neutron in 1967, our focus shifted to guidebooks: car repair, dieting, the environment. I adapted to the new regime. His unfinished conclusion to "2333" was orphaned. The working title was <u>The Tan Gun</u>, & it was to be about the end of the world & how to escape it. (Maybe it <u>could</u> have been a guidebook.)

Parker pleaded for me to sign him up, but my hands were tied. Two years later, he sent a Christmas card telling me how tall you were getting & that his wife—your mom—had "departed." I couldn't tell if she'd died, or left town, or got beamed up into space. He implied that Neutron's fate hastened the split, mortal or domestic or cosmic. To be fair, my other authors were having nervous breakdowns, too. Only Kim Tollson, midwestern nurse by day, followed my lead. She switched from

her chronicles of an intergalactic priest to books like <u>Beekeeping</u>, <u>Your Dune Buggy</u>, & (as T. S. Kim) <u>Foods of Korea</u>.*

Hélas! Four weeks have passed since I started writing you. But the break jogged loose something that I meant to get off my chest. Although Parker & I were a "team," we never met. We knew each other well, & also not at all. Let me explain: I first heard tell of him from my cousin "Zeff" Zephyr, who your father might have mentioned, though he died young. They knew each other from Korea, two black men in the so-called integrated service—or, rather, right after: they met while recuperating, somewhere in Tokyo. Zeff (Army) telegrammed, saying I should get Parker (Air Force) to write a book for me. Your dad had <u>seen</u> things. "You could call them flying saucers," Zeff wrote, "though that makes me think of Cora chucking a dish at my head when we're fighting!" (Zeff's first wife <u>was</u> a rhymes-with-rich, as Mrs. Bush would say.) Parker could also "type up a storm," despite losing a finger.

When he arrived stateside, Zeff kept bugging me about your dad. In 1954, I wrote Parker care of Jot Electronix, asking if he had any interest in "jotting" some stories. (Couldn't help it!) No reply for a year. Then <u>2333</u> landed in the Neutron office. First page—good; second page—<u>better</u>! We were ready to roll!

What I'm about to say colors this account. Cousin Zeff <u>passed</u> for white, but I never did. I blame myself for not asking Zeff directly if Parker <u>knew</u> I was black. What if he didn't? I was pretty paranoid back

---

* Fast-forward to 1985, & the Book-of-the-Month Club spotlights <u>Man in Korean Costume</u>, a splashy historical romance by... T. S. Kim. But though the jacket photo shows a slim Asian model who "divides his time between London & Seoul," I bet the words are all by Ms. Tollson, who divides <u>her</u> time between Kansas City, Kansas, & Kansas City, Missouri. Not only would I know her style anywhere; the novel lifts paragraphs verbatim from <u>Foods of Korea</u> and her other books, <u>Music of Korea</u> and <u>Korean Scenes</u>! Good for her!

Neutron Books, by the way, is nearly kaput: Last I heard, Auroch Bros. wants to sell it for parts.

then, & kept my authors in the dark about such things. Did I assume your father's "whiteness"—or have a hunch it was otherwise?

After we went our separate ways in '67, Parker didn't cross my mind for years. Life got hectic. I jumped from a mediocre marriage to a bad one, & fled to Canticle Publications as Neutron withered away. While I was skimming the <u>Boston Herald</u> at lunch, a headline grabbed me: BLOODY RACE PUZZLE IN BFLO. Someone had stabbed a night watchman, less than 48 hours after two men were murdered in cars in different parts of Buffalo. All three were black. This maniac cut out the hearts of the first two victims, stuffed the bodies in the trunks. I kept reading. Police thought the murderer was <u>also</u> the .22-Caliber Killer, still on the loose after shooting four Afro-American men earlier in the fall. Only at the end did the reporter reveal the name of the third stabbing victim: "Parker Jotter, 50, is in serious but stable condition."

I was relieved my old author was alive. Then the sadness hit. Our shared past felt cursed with missed chances. Not only had we failed to meet in person, but we never even talked on the phone. (Would our voices have given us away?) You could say we were both white by default, hidden on either side of the page ...

One last thing, Tina. I've sometimes wondered if your dad had <u>me</u> in mind when he wrote <u>Extradition to Gambrinus.</u> Like he suspected the truth. This was 1962. You know the plot: black author pens novels for wealthy patron, whose fetish is to burn them without reading a word. We assume this cruel weirdo is white. What you probably don't know is that in the original, the patron was black, too. Right before press, I cut the last page, so the reader never learns this fact. (If Parker noticed, he didn't say.) So ... here, at last, are some unburnt pages. Thank you for letting this dotty Dot dodder on ...

Sincerely,
Dorothy (Dot) M. Zephyr

12/8/80

Dear Diary,

Dr. Sin says tell you everything, no matter how minor. Calls it *wild-wording*. Made-up term or actual psychiatric tool? Regardless. The shrink says write, so I write. I put pen to paper in Room 625 of the Erie County Medical Center (ECMC), with a view of Grider Street, or at least the sky above it. From the bed, I only see a white swirl: the first snow of the season. When I was a kid, the moment had a religious intensity. The world became silent, soft, and sweet. Parked cars doubled in size, monster meringues. Bare branches, stark an hour before, looked heaped with frosting. (I'm getting hungry just thinking about it.) Our house was a rocket ship, docked on a new planet. But these days, every year, those first flakes fill me with dread . . . (More later—I have rehab with Dr. Sorrow now.)

12/10/80

Dear Diary,

Dr. Sorrow scolded me for straining myself. Apparently, even yesterday's short entry was too much for my mangled wrist, and she wants a word with Dr. Sin. (Sin and Sorrow do *not* get along.) So I'll be left-handing it today. Luckily, I became ambidextrous, back when I was trapped in Korea. Let me explain. (Dr. Sin says don't worry about jumping around in time and space, he'll piece it together later: "That's the beauty of wild-wording!") After my plane went down that snowy December dawn—28 years, almost to the day—the Reds put me in a prison camp in the far north. (By "Reds," I mean North Koreans, mixed with Chinese, some Russians for decoration.) I was battered but intact, save for the loss of half my right ring finger: a clean, almost surgical cut, neatly stitched up.

They sat me at a small desk, in what looked like a former elementary-school classroom, and ordered me to write my life story.

I whined about my wounded mitt till an officer stuffed the pen in

my *left* hand. I stared at him in disbelief but he told me to get on with it. That's how I jotted my first piece of fiction. The only real things in that document were my name, rank, and serial. I invented the rest: the left-handed story of my made-up life. My birth year was '27 instead of '29, my hometown Akron, not Buffalo. My folks were now clockmakers, not a steelworker-turned-shopowner and a teacher-turned-housewife. I gave myself three siblings. My wife's name, Flora, became our street's. I told them I had no wife. Jotter the bachelor.

My sinister chicken scratch grew smoother. Two weeks into this exercise, a new officer came by: Chinese, with long, elegant fingers and small round glasses. Name was Wilson, like our old president. He read over my masterpiece, then said: *Now tell us who you really are.*

What choice did I have? I rewrote my life, closer to the facts. The Parker Jotter on the page moved through the years, from a kid dreaming of outer space to a pilot in Korea. Soon, I was recalling my final flight. How the snow fell as I got to the cockpit, white pinpricks on my jacket like a universe being born. How the storm erased the drab hills below, like mistakes painted out of a canvas. I told them about seeing a huge white airship, big as a city, but didn't say I gave chase. I just said that my Sabre stalled; that I blacked out.

Comrade Wilson liked this version of my story, though he crossed out the line about the pinpricks. ("Too poetic.") But there was a *specific* scenario that was missing, he said. He told me not to play dumb. A lackey pulled down a screen and they ran a film of heavy clouds, feathers drifting down. No sound. Then a shot of city streets, men and women crying out in the rubble as skin slid off their bones. A lackey held my head so I couldn't look away. Comrade Wilson explained the scene: Americans had doused thousands of feather packets with germs, packed them into bombs, and exploded them over Pyongyang and other big cities in the North. Loathsome diseases were spreading everywhere. On the screen a child in a strange coat clawed at the door of a house, locked out by his parents. Only when he collapsed in the road did I see that his arms were bare, covered shoulder to wrist with overlapping blisters.

"Actor," I sputtered. "He must be an actor."

The film cut to footage of a downed Sabre, its poison payload revealed. I blinked: that was *my* plane. The Jotter symbol, painted on by my friend Horowitz to strike fear into the enemy, was clearly visible on the side:

I couldn't make sense of it. What evil staging was this? Yet I had no choice but to watch, over and over. I picked up the pen and delivered a damning account of the top-secret mission, plus a ten-page apology to the people of North Korea.

My writing got so good, I began to think I'd done all the things they told me to say I did.

12/13/80

Dear Diary—

Dr. Sin (I almost wrote "Comrade Wilson") read these entries yesterday, found them satisfactory. Asked me about the "huge white airship" I saw on patrol. A cloud, maybe? Flock of cranes? I just nodded. Even I know not to talk UFOs in front of a psychiatrist.

Dr. Sorrow rang while I was in Sin's office. Chewed him out. She said the wild-wording might undo all of my healing progress. My body is much better but not 100%. It could have been worse, Dr. Sorrow says. If my old Zippo hadn't been in the pocket of my workshirt when the killer came for me that night, his knife would have gone straight through my heart. I keep the lighter nearby. My good-luck charm. Wouldn't you?

Dear Diary—

A dream of Tina. My daughter. We're in some bewitched version of our old house. Outside, it's snowing. Tina's a baby. She's on that bright green hall carpet, prying the lid off a box. Flora scolds her, says opening boxes is bad luck. The box is actually a book, thick as a dictionary. I try to help, but Flora grabs me, throws me to the floor. . . . Woke up to shooting pain: my own fingers, clenched around my wrist and real snow outside my window.

Tina's on my mind today. I remember taking her to college. Three years ago! Sometimes it seems like *twenty*-three years have passed. We stuffed the Caprice Classic with suitcases, plus the Shalimar, which I'd repaired as a graduation gift. It was so heavy she didn't want to take it, but I told her every student needs a typewriter. Plus Tina had a special gift for it; the Shalimar could be temperamental in (or under) the wrong hands. I drove the speed limit the whole way. Trying to make it last, even as I sensed her impatience. Nine hours later, we were there: Penumbra College. Vermont was as green as advertised. Moving her into the dorm took all of fifteen minutes. I stood around for ten more, then drove back home.

The summer after freshman year, Tina stayed with me in Buffalo. She planned to do an oral history of the newspaper where Flora had worked as a teenager in the '50s. But all she did was sleep in, after late nights on the phone. Then I saw the bill: long-distance charges to San Francisco. That's when Tina told me she was "getting serious" with some boy at Penumbra. Winston Pang.

"Ping?" I asked. "Wilson Pong?"

"Pang," Tina said. "Winston Pang. He's a junior."

"Black?"

"No. There are about six black students at Penumbra."

"So he's white."

"No." She took a breath. "Chinese."

"Watson Peng, was it?"

She stormed out. Back at Penumbra that fall, Tina wrote with the news that she was bringing Winston home over the long Christmas break: "We'll stay in a hotel." A hotel! "He'll pay for it and everything."

I told her they'd do no such thing. They visited. I made young Winston sleep in the basement. I should have been nicer. Here he was in Buffalo, city of ice, instead of under the California sun, just to be with Tina. The boy was polite as hell. He asked questions about the machines I had going in the basement—all my half-built typewriters and computers. Gave my inventions a test run. Said he could see them selling well. Yet I wouldn't give him a chance. His face, nice as it was, still reminded me of my captors, all those years ago. Anything he said, I contradicted. Only later, after they left, did the scale of my rudeness become clear. How I kept bungling his name, calling him "Wilson" a hundred times. How I found the entire Orient hell on earth, based on experience. For five days straight, I said things I couldn't unsay.

The day after Tina and Wilson left, a blizzard shut down the city. I woke in tears from a dream in which the snow buried the house, the house in which I lay dead. No one could find me there. No one even thought to look.

12/17/80

Dear Diary—

Today I got mail from Horowitz, a war buddy: a news clipping from October with the gentle headline "Buffalo Slay Fiend on the Loose." "This you?!" he scrawled at the top. "Hope they string the bastard up by the nuts." It was strange reading about myself, like I'd become part of history, a name in a tattered scrapbook. . . . The attack occurred "two days after a fatal stabbing in nearby Tonawanda and four days after one in the town of Amherst," which, in turn, followed four point-blank shootings in September. All the victims were black men. It says the knife "was stopped by a cigarette lighter in Otter's [sic] breast pocket." A vivid piece of writing. The capsule biography checks off the highlights (Korean War vet, night watchman at Chatillion Academy) but

omits any mention of my writing. I told them about the original *2333,* and recounted the plot of *Extradition to Gambrinus,* but journalists are always dubious when subjects say they've written books.

At least Dr. Sin shows interest in my literary side. Maybe too much. My oeuvre is a subject of fascination. I've tried to be a good patient, recalling details. Alas, too much time has passed since I wrote them, and my new medication keeps me foggy.

Dr. Sin won't drop the topic. Last week he said, "I would like to read them."

"No chance. Even the publisher is on its last legs—no more science fiction. A place called Neutron Books, in Boston."

"Ah." He made a note.

"Their star writer was Kim Tollson."

Scribble. "I see."

I listed some other Tollson titles, as much as it pained me. No response. "In any case, Neutron let me go, right around when Flora left me. I'm talking a million years ago."

"You must have felt twice abandoned." Another scribble. "Wife, gone. Books, gone."

"I have a few copies in my basement. I'll send you some when I finally get out of here."

"Only if you remember! My son likes those space stories. He's ten."

"They say that the 'golden age of science fiction' is when you're ten years old," I said, unsure he would catch my meaning. "That's when I started reading the magazines, listening to the serials on the radio . . ."

"Yes, yes. He reads anything with rockets, robots, aliens with purple skin."

Like I said here already, I tried to describe what happened in the books. But I resorted to making things up. I couldn't even remember the basics, like the name of Tina's favorite character. It was on the tip of my tongue. . . . Later, back in Room 625, it struck me that Dr. Sin might have thought I was deluded. That I wasn't a former novelist, just a UFO nut gone mad . . .

At our next meeting, Dr. Sin was pink with excitement.

"Guess what?" he said. "I asked my son if he had read any Jotter. He said the name sounded familiar!"

"Oh yeah?"

Turns out his kid, Arthur, had recently scooped up some paperbacks at a garage sale, including a tattered specimen with the Neutron Books logo: a head in profile, an atom for an eye. (The novel was Kim Tollson's *An Alien Alphabet,* about Martians whose messages of peace keep being misread as declarations of war.) Dr. Sin flipped to an order form in the back, listing other Neutron titles. And there I was. *2333: Return to Tyosen!*

"Only 75 cents. How did we ever make money?" I marveled. "Ah, that's right—we didn't."

"Are your books about Korea?" he asked. "About the war?"

I was taken aback. "Not at all."

"What about the title? Do the stories all take place in the future—in 2333?"

I explained how the number meant different things in different books. "In one, it's the time of day a crime takes place." My memory was hazy. "Military time—23:33."

"Eleven thirty-three at night." He made a note. "But why that *specific* number??"

"Truth is, I didn't mean to use it in *every* book. But the editor at Neutron—fellow named Zephyr—liked it in the title, so I found fresh ways to use it after that."

I could hear his pencil move.

12/29/80

Dear Diary—

Dr. Sin's questions have put me on edge. He wants to know more about the books. And I just want to leave. Dr. Sorrow says there have been some setbacks. My wrist's not healing like it should. Just a few more weeks, she says.

Last week I asked if I could start reading the papers, so Nurse Bonnie brings me a copy every morning. Today I wish I hadn't. News of another killing. It never ends. Two days ago, a black man here in Buffalo was stabbed to death at a bus stop. Yesterday, the same thing, this time in Rochester. Are these murders related to the knifing of three black men in New York over Christmas? Can one person do so much evil? Are there copycats on the loose?

The press can't resist. They're calling him the .22-Caliber Killer. He uses a sawed-off rifle—except when he uses a knife.

I told the nurse's station not to bother with the paper anymore. Maybe just the sports.

1/1/81

Dear Diary,

Up at 9. A late start to the new year. I go to the window. It snowed overnight. I can't decipher the view. I'm not in ECMC. Where have they brought me?

I breathe in—ten seconds—then let it go. Again. One more time. Ten and out. A calming technique taught to me in Tokyo, from Nurse Doe. I haven't mentioned her to Dr. Sin yet. I met her after getting freed from the prison camp in Sinuiju, when they brought me to an American base in Japan. They treated me like a hero at first. They wanted me 100% before I went home. I wrote happy letters to Flora, counting the days.

Days became weeks, weeks stretched into months. Different doctors came by with cold manners and new gadgets. They stuck wires to my head, drew fluids. I was something to be monitored. One doctor worried about radiation. Another said my balance was off. I had previously walked without difficulty; after his remark, I swayed anytime I moved. No one could tell me how much longer I had to stay.

One day, they treated me to an exclusive movie screening: a propaganda film in which I was the star. Brow glistening with sweat, a haggard version of me addressed a North Korean camera crew. The

impostor admitted to germ-bombing three of their cities, on the orders of his government. My double denounced America, pledged his loyalty to the Great Leader Kim Il Sung. His eyes only looked up from the script once, at the very end. He met my gaze, unable to grasp the identity of his future observer.

After this performance, my American doctors regarded me warily. Nurse Doe knew I wasn't a traitor, just an American who had been through hell and was just trying to get home. She told me to breathe. Count to ten, let it out. At first, I took her for Japanese; we were in Tokyo, after all. Turned out she was Korean. She might have been forty. She had come to Japan before World War II, to work in a munitions factory, if I understood correctly; after the surrender, she picked up English assisting at American hospitals.

Nurse Doe watched over me most nights, to make sure I fell asleep. Sometimes we'd talk. She imitated voices of the other staff, made me laugh so much my old wounds started to hurt. In the dark, she asked what it was like flying the Sabre, facing MiGs head-on. She asked about Flora, who had dimmed in my mind so much that my description sounded unreal. The Americans thought I was lying about the floating shape I'd seen on my mission—that I'd made it up to appease my captors, make them think some giant American death-ship was stalking the skies—but Nurse Doe believed me. I confessed I no longer knew what was real and what had been put in my head, what I actually saw versus what I had turned into fiction to save myself. Cloud or aircraft, feathers or snow—even a visitor from out of this world.

Nurse Doe said it didn't matter, said that things and their stories can never be separated. The mythical founder of Korea, she said, came down from the skies, brought order to chaos. Now, thousands of years later, some Koreans looked to the heavens again for a powerful visitor to deliver them from strife. Maybe it was *me*!

"I'm flattered," I told her, "but as you can see, my power is limited at the moment."

Other nights, I tried speaking Korean. She laughed at my attempts.

I told her about my cellmate, the doomed Ko. I showed her the Zippo he left me.

"K.P.G.," she said, tracing the letters engraved on the side.

"His initials." For some reason, I could only recall his surname, Ko.

Nurse Doe flicked it on, and the dancing flame lit up her face. I remembered poor Ko cupping the fire with his palm. I watched her watch the light. Though it had become a lucky charm of sorts, I wanted her to have the Zippo. Besides, I didn't smoke.

But the day before my departure, Nurse Doe was nowhere to be found. The covering nurse didn't know who I was talking about. Growing alarmed, she hailed one of my tormentors, a constipated Texan, who said I was lucky to be alive.

"We almost had her," he said, shaking his head in disgust, "but she escaped."

"I don't understand."

"She doesn't work here. Now, tell me straight. What kind of questions did she ask?"

"We didn't talk much," I said. "Nurse Doe helped me get to sleep sometimes."

"I'll bet she did, Jotter."

I ignored the innuendo. "If she doesn't work for you, who does she work for?"

"The Koreans," he sighed, "but not *our* Koreans."

Had I been talking to a spy? I counted to ten, then breathed out. I tried to remember everything I told her. Too much. "You mean she's with the North?"

He shook his cue-ball head. "Not the South, either. These are some unruly third kind of Koreans, Jotter. Best we can figure, they don't like *either* side."

My phantom digit ached. "How did she even get inside the hospital?"

"These slopes all look alike, is the main issue," he said. "We found one of our nurses tied up in a locker downstairs. Clothes torn off."

"I don't understand."

"Your 'Nurse Doe' wasn't a nurse. Just had the uniform."

Thinking about this now isn't relaxing me at all. Ten and out. Ten and out.

1/5/81

Dear Diary—

Dr. Sin came in just as I was sinking into the sports section.

"Sabres Skate to 2-2 Tie," I read aloud. "Don't you love how they use that verb, Doc? 'Skate.' Like the boys went out and did a few figure eights, then came in for hot chocolate."

He set his briefcase down. It looked new: light brown leather and bright brass latches.

"Catch any of last night's game?" I asked.

"No, but I watched the Bills lose on Saturday."

"That must have been torture. Who did they lose to this time?"

"Chargers." Dr. Sin rubbed his forehead furiously, as if to erase the memory.

"My advice is to forget football. Hockey—there's a sport. The speed appeals. Maybe it's the jet pilot in me. Fastest game on two feet."

"Nobody has teeth. My son, he wants to play, but—ah, I don't know."

"I bet the Sabres and the North Stars got rowdy last night. Minnesota coming to the Aud is always a free-for-all."

"The Odd?"

"Memorial Auditorium."

"Ah."

"The North Stars hate us." I scanned the article. "Three years ago, I caught a Sabres-Stars game. It was hand-to-hand combat, but we won 9–2. Korab and Savard both got hat tricks—Korab and Savard!"

A blank gaze, as though I were discussing an Austro-Hungarian legal firm.

"It was a madhouse. A Sabre fell in front of their net, and the goalie chopped him on the head with his stick. I could hear it, all the way up

in the blue seats! The crowd went crazy. I'm surprised Minnesota made it out of the Aud alive."

Scribble.

Normally I looked forward to our sessions, but something was off. "You know what a sabre is, right?"

"A sword."

"Sure. But why is *that* the name of our team? Does Buffalo have a long fencing history? Negative. Is it a city where such weapons were manufactured, in days of yore? Not a chance."

"Why, then?"

"Way back when, the owners asked the public to send in ideas. Hundreds of entries came in and they picked mine."

He looks up from his note taking. "Do you mean that you came up with Sabres?"

"The most popular thing I ever wrote."

1/21/81

Dear Diary—

More snow. Did slow-motion jumping jacks with Dr. Sorrow. She said we're on the right path. After lunch, a nurse wheeled me into Dr. Sin's office. I was left to my own devices for a few minutes; he came in ten minutes late, the *Courier-Express* under his arm. The headline said INAUGURATION DAY. It occurred to me I'd been inside a long, long time.

"What's your take on President Reagan, Doc? Not too old?"

"In Korea, we elected Syngman Rhee when he was 73."

I remembered Rhee. Went around calling himself the Korean George Washington. I'd fought for *him*, in a way. "And how'd that work out for you?"

"He rewrote the constitution and got himself elected four times." Dr. Sin looked out the window, lost in the past. The snow was still falling hard. "I marched against him, you know. He ruined the country, so we kicked him out at age 85."

"I guess he *was* too old after all."

"Maybe so, maybe so," he said, and waved away the memory.

1/23/81

Dear Tina,

Dr. Sin says I'm ready for the next step in "wild-wording." (Or is he say-ing wired-wording? Wide-worlding?) He tells me to write letters to the person I miss the most. He probably expects I'll spill my guts to Flora, but of course it's you I'm thinking of. There's no stationery, so I'm sup-posed to jot them in here for now. Do I ever send the letters to you, or are they for his eyes only? (There are nuances to wild-wording yet to be revealed.) One problem with the former option is that I don't know your address. . . . I'd apologize if I knew how to reach you.

Last I heard, you had eloped with Winston and were moving to New York. Not that you told me. I got it from our old neighbor, Mrs. Nowak, who heard it from her daughter, who I guess you still write to now and again.

I'm not even sure what you go by. Are you Tina Pang, Tina Jotter-Pang, Tina J. Pang? Or still just Tina Jotter? I can't imagine it's a good sign when you don't know your own child's name. I'll try again later.

2/3/81

Dear Tina,

In Korea, I would spin stories to distract whoever I was sharing a cell with or just to entertain myself, the times I was alone. Some of these ended up in my books, those paperbacks Flora called blasphemies. Lately I've been talking to a doctor here about them. He thinks they're important. He thinks they're *really* important.

Dr. Inky Sin is from Korea, of all places. What are the odds? His English was hard to understand at first, but I'm used to it now. I learned that he came to Buffalo fifteen years ago, after a stint in the Army, to finish his medical education. He has everything he wants here: a house,

a wife, a job, a kid. When he stepped on that plane, he said, there was no going back. . . . Now his ten-year-old, Arthur, is a sucker for science fiction. "Don't worry," I joked, "he'll grow out of it." (Just like you did.) Arthur loves wordplay, does the Jumble in the paper every day before his dad gets a chance. (Just like you did.) His teachers say he's shy and doesn't talk much in class. (*Not* like you!)

Anyway, Dr. Sin keeps asking about my books. He wants to know how I thought up the strange names: Planet Tyosen . . . Greena Hymns . . .

"I don't know," I say. "It was a long time ago. They just *sounded* right."

"Why is the series called *2333*?" he asked.

I told him about your discovery, Tina—that the numbers actually were a tribute to your mother: her birth date, February 3, 1933. (She would be 48 *today*. I wonder if you ever hear from her. I don't think I'll ever see her again.) For some reason, Dr. Sin thinks this is just coincidence. That I'm hiding the real reason—maybe even from myself. Is this what wild-wording is supposed to unlock?

Dr. Sin says he's been hunting for my books at library sales and Salvation Army stores all over Erie County. Today he comes in with a grin and a copy of *2333: The Louse*.

"Garage sale?" I ask.

"No," he says. "I bought it from *you*."

He points out an ink stamp on the top edge of the pages.

It's a mark that you might remember, Tina, from stamping all over your coloring books. That's right: the long-lost insignia of Jot Electronix!

"You sold the books at the store—Michigan Avenue, yes?" He was getting excited. "I went there once, when my wife and I lived close by. Before Arthur was born. I was so confused when you put the book in my bag. An American custom? I didn't know you were the *author*."

"A blender." The distant memory returned. "You wanted a blender."

"A *brender*," he said, mocking the accent of his younger self.

The Louse must have been misplaced during one of their many

moves, at some point migrating to his study. Then, this past weekend, his son had gone poking through the shelves. Tucked behind a wall of Freud were a dozen pop-psychology paperbacks he'd accumulated over the years: *Passages, Your Erroneous Zones, In and Out of the Garbage Pail.* Somewhere in the pile was *The Louse.*

Dr. Sin showed me the book—the cover had nearly fallen off—and somehow just seeing it jogged my memory. Remember the story? The Louse is a 14-year-old custodian at a run-down grocery store. He wins a rickety computer by sending in hundreds of cereal box tops. When he flicks on the machine, it runs a program that gives him control over the whole planet. At first, the Louse has fun with it. He types out whimsical decrees: on Tuesdays, everyone must wear purple; on Fridays, the theme song from his favorite cartoon blasts over loudspeakers in every town square. But after he orders that his picture be hung above each doorway, things take a darker turn. . . .

Arthur finished reading it in a day, and Dr. Sin picked it up after. He had questions for me. He brought out his tape recorder, which he'd done a few times in the past.

"How did the Louse pull it off?" he asked. "A sort of hypnosis?"

"I'm sure you're right. I can't recall."

He looked skeptical. "Why is he called the Louse, of all things?"

"Just a nickname," I said. "He had lice as a kid. The other boys used to tease."

Dr. Sin looked dubious. I wanted to help, but for the life of me, I couldn't tell him why I chose to build a book around *that* word. As we argued, I felt a twinge. A pricking. That otherworldly tingle I used to call the Freak.

Now, alone in Room 625, I wonder when I'll get to leave. The mind goes to bad places. What if I'm not at ECMC but some made-up "hospital," with a "nurse" to check my "vitals" every day? No. I'm at ECMC. Get real, Jotter.

But I've decided I don't trust Dr. Sin enough to let him read these letters, this diary. Now what? I've got a big envelope, enough stamps,

too. (I swiped them from his office—see 1/21.) I wish I knew your address, Tina. For now, I can think of a place where all this will be safe for a while: Zephyr's office. (Despite what I told Dr. Sin, Neutron Books is still around, as far as I know.)

They say that if the average citizen finds a stamped letter on the street, he'll drop it in the nearest mailbox. Let's see if that holds true. My window should open just enough for me to slide the envelope through. I see a walkway below, with people. If you get this, Tina, please find me.

I need you—

FOR DAYS AFTER READING DREAM TWO, with its cast of doomed gunmen, I had a flickering memory of . . . a rock. A vexingly vague image, its dimensions and color in flux. What was it? Late one night, in the midst of searching for more information on the real-life assassins, I was swayed by ads to do some shopping on GLOAT. In a consumerist daze, I bought some mementos from the Pan-American Exposition, where Nobody killed McKinley: drinking glass, postcards, map. I bought laundry detergent, because I knew we were running low, and a jumbo pack of almonds. Impulsively, I got Story a green Hegemon backpack, decorated with UFOs. I kept adding items to my cart. The next day, a blue-and-red cardboard box from GLOAT appeared on our porch, long as a coffin, its contents a snapshot of my scrambled mind.

I kept seeing the rock.

I played with GLOAT's Spaticon function to see where the shootings of Ito Hirobumi, Durham Stevens, and President McKinley took place. Spaticon was still in beta, an enhancement to our popular mapping program; the vaguely disgusting term derived from a shortening of *space-time continuum.* I entered the years and locations, then watched as Spaticon smoothly rendered the Harbin train station in 3D, based on pictures taken by drones and self-driving cars. First I saw the station as it stood now, lit up and thronged. Then the modern touches melted away. A flood of previous incarnations appeared and disintegrated, until I was looking at what Thomas Ahn must have seen from his hotel window back in 1909: a vaulted structure, like the

skeleton of a whale. It took a half an hour, but I was hypnotized. I expanded the view and moved along the platform.

Of course, the program didn't have a thousand photos of this earlier station. It lacked the visual archive that allowed it to reproduce contemporary buildings down to the screws on the light fixtures. But Spaticon diligently scoured the internet for enough period detail to mimic brick textures and clothing patterns, and even conjured a murmur rising from the polyglot crowd. Chinese, Russian, Japanese, and even Yiddish. I knew Spaticon was already enriching game environments based on the real world; I wouldn't have been totally shocked to see Story's Hegemon avatar popping up, on a quest for pieces of the Tan Gun. For now, though, only GLOAT workers of a certain rung could access the experience.

A train arrived, disgorging its passengers, anonymous figures from old portraits, animated for a walk-on part. Their breath was visible in the air. Next, I visited the Ferry Building in San Francisco, watched as the filter hurled the scene back across the decades until it was the morning of March 25, 1908. The soft sound of water and the harsh cries of gulls enveloped me. I was *there*, with Chang and Chun, waiting by the docks for Stevens. I clicked for the final scene: the Temple of Music, Buffalo, New York. The afternoon of September 6, 1901.

Instead of a rose-tinted meeting hall, I got a rock. Pink and gray, knee-high. It was the one that had been lodged in my head. Onscreen, it sat on a patch of grass, bathed in sunlight. I walked my virtual body around it, taking in the unremarkable shape. On the opposite face was an unloved plaque, dark with years. Before I read a word, I knew what it was: a commemoration of McKinley's shooting, which had taken place on that spot, where the Temple of Music had once stood.

I'd seen the rock in real life. I attended Chatillion Academy in Buffalo for a while, beginning in sixth grade, when our teachers devoted a month to local history. We learned about the Seneca Nation and the Erie Canal, Grover Cleveland's swift rise from local sheriff to American president, and a hodgepodge of other things. The dramatic high point was the Pan-American Exposition. We walked a few streets over to look at the very rock now on my screen. As the plaque explained, the Temple of Music had once stood here

but had been taken down, along with all the other grand plaster structures, eighty years ago. One teacher said that the tragic end to the Pan—McKinley's assassination—marked the start of Buffalo's decline over the twentieth century, as it went from a thriving city to Rust Belt casualty; another teacher accused her of *post hoc, ergo propter hoc,* saying it was silly to assign such weight to an unfortunate incident. The debate intensified as we headed back to the classroom.

What is history?

Now, staring at my screen in Dogskill, I tried going back to 1901 using Spaticon, but it kept showing me the rock and its lowly plaque. Perhaps it was because the dream world of the Pan never actually existed. Even though there were photos of the Temple of Music, and maps of the exposition grounds, Spaticon glitched. It couldn't place the artificial over the real. I was stuck on an exquisitely dull residential street, as SUVs rumbled past in the background.

Who was Echo, to write so confidently about such remote events and people? I wondered which parts were true, which invented. I poked around GLOAT, dipping into /koreana, /assassins, and other forums. I confirmed a few facts, but much remained elusive. There *was* a Korean Provisional Government, but its power seemed largely symbolic. With members scattered across the globe, the KPG could issue proclamations, but no country would recognize it. Infighting was rampant. It was a historical footnote, nothing more.

Was that the point of Echo's book—that the KPG did its great work undercover, outside history? I didn't know what to believe. Maybe reading the whole book would resolve matters, but no one at the Slow Press was getting back to me. I reread the two Dreams. Echo had an uncanny way of inhabiting the minds of his various killers, an atmosphere enhanced by the pages themselves. Sprout's toothmarks and the grime on the unearthed chapter added to the unsettling vibe. For my own mental upkeep, I needed some distance, so I spent as much time as possible in the most antiseptic place I could think of: the office.

. . .

THE ONLY WAY I could get to my job any quicker would be if they perfected teleportation—which, knowing GLOAT, was probably in the works. We had a car now, a car and a van. I usually took the former unless Nora needed it. The van was fine except it said DAILY DIVAS on the side in huge pink letters.

I drove out of Westgate Estates, hung a left at the light, and went uphill. Soon the trappings of Dogskill vanished. For a full minute there was no glimpse of civilization apart from the road itself—not a single sign, tower, building, or wire. An electronic sentry disguised as a tree read my license plate and a row of spikes, hidden among stones, receded into the ground. As the car crawled through the thin zone where the scanners were focused, I imagined it going bright with information, casting off data like sparks. As of May, I had my own parking space with a sign that said SHEEN, a bit too suggestive of my future tombstone.

Nora called as I got out.

"Have you seen Sprout?"

"No."

"He's missing. Story's worried."

"I'm sure he's just exploring."

"For three days?"

It was unlike me not to notice. The neighbors knew Sprout and wouldn't hail the pound, but I feared he'd strayed too far. Coyote sightings had made the news. Then I remembered that he had his GLOAT collar on, so I looked up his whereabouts on my phone. Something was off, though. It said he was in the car.

The collar turned up in the back seat. The dog in question was nowhere to be found.

"Come on back, buddy," I whispered, then put the collar around my wrist like a bracelet.

CAMPUS WAS A RORSCHACH. Sane people had compared it to a starfish on steroids, a certain kind of Portuguese pastry, or the long fingers of a small hand. To me it looked like an asterisk. No one else called it that. You didn't

get a sense of the layout from the inside. For a long time, a blueprint in the lobby showed seven spokes radiating from the hub, whereas official maps indicated only six. It took me a few years to note the discrepancy. Soon after, the drawing was gone.

Entering the center, I waved to Otto at security.

"What's the good word, Bruce?" he said.

Otto always called me Bruce, after Bruce Lee. Sometimes I pretended to brandish nunchucks, let out a feline yowl. Otto usually had a book nearby, for the mellow period after the morning rush. Today, however, I saw a game of Hegemon paused on his phone.

"Are you close to putting together the Tan Gun?" I said, like one in the know.

He gave me a look of pain and longing. "Not even close, Bruce."

People were heading in. I had to move. Another day at the Asterisk. Another day of building the future. My phone was already humming with Dr. Ubu's demands. I walked to the ramp for the southeast-pointing stalk, then shrugged my right shoulder to align the Freckle—a freckle-sized chip in my arm—with the door's sensor. (The stoop was vestigial, from when I used the standard lanyard; the sensor would have picked up the Freckle's signal even if I whizzed by on a skateboard wearing a lead wimple.) A machine voice politely said, "Rung 10," announcing my rank. Then I went up to the third floor, where I walked through acres of open plan to get to my work-womb.

A sensor read my Freckle, and a small black plaque flashed my name in soft teal letters. Before I entered, I shouted, "Here we go!"

"Here we go!" my teammates shouted back. Then we proceeded to not talk to each other for the rest of the day.

Parking slot and Freckle chip and office womb were perks of my longevity. Turnover at GLOAT was high, with new hires lasting eighteen months on average. I had survived and thrived for over a decade. When I wasn't out playing Korean drinking games, I was a competent company man, as stable as they come.

In addition to managing my early literary career, my friend Tanner Slow had set me up at GLOAT, where he was briefly SCM, or Supervising Con-

tent Megalomaniac, when the company was based in Lower Manhattan and the corporate culture embraced whimsical business cards. Later he was DHM (Dude Handling Marketing), then CPO (Chief Procrastination Officer). Such self-deprecation suggested hidden depths, or so everyone liked to believe.

I started as an NCD (Nicely Compensated Drudge) on a grim February morning in 2002, less than a year after *Pretenders* came and went without a ripple. My remit was to generate content—back then, a term ambiguous enough to convey cachet. Specifics were hazy. Did Tanner want me to recap TV shows, lead a virtual book club? (No.) Do a rundown of the deadliest tornadoes, a listicle of bankrupt Olympians? (Not quite.) Publish flash fiction or a daily poem? (God no are you insane.) I accepted strange, time-consuming assignments, like transcribing all the entries in an anagram dictionary or creating a directory of defunct websites. "It's all mill for the grist," Tanner would say, "or, rather, mist for the grill, that is to say—you know what I mean." He was distracted by intrigues around his father's fortune (a great-aunt's lover's grandchild had materialized to stake a claim) and thus was unclear about my deliverables. I took long lunches, wandered the halls, ran errands. None of the other NCDs lasted long.

One Friday morning, with unusual urgency, Tanner tasked me to build acronyms that might catch fire. These would populate the various GLOAT networks—the chat rooms and bazaars, the galleries and aggregators and coupon swaps—where, with any luck, they would percolate, alchemize into ad dollars. The model never made sense to me, but grander forces were at play. Mist for the grill. S-D profiling. On a whiteboard, I free-associated letter clusters, then fit words to them. Nora, who put in superhuman hours at Daily Divas, called my gig a dream job, but I found it taxing. My hair started to fall out. I'd sit at the keyboard and let my fingers fly blindly for five minutes. Out of a heap, a few combinations would spark something that got traction, once GLOAT put them out in the world: the mild complaint AWAM (*And what about me?*), the adventurous YOLT (*You only live twice*), and the versatile expression of surprise WITAF (*What in the actual fuck?*).

Overhearing one of my winners still gave me a thrill. People would use them in casual conversation, unaware that they had an author. My work was

nameless but everywhere, a step up from my mute toiling in the fields of fiction. My hair grew back, lush like a teen's.

"It's a medical miracle," Nora said.

IAMM, I thought.

SEVERAL YEARS LATER, GLOAT made Dogskill its new East Coast hub. Tanner Slow was long gone by then, building up his new publishing venture. Story was almost five, already acquainted with the dance of pawn and knight. Nora wasn't opposed to relocation, as her trio of upstate Daily Divas were thriving. GLOAT secured us a place in Westgate Estates, where every neighbor had some connection to the company. The house dwarfed our Manhattan apartment, the entire contents of which could fit in our new basement. I had room for all my junk: old books, hockey cards in Mylar sleeves, every movie tchotchke and rock-club handbill accumulated over the years. I'd tell Nora all of it might be valuable someday—a theory she blithely tested (under username hoarderwife_78) when GLOAT opened its e-auction platform.

We walked in a daze from room to room, going up and down stairs, shouting at each other just to be heard. Sprout rubbed his coat against the walls, to mark every new space with his scent, but gave up halfway around the kitchen.

Story's school, Measures, emphasized that the margin was the center. Most of the kids there were white like her, though the curriculum appeared geared to nonwhite kids in nontraditional family arrangements. Every time I visited her classroom, there was a new poster celebrating the wisdom of the Buddha, or the Maya calendar, or Inuit ingenuity. The LGBTQΩ Alliance had a large presence, and decorating the walls were scrolls of colored paper with slogans like "You Can Love Anyone You Want + Be Happy." I was getting old: I didn't know what the omega stood for; it would have been gauche to ask.

For that matter, I wasn't clear on what the letters in GLOAT signified. Possibly nothing. Or else many things: the phrase in question ever changing, apt for a company based on change. ("Good luck on all that," we'd say to each other, at least once a week.) The practice of matching sayings to the letters worked its way into campaigns for various GLOAT ventures. Users

came up with their own interpretations all the time. Most infamously, they mangled the catchphrase "Greatest Love of All Time," for GLOAT's dating site, into "Get Laid on a Train."

Shortly after relocating to Dogskill, I shifted into Digital Penetration, where I continued to toil. We brainstormed in a kidney-shaped conference room known as the Dig Pen. The walls were decorated with seventies album covers, a deconstructed hi-fi system, a pair of well-worn bell-bottoms. We were too busy to ask what the metaphor was. Our aim was to maximize click rate and impression time by taking copy through multiple iterations, so that GLOAT could learn to do it better on its own. We were paving the way for our own obsolescence.

THE AMBUSH OCCURRED RIGHT before lunch, as I made my way to one of the cafés on the third floor. Suddenly everything went dark.

"Guess who?"

I couldn't recognize the voice, nor the texture of the palms clapped over my eyes. Man, woman, tall, short, young, old? I caught a whiff of aloe and coconut.

"Loa," I said. "Loa Ding."

She pulled away her hands. I turned around.

"How did you know?" she said.

"My secret talent."

"What's up with your lip?" She tried to dab my mouth with a corner of tissue.

"What?" I touched my face. "Ah, right. I'm building out a mustache." *To make me look like a doomed Korean assassin.*

"I thought maybe there was some ink from a newspaper."

"It'll look more grown in next week."

"Good luck on all that."

The situation was that GLOAT had finally absorbed *slanted+enchanted,* and Loa was in the midst of onboarding. She would be operating out of the Asterisk the rest of the year. Her desk in the southernmost arm overlooked a loading dock. Trucks moved in and out all day long.

"I pretend they're whales," she said. "I might be losing my mind."

"In that case," I said, "let me take you to Little Eden."

After swearing her to secrecy, I told Loa about the patch of land that the internet forgot. The idea repelled and attracted her. Who was Loa without constant contact? We picked up sandwiches and two canisters of Marshlands—GLOAT's brand of lime-inflected, gently carbonated H_2O— and exited through a discreet door in the fifth spoke to the last unmapped scrap on earth. The days were getting cooler. No one else was there. I gave her one of my spare keys and told her to guard it with her life. We unwrapped the food. Loa took out her phone and laughed at the image on her map: "You are somewhere in this circle," it said. The circumference covered most of the Western Hemisphere.

"What's next for *slanted+enchanted*?" I asked between bites.

"Now that I've sold it, I feel so *liberated.* I took most of the payment in Gloatables. I hope that was the right move."

"Probably."

"It's like getting stock, right?"

"Probably not."

Loa was unruffled. "You know I used to be a GLOAT intern, right? Back when it was still in New York. I reported to Tanner Slow. Well, to his assistant."

"What were you, twelve?"

"Very funny. I was sixteen. I had just started college, early. You hadn't been hired yet." I sensed her debating whether that meant she had seniority now. "I heard Tanner got spooked. That he walked out of the office one day after seeing something and never came back."

"An urban legend," I said, though there was some truth to it. Even now, he changed the subject whenever anyone brought up his time at GLOAT.

"Still, it feels like I've come full circle. I'm returning to my roots."

"How?"

"Well, *slanted + enchanted* started out as a zine. That's how I built community. I'm using my platform to launch a storytelling mentorship program for underrepresented voices of the Asian diaspora."

I was certain she was sincere. I was also convinced that this was a care-

fully crafted message, vetted by GLOAT's comms arm. "Sign me up. I could use mentoring."

"You're funny. The program is called Tell It Slant."

"Not crazy about that name."

"It's from Emily Dickinson."

"Even so."

"The team's just spitballing now. Having a blast. Maybe there could be a—"

She screamed as something bolted from the brush. Before I could react, she dragged me in front of her as a shield. The beast came so close I could feel its breath. The gray fur was clumped and knotted, and burrs on the legs gave the appearance of knit socks. The D part of my S-D quotient surged. If it killed us, would anyone find our bodies? I couldn't remember who else had a key to Little Eden. The thing circled, barked, and attacked the ground with its paws.

"Just a dog," I said, relieved, as clods whizzed by and my heart pounded in my ears.

"Is it rabid?" Loa gripped my arms. Her faint island scent was making me dizzy.

"It's not." I pulled myself away from Loa and approached the shuddering mass. "It's *Sprout*."

I took his GLOAT collar off my wrist, switched it on. Normally it gave off glints as it processed his health, but it had gone dead here in Little Eden. He whimpered as I brushed an ear with one hand and started plucking out burrs with the other.

"Whatcha got there, pal?"

Sprout was exhausted, but his panting mouth seemed to smile. He licked my hand, then went for my face, nearly knocking me down.

"Down, boy—easy."

Sprout rolled over. While I rubbed his belly, Loa inspected the treasure he'd dug up.

"'Dream Three'?'" she read. "I mean, I knew GLOAT was a strange place, but wow."

"It's . . ." I fluttered my fingers, as though the mysteries of this unrecordable acre extended to all creatures and objects within it. Sprout was on the verge of collapse. I casually took the filthy pages from Loa, as though they were just so much litter, bound for the trash. But she could tell I wasn't going to throw it out, so I told her about Echo's Dreams, Sprout's disease. The three of us left Little Eden. I headed straight to the parking lot with Sprout. At home, I gave him a bath, reattached his GLOAT collar a notch tighter, and read the next of Echo's infernal Dreams, while the 3D printer slowly manufactured another game piece for Story.

DREAM THREE
1884–1965

[The KPG] is the sole representative of the Korean people, whether they are resident in Korea proper, Manchuria, Siberia, China or elsewhere, and regards itself . . . not as a free movement in any sense whatever of that phrase, but as the only government agency of Korea that is in existence.

—Syngman Rhee to Secretary of State Cordell Hull

1. Composition

Time enters these paragraphs without staining them. Some were written before you were born. Others will be written tomorrow.

This is the third dream of the Korean Provisional Government.

2. Metamorphoses

Bae Boonam becomes Udam becomes Dayama Sadako becomes Bae Boonam again, a double or triple agent. Kim Jongsook of Manchuria becomes Vera Kim. Franziska Maria Barbara Donner of Vienna becomes Francesca Rhee, the frugal "Martha Washington" of South Korea. All are members in good standing of the Korean Provisional Government.

3. Becoming Sadako

Bae Boonam is born in Seoul in 1870, to a family employed by the royal court of King Kojong and Queen Min. The court is aligned with China, but some see Japan as a model for modernizing Korea. Bae's father is purged from the palace for such views; her mother goes blind with grief. Destitute at twelve, Bae trains as a *kisaeng* for the delectation of the elite. She recites poems and declaims her own, every bit as good. A double

drum, shaped like an hourglass, produces a low sound and a high sound as she beats it with mallets. Bae's whole self becomes an instrument for the most rarefied dancing and music and poetry; but as a *kisaeng* she is subject to the baser things as well, the pawing hands of men older than her father. Low, high, low, high. She eludes her fate for a while by becoming a Buddhist nun, renamed Udam. But her scandalous *kisaeng* past causes a stir among the sisters, and she has to leave.

Bae looks east. The rest of her life goes something like this: A Japanese merchant—an ardent patron of her *kisaeng* talents—whisks Bae to Tokyo, where she takes the name Dayama Sadako. She meets other Koreans, like the dashing, disgraced reformer O. K. Kim.

O.K. has been living here a couple of years. He fled Seoul in 1884, after a botched palace coup, engineered with Japanese backing. (One co-conspirator fled for America and renamed himself Philip Jaisohn.) Sadako recounts her father's death at the hands of the same Korean court. The sympathetic O.K. grows besotted, but she marries another exile, a man named Jun, and bears a child. Jun dies. O.K. introduces the widowed Sadako to Prime Minister Ito, who "adopts" her, crows that she's the daughter he never had. (Baffling, as he already has a daughter.) The most powerful man in Japan flaunts Sadako in public, but his tastes are so well known that most gossip fails to shock. A year earlier, rumors that the PM bought the virginity of a fifteen-year-old geisha were met with a shrug, even a sort of patriotic admiration for how he's sustained a deep-rooted folk practice.

At seventeen, Sadako has porcelain skin and a knack for survival. At forty-six, Ito is wrinkled but still lean as a cat, every inch a samurai. They look like different species. The adoption reads as political allegory: *Japan and Korea can live harmoniously under the same roof.* In reality, his family shuns the new addition, so Ito installs her in posh quarters not far from his own grand

house. He hires someone to raise Sadako's son, so she can finish her schooling and focus on being his mistress.

It's the mixing of races that stimulates. In Britain as a youth, he sampled tarts white as paper. On his continental tour, he tasted the confections of Vienna and Paris. But he considers a Korean girl the most tempting: so close, yet so despised. Sadako will be his to civilize.

The prime minister visits every day, while out with his dog for a walk. He lashes it to the banister and goes upstairs. For these encounters, Sadako dons outfits native to her country. Her wardrobe is stocked with *kisaeng* gowns, the drab robes of a Buddhist nun, and the monumental headgear of ladies-in-waiting, into which one can deposit jewels, coins, entire documents, with no one the wiser. Though Sadako knows Japanese, Ito instructs her to speak only Korean.

4. Six Seasons

Ito has Sadako call out to him in her tongue: *Pabo*, fool. *Yisang*, strange. *Yobo*, spouse. This is how he learns Korean, in shouted bursts. Every so often, during a meeting with his ministers, this new vocabulary rises to his lips. Articles of clothing: *shin, paji, moja*. Facial features: *noon, mori, eep, kwi*. The words are like a sweet infection. Once he hears them, he does not forget. In idle moments, he catches himself saying them to his wife, his children, his dog. All of them recoil in disgust, except his faithful *keh*, who understands.

Ito and Sadako will have but six seasons together. Advisers catch wind of blackmail schemes, urge Ito to end this affair. To be with a Korean is unspeakable. Sensing that Ito will cut her loose, Sadako moves to secure her future. She seeks advice from O. K. Kim, now going by the Japanese name Iwata Shusaku. He sees qualities that would make her an invaluable special agent, and introduces her to a spymaster. In eight months, she learns it all: how to communicate in cipher, how to

kill with a lacquered hairpin dipped in homemade toxin, how to vanish. She can speak Chinese with a Japanese accent, Japanese with a Chinese accent, Korean with a Japanese accent, and Russian with a Chinese accent. With the right clothes and makeup, she can play prostitute or priestess, roles she already knows. Binding her bosom, lowering her voice, Sadako passes as a boy or young man.

She can turn spoons into skeleton keys, take down a foe with a sweep of her leg. She can fire two revolvers at once on horseback, bullets hitting the same target within inches of each other.

5. Shapes in the Sky

Meanwhile, O. K. Kim is summoned to Shanghai to meet with the Chinese. He has a bad premonition. He leaves his diaries with different friends in Japan, including Sadako. He confides that hers is the most crucial one, covering the mid-1880s. To her dismay, it contains no account of his failed coup, but instead is taken up with gassy reflections on Korean history, his storied lineage, and above all, the weather. She puzzles over sketches of what appear to be shapes in the sky. She will ask him later what they mean.

Unbeknownst to Kim, a Korean named Hong has been tailing him in Japan ever since he arrived. Hong follows O. K. Kim onto the ship, shoots him at sea. His body is brought to Korea, cut up, and displayed, to warn collaborators of their fate. Sadako knows that Hong or his henchmen will find her if she stays in Japan. She looks for signs from the heavens, shapes in the sky.

6. Queen Min

In 1894, then, agent Dayama Sadako—born Bae Boonam—returns to her native Seoul as a translator for King Kojong. If her interpretations are less than faithful, at times outrageously

brief, it's because she doesn't think the king deserves the whole truth. Anytime she catches a reference to Kojong's wife, Queen Min, she discreetly spits into a handkerchief. (It was the queen's powerful family who ordered the death of her father, back when she was a child.) Sadako has a red hairpin she'd like to introduce her to. She maps the palace, describes down to the smallest mole the girls who serve as the queen's decoys.

Once a week, Queen Min receives an American visitor: Lillias Underwood, wife of the missionary Horace Underwood. The meetings always begin with Lillias practicing her Korean and end with her teaching the queen some English, which has the unintended effect of improving the English of Sadako, who sits behind a screen.

Lillias is an accomplished woman, a doctor from Chicago. She now acts as the queen's private physician, though she has no official standing. Her predecessors—all of them Korean men—used to take Queen Min's pulse by tying a cord around her wrist, then gathering in a different room and holding the other end, searching for vibrations. They dared not touch her, or even breathe the same air. Queen Min is forceful and controlling; more than one foreigner dubs her the Lady Macbeth of Korea. But Lillias finds her face beautiful, her presence calming. She is not afraid to touch. Sadako coolly reports on their meetings.

In the early hours of October 8, 1895, Queen Min is murdered at the direction of Japan's minister to Korea—and aided by Sadako's preparations. Horace Underwood and another American missionary, Homer Hulbert, stand guard by King Kojong's chambers. They permit Sadako to weep her condolences, not knowing she is actually Korean. Privately she relishes the accounts of the gruesome crime, whispered by servants. In Japan, Ito makes noises about bringing these rogue *ronin* to justice, but in fact all is according to plan.

King Kojong is a wreck, practically mute. Sadako sneaks

news of his condition to her Tokyo taskmasters. She learns of a scotched plan to dress Kojong as a girl and move him from Seoul to Vladivostock, a precaution against future plots. All the while she keeps a poison pill in a locket, in case her true self comes to light.

7. No Heirs

The consumptive poet and KPG operative Yi Sang doesn't have children. Kim Sowol, the suicidal, azalea-strewing, anticipatory shaman of the KPG, is not a father. Nine-fingered Catholic assassin Thomas Ahn is without issue. The thirteenth-century Buddhist monk Ilyon, author of the *Samguk Yusa*, leaves no heirs. KPG president Syngman Rhee declares, *I have no children, but all young Koreans are my sons and daughters.*

In 1890, Rhee marries P., by parental decree. They have never met before. Astrologically, it's a propitious match: Year of the Pig, Year of the Rooster. He is fifteen, and P. is two years his senior. The union will stay unconsummated for four years. P. has a quick mind but is slow to speak. On her chin is a hateful black mark, dark as ink, a comet or comma. It soon becomes the *only* thing he can look at. It finds a way into his dreams, school-books, math problems. *Let P = darkness.*

8. Horace and Homer

In 1896, at age twenty-one, Syngman Rhee is jailed and tortured for his involvement with the Yes or No Club, the debate society started by Philip Jaisohn. At one point, he hovers close to death, and a sympathetic guard takes over. Instead of whipping him, the guard thrashes the floor, and Syngman screams. It's a fine performance. Sometimes fiction has the advantage over truth. Slowly he regains strength.

The American missionaries Horace Underwood and Homer Hulbert visit him frequently. They praise his oratory, encourage him to deliver sermons. They smuggle in a Bible, translated into

Korean with the English *en face*, and hymnals with the words done phonetically.

P. gives birth to a son, Bongsu, but she deems it bad luck to bring an infant into the jail. Syngman plots an escape to see his child. Cho, a fourteen-year-old trusty, supplies him with a revolver. But the gun backfires, and the jailbreak fails. To his horror, more years are piled onto his sentence. Syngman's mother dies during this extension.

Now Syngman wears a neck stockade half the day, a heavy plank anchored to the ground that yanks his vision downward. Even from this humbled state, he exhorts his cellmates, his new brothers-for-life. They look up to him, though he can barely lift his gaze from the floor.

When P. finally visits, holding three-year-old Bongsu, Syngman cries out with joy. The boy looks different at each subsequent meeting. Watching his son get older in this way is like trying to read a book that has entire chapters missing.

In 1904, as war erupts between Japan and Russia, Syngman is granted an early release. The conflict spells a death sentence for Korea. The two neighbors want her, each for its own purpose: Japan for a foothold on the continent, Russia for access to warm-water ports. Horace or Homer sermonizes: *Same bed, different dreams.*

Syngman Rhee is desperate to leave. Through the good offices of a missionary he's impressed, he finds passage to America. He takes Bongsu, now eight, on the long journey, while P. stays behind to look after Syngman's widowed father. Over the next several months, Syngman and Bongsu go from Hawaii to San Francisco, New Hampshire to Philadelphia, Long Island to D.C., where Syngman enrolls at George Washington University. He secures a scholarship with a tacit promise that he will join the ministry.

Bongsu wants to know the words for everything. Rhee hires a tutor, and in a year the boy speaks English as well as his

father. Not that it matters much. They will return to Korea once Syngman completes his studies. The family will be reunited, the country redeemed.

9. The Second Bae

After the death of Queen Min, the spy Sadako moves to a different part of the palace. She takes Bae Jeong-ja as an alias—reclaiming her Korean surname but altering the rest, in case anyone in the court recalls a girl named Bae Boonam. Bae marries and divorces twice more, each husband attaining a plum government post. Her brother becomes mayor of Seoul.

After stepping down as prime minister for the last time, Ito Hirobumi visits Korea regularly. In 1905, he is appointed the first resident-general of Korea. He stays at Sontag's Hotel.

Bae knows that it was Ito who renamed the country Chosen. Ito, her father and lover, master and slave. She never wants to see him again, but every day the part of her that is still Sadako wonders if he will make contact. She sends notes in code. Bursts of longing, verbal maps of her body: its hollows and dips, pale skin like a snowfield. The old fool doesn't catch on.

One morning, she receives instructions to meet at a dilapidated pavilion on the edge of the palace grounds. There she relates events at court, while Ito sits on a mountain of rags and strokes his beard. It looks grayer than when they were lovers, or father and daughter, or both. Is it possible he has forgotten her? He could be senile. Or playing a different game entirely.

10. The Reign of Stevens

In 1904, Ito installs an unpleasant American named Durham Stevens as special adviser to Kojong. Though informed that Bae is an agent of Japan, Stevens mistrusts her. He mixes her up with a certain Lady U., who doesn't know Japanese at all. Stevens thinks Bae is spying on *him*—for King Kojong.

In 1905, Durham Stevens catches the mayor of Seoul calling her *sister*.

In 1907, King Kojong, in a flash of courage, writes secret letters to be presented at The Hague: a plea to the sovereign nations of Europe. He paints the Japanese as scoundrels, invaders who took advantage of his gentle nature to wrest all power from his hands. Bae steals each missive before it leaves the country, though, and hands the stash to Stevens. Like a good dog, the American delivers them to Ito's suite at the Sontag. Thus Kojong is caught: the communiqués never leave Seoul. Bae hopes this will convince Stevens that she is on his side.

Kojong's palace is now a prison. He stops making his public excursions—those red-dirt affairs that give the people hope. Meanwhile, his allies hunt for the interloper, and Stevens slyly directs them to Bae. Believing that the royal guard is closing in, she swallows the poison pill, but it has lost potency. She sees double for a day. In this heightened state, she lures Ito to their hidden pavilion one last time. As their reunion reaches its crescendo, however, the odious *Suh-tee-bun-suh* pokes his head in.

Beg your pardon, he sneers, unaware that it's Ito she mounts.

11. Proper Touch

Boston, 1907. Syngman eats alone while his son is at school. He likes American food, but it still does not agree with the frail Bongsu, for whom chowders and casseroles are a torment. Even steamed-vegetable fare is hard to keep down. Some weeks he lives on nuts.

In the Public Garden, Syngman ponders his Harvard thesis. Pigeons walk soberly alongside him, as though musing on their own avian dissertations. Something brushes his shoulder. A pack of boys, not much older than Bongsu, are pitching pebbles, twigs. He walks faster. A handful of gravel hits his hat. The boys call him Chinaman, cry out like the laundry: *No tickee, no shirtee!*

Syngman turns and says *Korean*, pointing to his heart. *Korean!* He might as well be saying *chorine* or *Maureen*. What would they think if he told them he was studying *their* Constitution? More rocks, probably. At Harvard, across the river? A boulder.

The gang loses interest at last. On Boylston Street, an iron-haired woman and a neatly tailored man stand at a table around the corner from the Bryant & Stratton Commercial School. On display are several booklets bound in red cloth. Syngman tips his hat and picks up *Exercises in Typewriting*. His rooms at Harvard came with an Underwood heavy as an anvil, but he hasn't touched it. He writes his papers in longhand and hires a girl to bang it all down.

Perhaps he should do it himself. Typewriters helped Christianize Korea, after all. Horace Underwood, the Presbyterian missionary, arrived in the 1880s, funded by his brother John, who ran the family's typewriter concern. Horace lugged a writing machine along, to peck out strategies and reflections. When Syngman was in jail, Underwood's weekly letters buoyed his spirits.

On Boylston Street, Syngman Rhee fondly recalls those cheering missives. Underwood on an Underwood! The natty man gently pulls at the book.

"Ah, that isn't for sale."

"Then why do you offer it?"

"We are not selling books," the woman says. "We are offering a *course of study*." She enunciates, as though to a child. He at once senses her annoyance. "We are enrolling students for spring classes."

"I don't have time," Rhee says, putting the book back.

"Wait," the man says, as he starts to walk away. "Are you, ah, a Chinese?"

Rhee shakes his head.

"Japanese, then?" the woman guesses. Rhee flashes a withering look.

"Japanese!" He slaps the table with such force that the assorted booklets jump. "HA!"

The man's face turns red. "What—what else could it be?"

Syngman Rhee is in no mood to explain about Korea. His simmering ire at the rock-tossing boys explodes. He grabs *Exercises in Typewriting* and declares, "I am TAKING this book!"

"Please—yes—by all means," the man stammers.

That evening, when Bongsu is asleep, Syngman studies the book. It is twenty-nine pages, bound along the top. He removes the rigid cover from his Underwood and follows the directions: Sit erect; elbows close to body; feet flat on the floor. The object is CORRECT FINGERING and PROPER TOUCH.

Strike the SPACE BAR with the thumb of either hand.
USE A QUICK, SHARP, EVEN TOUCH.

The woman was right: the book is of limited use outside of a class. It consists of sixty lessons, of increasing complexity. These largely involve typing up words, sentences, clusters of letters. They must be completed accurately, or points are deducted by the instructor.

He closes the door. Elbows in. Feet on floor.

LESSON 1.
Required mark, 70.

```
asdfgf  asdfgf asdfgf asdfgf asdfgf
asdfgf  asdfgf asdfgf asdfgf asdfgf
asdfgf  asdfgf asdfgf asdfgf asdfgf
asdfgf  asdfgf asdfgf asdfgf asdfgf
```

He starts to type, spirits high. Then he goes over the lesson, looking for errors. He keeps at it for an hour, pecking out columns of nonwords. Bongsu awakes to check out the racket.

Syngman gives up his seat, instructs him in the proper posture. They type out their names.

```
bongsu &  syngman               rhee
```

Every morning, before cooking up oatmeal, Syngman does a couple lessons. He types simple words, longer words. He checks his work while he eats.

LESSON 11.
Required mark, 85.

Write the following:

```
one     any    man    men    our    are    him
day     tell
```

LESSON 15.
Required mark, 85.

Write the following:

```
whom    want    away    with    your    what    were
none    when
```

The typewriter is anonymous. Looking at the page, no one could tell that the output was the work of a Korean. For fun, he writes a letter to Horace Underwood on the Underwood, signing off:

```
Guess who?
```

12. Nature Manner Matter

Over the Christmas recess, Syngman Rhee leaves Bongsu with friends in Philadelphia and heads to California. He has no love for Harvard and is impatient to finish his studies—Princeton

awaits. All he requires is that Professor V——— sign off on his thesis, which he submitted months ago.

In San Francisco, he rents a typewriter.

LESSON 19.
Required mark, 90.

```
above  about  until  truth  which  equal quite
could  cared
```

He meets with two groups of expatriate Koreans; their mutual dislike threatens to thwart the common cause of freeing the motherland. Most of these men have arrived not directly from Korea but after a sojourn in Hawaii, where they worked on farms for pennies a day. Yet even men of such similar back-grounds find a way to squabble. Rhee ponders whether this is indeed a *Korean* trait, but then thinks of the rifts among Amer-ica's Founding Fathers.

Founding Father. Syngman Rhee likes the ring of it. He pic-tures his face on currency.

LESSON 23.
Required mark, 95.

Write, as instructed in Lesson 21, the following sentence:

```
beyond entire nature manner matter myself
either though valued
```

13. The Wings

The bad blood among the San Francisco Koreans in 1907 fore-tells the rifts that will appear in the Korean Provisional Govern-ment, shortly after its founding in 1919. Some push for armed resistance, others for diplomacy. KPG members will excommu-

nicate one another, form tenuous alliances, even resort to murder. By 1930, two definite wings will have formed. Each operates in secret and tries to subvert the other, even though both have the same goal: a free Korea.

14. Too Late

Meanwhile in Philadelphia, separated from his father by thousands of miles, twelve-year-old Bongsu is at war with his stomach. Nothing stays down. Vomit surges through him like a poisoned river. At this time, Philip Jaisohn—former teacher of Syngman, future surgeon general of the KPG—is a physician in the City of Brotherly Love, but he has lately given up his failing medical practice to run a failing printing business. When Dr. Jaisohn is finally located, Bongsu is in a terrible state. Thin as sticks, he has no words. He smells of rust and fear.

A telegram summons Syngman from San Francisco. On the train, he bargains with God. If only his son can live, he will take Bongsu back to Korea and gladly call it Chosen. Return to his wife with the blot on her face. Surrender his mission completely, take on a Japanese name. Yes, all of Korea can be signed away, right now—if only Bongsu can live.

These negotiations fail. At the start of 1908, Syngman Rhee loses his only child. Bongsu's death marks the end of his family line.

LESSON 26.
Required mark, 95.

An Exclamation Point is made by striking period, back spacer, then apostrophe.

```
              ring awful words ears late
In his ears will ring the awful words,
Too late! Too late!! Too late!!!
```

15. Village Rumblings

Around this time, Korean spies learn of Bae Jeong-ja's double life at court. She is confronted with her real name. Some call for her head. Ito Hirobumi acts stunned by her duplicity. He protects her just long enough that she gets exile instead of the hatchet. At his suite in the Sontag, Ito assures her they will be together before long.

Far from Seoul, nobody knows who she is: translator or spy, Bae or Sadako, *kisaeng* or thrice-married nun. Anonymous, she observes that protests against the foreign presence are louder in the villages than the capital. One fiery manifesto, signed in blood, declares that the *ten million able-bodied men of Korea* will rise up at the appointed hour, beggars and tradesmen alike revealing their true avenging selves. Arrows will be notched, sharp knives drawn. *We will destroy the railway, we will kindle flames in every port, kill Ito and all the Japanese, we will not leave a single rebel against our Emperor alive.*

A yearning stirs inside her. *Yes! At last!* Then her late father's voice asks, *What has Korea ever done for you? Murdered me, drove your mother blind, pimped you out.* The ember fades. She stays in Tokyo's employ. Calls herself Sadako again.

16. Cut Fingers

In January 1908, the spy Sadako stalks an agitator and former schoolteacher named Thomas Ahn, following him all the way to Vladivostock. Her cover is chef at an *udon* shop. She infiltrates his group, the Cut Finger Club, presenting herself as a *zainichi*—a Japanese-born Korean, orphaned as a girl. She devises an elaborate accent to throw them off her scent. None suspects a connection to Ito, target of their fury.

At thirty-eight, she is one of the oldest of the Cut Fingers, though she gives her age as twenty-five and, indeed, could pass for younger. On the night they earn their moniker and consecrate their bond, she makes a speech to match Thomas

Ahn's, with lines gleaned from the manifestos she read in the Korean hinterland. *It is better to lose our lives now than to live miserably a little longer, for the king and our brethren will all surely be killed by the abominable plans of Ito.*

The cleaver echoes. She stifles a scream, stamps her foot instead. Blood pours out as if from a tipped inkwell. After, Sadako sports a dark blue glove with the ring finger sewn closed.

A year later, Sadako trails Thomas Ahn to Harbin. He signs into the Grand Hotel as Taro Tsujimoto. She procures a room on the same floor. She follows him to the restaurant, smiles when she senses his indigestion. (She, too, can hardly stomach the food.) She relays her position to Ito, via the Lover's Cipher. (Her index finger is the same circumference as Ito's little finger.) One restless night, she ducks into the cinema down the road. She has never seen a movie before. A Chinese lutist and Russian flutist lend color to the silvered scenes. Despite the novelty, she melts into slumber in the dark.

Laughter wakes her, and for a moment it's as if she's entered a dream inside a dream. There, two rows ahead, sits Thomas Ahn, doubled up at the sight of the cartoon dancing onscreen. He slaps his thighs, then winces. His bad hand's in bandages, infected again.

Sadako removes her hat and whisks the long pin out of her hair. She can stop him right now: a quick thrust through the ear into his brain. He would be dead in minutes. But Sadako, a.k.a. Bae, is half in love with Thomas Ahn, this man of fire nine years her junior. She keeps the pin in place, lets history unfold without her.

17. The Torn Card

October 23, 1909, Grand Hotel, Harbin. Sadako receives the message she has been waiting for. Ito has solved the Lover's Cipher by wrapping it around his finger, and has sent back . . .

the king of hearts, torn in half. She inspects it carefully. For some reason, the word *Geronimo* has been scrawled in English near the monarch's blade. On the back, masked by the dense blue design, is a shard of English that sounds Japanese: KALEIDO. On the face, near the sword, Ito has written in tiny *hangul* letters the details of his upcoming stay in Harbin.

Arriving from Mukden in three days. Nine a.m.

He wants her to watch and wait. Sadako encloses the card in a new envelope, with two large bills and instructions to the clerk. The contents must be delivered immediately to the room of *Mr. Taro Tsujimoto of Nagasaki.* Thomas Ahn's nom de guerre. She slides it down the mail chute.

18. The Beggar

On October 26, 1909, Dayama Sadako gets to the station at dawn. She hacked off her hair the night before; the chill wind freezes her nape. Wearing a sailor's cap and blue gloves and a tattered Russian greatcoat, she kneels on a wheeled platform under a dirty blanket. It gives the impression that at least one leg is gone, blown off in the war. Shaking a can, Sadako sets her voice low and becomes a man. When a Japanese approaches, Sadako begs in Russian; when a Russian does, she trots out her Chinese; when a Chinese does, she plays mute.

At quarter to nine, she glimpses Thomas Ahn in the waiting room. One hand clutches a lunch box from the Grand Hotel; the other crosses himself. Lips form a silent prayer.

Sadako drags herself around the platform in a slow figure eight. At one point her circuit intersects with Thomas's path, by the newspaper kiosk. She begs for alms. He opens the pail and gives her his meal, neat shapes in waxed paper. She nearly cries as he intones a Bible verse, something out of Proverbs. Peeking out of his breast pocket is the card she sent him. The

king of hearts, torn in half. It's like the setup for a magic trick. Is she the magician or the audience?

Gamsahamnida, she says, thanking him between bites.

The Korean word startles them both. She wheels off without a word.

19. The Fool

A cheering crowd greets Ito's train. For a second its plume of smoke wraps around the scene like an ermine stole before vanishing forever. The Russians waiting in the station house exit and walk briskly across the platform into the main car. The train's shades are drawn. Outside, Thomas paces, left hand warm under the handkerchief.

At last, the Russian delegation exits the train, followed by the Japanese. She sees Ito with his long cane, which hides a long, thin blade. Thomas draws the gun from the lunch pail, shouting as he fires.

Ito looks offended. *Pabo*, he says. Sadako sees him sitting on the ground with his legs splayed like a baby's, as a wave of men fall upon the assassin. *Fool.* Her gloves come off.

There is a fatal flaw to Thomas Ahn's plan: If Ito dies, Korea will die, too. Japan will retaliate ten thousand–fold.

As Sadako runs, she pulls a pistol from her boot. To follow through on her oath to the Cut Finger Club—to Korea—is also to fulfill a vow to destroy Korea.

Pabo, she snarls. With gun held low, she shoots through the fracas, then pitches her pistol onto the tracks.

20. Syngman in Seoul

Seoul, 1910. Funded by the missionaries, Syngman Rhee returns to occupied Korea to see his wife, P. He is shocked to find a boarder in the house, though she has mentioned this fact in her letters. All of Rhee's friends insisted that P. has been faithful, mourning their son from afar, patiently looking after Syngman's

aged father. She had to take in renters because Syngman never sent a cent from all his scholarships and stipends.

But he cannot control himself. He yells at the boarder to appear, throws a bottle at him when he does. The man—the student—takes off into the night. Syngman shouts at P., denouncing their marriage as an evil dream. He curses the blot on her face, the men in her bed.

The guests stare at the table. P. whispers their son's name and leaves the room. Everyone now thinks: *While she was caring for his father, he abandoned Bongsu and let him die.*

21. N. H. Osia

In 1921, two years after the founding of the Korean Provisional Government, an unknown writer with the exotic name N. H. Osia pens a novella in English that resurrects Syngman Rhee's late son, imagining him as a fearless, globe-trotting freedom fighter. Osia's grammar is scrupulous, his vocabulary multisyllabic. But the result is doggedly awkward.

> *Bongsu was nearly a head taller than most of his friends and had the high forehead and clean-cut oval face that denoted intellectuality.*

> *His blue black hair was closely cropped and his habiliment was a mixture of European and Oriental fashions.*

The young hero is bound for Seoul, there to commence a traditional scholar's life. Before he can board the train, however, a scuffle with a Japanese stationmaster lands him in jail. His patriotic bona fides have been announced. Later, Bongsu escapes to Moscow in time for the Great War, enlisting as a machine gunner with the Russian army.

He serves with a division of Korean Siberian recruits in Poland, which gets shot to pieces and sent back home. After bureaucratic delays, Bongsu returns to Seoul. On March 1, 1919,

he joins the crowd at Pagoda Park to hear a man read aloud
the declaration of independence. He thrills to this mass protest.
But the Japanese come down hard on the throng, and Bongsu
flees for his life. Later he meets Marcella Jurng, an educated
young Korean tortured so badly after the protest that she is
missing a hand. He sails to Shanghai and hobnobs with the
newly formed KPG. Throughout the book, he's on a hair trigger.
For N. H. Osia, this is precisely Bongsu's appeal. He lashes out
at the slightest insult.

Heading to America at last, Bongsu meets one Mr.
Hugheston, president of "Northern University," who is curious
about his homeland. Bongsu gives an impassioned summary of
Korea's woes, leading Hugheston to conclude, *I feel America
owes Korea a moral as well as legal obligation to see that she is freed
from the militaristic yoke of Japan.* Then he offers Bongsu an education at Northern U.

N. H. Osia can't resist adding another happy ending. It turns
out that Miss Jurng, the one-handed patriot, is also on board.
Bongsu proposes marriage, then issues a statement fit for a
notary public: *It is the custom in America to sign and seal all contracts, therefore let us seal ours.* They kiss.

22. Hansu's Journey

N. H. Osia changes the title of his debut from *Bongsu's Journey*
to *Hansu's Journey*, for fear of upsetting Rhee. The tale is serialized in the newsletter *Korea Review*, then brought out in 1922 as
a small book by Philip Jaisohn's press, there on Chestnut Street
in Philadelphia.

"N. H. Osia" is none other than Philip Jaisohn himself, who,
among other things, is the editor of the *Korea Review*. For this
book, his only work of fiction, Jaisohn reverses and amputates
his anglicized name, like a sacrifice to the spirit of his friend's

lost son. Bongsu is the casualty of exile that Syngman never speaks of.

Strident and mawkish, *Hansu's Journey* nevertheless has a dreamlike intensity. Rather: it *is* a dream, one in which Korea's plight is recognized by the rest of the world, her misery validated. A dream in which vengeance is wreaked. A dream in which a dead child is born again, made invincible, and delivered at last into a sort of heaven called America.

Hansu's Journey is one of the secret bibles of the Korean Provisional Government.

23. The Fräulein

In 1933, eleven years after *Hansu's Journey* comes out, and twenty-five years after the death of his son, a dejected Syngman Rhee is staying at the Hôtel de Russie, Geneva. He has devoted his life to Korea, yet has little to show for it. This European trip, backed by the KPG, is as much a crucial mission as it is respite from the hot monotony of Hawaii, his base of operations.

In the hotel library, Syngman leafs through an old issue of *Time*. There's a review for a movie with the incredible title *King Kojong*, a fantastical tale about a giant ape run amok. (Alas, he blinks and the extra letters disappear.) In his gloomy state, the news of the day washes over him, until a small item on the page stops him: Woodrow Wilson's daughter Jessie has died, only forty-five, after a surgery. In a flash, he sees her as she was, hair like gold. In truth she was all that he looked forward to, those nights around the piano in Princeton. Her tresses grow wavy as his tears soak the magazine. If she could see him now, in Europe, sole ambassador of his race! In his head he drafts a note of condolence to Woodrow Wilson, only to remember that he died years ago. Rhee is near sixty himself. Half the people he's ever met are in the ground.

In the dining room that night, the maître d'hôtel seats a sad-sack Syngman at a table with a woman twenty-five years younger, Franziska Donner of Vienna (and, alas, her mother). Serious eyes in a soft, round face. Franziska's father runs an ironworks. She is in Switzerland as an interpreter for Austria's delegation to the League of Nations. Fräulein Donner has followed Rhee's progress, or lack thereof. Brief items in the paper—Rhee always works the press angle. The talk is lively. They see each other the rest of the week, for long morning walks and afternoon coffee. Then Syngman heads to Moscow, for another doomed stand in the name of the KPG.

The couple contrives a Roman rendezvous for August. (*Unchaperoned,* he insists, in a letter that she burns.) Franziska tells her sister that she's attending a conference. At the hotel, she signs her name Francesca RHEE. Makes sure he sees her do it.

Syngman is aware of the spectacle they present, this old Oriental with a sprig of edelweiss. His face flushes over lunch when he overhears a waiter saying *the yellow man and the girl.* They use English. She wants to know Korean words, but if he breathes a syllable, everything will crumble, his life will revert to a dream, he will wake up in his old jail cell in Seoul. *Not now,* he says, *not yet.* Francesca confesses that she was married before, to a race-car driver—a friend of her father's. It didn't last a year, and there was no passion. *Of course,* Syngman says, *of course.* (Still: a *race-car driver?*)

Syngman tells Francesca about his arranged marriage at age fifteen. A favor to his parents. It was seen as a boon for two depleted clans that were, as his father put it, like tapestries worn down to their last bits of thread. All of this was a lifetime ago. He remembers the nineteenth century.

Francesca asks what his first wife's name was.

P . . . b . . . p . . . His throat catches, refuses to release it into the thick Roman air.

24. Earway Inoué

After lunch, Syngman and Francesca roam in the heat. The sun is heavy as paste. They cling to the sides of buildings, seek whatever shadows can be found. At an open market, he catches the conversation of a group of Americans. One of them bursts into giddy song, but what reaches him is insanity. *Earway inoué, athey, UH-nee-may.*

Francesca, the translator, identifies the strange language. She explains the construction of Pig Latin.

"*We're in the money,*" she says. "It's from a movie."

"Oh?"

"*Gold Diggers of 1933.*"

"Ah."

"Ginger Rogers." He thinks she means the root. "When's the last time you saw a movie?"

"In 1919."

"Did you like it?"

"I did not."

Francesca is different in Italy than in Switzerland. Her hair is wilder, her accent lovelier, and for a minute he imagines she's a different person entirely. What if Francesca is an agent of the Japanese, sent to lure him from his goal of a free Korea, discredit the KPG? In Rome he is losing his mind.

25. Who Were the Koreans?

In Europe he is twice a foreigner. How many Koreans have ever set foot in the Eternal City—fifty, twenty, *ten*? The Japanese have been all over the Continent. He thinks of how Ito, long dead now, cleverly stocked his mind in Berlin and Vienna, London and Brussels, carefully studying the ways of the West to make Japan the equal of any nation. Meanwhile Syngman Rhee walks in circles with someone young enough to be his child, her dress the color of the sky.

Siggy! Francesca cries, as they approach another field of

ancient clutter. A carved column draws them closer. The surface swarms with hundreds of figures. At the base a broad-
backed river god watches bemused as the Roman troops
march against the Dacians. Syngman prides himself on his
knowledge of European history, but he's never heard of Dacia.
The column might as well have fallen from the sky, a message
from a different planet.

Francesca flips through her Baedeker. Ah yes: Dacia was
the domain of what's now Romania. *Two thousand years ago,*
she reads aloud, *border skirmishes compel Emperor Trajan to
invade and subdue the Dacians once and for all.*

The story scrolls upward. The more he looks, the more he
sees, the less he understands. Amid scenes of bloodshed and
building are weird interludes: Romans crossing the Danube on
a bridge made of boats or hoisting their shields overhead like
a turtle shell. Who were the Dacians? The cylinder seems to
spin, the world's longest comic strip drilling into the sky.
Syngman steadies himself on Francesca's shoulder, as drops of
rain wet his hand. As far as he can see, there are Dacian
soldiers falling to Roman spears or killing themselves in
despair.

Someday people will wonder: *Who were the Koreans?* After
the Romans conquered the Dacians, did the exiles establish a
Dacian Provisional Government?

The spattering raindrops are Syngman's own tears. Francesca takes his hand as he shudders. The KPG will do as much
good as the DPG. Her thumb goes over the scars on his knuck-
les. He holds her in the hot middle of the day, tastes the sweet
wine on her young mouth. The guidebook falls as she leans
against the shaft. A hundred bells go off in the distance to
mark the hour or just to ring. She takes his wrist and lifts her
hem and rubs with his palm until the worn fingers come to
life.

26. Missing Pages

Their time in Rome runs out. Francesca returns to Vienna to tell her family that she will marry again, and Syngman heads back to America at last, having been absent the better part of a year. The funds of the KPG are at his disposal, but they are not unlimited. And what would the treasurers say if they knew what he'd been up to? Henry Kim, the aide who has covered up Syngman's past indiscretions, would go mad.

Syngman knows what the KPG will say. They will quote his words back to him: the times he had inveighed against race mixing, the dilution of blood. To scold him, Henry Kim will track down the chapter in *The Spirit of Independence*, written in prison, entitled "The Five Races." Time was, few things more reliably sent Syngman into a fury than Ito Hirobumi's goal of *amalgamation:* for Koreans and Japanese to interbreed, so that in two generations there would be no distinction on the peninsula. Future Koreans would not revolt, because they would *be* Japanese.

Who today could trace their lineage to Dacia?

His mentor Philip Jaisohn would understand. He's been married for decades to Muriel, née Armstrong, a Caucasian. Then again Jaisohn (né Suh Jae-p'il) wants to *be* white, and Syngman does not. The last time Syngman saw his old friend, it was obvious that certain procedures had been undertaken, so many that his eyebrows had fallen off. The skin looked streaked with rust, and the nose had been built up clumsily to ape a Westerner's. As grotesque as a ventriloquist's dummy. What on earth does his wife think?

Rhee slices the Roman episode out of his diary, drops the pages into the cold Atlantic.

27. Here Comes the Bride

In 1934, Francesca Donner applies for a visa to be with Syngman, but her stated reason for immigrating—*to marry an*

Oriental—marks her case as the lowest priority. *To join the circus* would have met with more success. For months, Syngman pulls every string. With KPG money, he hires a D.C. gossip columnist to make some high-minded noise in the papers. The way Syng-man sees it, anytime his name appears in print, it's an advertisement for the Korean cause.

At last, his fiancée boards the *Europa* for the transatlantic trip. The two are married in New York at the Hotel Montclair by his old friend Reverend P. K. Yoon. The Koreans in attendance say her name like this: *Puh-ran-che-suh-ka Dah-nuh-ruh.*

HOTEL MONTCLAIR · LEXINGTON AVENUE · 49th to 50th Streets · NEW YORK

28. #13

In 1934, Yi Sang the Strange—tubercular poet of occupied Chosen—runs his Seoul teahouse with its miniature furniture while his lover, Gum, the former *kisaeng*, is home. Entertaining. On their bed. His lungs feel like they've shrunk along with all the tables and chairs. He is obsessed with the number 13. He holds his breath to a count of 13.

On a rainy afternoon, with the windows blurred and the teahouse empty, Yi Sang the Strange writes a poem in which children run screaming down a road, one after another. He doesn't say what they're running from, leaves the horror

unnamed. A maniac with a knife, a microbe, the blood-dimmed tide of history itself.

> ~~The #13 child~~
> ~~The #13 child says~~
> ~~The #13 child says he is~~
> ~~The #13 child says he is scared~~
> *The#13childsaysheisscared*

He tries other, lower numbers—four kids running, then eight—but only at thirteen does the poem pulse with terror. A former architect, he knows that it's numbers which underlie reality. Each one has a character, holds dimensions beyond language.

While working as a draftsman for the governor-general, Yi Sang designed the cover for *Chosen and Architecture*, published by the Japanese. Yi Sang begged the magazine to run his poems. They published the whole bizarre batch under the title "Bird's-Eye View." The few who paid attention took it for an extended architectural in-joke, full of spooky spaces and weird math. One poem repeated the equation 3 + 1. Another posed a stumper: *Why did the straight line murder the circle?* (A reader writes in: To get to the other side.) Another was a grid of numbers, running 1234567890. He put himself into a trance, whispering the digits.

Later, ailing from TB, he leaves architecture behind. He becomes poet, invalid, cuckold, genius. He writes his new poems in Korean, including the same grid, *reversed*. "Diagnosis" is a poem you can't recite.

He calls this new, even weirder series "Crow's-Eye View." Yi Sang submits the poems to a daily paper in Seoul. Everyone hates them but his friends. No one understands them but Gum.

One day, he keeps the teahouse closed and hides in the

trees by his house. Periodically he looks to see if a man has entered, judging by whether a pair of shoes is by the door. Over the course of the day, he counts five, eight, thirteen different pairs. Same bed, different dreams.

29. Wanderings

In the end, the arrangement proves too much even for the unconventional Yi Sang. He breaks up with Gum and marries a friend's sister, Pyun.

One day, walking with Pyun, Yi Sang bumps into a woman who looks exactly like Gum; she turns out to be her sister. She tells him that Gum is not well, wants to see him one more time. Pyun objects, but the poet goes anyway. How can he not?

Gum's eyes are gray, and her skin looks like leather. They drink and sing songs from the north and songs from the south. Then she sings one he's never heard, a song she learned from an older *kisaeng* named Bae. The words apply to their situation. The singer and her lover are both unfaithful (runs the song), but it was all a dream anyway. Life is but a wandering dream or a dream of wandering. The last line, before she passes out, is: *Set fire to your shadowy heart.*

Pyun is furious when he comes home stinking of wine, but she was furious before then, too. He kept putting her in his stories, blending in elements of Gum. Made her out to be like that whore. She's had it. Yi Sang knows he's gone too far. He starts telling his friends he's moving to Japan, says it so much that eventually he follows through. Gets ready to set his heart ablaze.

30. Guns, Money, Goods

Yanji, Manchuria, 1935. A sixteen-year-old orphan named Kim Jongsook joins a Korean guerrilla unit of the Northeast Anti-Japanese United Army. Instead of taking up arms against the Japanese, Jongsook cooks and cleans. She scours the moun-

tains for ingredients. She sharpens bayonets, packs grenades, keeps the unit honed.

Their great leader, Kim Il Sung, is seven years older than her. He has scars on his chest, burns along his arms. His jolly face goes pink with rage or joy. There's a pea-sized growth poking out of his neck. It pulses when he gets excited, as he delivers his daily communist catechism. Jongsook listens closely. She's the only one who really pays attention.

The bounty on Kim Il Sung's head swells by the month, and so does the growth. The Japanese spread rumors of his death, rumors of a double. Harried across the Manchurian waste, Kim's group is in constant need of supplies. After taking over a village, he demands, *Guns if you have guns, money if you have money, goods if you have goods.*

He adds to his forces by taking hostages. Sometimes he just lets them go, to spread the news of his might and magnanimity. Sometimes he cuts off an ear. (You only need one.) In the future, Kim announces to every captive, he will lead a free Korea. Too many times, he weeds his own ranks, hunting for traitors—indeed, when Kim Jongsook first came to him, he was certain *she* was a spy. She won him over with soups and sewing. Inside his tent it was discovered that they fit together perfectly.

Kim and Kim marry in 1939, before a gathering of Korean guerrillas, Chinese mercenaries, and Soviet advisers. In 1941, twenty-nine-year-old Kim Il Sung and company cross over into the Soviet Union and lie low. Japanese scouts are in hot pursuit, but he shakes them off. Jongsook gives birth to their first child in 1942. They give him a Russian name, Yura. Brother Shura is born a few years later. The Soviets love Jongsook's hearty cooking. They call her Vera.

31. Japan Inside Out

Throughout his life, Syngman Rhee sends letters of supplication, letters of protest, letters of passive-aggressive explica-

tion. Letters to Woodrow Wilson and Philip Jaisohn. He writes a letter to the emperor of Japan, giving him one last chance to do the just and moral thing and tell his ministers to allow Korea to stay independent. (It doesn't take.) Letters to President Theodore Roosevelt in the aughts, President Franklin D. Roosevelt in the forties. Letters to keep other members of the KPG in line.

In early 1941, Syngman and Francesca and his trusty Underwood move to Hobart Street in Washington, D.C. Like Yi Sang moving to Tokyo, he is getting closer to the source of power. Syngman recalls an episode from his student days at George Washington, when he met the British author H. G. Wells. What a writer—what a man! If only "real" statesmen knew as much history as Wells, that brilliant mind who could concoct a war of the worlds *and* immediately grasp the Korean conundrum. Despite having written *The Spirit of Independence,* and thousands of letters, and his Princeton dissertation on neutrality, Syngman Rhee is no writer.

How would the great Englishman warn humanity? Rhee at last finishes *Japan Inside Out,* a project that has consumed him for a year.

```
    years ago ix you heard faint whispers of impending
    trouble, it was so far away, it seemed as if it might
    be on Mars or some other planet. Later xkx you saw
    columns of smoke rising at a distance, at times
    even heard the crack of burning trees, yet it was
    still far enough away to cause you no worry
```

Who is the "you" that he writes about, that he scolds?

```
    bxx now that is all changed, you already begin to
    feel the heat, it is coming too close for your
```

comfort, you must move from your own home, you
must give up international settlements in the
Orient, you must lose your business investments

Who is the "you"?

Can you still say, "Let the Koreans, the
Manchurians, and the Chinese fight their own fight;
it is none of our business"?

Who is the "you"?

I cannot persuade myself to see how you can escape
clashing with a bully while making it stronger all
the time. Is it not clear that when he becomes
powerful enough to tackle you, he will surely attack
you as he has already attacked and robbed every
one of his weaker neighbors?

The "you" is the U.S.A.

32. The Alliance

The United States enters World War II that December, after the
Japanese attack Pearl Harbor. This is good news for the KPG.
Surely having a common enemy means there is hope for Korea
at last. Syngman Rhee urgently wires the Korean Provisional
Government, to hammer out a resolution. He writes to the State
Department: *The KPG will join the fight against Japan. America, we
are with you!*

The U.S. ignores Syngman Rhee and the KPG. In desperation, Rhee badgers a senator to make inquiries. The senator
tells him State doesn't want to offend the Japanese by recognizing the KPG.

In that case, the war is lost, Rhee says.

33. The Infiltrator

At the time of Pearl Harbor, Sadako is over seventy years old.

After the 1909 execution of Thomas Ahn for the murder of Ito Hirobumi, Sadako remains in Harbin, rooting out Korean terrorists, including members of the Cut Finger Club. (They are easy to verify.) She serves as a military spy in Siberia and Manchuria, dissuading the mounted bandits in the region from attacking Japanese soldiers. She infiltrates Korean independence groups in Shanghai and Seoul, including the KPG. And in a twisted reprise of her own history as a young *kisaeng*, she tricks Korean girls into becoming "comfort women"—sex slaves for the Japanese forces in the South Pacific. Her life becomes rumor.

As if a single person, through sheer force, could destroy Korea once and for all.

34. The Return of Kim Il Sung

Japan surrenders to the Allies in 1945. What will become of its colonies? That Communist spitfire, Kim Il Sung, arrives in Korea. It's his first time back since leaving as a child. Wife Vera and sons Yura and Shura have never seen it before, wondered if Korea was a myth.

Kim Il Sung is thirty-three. He installs the family in a house that once belonged to a colonial officer. At last, a new future can be written. Soon enough, Kim establishes himself as the leader of half the peninsula, which he will rule for nearly fifty years. As for Vera (née Kim Jongsook), her future is much shorter; she dies giving birth in 1949. (The baby, a girl, is stillborn.) Her husband's grief is an unexamined factor in the origins of the Korean War.

35. Revisions

Sadako is seventy-five when World War II ends. She prostrates herself before the authorities in Seoul—then reveals, with a tug

of a glove, that she actually was *part* of the Cut Finger Club. That she grew up Bae Boonam, daughter of an officer of the old Korean court. That *she* was the one who lured Prince Ito to Harbin in the first place, back in 1909, to put him in the path of Thomas Ahn's gun. Is this just the doddering account of a crone? (Her confusing saga involves a cipher, a playing card, any number of pistols.) She insists the story is true.

There's more, she claims. Beginning in 1919, she secretly worked for the Korean Provisional Government. She was so deep undercover that only one officer knew of her position: Yi Sang the Strange. The poet-spy's *real* reason for abruptly moving from Seoul to Tokyo in 1936, she insists, was to begin an important new mission with her. They belonged to opposing factions of the KPG, but this project would unite them, help heal the schism.

Unfortunately, the secret police arrested Yi Sang just hours after their first rendezvous, on the charge of *thought crimes*. She never sees him alive again. The mission is abandoned before it's even begun—indeed, before she even knows what it is.

Her brain would overheat as she scoured his cryptic poems. *Did the straight line kill the circle? 0987654321. 3 + 1 = 4.*

They reminded her of the scribblings of an earlier doomed Korean, another transplant on Japanese soil: O. K. Kim, who she met in her youth. O.K. had given her one of his diaries, full of inscrutable calculations and odd prophecies, for safekeeping. He cataloged unusual aerial phenomena, looking at royal annals, Taoist texts, and the thirteenth-century *Samguk Yusa* for examples: from cloud-riding monks, to comets heralding war, to the deity who descended from the heavens four thousand years ago and sired Dangun, founder of Korea. She used to think it was madness but now she's come around.

36. Above Hwajiri

Perhaps both men had seen something, up in the skies, and their jottings attempted to foretell when a savior might swoop down to rescue Korea. Or did they hope to *summon* such a being?

Inspired by Yi Sang and O. K. Kim, Sadako claims, she launched a secret project for the KPG, to hunt for shapes in the sky. In the '20s, she recruited young women in the countryside to report any unusual sights as they tended to household tasks. Her best recruit, in the hamlet of Hwajiri, was a girl who went by only her family name, Doe. Doe kept watch on the sky and collected sightings from nearby towns as well. A shooting star viewed above Hwajiri appeared as a glowing disk one town over, while a hunter camped out at the edge of the woods witnessed a green radiance but nothing else.

Doe married and had a son in Hwajiri. Doe's work got reported to the Japanese as suspicious. Upon learning that her protégée was in danger, Sadako helped her flee Korea. On the boat, Doe flipped a coin. If it landed dragon side up, she'd see her family again. If not, then . . . Sadako batted it out of the air. An agent of the KPG could not afford to be homesick.

"Maybe you'll live to see your grandson," Sadako said, doling out a measure of hope.

"Me, a *halmoni*?" Doe laughed bitterly, imagined her young arms veined and speckled.

Syngman Rhee, now president of South Korea, pardons Sadako, née Bae Boonam, saint or saboteur. She dies in 1952, while the Korean War grinds on. Like Yi Sang and Thomas Ahn, like any legend worth their salt, her final resting place is unknown.

37. The One

In 1960, at age eighty-five, Syngman Rhee steps down, forced out by his own people. He returns to Hawaii for his final exile. One of his few friends is a banker named Borthwick who used

to run a funeral home in Hawaii. They talk about the old days until Rhee's health declines. He dies in 1965 at the age of ninety.

Doe learns about it in New York, where she escaped after her cover was blown in Tokyo. In America, she takes on aliases. It is easier to hide here, to do the hard secret work of the KPG. Part of this involves an import/export company called Halmoni, a front. Other merchants have trouble pronouncing the name, and she eventually changes it to Harmony. She is fifty years old, too young to be a *halmoni* yet, she thinks. She wonders what became of her son, back in Korea.

Rhee's widow, Francesca, outlives him by twenty-seven years. When she passes away, a bolt of silk is draped over the coffin. It bears four words in her husband's strong hand: *Nam Buk Tong Il*. A dying dream, the only dream. *South and North as One.*

It is, of course, the motto of the Korean Provisional Government, of which this has been Dream Three.

2333: The Exposition (1993)

THE SWISS MAN ISN'T SWISS, AND you're not even sure he's a man. The handwriting resembles your mother's cursive-print hybrid. Flora used to put notes in your lunch bag, back before she left for good. Bible verses, but you didn't mind. Your dad ink-stamped the logo of his store on the bag: Jot Electronix. Parker Jotter was a big believer in free advertising.

The Swiss Man faxes every weekday, each time from a different number in Geneva, to one of four machines in the tristate area. He's set you up as a freelance photographer at foreign-language newspapers serving the Polish, Honduran, Irish, and Indonesian diasporas. You head into the respective offices Monday through Thursday. Your shots aren't Pulitzer material, but you know to account for the light.

The faxes are in English and addressed to you, more or less: Dear Mrs. Tina Jotter, To Ms. T. J. Pang, ATTN Mr. (!) T. Jotter-Pangoo, Hello T. J. Phang, and your favorite, Dear Tiny Pang. The transmissions appear to be chatty press releases touting eateries and cultural events, with handwritten personal postscripts. Everything is fiction, though. The addresses don't *quite* exist; the phone numbers are bogus.

The postscripts encode a message only you can unscramble, a process that involves your Friday morning freelance gig at the North Korean consulate on Park Avenue. The staff is youthful, friendly, fashion conscious. (You did a double take in the ladies' room when Comrade Cha pulled her cardigan over a Soundgarden T-shirt.) Your job there,

arranged by the Swiss Man, is to proofread Pyongyangian propaganda, equal parts anti-Western tirades and patriotic slogans: *Let's harden our revolutionary spirit like a rock!* You could do most of this from your West Ninety-fifth Street digs, but you need access to the consulate's fax. The Swiss Man transmits a fresh cipher every week, which you apply to the first five sentences of each of the newspaper-office faxes, which gives you a new sentence. *Did the straight line kill the circle? The #2 Child Is Scared.* It reads like ghostly poetry. For the last step, you work the decoded sentence into a bogus complaint that you fax to a frozen-food company in Chicago. Someone else takes the baton from there.

ON SATURDAY, YOU and Mercy catch a matinee before drop-off at her father's place. Sunday you clean the apartment, discover more mementos of the dreaded ex, Winston Pang: T-shirt for a charity 5K, box of floppy disks, old Kinks tape called *Give the People What They Want.* Years later, his crap still pops up in closets and drawers. The only escape would be to move out of your building, the Sans-Souci, with its anemic elevator and peeling hallway wallpaper and fire escapes painted hooker red.

You fill a plastic D'Agostino bag with Winstonia and drop it down the chute, wait to hear that satisfying *smack.* A neighbor's old papers sit in a stack on the floor of the garbage area. A headline in the lurid *New York Whip* jumps out: J. CHRIST. DEAD. The name takes a second to register. Joseph Christopher. Your hometown serial killer, circa 1980. A native of Buffalo, like you.

It's over, you think. *It's finally over.*

He had been in Attica since 1985, with a retrial halfway through for a new insanity plea. It didn't take, but maybe he *did* hear voices saying, *Kill, kill, kill.* Thirteen years ago, Joseph Christopher, a white man, set out to murder Black men in Buffalo. In the parking lot of a Tops grocery store. Outside a Burger King. In the middle of the street.

Black men like your father.

The press called Joseph Christopher the .22-Caliber Killer, after his

weapon of choice. But he was also handy with a hunting knife, which is what he used on Parker Jotter. As the police got warmer, Joseph joined the army. He had tried a year before and failed. This time it worked. His late father would have been proud. Down in Fort Benning, Private Christopher attacked a Black soldier, who fended him off. In sick bay, Joseph bragged to a nurse about what he'd done up north. Claimed he'd killed thirteen. It was too crazy to believe. He healed up, escaped to New York. To Times Square. To kill again.

He got caught and brought to Buffalo. Maybe the *voices* told him to stand alone before the judge. *No jury.* One psychiatrist said this represented a wish to be judged by his father, a manly man whose death had weakened the son's mentality. With his soft face and faraway eyes, Joseph could never impress him in life.

Maybe, you think. Or can someone just be pure evil, all oedipal conflict aside?

You toss the paper aside. Then you call *your* father, Parker Jotter.

FOR THE PAST six years, Parker has lived at Ironheels, a group home for veterans. He shares a room with a former coast guard lieutenant named Russ. They seem to get along. Your father has good days and bad. He recalls sports minutiae, hockey highlights of the Buffalo Sabres, but gets foggy when you mention the name of his attacker.

"Joe Christmas, was it?"

"Joseph *Christopher*," you repeat. "The one who tried to *carve out your heart.*"

"Nothing was ever proven, Tina," he says. He sounds like a lawyer on TV.

True, the DA never prosecuted the specific incident, the stabbing. He focused on just a few cases out of the dozen likely killings. He wanted J.C. dead to rights, put away for good, so he kept it simple.

"Well, it *was* him," you say, pacing the kitchen. "Your description matched."

"We sure about that?"

He's said this before: that he doesn't trust his memory of that night. He suggests it was someone else, maybe a hired thug or drug-addled drifter. He didn't really get a good look. You think: he survived, but a part of him did not. Or else this is just his way of changing the topic.

"Consider, it was a stressful moment in my life," he says, "seeing how my *arm* almost got severed and a nine-inch blade was sticking out of my sternum." He makes a vibrating sound, like a cartoon diving board. "B-b-boing!"

"Pops!"

You haven't called him that in years, and the word makes you sad. Before the attack, communication between you two had petered out. You'd take a month to answer a letter, and there was a letter every week from him, endlessly curious and concerned—Parker full of words, and you with nothing to say. The letters piled up in your drawer, half read. It was strange; you used to be so close, with your mother out of the picture, but once you left home, you started to erase him. You had thrived in college. You were about to graduate early, waiting to hear from law schools in New York, eager to join Winston in the city. Winston Pang was so lovely then. There was a life together to look forward to. The plan was to elope. You said nothing to your father. It was months before you learned what happened. How much pain he was in. How alone he felt. You were so in love with Winston, you left your dad behind. For that, you can't forgive yourself.

This is the voice saying: *Forgive yourself.*

PARKER JOTTER WAS one of a handful of Black pilots who fought in Korea. You know just the outline. He was close to making double ace when his plane went down. Lost a finger, spent a year in a POW camp, and was moved to an American hospital in Tokyo after the war ended. Returned to Flora, who was, he said, already losing her sense of things. Took over his father's store, painted a sign with its new name: Jot Electronix in blue, above a pair of gold lightning bolts crossed like swords.

In the back room, he repaired castoffs for resale and devised gizmos

like a ballpoint pen that played music when you clicked it. At home, he wrote six books of a sci-fi saga—well, five that you know of. The sixth never got done. Sometime between books one and two, you were born. You were a kid when you read the first installment, *2333*, around the time your mother was waiting for the world to end.

But *2333* wasn't like the stories you read for school. Nothing was real—cars that ran on magnets, a moon shaped like a seashell, from which no sound could ever escape. Some sentences had an eerie quality, as though a second meaning hovered in the white space, written with invisible ink. Your favorite was *Escape from Tyosen!* Even as a kid, you thought it was *really* about his time in Korea, only set on a planet of ice and wind in a distant dimension. Pops insisted that nothing from his real life leaked into those pages. Names and plots came to him out of a clear blue sky. The denials made you dig deeper, read between the lines.

At age seven, you "solved" the secret behind "2333." Pops said he picked the number to sound futuristic. But you showed how it could be read as 2/3/33—Flora's birthday.

"Okay," he conceded, "*maybe* there's stuff buried inside."

YOUR PARENTS SPLIT up soon after. Flora spent most days with the Divine Precepts, still waiting for the end of the world. Parker called them a cult. A few times, when he wasn't around, she tried to interest you in DP teachings. She gave you pamphlets explaining how it was the *real* Christian religion, unlike the watered-down faiths your friends followed. You pretended to read them but didn't let her take you to a meeting.

One October afternoon, in the fifth grade, you came home early from a half day at school. Flora was filling a suitcase. She said she was bringing old sweaters and blankets to a church drive downtown. She'd be back in an hour. It was strange but nice that she hugged you. The next time you heard from her, it was by letter. She and four of her fellow Divine Precepts had made it to a commune in Kansas, a five-day trek.

Their new home. Flora said someday she would come and take you there, but you never wrote back.

The voice repeats, *Forgive yourself.*

These days, to sort things out, you see a therapist named Meta. Her office is on East Ninety-fifth. You cross the park every Friday to see her before your regularly scheduled visit with the North Koreans. Sometimes you wonder if they're spying on your sessions. For Meta's safety, you don't mention the work you're doing—the faxes, the ciphers, the Swiss Man. You don't mention work at all, which can be awkward. Mostly you talk about Winston, Flora, Parker. That's more than enough.

YOU'RE STILL ON the line with your father, who's trying to hang up.

"I've got a lot to do," he says. "Finishing touches."

For years, Parker has toiled on a how-to guide, *Wildwording.* The book distills the wisdom of history's great authors, which means his research is endless. It promises a revolutionary set of methods to jump-start anything from one's novel or autobiography to a poem, or even a diary entry.

You once were keen to read it. You've tried scribbling stories yourself on occasion. Not science fiction like your dad, not really fiction at all. More like semi-memoiristic prose blobs that don't quite come together. But you had trouble following the tenets, which have expanded from five to nine to something like fifty-three. The whole thing throws you into a panic, frankly.

It's good that he has a project to pour his energy into. What's not so good is that he wants to send *Wildwording* to his old publisher at Neutron Books, which he last wrote for thirty-odd years ago.

"Wait—*stop*," you say. "This is important. Joseph Christopher is dead!"

"Like the saying goes, never trust a man with two first names. How'd he kick the bucket?"

"It said breast cancer."

"We sure he was a dude?"

"Pops."

"Russ!" he shouts to his roommate, whose stated goal is to read every detective novel written between 1925 and 1975. Everyone at Iron-heels is some kind of obsessive. "Remember that guy who sliced me? Turns out, I almost got killed by a dame!"

Russ cackles. He's a bad influence. Parker says, "Well, it's back to the salt mines for me."

Every day he burrows into a pile of books and old magazines, to glean more examples for *Wildwording.* Paper rises around him.

"Please," you sigh. "Talk to me for five minutes like a normal person."

Silence. He doesn't want to think of Joseph Christopher for one more second.

"You're so far away," he says, his voice all hazy. "I want to see my granddaughter. Heck, I want to see my *daughter*-daughter."

"We'll visit. I promise we'll do a big visit soon."

"Say you will, but never do."

It's true. "Labor Day at the latest. Mercy would like that."

"Bring Wilson, too," he says. He thinks you two are still married.

"It's Winston," you mutter. You shouldn't be pissed, but you are.

WINSTON PANG LIVES down the block, which makes the Mercy hand-off relatively smooth. It's amicable—a word only used in the context of divorce. You've thought of ditching his last name, but it's your kid's, too. (The one perfect thing you've done is name your daughter Mercy Pang.) Keep it simple for now.

Someday you might go back to being Tina Jotter. Good name for a hit woman.

Maybe that's what tomorrow's top-secret job interview is for. Your instructions are so elaborate they approach parody. The Swiss Man says to rent a teal Subaru from Pablo at the place on Ninety-sixth by the West Side Highway, drive it to a diner in Hastings-on-Hudson by ten forty-five A.M., and sit in the third booth on the left. The interviewers

will join you at eleven. While you wait, nurse a cup of tea. Refuse to accept a menu from a server named Amber. Then say, in this precise order: "I would like to wait for the rest of my party."

You practice in the mirror. *I would like to wait for my party*—no. Pleasant voice. *I'm waiting for the rest*—damn. *I'd like to . . .* argh.

Don't rush it. Deep breath. *I would like to wait for the rest of my party.*

There you go.

What's it all for, anyway? You're fine at your current post. But the Swiss Man insists. You don't know if the new job would pull you out of his orbit or draw you closer. These things can get confusing, even for an agent of confusion like yourself. For instance, you've been working for the Koreans, but it's not clear *which* Koreans. Most likely, it's the South Koreans; after all, you have access to their enemy's consulate. But maybe that's what Pyongyang wants you to think.

Whoever's in charge clearly doesn't want people like you to know certain things. As long as the funds keep landing in your bank account, you're good. Most jobs are like that. Games are being played above your head, dice thrown by people you'll never meet.

You tell yourself you're not doing anything illegal. But you don't always believe it. Then you tell yourself it's all for your daughter, Mercy Pang, your quiet and sensitive nine-year-old, a.k.a. the best person in the world. That's enough of a thing to believe in.

Now and then, when life gets crazy, and the voice asks how it feels to be such a failure, you recall how this business with the Swiss Man began. Three years ago, when you didn't make partner at the firm, you quit on the spot. You and Winston had had blowups before; now he said you were *erratic* and he wanted out. Not your finest hour, sure, but it could hardly be said to indicate a pattern of behavior. Plus, Winston always scolded you for things that he himself did: speeding through yellow lights, using the wrong toothbrush. As far as erratic went, Winston had switched jobs six times in eight years. On a tip, he bid a grand at auction

on an unclaimed shipping container, convinced of the treasures within, only to be left with two thousand pairs of argyle socks. He had just bought a time-share in Philadelphia, while attending a convention. *Philadelphia.*

You picked up a medley of jobs. Fridays you tutored a French newscaster in English. Marie was a fascinating creature, younger than you, with a face like a doll's. She'd set up shop at the periphery of break-ins, three-alarm blazes, ask passersby for comments. No one could understand a word. "You're asking what I think about the fire?" It was all a little heartbreaking.

The tutoring money was good. One thing led to another. That thing led to yet another thing and you became closer. None of this was forbidden. She was married to a famous sports agent named Robb with two *b*'s who worked in midtown. Marie told you Robb had a boyfriend (a Rob with one *b*), which didn't stop *New York* magazine from listing Robb and Marie as one of the city's new power couples.

The first time you ran into Robb on the street, you and Marie were holding hands. Robb's smile never faltered. Perhaps tutors and tutees strolled together down the Champs-Élysées. Robb was tall, and Black like you, with a roguish accent and scrunched features that somehow looked *très agréable.* He didn't suspect anything, or else he did and liked it.

The second time you met Robb, you were in line for a buttered everything at H&H. Robb's eyeglasses were steamed white in the heat of the bagelry. But it was like he knew you'd be there. He tapped your shoulder and asked if you could tutor him. You said you'd think about it. He slipped you a business card when you shook hands goodbye.

You and Marie grew apart. A Belgian broadcaster hired her, and she'd deliver *l'angle américain* three times a week, in the thankless twelve-fifteen A.M. slot. She had a harsh pageboy. Some nights you'd close your eyes and listen till you fell asleep.

Scrounging for work, you fished out Robb's card. The company's name was scratched out. What was this shit? The number was L.A., but the call went to Geneva.

"Allô," said a high, unflappable voice.

That was your introduction to the Swiss Man.

. . .

When Neutron Books discontinued its science fiction line, some-time in the sixties, Parker's run as a novelist ended. Still, for as long as you lived in that poky house on Oak Street, Pops kept going up to the Carrot every night. That's what he called the attic room where he'd written most of his books, because of the dark orange rug. (Only years later, taking a snoozy seminar on the Romantics, did you realize that Parker had been saying *garret* all along.) The Carrot was prone to mildew, home to daddy longlegs. Parker kept a blanket-lined nook just for you. A series of extension cords snaked from the upper hall to power a battalion of lamps, fans, and electric typewriters. In winter, he turned on a space heater, its innards glowing like a fiery script. It clucked gently as you drifted off, arms tired from hoisting up your book.

You're thinking about the Carrot as you sit in the booth at the diner in Hastings-on-Hudson, because Amber (red name tag) mentions that carrot cake is one of the specials. She says this as she slides you a menu. You hand it back.

"I would like to wait for the rest of my party," you say, following the script.

"Of *course,* dear," says Amber, with a warm voice and blank face. "Coffee?"

You want tea. You are supposed to have tea. But you are not supposed to say anything beyond that sentence. You shake your head.

"Tea?"

You nod. She brings a cup of hot water, a Lipton's bag and lemon on the saucer. The trees that fringe the parking lot sway in a breeze that turns the leaves electric. Only a few tables are occupied. An old man sits at the counter, lingering over a magazine. You can see a horse on the cover. At eleven on the nose, a young Asian couple slides into the booth. They have a throwback dapper-criminal look, like any minute they might start swing dancing. Amber comes by with menus for all. You sigh, relieved at passing the first test. The man orders a club sandwich and coffee, black. The woman asks for meat loaf with home fries. And a beer.

The man gives her a sharp look, but she ignores him. She says to you, "Azaleas."

"Huh?"

The pair studies your reaction.

"A-*za*-le-as," the man repeats.

You panic. Did you forget part of the script? You get up, flustered. "Sorry to waste your time."

They look at each other, satisfied.

"Relax," she says, with a lovely soothing smile. You sit back down.

"We just needed to know it was you," says the man, sipping his coffee. "We're here to talk about *2333*."

They introduce themselves as Joon and Misa. They're from a computer game start-up called Corewar. They want to make you an offer.

"I don't understand."

"We want to negotiate interactive rights for the *2333* books," Misa says.

"With me?"

Amber comes by with their orders.

"You're the rights holder," Joon says. He takes a file from his briefcase: a printout as fat as one of Parker's books. You flip through the legal considerations. The signature page is dated March 7, 1983. Under your father's name, assorted stamps and initials decorate the bottom, like some nineteenth-century peace treaty.

Misa and Joon speak the truth: Parker Jotter signed over all current and future rights regarding the books to you, his daughter and sole issue. Dr. Inky Sin, a psychiatrist who he saw for years after the stabbing, attested to his sound mind. Was it the good doctor, then, who arranged for a lawyer? You never met Dr. Sin, only heard about him from Parker.

Clauses from the original Neutron Books agreement appear, dated 1957, photocopied into the current document. Parker ran the store back then; any book money was gravy. (He once told an interviewer that his books were attempts to describe a frequency only he could hear.) Still, he should have paid more attention to the contract.

"What are *interactive* rights, again?"

"We thought you went to law school," Joon says.

"Parker and I didn't interact much back then."

You notice Amber ushering the last customer out and flipping the sign to CLOSED.

"Interactive extends to any type of electronic or nonelectronic game, including but not restricted to board and card, as well as any computer program or future technology yet to be devised."

You return to the pages from the 1957 contract, which lacks such language. All of it comes from the 1983 revision.

"How about microchips in the head?" you joke.

Joon thinks it over. "Yes. If it comes to that."

"When pigs swim," Misa says, a spot of beer foam on her upper lip. "I mean fly."

Joon writes a number down, so large it must be a mistake. It could sustain you and Mercy for a long time to come. Joon says he can go to this number if Corewar can possess *all* of the rights, including publication and performance, for his novels and any unpublished writings.

This windfall could get you out of the dumpy, occasionally scary Sans-Souci. Pay for Mercy's future schooling. Get you started on whatever you wanted to do next in life.

"No pinches," says Misa sternly.

"She means you don't have to pinch yourself," Joon says. "As in, this isn't a dream."

"I'll need time," you say.

"The clock makes noise," Misa says.

"She means it's ticking."

Misa finishes her meat loaf. Joon's meal remains untouched. He takes a bite of his sandwich, offers you some fries. You're ravenous, but you decline.

"Why all the cloak-and-dagger?" you ask. "Renting the teal Subaru. This diner. Tea, not coffee."

"We had to make sure it was you."

You almost laugh. "Who else would I be?"

"The Swiss Man has a lot of enemies," Joon says carefully. "We put out false instructions on channels that we suspected of being compromised."

"I don't understand." Though given your experience posing as a photographer and fielding false faxes, you have some sense of larger forces in motion. It's around this time that you start to get scared.

"Pablo radioed that you rented the right car. If you'd picked, say, a Honda—that would be a tip-off. Here, Amber paged us after you ordered tea—the green light for us to come in."

"Tell her about 'azaleas,' " Misa says, face flushed from the alcohol.

The word they said at the start was meaningless: bait to catch any pretenders. Joon says that a fake Tina Jotter would have responded differently—by reciting an old poem, thinking this would confirm your identity with them.

You wonder what's so special about your father's books that would make Corewar want them so badly, and make others want to stop them. If you weren't you—if you got the Honda or a Coke—would Joon and Misa have entered with a silencer and a tarp?

"I get it," you say coolly.

"Plus, we want to make sure the Swiss Man *is* the Swiss Man," Misa adds.

"That's all we can tell you for now," Joon says, irked that his partner said too much.

"Does he work for you?" you ask.

"Other way around!" Misa says. Joon glares at her.

"And he's really Swiss?"

"No, but he's in Sweezerland a *lot*," she says. "His sons go to school there. Went to school. I mean, one of them *went,* a younger one *goes.*"

You make an educated guess. "So the Swiss Man's Korean, then."

"Oops. The cat escapes the sack."

"The cat is indeed out of the bag," Joon says, exasperated. "Let us know soon about the offer."

. . .

ON MONDAY, YOU pick up Mercy from Winston's to take her directly to school. She's waiting alone in the lobby with her weekender and schoolbag. You could strangle him. He couldn't wait five minutes to make sure his daughter got picked up okay? Asshole.

You get a hug, lug the weekender. Supers water down the sidewalk on this fine morning, turn their hoses away modestly as you pass. Nurses in pastel scrubs wait for a bus to the East Side hospitals. You turn, walk north, displacing a mob of pigeons.

"So what did you and Dad do?" you ask.

"Oh, he went out," Mercy says.

"Without you?"

"Dad *asked* me, but I wanted to stay in and finish my book."

"Where was he going?"

"La Rosita. With a friend."

You and Winston used to go all the time. Cuban sandwiches and Mexican soda. The voice says: *Don't ask* which *friend.*

"I hope he wasn't out late." Pigeons scoot from your path. "What were you reading?"

"Gramps' book." She swings around her backpack and pulls out *Return to Tyosen!* "It's so freaking good."

"Language, Mercy."

"It's so 'damn' good?"

"Well . . . okay."

She never reads, so you cheer this development. Mercy is more of a visual person. That's your line these days. You took her to the Magritte show at the Met last fall, and for months she'd sketch a tree on a canvas in front of a window. "Refresh my memory?"

"There's a big battle, and a pet ferret, and then another battle."

"Does that book have Greena Hymns?" Your old favorite. "With the long white hair?"

"Yeah! She gets her finger bitten off by the ferret. On purpose."

"To fool the guards or something, right?"

The shorn-off finger was something Parker shared with his creation,

a similarity even he admitted was deliberate. But Greena wasn't just him. She was *you*. Fearless. A problem solver. Loyal till the end.

"Also," Mercy says, lowering her voice, "I might have ESP. Like Greena. She sees things happen before they happen."

"You don't say."

"Think of a number, one to a hundred?"

"Eight."

"You're not supposed to tell it to me!"

"Sorry. Okay, I have a new one. Go ahead and guess."

She closes her eyes, keeps walking. You guide her by the elbow as you cross the street.

"Fifty-three."

"No."

"Seventy?"

"Uh."

"Twenty-two."

"Sorry, pal."

"Rats, I can't do it. The conditions aren't right."

"We'll try later, sweetie."

She holds up a finger. "Was it . . . ninety-nine?"

"No."

She rubs her forehead, to draw forth any dormant psychic powers. "Four . . . teen?"

"Not even close." You're at Mercy's school. "Want me to walk you up?"

"Parents aren't allowed," she says. "Tell me the number."

"It was zero."

She whacks you on the arm in excitement. "That was my next guess!"

MERCY PERMITS A kiss goodbye. You walk back home, her weekender slung over your shoulder. You don't have to visit the *Nowy Dziennik*

office today, or ever again. The Swiss Man, pleased that you made contact with Corewar, has released you from your duties. It feels strange not being near a fax machine. You give your father a buzz.

"Pops, this company approached me yesterday? They want to buy rights to the series?" Inflection like a teenage girl's. "*Your* series—*2333*. This company, Corewar, makes computer games . . ."

You try to sell him on it for a while, not that you need his permission. But his mind is somewhere else. You clench your stomach, ready yourself for the blow.

"What is it this time?" you ask.

"Kim Tollson is T. S. Kim."

"I'm sorry, what?"

"That author, T. S. Kim. Who wrote *Man in Korean Costume*."

The title rings a bell. A historical novel Winston liked. "What about him?"

"He's the same person as Kim Tollson. My nemesis at Neutron Books."

"Right." He's griped about her in the past, but this is more alarming. "Hold on. You're saying that T. S. Kim, a Korean author from the eighties . . . once wrote science fiction as Kim Tollson in the fifties?"

"There's a reason no one knows much about T. S. Kim," he says. "He's never given interviews. There's only one picture of him. A little too chiseled. Clearly a *model*."

You know the photo. T. S. Kim gazes into the middle distance, hair like a raven's wing. Winston tried to style his that way for a while, but didn't have enough to work with.

"No one even knows if he's still alive. Wouldn't you say that's very strange, in this day and age, for the author of such a popular book?"

"So is it a white woman masquerading as an Asian man, or the other way around?"

"That's what I've been trying to find out!"

"Honestly, I wouldn't lose sleep over it."

He's not listening to you. "Did you ever read *Man in Korean Costume*? I found a copy in the library here. It's about the first Korean to be

seen in Europe. Inspired by a Rubens drawing. The figure is in a loose Korean *hanbok,* with one of those tall hats they wore. It's black and white, a trace of color around the lips. No one knows who he was, but T. S. Kim turned him into a cross-dressing servant."

"That sounds fun."

"He smuggled diplomatic secrets in pasta recipes. Made for a decent page-turner, I admit. A decent page-turner. But something reminded me of Kim Tollson's books. The tone. Certain descriptions. Similes and whatnot. Once or twice, I would have said it's just coincidence. But then there's a part in which the servant, named Correa because he's from Korea, meets a handsome priest in a small village where a strange rock has landed. Correa correctly identifies it as a meteorite, tries to explain that it came from space. The villagers nearly burn him—sorry, 'her'!—on the spot. She escapes, and months later hears from another servant that the priest went mad, that his followers began worshipping the rock, having orgies, blaspheming Christ."

"Wow."

"Don't you see? That's the plot of *Priest from the Stars*! Kim Tollson's first book, from '57. Nobody remembers it now."

"Maybe it's a coincidence," you say.

"Also, there's a clue near the end. The servant has been in Europe so long that she's forgotten how to speak Korean, even forgotten her real name. Then a flock of birds crosses the sky, and another, and another. She's looking out the window, and she thinks the birds are spelling something out in Korean. Then they fly the other way, the shapes change to Roman letters . . . her last name Kim, then her first name D-O-L-S-U-N."

What was he getting at? "Ah."

"Consider, right, that 'Dol' can also be spelled 'Toll.' And 'sun' in the sky sounds like a boy, a 'son.' So the book is basically giving out the name Kim Tollson. Do you see?"

"Sort of," you say, but you don't. You hate this conversation, hate where his mind has gone.

"Now reverse the names, Western-style. Which gets you to Toll-son Kim. Abbreviated T. S. Kim."

He pauses, expecting you to be bowled over.

"Talk later, Pops," is all you can say.

BUT YOU DON'T talk to Parker much that summer. It's information overload. He sees connections where there aren't any, or connections that don't matter. Over Labor Day weekend, you borrow Winston's Volvo and drive west to Buffalo with Mercy. She's looking forward to seeing him. Highway signs pair town names as the exits draw near, sounding like characters you'd see in an old play: Chester Florida, snooty Cadosia Hancock, that rakehell Newark Phelps. Mercy reads aloud from the final *2333* book as you drive. For one exciting chapter, somewhere past Syracuse, rain coming down, she keeps pausing to draw out the suspense. Then there's one lull that lasts so long that you finally look over to see she's fallen asleep.

You make it in just under seven hours, check into the Marriott by the cloverleaf. On Sunday you visit Ironheels. The facility occupies a pair of century-old mansions off Elmwood, the elegance marred by a modern passageway. There's no one at reception. You and Mercy find Parker's room, where you're met by the director, two nurses, the chaplain, the chief medical officer, and his pal Russ.

The director spots you and Mercy. "This way, Ms. Otter—er, Jang—ah, Jotter-Pang, *right this way*!"

He ushers you and your daughter into a drafty parlor hung with torrid paintings of Niagara Falls. Mercy sits on the bed and reads *Return to Tyosen!* Her copy is mostly intact; only the last few pages have fallen out, the binding weak after thirty years. She's left them in her nightstand in New York. She'll get to the end when you return.

"What's going on?" she asks. "Where's Gramps?"

. . .

YOU DIDN'T GIVE Corewar an answer right away. There's been a lot to deal with. The burial, the will, and, most daunting, all the *paper*. Russ gives Mercy her grandfather's busted Zippo, a trophy from the war. The director takes you to the basement storage locker. The boxes are buildings in a city of the mind. Easily ten thousand pages' worth of Jottings reside inside. Surely this can't all be for *Wildwording*. Maybe the last unwritten volume of *2333* lies within. Or it's a lost diary from the war. Maybe everything you wanted to know about him is in this locker, these boxes.

The storage unit is crammed with other printed matter: repair manuals, foreign-language dictionaries, pamphlets on the paranormal. Sober tomes on the Korean War, its causes, the causes of the causes. Six lineal feet of magazines, from *National Geographic* to *Foreign Policy* to a linotype rag called *CinéFreak*.

"This is what happens when you don't throw anything away," you tell Mercy. You mean it as a warning, but she looks excited by the mess.

The mystery of Parker Jotter, the secrets of the Carrot. All of it is here. Correspondence stuffed into coffee cans. Pictures cut out from newspapers. At the far end is a crate of videocassettes: talk shows, hockey games. Mostly there are movies, the labels a palimpsest of titles.

You can sense your daughter trying to connect the book she's just been reading to all this junk, both by-products of the same person.

"I think I've been here before," Mercy says.

"We haven't been here before, sweetie."

"But it feels so familiar." There's a cumulative three square feet of vacant floor space. Mercy slips around the maze of dusty boxes. "We have to keep it all, right?"

YOU CALL JOON and Misa from the hotel, using a number the Swiss Man gave you. It's twenty-two digits long and there's no way it will

work, but they pick up on the first ring. Misa says she's glad you called. Corewar is eager to get started. She asks if you can meet at their office in two days. You say you'll need more time, that you're in Buffalo right now.

"What a coincidence," she says. "So are we."

Misa gives you an address. It's close, off Main near the university. In ten minutes, you and Mercy arrive at a neatly maintained ranch house on a residential street. No signage, just the letters C.W.G. on the mailbox. You step into a surprisingly grand stucco-walled foyer. In the main room, Misa's on a stepladder, dusting the chandelier, as Joon buses empty coffee mugs to the kitchen.

"Is this your headquarters?"

"Yes and no," Misa chuckles, climbing down. She's wearing an apron and a hairnet.

"Most of the work is in other cities," Joon explains vaguely, before she can go on. "But we held on to the original office."

The original? It doesn't compute. One section of wall is hung with old maps, an antique gun, and other dusty knickknacks. Mercy wanders across the maroon shag to investigate, nearly tripping on a heap of classical records and hand-labeled videotapes.

"Don't touch," you say, but of course she doesn't hear you. She picks up a toy telescope, puts it to her eye like a pirate.

"Let's talk about the turkey," Misa says, as your daughter focuses on her.

"She means 'talk turkey,'" Joon corrects. "About *2333*. We're prepared to go higher."

"We love it all," Misa says. "The planet within a planet, the computer that programs itself!"

"The war between the F'falo and the O'rë," adds Joon, pronouncing the alien names with such crisp authority you don't recognize them at first. "Talk about epic."

You cut short the gushing. "I need something from you."

"Anything," Misa says.

"The situation has changed. My father is no longer alive." They don't say anything. "As in, he *just* passed away."

"So sorry!" Misa says. She puts down the duster, lays a comforting hand on your hand. "We thought it happened long ago."

"Our condolences," Joon says guardedly. Mercy trains the telescope on him.

"I'm surprised you didn't know my father had died," you say, sliding your hand from under Misa's, "given how you're so fixated on his work."

Joon doesn't blink. "We follow the rights holder."

"Then you're in Buffalo by pure coincidence?"

"This is technically the home office," Joon says coolly, "though we've only been in this particular building for a decade or so."

"Why this house?"

"Oh, just something that came on the market. A distress sale of sorts."

He says that Corewar started almost a century ago as Kaleido-Pan Games, a few miles from the current site. The company made novelties for the Pan-American Exposition: puzzles and kites, playing cards, and kaleidoscopes, of course. (So *that's* what Mercy's looking through.) It became K.P. Games in 1902, to distance itself from the event, which had culminated in McKinley's assassination. K.P. found modest success, but ran out of ideas by the '50s. In the late '60s, it was renamed Corewar and was putting out board games that re-created famous battles from history. They marketed them to schools as educational aids; the boxes would sit in closets, unplayed, for another decade.

Misa mimes drifting off to sleep, and it's true that Joon's corporate history gets too detailed, as he lists Corewar's hit titles. At the dawn of home computing, it went all in on producing an ambitious game on disk (*Falklands!*), which proved a flop. Soon it was a company in name only; the current owner—Joon and Misa's father, you take it—bought it five years ago for a song.

"Time to talk about the turkey," you say.

"Indeed." Joon looks apologetic.

"There's a locker full of stuff that Parker's been writing for the past million years."

They perk up. "The last book?"

"I've only sampled—it's overwhelming, but I think it's important." You bluff, wishing you were more up to speed on the work of Parker Jotter. "The Fool-ya, the, uh, Rey—Reo—er . . ."

"The F'falo and the O'rë," your daughter chimes in. She's using the side of Parker's old Zippo to redirect a slice of sunbeam around the room.

"Thanks, Mercy." Cough. "Indeed. The origins of that war lurk somewhere in these boxes."

You practically hear them salivate. "The . . . origins of the F'falic-Orëash War?"

"Uh, yeah." You don't mention *Wildwording,* his impossible book that must exist in dozens of squabbling versions in the storage locker. "The origins. And the, ah, last book."

"*The Tan Gun?*" Joon asks.

"It's *amazing,*" your daughter says, a devilish look in her eyes.

"Yes. And it needs to be preserved."

You're smiling at Mercy, at your mutual lie.

"And we would have all rights to the content," Joon confirms, exchanging a look with Misa.

"Sure. The . . . content." The word sounds false, like you're discussing a quantity of cooking oil or pistachios. But you let it go.

"That's no problem!" Misa chirps. "We photograph it, transfer it all on computer."

"Give us a month," Joon says.

"And I need a copy."

"Of course," Joon says. "Do we have a deal?"

Mercy's looking through the wrong end of the kaleidoscope as she flicks the busted lighter. Your father always kept it near him, up in the

Carrot when he was writing. With the Zippo as a mirror, she funnels a sunbeam through the cardboard tube. Aims it at Joon's heart, then Misa's cheek.

It occurs to you that if Corewar wants the fruits of your father's imaginings so badly, there must be someone *else* who does, too. Someone they want to keep it from. But you don't want to bargain, or shop around, or wonder what it is they want it for.

You say yes. This is the last thing you will do for Parker Jotter.

THE SINS OCTOBER PRETENDERS

AT THE START OF OCTOBER, Monk Zingapan got in touch. Due to unforeseen developments in Seoul, Echo was postponing his guest lectureship at Rue University Extension Campus's Wildword program yet again. Monk was having trouble finding a replacement.

"I knew I couldn't trust him," Monk said.

"Sometimes life just gets in the way."

"He reminds me of someone who gets in other people's way, if you know what I mean. A total Korean fake."

"Korean fake?"

"I said *flake.*" He laughed.

I understood being sore at someone for flaking out, but Monk seemed to cross the line. "Echo seemed pretty solid."

"Not that Koreans are flakes," he assured me. "Take you, for instance. Slogging away at GLOAT, twenty-four/seven. We could use someone like you. Which is why I'm calling. Are you down to teach?"

"No."

"Just the one class," he said. "For the spring."

"I can't." I felt bad that Monk was in a jam, but he was being absurd. "I don't have the bandwidth."

"God, you've turned into a *computer* working at that place."

"What? Lots of people say 'bandwidth' now."

"Beep, beep, beep," he said. "Zeros and ones, zeros and ones."

"Guilty as charged." I studied my reluctant mustache in the glass of the

microwave door. Its two wings angled down sharply, like a circumflex. "One problem is that I never totally understood Wildwording. I don't think I'm qualified."

"Wildword," he corrected. "In any case, I'll teach you the basics. The beauty part is, it's not just a writing method but a therapeutic practice. So even if the students can't write worth a damn, they get something out of it."

"Therapeutic how?"

"In a nutshell, it's like yin and yang—darkness and light, good and evil, water and fire, you know? The true Wildworder uses the *opposite* of his or her strength to produce weakness."

"I'm not sure I follow."

"If a student habitually writes in the past tense, I'll ask him to compose in the present. If someone defaults to the first person, I'll make her switch to second person. In this way you create harmony."

"Sounds complicated. What if they like a close third?"

He ignored me. "It's time to come back, Soon. Unplug from the motherboard and reclaim your humanity. Like the slogan says: Dreams Come True at Rue." In a quiet voice he appended, "Extension Campus."

"You're saying I should reclaim my humanity by coming to RueXC as a temp," I clarified.

"It would be for the spring," he said hopefully.

"Who's filling in now?"

"Amy Ma. Know her? She stepped in at the last minute. This erotic poet from Melbourne. She pronounces it Mal-bone. Amy's better known here for her anthologies. She has one called *Sextinas* and another one that just came out, authors doing smutty rewrites of Proust."

"Why can't she do the spring?"

"Some visa drama, I think—I don't know. It's hard to understand with that accent. She might be saying *visor*." He sighed. "Come on, Soon—help a brother out." He paused. "Do you think anyone remembers *Predators*?"

"*Pretenders*," I corrected.

"I rest my case!" Monk wheezed. "Check this out. The other night at the Awkward benefit, I mentioned to Padraig that you should be a judge

for its fiction award. Yuka Tsujimoto was there. She says to Padraig, 'Soon *who*?'"

"Ouch."

"She was joking. Said you were like a brother to her."

"No comment."

"Point being, your cred is on life support. It might be too late. Do you think a single person has picked up *Pretenders* this year?"

"My cousin Gemma did. She was at the dinner, too."

"You know Padraig has a thing for her, right?"

"Still?"

"Let me ask you. How much play do you think he gets?"

"I don't know. A lot?"

"Word on the street is he can't get it up. Too weird, right? Take an ugly bastard like me. Ready anytime, anyplace. Three A.M.? No problem. Afternoon delight? Roger that. At the bakery, behind the dog run, in the bathroom at the Nuyorican Poets Café."

"Tell me which bakery so I never, ever go there."

"Back seat of a gypsy cab—check. Observation deck of the Empire State Building—check. The Starbucks on Astor Place—check. Floor of the New York Stock Exchange, after hours. Subaru dealership in Bay Ridge, Brooklyn."

"TMI, Monk." I suspected he was immersed in a Wildwording technique, for a poem in progress. Maybe he could work for the company making the Louse. "We should all be so lucky."

"You got *that* right, buddy," he said. "I won't complain. Neither will my wife."

I'd forgotten he was married. Or had I ever known this? There was a lot about Monk I still didn't know. When we first met, back in our *NY Whip* days, he asked if I knew who my parents were. He explained he once got fired from his job at a game company on the Upper West Side for knocking up the boss's daughter; it was so long ago that the kid might be close to my age now. A kid he'd never met. My Koreanness was no impediment to his theory that we might be flesh and blood.

"Poor guy," he said, of Padraig. "So—you down to teach?"

. . .

AFTER DINNER, THE LANDLINE rang again, just as I was starting the dishes.

"Yellow?" I answered.

"Is that like a 'yellow power' thing?" It was Padraig Kong, apparently calling from a rave.

"Probably not."

"Hey, man," he said. "Need a favor."

Everybody wanted something from me tonight. "Are you okay?"

"Do I sound different?" Muffled club beats ate into his words.

"What's with the music?"

"Reality."

He meant the group. "My daughter's favorite."

"Confession: I took a pill. Actually, two pills. But fear not. They're going to, uh, neutralize each other."

"That's something Monk Zingapan used to say."

"Aw, snap! Come on, Soon. It's your boy Paddy *Kong*." He sounded like he'd taken six pills, though that made him neither more nor less annoying than usual. "Need to get in touch with Gemma."

"My cousin?"

"Yes! And *soon,* Soon." He paused. "Dude, your name is an adverb."

"Good night," I said.

"Wait. Need your help. The email she gave me sucks. I keep getting bounce-backs."

"What's the address?"

"Uh, hold on. It says, stay dot away dot please at disinterested dot org."

That "dot org" was a nice touch. Even Padraig had to laugh. "Time to move on," I said.

Story wandered into the kitchen and put a bowl in the sink. "Tolga," she said, instinctively addressing the artificial intelligence module on the counter. "What time is it?"

"*The time is eight forty-seven p.m.,*" Tolga replied, in a starchy British accent.

"Tolga, what's an anagram for 'Dogskill'?"

The device had a limited set of abilities, but GLOAT added more each week.

"Kill dogs," it said, inspiration at a low ebb.

"Time for bed," I told my daughter, who pretended not to hear. Around her finger she twirled a gray plastic doohickey, which I suspected was a 3D-printed game piece for Hegemon.

"What's the story with Gemma's husband, the Incredible Hulk?" Padraig asked. "The German guy."

"The anagram for 'German' is 'manger,'" Tolga offered, picking up on my conversation.

"Korean German," I said. "He grew up there."

"In Germany? How does a Korean wind up *there*?"

I could hear Story asking the device: "Tolga, what's an anagram for Korean?"

"No rake."

"Tolga, are you good or evil?"

"Sometimes I wonder that myself."

Story laughed. The device was loosening up, its banter quotient improving with each interaction. "Tolga, try again. What's an anagram for 'Korean'?"

It considered. *"'Near OK' is an anagram for Korean,"* it said at last.

"Get ready for bed," I whispered to Story, making a "zip it" motion.

"Hello?" Padraig said. There was a break in the pulsing music. "Still there?"

"Yeah." I told him what I knew about Hans. "His dad was brought over in the sixties to work in the mines."

"Coal mines or gold mines?"

"I just know 'mines.'"

"Old man, you're not being a great help here, no sir. You are not being a major supporter of the cause." He made everything sound like a pledge drive. "I swear I saw her at the Princeton Club. This mixer-benefit, which by the way, why weren't you there?"

"I wasn't invited."

"Sure you were. It was for Awkward Enterprises." Padraig Kong was very

ambitious, determined to turn a respected but obscure Asian arts organization into some sort of multimedia juggernaut. He envied slanted+enchanted, Loa Ding's branding business, and the two were always either announcing collaborations or at each other's throats.

"AAWCWA's launching a video series," Padraig said. The music faded for a bit. "An Asian American cultural news vertical. That you watch on your phone. I decided it's a new era, and so we're getting rid of paper mailings. The future is online, old man. The future is in the cloud."

He forgot that I worked for GLOAT. "Right."

"Gemma would make a great host. Working the culture beat. Interviewing poets and actors and whatnot."

"She doesn't actually like culture."

"What does she like?"

"Money."

I could hear Story ask an old favorite: "Tolga, what's an anagram for 'Tolga'?"

" 'Gloat' is an anagram for 'Tolga.' "

She cackled. When Story first made the discovery on her own, months ago, she thought she'd unlocked a secret, leveled up in some way. I didn't have the heart to tell her the similarity was likely intentional. Then again there was a chance she was on to something absolutely crucial, hidden in plain sight.

"Why won't Gemma give me a chance?" Padraig shouted above the noise. "It's because I'm not Korean, right?"

"I would say it's because she's married."

"You Koreans are so freaking close-minded. That whole Hermit Kingdom mentality. Hide away from the world. Keep the bloodlines pure." Perhaps remembering that my daughter was white, Padraig retreated. "Can you tell Gemma I'm practically Korean myself? My mother's half. Well, a quarter. Meaning I'm an eighth. But why haggle? Just tell Gemma 'half.'"

Then he badgered me about her Korean name, how to spell it in *hangul*. I described the letter-shapes the best I could. I thought of Jack London, reporting on the Russo-Japanese War. Circles and lines, circles and lines.

Story wandered back, toothbrush in hand. Her pajamas showed a snow-

haired woman crouched atop a flying saucer, contrail dissolving into stars. It was Story's avatar from Hegemon.

"Tolga, set a timer for two minutes." Story was fastidious about her brushing routine.

"Two-minute timer, commenced."

She headed for the basement, where we had relocated the 3D printer.

"Just forget Gemma," I said at last to Padraig, as the dance music returned with a vengeance. "You wouldn't want to get on the wrong side of Hans."

"Pfft, Hans." He sounded sad even though he was shouting. "This isn't something I ever say, but I feel like Gemma's my destiny."

I could, in fact, think of numerous occasions when Padraig had dropped the D-bomb. It meant he was in a fragile mental state, apt to go off the rails. Meanwhile, Tolga was already at that point. For reasons unknown, the all-hearing pyramid was reciting the state capitals, in a pattern I couldn't discern. Tolga was in less than a thousand households at that point, so glitches were expected.

"Think about it," Padraig said. "We'd be related!"

"Topeka . . . Harrisburg . . . Atlanta . . ."

I tried turning Tolga off by growling *"Off"* at it. They'd built it without any discernible switches, buttons, or dials. The easiest thing would have been to pull the plug, but they'd omitted that, too. I threw a paper bag over it.

"I have to split," I said.

"Let's get coffee sometime." His voice cracked. "I miss you, dude."

"Sure." I pictured Padraig sobbing into a long, expensive scarf. "I'll be in the city more soon," I lied. "I might be teaching."

"Providence . . . Olympia . . ." Tolga said from under the bag.

"Oh. I was thinking maybe . . . now?"

"Now? But it's almost nine. And I don't live in the city anymore. You know that."

"I can come up to your neck of the woods! It's no biggie. Except that I'm extremely high at the moment."

"Don't get in the car."

The music got louder on his end. Something crashed to the ground.

"Where *are* you?" I asked.

"A club in Chinatown. At least I think it's a club. I was brought against my will. I started the night at the Museum of Sex. A launch party for Amy Ma's latest erotic anthology, *Remembrance of Thongs Past.*"

"I'm getting another call," I said. "Don't do anything crazy, Padraig."

MY PHONE GROANED, as though burdened by my sudden popularity.

"*Soon dubu jigae!*" It was none other than my cousin Gemma.

"This is so weird," I joked. "I was just talking to your boyfriend."

She didn't miss a beat. "Jorge or Boomer?"

"Padraig."

"Who?"

"Padraig Kong, from the party."

"Ah, my stalker. Never mind him. Listen up, cuz. Speaking of the party: something bizarre happened. Yesterday I brought the Hyundai in for inspection. I had to drive it all the way to Queens." She unwrapped something. "Sorry—haven't eaten all day. Anyway, I dropped the car off around noon and went hunting for coffee. It was the middle of nowhere, even for Queens. I felt like I was going to get thrown in the back of a truck. I was walking forever. My phone was running out of juice. Then I found a mini-mall, got some boba. I was hoping I'd see a Daily Divas so I could get my nails done while I waited. Doesn't Nora have a branch in Queens?"

"Yes, but it's a big borough."

"Tell her there's a mall where she could make a killing. I was walking by a *naengmyun* place when I bumped into *him*. The author from that book party."

"Echo?"

"Yeah, except he wasn't all gussied up. He looked like a driver or deliveryman for one of the restaurants."

"It couldn't be Echo. He's in Korea."

"That's what I thought. But I swear it was him."

"Did you talk?"

"I said, 'Fancy meeting you here,' and he jumped ten feet. I could tell he remembered me, even as he was backing away. I tried talking in Korean. He *almost* said something back—then caught himself just in time. My phone was already out, because I was waiting for a text from the auto shop, so I took a picture. He more or less sprinted away. A magazine fell out of his back pocket, but there was no address or anything."

"What was it?"

"Some kind of horse-racing rag. I didn't pick it up—the cover was all greasy. I told him he dropped something, but he kept going, ran outside. I would have followed, but I didn't have the right shoes," she said. "Anyway, it was so strange. Why didn't he say anything, or even acknowledge that we'd met?"

"Probably because it wasn't him."

"It one hundred percent was. And it got me thinking. What if Echo isn't Echo? Like, what if the guy I saw today was *hired* to be the face of Echo. Just some guy living in Queens."

"I don't understand."

"Stay with me, Soon. After that dinner, what if . . . what if he didn't exist anymore—or only appeared when needed? Maybe he didn't get on a plane back to Seoul, because he hadn't come from there in the first place. Maybe someone wants him—needs him—to exist."

Gemma always had a wild imagination. "Who?" I asked.

"Beats me. Probably your friend Tanner Slow doesn't even know. I bet most of the people at that party had no clue this Echo guy was just a stand-in. A pretender, to quote your awesome book that I haven't read yet."

"What about your husband?"

"Hans had no clue. He thinks I'm seeing things. Hang on—let me send you the picture."

My phone blooped. I opened the text. The top of the man's head had gotten lost in a halo of light, but from the forehead down there was a resemblance. His face was flushed. His thin zippered jacket had a name on it, perhaps the noodle shop's. His hair was shorter, grayer.

"I don't know," I said. "It doesn't really look like him."

. . .

DISHES DONE, I STUDIED Gemma's photo again. It couldn't be Echo. The nose was off, the hair too scraggly. But when I wasn't looking at the screen, the possibility haunted me. Echo *was* missing, had been AWOL awhile, according to Monk. Was he hiding in New York rather than Seoul? Perhaps he was overly anxious about making his stateside debut with *The Sins*. If that was the case, I could have settled his nerves by telling him that exactly zero previous Slow Press books had garnered even a cult following.

I thought about Dream Three, the most involved one yet, detailing the exploits of the KPG's far-flung members. As strange as the whole thing was, I'd gotten the hang of Echo's fragmented style; the collective "we" voice of the Korean Provisional Government, unnerving upon first encounter, felt more familiar. There were humanizing touches. This Dream gave a double portrait of the '30s, showing both the future North Korean ruler Kim Il Sung falling in love with comrade Kim Jongsook during his youthful guerrilla-warfare days in Manchuria, and an older Syngman Rhee meeting Francesca, his Austrian wife-to-be, in Geneva.

But other parts of Dream Three puzzled me. It alluded to factions within the KPG that were at each other's throats but didn't say who was on which side. (Was the modern KPG now presenting a unified front?) Then there was the way it restaged Thomas Ahn's assassination of Ito Hirobumi, from Dream Two. In this version, we see that it wasn't Thomas—the leader of the Cut Finger Club—who did the deed but, rather, Dayama Sadako. She had been Ito's lover, or adopted daughter, or both, a Korean who spied for the Japanese for years, and who insisted in the end that she was with the KPG all along.

Logging on to GLOAT, I found numerous accounts of Thomas Ahn's notorious crime. But there were only hazy mentions of Sadako, under any of her several names. There was not a word—at least not in English—about her infiltration of the Cut Finger Club, indeed no sign that she'd ever crossed paths with Thomas Ahn in Vladivostock or Yi Sang in Tokyo. Was she real or Echo's invention? I reminded myself this was fiction. That Echo called the parts Dreams for a reason.

My phone trembled: a message from GLOAT analytics informing me it had made a facial-recognition match. Gemma's shot of Mr. Queens was side by side with the single poorly lit picture of Echo I had taken at the Admiral Yi, as he presided over the drinking game.

Ludicrous. There was barely enough visual data for GLOAT to go on, in either picture. I let my phone charge on the counter and went upstairs.

STORY WAS IN BED, Sprout at her feet. She was nestled in the arms of a mysterious alluring woman who was reading aloud from *Memoirs of a Korean Queen*, an autobiography from the eighteenth century. My daughter's blue eyes were already closing.

"Good night, everyone," I whispered. "I love you."

"Good night," murmured the strange woman, who I now identified as my wife. Nora. She was always working late these days. We hadn't seen each other in a while.

"When did you get home?" I whispered.

"Shhh. You were on the phone."

"Bad things happen in that book," I said. I had read the memoirs more than twenty years ago. A college seminar on the domestic perverse. "For starters, the prince is insane and the king starves him to death inside a wooden chest."

"Typical Korean family dynamics," she said.

"A little intense for a seven-year-old, no?"

"Story saw it on the shelf. It was her choice. No point covering up what happened. That's what history is all about."

Nora put the grisly reading matter back and walked gingerly out, headed for our bedroom. I shut the door. Sprout followed me down to the kitchen, and I gave him his Dorchester medicine. In seconds he was asleep, sprawled by the fridge.

I said, "Hey, Tolga, what is history?"

The silver pyramid was pensive, blue light swirling. At last it said, *"Sorry, I can't help you at the moment."*

"Thanks for nothing."

"Cheers."

I went back upstairs. Nora was flossing while looking at her phone. Somewhere in her dresser, the Louse was already coming to life.

"Do you know anything about Gen-Era?" Nora asked.

"Sure," I said. "DNA testing." GLOAT had acquired the ancestry-tracing venture last year. It had the power to connect users with long-lost relatives and, as a bonus, track down serial killers.

"I'm sending in a cheek swab," she said. She hadn't been flossing; she held up a Q-tip and sealed it inside a small tube. "I thought we could share the results with Story, use it as a way to discuss heredity and genetics."

"Then tell her she's adopted."

"Right. And she could choose to do a swab, too. Or not. Or do it later."

"Makes sense," I said.

I was distracted by visions of DNA helixes as the Louse kicked into gear.

When we were finished, right before sleep, I swear I heard Tolga blurt out downstairs: *"The anagram for Seoul is Louse."*

IN THE MORNING IT rained. I dashed out to nab the *Dogskill Daily* off the driveway, snug in its plastic bag. Out of the corner of my eye, I spotted a clump in the shrubs. At first I took it for a mangled bird, left by a rogue feline. But by some miracle, it was Dream Four, unearthed, as though Sprout had needed to look up some detail in the buried text. The ink had bled in places, and several pages were ripped, but it wasn't too bad. I worked it over with a hair dryer, then hung up a few of the damper chunks on the towel rack. I started reading before they had a chance to dry.

DREAM FOUR
1945–1953

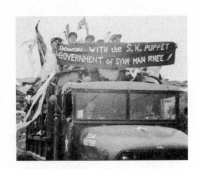

1. Endings

We believe that the Korean War (1950–?) never ended, just as we maintain that the National Hockey League's 1998–99 season continues to this day, absent a legitimate victor.

A cease-fire *was* declared on July 27, 1953, but North and South Korea technically remain at war. And Brett Hull *did* shoot a puck past Dominik Hasek in the early hours of June 20, 1999, which let the Dallas Stars triumph over the Buffalo Sabres in the Stanley Cup finals, but the goal *should* have been disqualified, as Hull's skate was clearly in the crease. As this violated league rules at the time, we consider the game, series, and season to be unresolved.

This is the fourth dream of the Korean Provisional Government.

2. The Sabres

How did Buffalo's hockey club get its name, circa 1970? According to team lore, a contest was held. Some anonymous poet must have grasped the similarity between the blade of a skate and that of a weapon for hand-to-hand combat—sporting yet deadly.

We actually know who devised the winning entry: Parker

Jotter, an air force vet who had once flown the signature jet of the Korean War: the F-86, known as the Sabre.

3. The North Star

Parker Jotter died in 1993, six years before the disputed series. Significantly, he predicted that the *Sabres* would one day face off in an epic clash against the newly formed Dallas *Stars*.

As he writes: "When we talk about Stars vs. Sabres, we really mean North vs. South Korea." Consider this: In North Korea, the country's founder, Kim Il Sung, and his son and successor, Kim Jong Il, are frequently hailed as the *lodestars*—i.e., the North Stars—of the people. (The N.K. flag features a red star in a white circle.)

Consider this: the Dallas Stars were originally the Minnesota *North* Stars.

4. Proxy War

"This will be a proxy war between the North and the South," Parker Jotter wrote toward the end of his life. We picture the former science-fiction writer and part-time prophet in the computer lounge at his group home in Buffalo. "A test run for something bigger."

5. The Wrong Picture

A paid notice in *The Buffalo News* preserves some biographical highlights. Parker Jotter was born in 1929. As a boy, he listened to Buck Rogers on the radio, read Flash Gordon in the funnies, and dreamt of outer space. He convinced his father to stock titles like *Astounding* and *Weird Menace* alongside the electronics magazines at the family's appliance store. Shortly after the start of the Korean War, Parker joined the air force, training at the base in Sampson, New York.

He met his future wife, Flora Edwards, when she interviewed him for *The Buffalo Criterion*, a Black-run paper, where her uncle worked. Flora was eighteen, the youngest reporter in the news-

room. She began her profile of Parker while he was still in town. Days before his deployment, to her family's surprise, she took the bus to Seneca County, to get some local color. They were married at the courthouse in Romulus; the profile was never published.

Sent to Korea in the spring of 1952, Parker Jotter completed forty-three missions, achieving the status of ace. On December 1, 1952, his plane went down deep in enemy territory under murky circumstances. He was captured and sent to a POW camp near the Chinese border; freed in 1953, he convalesced at a U.S. military hospital in Tokyo. Upon returning to Buffalo, he briefly studied electrical engineering on the GI Bill and took over his father's store on Michigan Avenue. He wrote several science-fiction novels, deeply informed by his wartime experience. Later, he worked as a security guard at Chatillion Academy. His marriage to a local girl, Flora (née Edwards), ended in divorce; he is survived by his daughter, Tina Jotter-Pang, of New York City.

The death notice ran with the wrong picture. (He would have laughed at the irony of an Asian face atop his life story.) It was paid for by us. In truth, we had been following him for a while, ever since Tokyo.

6. Wildwording

The memorial for Parker Jotter was held at the Amigone Funeral Home. We asked his roommate, Russ, if Jotter had written anything during his last years. Russ handed us a pamphlet that the author had printed up earlier that year. We hoped it was part of the sixth book in his *2333* series, abandoned decades ago. Alas, it was part of an unfinished guidebook called *Wildwording*, which purported to teach authors how to unleash their true potential. The pages are a mix of military analogies, straightforward advice, and rambling philosophy. He includes diagrams of various typewriters he designed, and other inventions that never took off.

Jotter had sent copies to schools and the media. Russ admitted it was a lot to take in; even *he* wasn't sure what to make of it, though he had been a sort of research assistant. He didn't know what to do with the remaining copies. We bought them off him at a bulk rate.

7. A Note on the Text

Dream Four is a secret history of the Korean War. It skips around a lot, in the spirit of that book of Korean lore the *Samguk Yusa* or Parker Jotter's *Wildwording*.

8. The Dead Line

By most accounts, the Korean Provisional Government quietly shuts down after World War II. Its main goal, the liberation of Korea from Japan, transpires on August 15, 1945, seemingly without the KPG's help. (We said *seemingly*.) Two weeks later, an emissary for Emperor Hirohito surrenders aboard the USS *Missouri*. The yoke is cast off; at last, Korea will govern herself.

This doesn't happen, of course. The Soviet Union and the United States, allies just months before, enter an era of distrust. The former throws its support behind one of the many Communist movements, centered in Pyongyang, in the north. It is led by the former guerrilla fighter Kim Il Sung, recently back from Khabarovsk, where he hid from Japanese forces.

The U.S. pays scant attention to Korea, until it realizes the country could be a hedge against the looming Communist giants of Russia and China. After digging up a *National Geographic* to determine its exact location ("Is it 'Korea' or 'the Korea'?"), the world shapers in the State Department propose the 38th parallel as a dividing line. The deal will be that the Soviets can oversee everything above it, while the Americans monitor what's below.

This drastic cut, this unnatural border, alarms the Koreans. Nevertheless, Syngman Rhee and Kim Il Sung jockey for posi-

tion. At last, the Americans take Rhee seriously. The president of the KPG is a Christian who is fluent in English and staunchly anti-Communist—the ideal figurehead. His link to Woodrow Wilson doesn't hurt. Meanwhile, Kim—a *secret* member of the KPG—has already proven loyal to the Communist cause. His Korean wife and children have Russian names.

The Korean Provisional Government is broken. Rivals feud, turn to assassination. But despite these differences, the KPG persists. Its work remains crucial, if the country is to be united and free.

9. Acronyms

The United States Army Military Government in Korea tries to control the confusion. With an acronym that sounds like dark sorcery, USAMGIK occupies the huge, European-style Government-General building erected by Japan—and glimpsed in Na Ungyu's lost movie *Arirang*. Under the direction of Lieutenant General John R. Hodge, USAMGIK keeps many Japanese officials in place, as well as their Korean collabora- tors. (The Japanese might have been the enemy, but at least they knew how to *run* things.) Hodge's decision sets the natives seething. General Hodge dislikes Syngman Rhee and casts about for a new figurehead.

Other foreign agencies arrive, with their own maddening letter-cluster monikers. The United Nations Temporary Com- mission on Korea is convened to supervise this larval phase. Its initials are UNTCOK, which if you say it ten times fast sounds like a very basic description of a sex act. As Parker Jotter notes in *Wildwording*, "Even on a language level, that old beat-up country was fucked from the start."

10. Three Things

General Hodge jokes, "There are three things American troops in Japan are afraid of: diarrhea, gonorrhea, and Ko-rea." Still,

he brings them over. He doesn't believe the Koreans are ready to rule themselves.

11. Pee-rip

Hodge sees a leadership void. Which Koreans should be put in charge? Who among them listens to the United States? It's a mess: too many grudges, too much paranoia. A Korean might sign up with the Reds in the morning, then vow to hunt them down after lunch. Whatever it takes to save his hide.

Hodge convinces Philip Jaisohn, the old revolutionary turned American doctor, to return. But Jaisohn (né Suh Jae-p'il) insists on being called *Philip,* hard for the typical Korean to pronounce: *Pee-rip.* At a stadium filled with thousands of his countrymen, he delivers his speech in English, requiring an interpreter.

By 1948, the rift between north and south is so great that separate elections are held on either side of the 38th parallel. The south, under the supervision of the newly formed United Nations, elects Syngman Rhee as president; the north, monitored by the Soviet Union (which, confusingly, is also part of the U.N.), picks Kim Il Sung.

This is the time of capitalization, when north becomes North and south becomes South.

12. Insults

Syngman Rhee and Kim Il Sung are back home for the first time in decades. The two have never met. They are nearly forty years apart in age; Kim could easily be Rhee's son. They despise each other, which is not unusual when it comes to the passionate members of the KPG. In *Wildwording,* Parker Jotter floats an oedipal interpretation: the hot-blooded Kim is driven to destroy the elder Rhee. "In truth, they were *both* hot-blooded," he writes. "All Koreans are."

Kim begins a long tradition of the North jeering at the

South, calling it America's running dog, lap dog, bootlick, lackey. He becomes a *Roget's* of insults. Rhee, in turn, hammers away at the godless worldview of the Reds. Communism is a spreading stain, he tells his fellow Koreans, a foreign sickness as destructive as the Japanese occupation. Can't they see that Mao Tse-tung and Joseph Stalin will step in and take over, once Kim softens things up for them?

Same bed, different dreams.

13. Ahn and Ahn

Kim Koo is Rhee's sometime ally and a die-hard member of the KPG. In 1948, Pyongyang invites him north to hear out proposals from the arch-Communist Kim Il Sung. Though he regards the whole overture with skepticism, he makes the trip. The Syngmanites brand him a traitor, and a year later, he is offed by a man called Ahn, who some claim is a distant relation of the martyred patriot Thomas Ahn, the assassin of Ito Hirobumi.

14. Attack and Flight

The Korean War starts in the early hours of June 25, 1950. North Korean armor surges over the 38th parallel, beating a path to Seoul. Or it *doesn't* start then, but earlier: some KPG analysts claim that the North was simply reacting to smaller previous incursions by the South—that both sides were bristling for war, and to blame the North is academic. Just as the Korean War never ends, it can also be said not to *start*.

Regardless, on June 25, the North hits hot and fast, reaching Seoul in three days. The Korean People's Army boasts a force nearly twice that of the South, and it wants Syngman Rhee's head. Rhee and his fledgling government and his Viennese wife flee from Seoul to Pusan, from the northwest to the southeast. They sail out of Inchon, going around the tip of the peninsula. Others flee by land, the path roughly the one

described twenty years earlier, by the roaming black dot in Yi Sang's poem "Diagnosis":

```
·  0  9  8  7  6  5  4  3  2  1
0  ·  9  8  7  6  5  4  3  2  1
0  9  ·  8  7  6  5  4  3  2  1
0  9  8  ·  7  6  5  4  3  2  1
0  9  8  7  ·  6  5  4  3  2  1
0  9  8  7  6  ·  5  4  3  2  1
0  9  8  7  6  5  ·  4  3  2  1
0  9  8  7  6  5  4  ·  3  2  1
0  9  8  7  6  5  4  3  ·  2  1
0  9  8  7  6  5  4  3  2  ·  1
0  9  8  7  6  5  4  3  2  1  ·
```

15. The Major

On June 25, 1950, the bad news reaches Major Frank Hallsworth on an island off the western coast. He is in a room at the home of his Korean lover, the willowy Lim. Only one American officer was at the 38th parallel that morning, and the South's defense is in shambles.

Hallsworth must get to the mainland immediately. He is a compact man. Everything he owns fits in one suitcase. He has been stationed in Korea since '46, for what he thought would be a stable peacekeeping stint. Two years turned to four, and now there is something that looks like war.

Barbara, his glamorous, cultured wife, joined him last year. They haven't spoken in months. Frank spends every free minute with Lim: the grizzled Yankee with his Asian pearl. He knows what Lillias Underwood, the wife of the famous missionary, wrote way back when: *Korean women as a rule are not beautiful.* But have you ever seen a picture of Mrs. Underwood? The leggy Lim makes Lillias look like something you pull from the drain.

Barbara knows about this girl, though she never gets the

name right—Lamb, is it? Ling? She refers to her as *your Oriental cookie.*

16. Promises
In his bullfrog croak, Frank assures Lim that after things stabilize—once the North is pushed back—he'll divorce Barbara. He loves her, doesn't she know that? All Lim knows is that he is going away. She paces the perimeter of her house. Under the harsh sun, every surface hurts the eye. She knows it's over. Lim murmurs the last lines of Kim Sowol's poem "Azaleas." She's the abandoned lover, saying farewell without a word.

17. The Station Wagon
Meanwhile, in a quaint town ten miles south of the 38th parallel, folk dancers twirl to raucous drums. Inside an antiques shop, Barbara Voorhees Hallsworth haggles with the dealer over pieces she wants for her decorating company. Her plummy voice and stylish wardrobe clash with the rustic locale. It's clear she enjoys the ritual, each side confident of getting maximum value out of the exchange.

A radio announcement interrupts the banter: the North Koreans have crossed the 38th parallel and are heading for Seoul.

Pali pali, the dealer says to his men. *Hurry.* The radio blares the South Korean national anthem, its strains soon lost amid the hysteria. Tanks rumble into view, stars chalked onto turrets. They plow into thatched-roofed huts. Old men throw stones until bursts of machine-gun fire hurl them backward through the air.

It is already too late. Corpses clog the streets. The dealer tells Barbara to take his station wagon and *go.* A North Korean soldier shoots him as the car pulls away.

18. Five Korean Sisters
The bridge is alive. Fleeing villagers clamber along girders. Every so often one plunges into the river with a rending cry. A

white-haired man materializes before Barbara. His clothes glow, speckless, as though he's stepped out of a museum exhibit. Despite the tumult, his soft voice resonates. He calmly asks her to save his five granddaughters, who have just lost their parents. She says no. He looks so serene, as though already part of the spirit world. At last, Barbara relents. The kids pile into the wood-paneled car and they make their way slowly across the bridge. Ten seconds later, it's demolished—by the *South*, to slow down the marauders. Hundreds fall to their death.

Barbara remains poised, smudged cheeks and all. Brow sweat suits her. The morning started out so calm. How did she get stuck fleeing for her life—with five little girls to look after? Even if they make it to safety, God knows what will come next. Will she adopt them all, bring them to Philadelphia? Her sisters, those shrews, would have a field day. Meanwhile, her so-called husband licks his lips over some Korean cookie not much older than the eldest girl.

19. Wedding Day

Back on the mainland, Frank Hallsworth meets his friend Sergeant Henderson, who is Black. People here have heard the news but have yet to panic. *The North pushes down, we push up, life goes on.* A pretty Korean woman in a bright *hanbok* asks for a ride to city hall.

Frank tells Henderson to ignore her. *Give an inch, they'll take a mile. The Korean way.*

The woman, Mila, explains that it's her wedding day. She has a beautiful smile. She is not trying to trick them. Henderson and Hallsworth take Mila to city hall, where her fiancé, Pak, awaits with flowers in hand.

20. The Good Soldier K.

In Seoul, Kim Eunguk has just finished his first year of college. On June 25, he and hundreds of other young men are captured

and pressed into service with the Korean People's Army. Though Kim is originally from the northern city of Hamhung, he loathes the Communists, who imprisoned his father and executed one of his grandparents.

At training camp, he keeps his mouth shut, waits for a chance to escape. He reads European writers in Japanese translations, thin books by Camus, Kafka, Hesse. Every night for pleasure he reads one chapter of a fat Czech book called *The Good Soldier Schweik,* in a German translation. He signs letters to his parents "K." or, with irony, "The Good Soldier K." He doesn't send the letters because he doesn't know where they are anymore.

21. The First Shot

A soldier barks at Mrs. Barbara Hallsworth in Korean, trying to commandeer the vehicle as he trots alongside. If they lose the car, they lose their lives. One of her quick-thinking young charges opens the glove compartment and hands her a pistol. Barbara shoots the man in his chest. He looks as surprised as she does.

22. The Tokyo Bureau

Seven hundred miles away, in Tokyo, a room of jaded American journalists learn of the unpleasantness in Korea. "Who cares about the 38th parallel anyway?" gripes raven-haired Longfellow. It's too soon for another war, as far as he's concerned. His colleagues nod and sip their thirteenth cup of motor oil.

"I betcha *Truman* doesn't even know where Korea is," he sniffs, echoing Isabella Bird from fifty years ago, whose learned friends thought it might be somewhere near Greece.

None of the reporters gathered here has set foot on the peninsula. Japan suits them just fine. Dyspeptic Longfellow has an irrational dislike for President Harry S Truman. "S" is Truman's actual middle name, whole and complete. That sham initial rubs Longfellow the wrong way.

23. Henderson's News

The wood-paneled Ford carrying Barbara and the orphans breaks down. Fortunately, Sergeant Henderson, her husband's friend, spots her while on patrol. He's chipper despite the danger. He lifts the hood and enlists the five Korean lasses to help him fix the car. Barbara pitches in.

"Motherhood becomes you," he says. Barbara blushes. She's never wanted children, yet here she is. He says Frank is looking for her. She doesn't believe it. According to Henderson, her husband is desperate to know she's safe. He will pass along word.

She bemoans shooting the Korean who tried to take her car, but Henderson says to get over it. "Just one less," he says.

24. Marriage and Separation

Mila and Pak are married in city hall on that morning of June 28, 1950, only to get separated hours later as the North overruns the city. Captured by the Communists, Pak watches in horror as they prepare to execute the more defiant prisoners, who shout their hatred of the North.

Pak, a lawyer, bites back his fear and turns on the charm. Though he's never met the other prisoners before, he pleads on their behalf: *It's okay! They just misspoke! They'll come around—give 'em time!* A North Korean soldier shoves a machine gun into his hand. With a smirk, he orders Pak to kill the three holdouts, or else *he* will be shot. Pak clings to his lawyer's logic. He thinks of Mila, his bride of just a few hours. The plans they had together. If he refuses, he will never see her again. If he agrees, at least there's a chance.

Pak shuts his eyes and pulls the trigger. The three prisoners scream. The gun takes over. It keeps firing, even as he tries to let go. At last, he collapses in sobs.

In the commotion, several of the captured men—including the Good Soldier K.—make their escape.

25. The Flood

Meanwhile, Mila, Pak's wife of less than a day, is still caught up in the flood of people fleeing south, south, east. This is no nuisance, no temporary instability. This is war.

26. MacArthur

Douglas MacArthur is born in 1880. His first home is the barracks at Little Rock, Arkansas, formerly an arsenal of the Confederate army.

Douglas MacArthur's father is Arthur MacArthur. He was famous in his teens as the "Boy Colonel" who rallied Union soldiers in a battle near Chattanooga. He received the Medal of Honor. After the war, he married a southern belle, Pinky, who idolized Robert E. Lee. Arthur MacArthur commanded the U.S. military forces in the Philippines in 1900, a year before President McKinley was assassinated. (America got the Philippines by making a deal with the Japanese, who wanted Korea.) Things went downhill for Arthur MacArthur as he tangled with William H. Taft, the territory's governor-general, unwilling to cede authority.

Arthur MacArthur's name was a doubling, a curse.

Douglas MacArthur's last name carries his father's first. But he is not his father, a failure. He is not his father.

27. I Shall Return

Douglas MacArthur attends West Point. Like Arthur MacArthur, he wins early glory. Carrying out raids and reconnaissance in France during World War I, he collects over a dozen medals and earns the distinction of being the youngest division leader. In the sequel, he commands the U.S. forces in the Pacific. Japan hands the Americans a major defeat in the Philippines, which it now wants back. This is the place where his father's career had peaked thirty years earlier. Regrouping in Australia, he vows, "I shall return."

He does. Like his father, Douglas receives the Medal of Honor. He is not his father.

28. This Is Not a Pipe

Douglas MacArthur knows how to play to the cameras. He wears mirrored sunglasses and jams a huge corncob pipe in his mouth. The pipe is a prop of sorts, a way to get into character. It also serves as a distraction, a useful way to obscure his face while being perfectly present. There is something disturbing in its shape and texture, the divots that once held kernels giving it the appearance of a portable apiary.

29. The Sea

Douglas MacArthur is on the deck of the *Missouri* for Japan's surrender in 1945. Two of its cities have been leveled by atomic bombs and he thinks he can smell the radiation, hundreds of miles away. It's just the sea, he tells himself. Later he meets and towers over Emperor Hirohito, until recently a god among men. But at age sixty-five, the general's hands tremble too much, and even his most loyal aides worry about his health.

30. Uncommitted

"I wouldn't put my foot in Korea," Douglas MacArthur says, before he sees how dire things are. "I wouldn't touch it with a ten-foot pole."

31. The Greatest

In June 1950, when North Korea invades the South, MacArthur is still head of the Far East Command, guiding Japan's transition from wartime enemy to peacetime ally. His headquarters are located in a new office building that houses a life insurance company.

General MacArthur is eventually called on to rescue South

Korea. He mutters to his wife, Jean, that he's too old. She calls him *Sir Boss* and tells him he's the finest general in history.

He will lead a combined American and South Korean force, with soldiers from some other U.N. countries—not including the Soviet Union, of course, which backs the North. And he is not his father.

32. The Fifty-first State
Douglas MacArthur boasts, of the Korean conflict, "I can handle it with one arm tied behind my back." He promises Syngman Rhee that the United States will defend Korea as though it were California.

33. Pusan
Barbara Hallsworth and her crew of scrappy orphans find refuge at St. Mary's Mission in Pusan. Outside is a scene of triage. Barbara recoils at a dead soldier, facedown and shirtless. His hands are bound behind his back, and dried blood cakes his shoulders.

She tells the girls: *Look away, move along now, look away.* It is not the worst thing they have seen or will see, but to spare them this is a small mercy. Nearby, a Korean woman tends to a badly wounded American. He's Black, and for a second Barbara takes him for Sergeant Henderson. But this man is younger, with no mustache. The woman is Mila, the unfortunate newlywed. She carefully tears her heirloom bridal *hanbok* into bandages.

34. The White Brigade
Meanwhile, a North Korean platoon hits another Southern village. Just as it seems that all is lost, soldiers in white rise from the tall grass like vengeful ghosts. Frank Hallsworth is one of them, face concealed by a farmer's hat. The spectral soldiers

repel the attackers, shooting them down, save for one man whom Frank recognizes: Pak, the groom he met the other day.

Pak wears a red string around his arm. He moves as though in a trance, pumping round after round into a South Korean soldier. He might as well be shooting himself.

That's enough, Frank says gently.

Pak's eyes look dead. He puts the gun down at last and howls.

35. A Bloody Race

Pusan is the city closest to Japan, Korea's former foe; ironically, it's now the safest place to be—as far as possible from the enemy in the North. This time the aggressor is not some foreign horde but an army of countrymen: their brothers, their doubles.

As Koreans massacre Koreans, some wonder if the Japanese were right. That Korea needs foreign guidance—a helping hand—to survive in this modern world. Maybe that 1908 headline in *The New York Times* was accurate: KOREANS A BLOODY RACE. Maybe the Americans and Soviets and Chinese were right. They really *don't* know how to rule themselves.

The KPG rejects this line of thinking.

36. Taejon

Longfellow and the other journalists take bets on when MacArthur will be fired. Meanwhile, American boys are thrown into the grinder. Arch Newly of the 23rd Infantry Regiment is so far from his Montana home he might as well be on the moon. Near Taejon, halfway between Seoul and Pusan, the Korean People's Army takes him prisoner.

37. Magnets

August 23, Tokyo, Japan. Douglas MacArthur surveys the freshly painted map of Korea that covers a wall of his command post. Alexander Haig, a kid straight out of West Point, moves mag-

nets around with a long stick, solemn as a croupier. Seated alongside the American brass are commanders from U.N. countries like England and Turkey. A *police action*, Truman has called it. As if the word *war* would unleash the Korean version of Hiroshima and Nagasaki.

Yet what is it but war? As MacArthur talks, Haig repositions the magnets, each one representing a beleaguered infantry regiment or depleted armored division.

MacArthur brays, unable to gauge his own volume. But he is not his father. Every so often he pitches his voice so low that the officers hold their breath to hear the words. He twists reality, convinces them that the zone at the southern tip to which so many have retreated, the so-called Pusan Perimeter, is safe. It may seem like the South is curled up in one corner, but the North's position is in fact the weak one.

38. Chromite

Douglas MacArthur unveils Operation Chromite. On September 15, 1950, he declares, U.N. forces will launch a sneak attack: an amphibious landing at the port of Inchon, twenty miles from Seoul. Inchon and Seoul, he cries, will be the *anvil* on which his forces will strike.

Haig adds magnets to the big map, positions them with the stick. The American, South Korean, and U.N. troops will take the interior, cutting off the North's supply lines.

MacArthur fixes the room with a lunatic stare. *This, I promise you, will happen.*

He says, as though reciting poetry: *I can almost hear the ticking of / the second hand of destiny.* He says, *We must act now or we will die.* Then he plugs the corncob pipe into his mouth.

Few share his confidence. Only six years have elapsed since D-Day, but the audience considers amphibious landings passé. The commanders of the army and navy object, citing too many variables. MacArthur argues that this is *precisely* why they *must*

do it. *The North won't know what hit them.* Inchon, their target, is virtually unprotected.

Another complaint: September is simply too soon for such a fraught maneuver. One of MacArthur's men explains that the landing *must* happen on September 15 because that is when high tide will reach its maximum depth of twenty-six to thirty-two feet.

It's September or never, he says.

39. The Window

Adding to the madness, everything must happen inside a two-hour window on September 15. If they fail to make the landing then, the waters will recede, miring the amtracs in the mud flats, which extend for miles from shore. The North will reinforce. Tens of thousands of American troops will be sitting ducks. The odds are long but MacArthur, who is not his father, trusts in Operation Chromite.

40. To the Lighthouse

Not only must they strike within that two-hour period, but they *also* need to secure the lighthouse on a nearby island beforehand. The North has a small garrison there. The lighthouse has to be reclaimed right before Operation Chromite begins. It will be used to signal the forces to initiate the landing.

There's only one man the general can think of who can pull off a commando raid on the lighthouse. For a second, Haig thinks the general will say *his* name, so he straightens up, lifts his chin. But, of course, MacArthur is talking about someone else, a seasoned officer: Major Frank Hallsworth.

Frank gets the nod and assembles a crack team that includes his lover, Lim; Pak, the lawyer-turned-POW; and Saito, his enigmatic Japanese mentor, who lives on the same island as Lim's family. It's a bizarre assortment, on the face of it, but Frank has a genius for organization.

41. The Speech

The early hours of September 15, 1950, aboard the flagship *Mount McKinley*. MacArthur's generals are losing faith as they await news of the lighthouse. They urge him to call off the mission. He gloomily agrees. (*Is* he his father?) Pacing on the deck, an hour before dawn, MacArthur dictates a rambling message, acknowledging that Chromite has been aborted and—to the shock of those gathered—that he is giving up his command.

He thinks: *I'm on a ship named after a mountain named after a president who was killed.* At West Point they do their best to eliminate superstition. But this can't be a good omen.

Before he finishes, light pulses across the waters. Major Hallsworth has done it! His team has suffered losses, but they will be remembered for their valor.

42. The Oriental Millions

Operation Chromite launches under cover of night. Ships bombard enemy encampments teased out earlier in the week. Scores of amtracs rumble off boats into the water, huge treads rolling them to shore. The front panels open into ramps. Tanks and troops spill out.

Douglas MacArthur declares that Korea will be reunited, and peace will come to not just this battered peninsula but to all of Asia. The daring rearguard movement surprises Kim Il Sung's army. MacArthur's seventy-five thousand men take Seoul, against a garrison of ten thousand.

Douglas MacArthur says, "Oriental millions are watching the outcome."

43. Tommy's War

Upon learning of MacArthur's brash maneuver, British war correspondent Reginald "Tommy" Thompson leaves his vegetable garden to report on the war, arm throbbing with vaccinations: typhus, cholera, Tet-Tox, yellow fever. On the flight east he

views the Alps, Geneva like a jewel, the outlines of Crete and Cairo. Rangoon, Bangkok, Tokyo.

Memories of his greenhouse: *Astonishing plants dripping with tomatoes.*

44. Bird's-Eye View

Inchon sits on the western coast. The low houses resemble clumps of mushrooms. Puffs of smoke leak from guns, unravel in the upper air like fingers of a glove. Thompson hears talk that the war should be sorted in a week. A short trip. His tomatoes await his return.

45. Picks and Pans

Tommy Thompson gets along with some of the newspapermen, but the American correspondents rub him the wrong way. Longfellow and others resent having been dragged to Korea just as they were starting to enjoy the peacetime pleasures of Tokyo. Only 10 percent have experience in the field. The rest of the World War II journos, Thompson gripes, have become movie reviewers.

The movie version of this war is probably already in production. What will the critics say? *Too confusing, why are we there, everyone looks the same.*

46. Experience

Most of the American reporters carry guns, Tommy notes. *It seemed that every man's dearest wish was to kill a Korean.*

47. The Abiding Things

Tommy Thompson follows the marines from Inchon to Seoul, a twenty-mile trek. He has a knack for cadging rides. He loves the morning drives through hamlets that look untouched by the twentieth century. His eye delights at the roof tiles of splendid

homes, *upcurled like the toes of oriental slippers.* Emerald fields
and tall trees, a vision of bounty.

The people are glorious to him, ethereal. He's read old missionary accounts in which everyone is outfitted in drab sacks,
but the women today are swathed in marvelous bright greens
and reds, *bodies wrapped tightly to give them a tubular appearance.* Babes nurse placidly as the men reap their harvest.
Apples and pimientos grow on terraced hillsides. The sun
brushes everything gold as he talks with some French correspondents, older men like himself, of the finer things, *the abiding
things,* of art and music, Proust and Gide. He swears he sees a
Korean soldier reading Camus.

48. The Automatic War

Every night he returns to his floating quarters on the *Mount
McKinley.* Thompson hears a young marine say, *Today I'll get me
a gook.* Another describes shooting a Korean who walked out of
a rice paddy—maybe a Communist, maybe just a farmer, what
does it matter. *I let him have it in the fucking guts,* he says, *then in
the fucking head.*

Twenty bullets are used when one would do. This is a new
kind of automatic war, a push-button death. The young marine
says, *Fucking head split like a melon.* But his hands are shaking,
as though still holding the gun.

49. The Informer

The South Korean troops are hardly less restrained than their
American counterparts. In one village, Thompson sees a Korean
inform on his neighbors, leading the troops to the hideouts of
supposed Reds. Were they? Men are stripped and marched
away, hands on head. Their genitals swing morosely. He hears
of entire towns slaughtered, bodies rolled into mass graves. The
forces of the North are no less vicious.

50. The Anvil

Thompson is impressed neither by General MacArthur, the ego-maniac, nor by President Syngman Rhee, the corrupt egoma-niac. They know nothing of the horror and confusion of the average Korean citizen, pulled by forces he doesn't understand. White-haired Rhee is even worse than the great corncob pan-jandrum. A zealot and a coward who claims to speak for Korea after being away for more than thirty years.

He hears another general echo MacArthur's metaphor: *We are the anvil. The United Nations troops pushing up from the south are the hammer. Soon the enemy will be pounded to pieces upon us.*

The success of Operation Chromite is beyond dispute, but there's a problem with the imagery. Thompson strains to visual-ize this upside-down anvil. He sees it growing cracks, splitting up. He sees Korea itself as the cracked anvil.

51. You Only Die Once

The Associated Press bureau in Tokyo prematurely reports that MacArthur's forces have retaken Seoul on September 22, though the battle doesn't begin until September 25. The remaining Seoulites flee as the city is pulled down around them, belongings strapped to backs.

They could only die once, Thompson writes.

Communist forces are sparse in the capital. There is little fighting to be done. The enemy has disappeared, like figures in a dream.

52. Sewing Up

Heady with victory, MacArthur wants to keep going. Truman does, too, but wants his general to think of the idea himself. On September 27, Truman authorizes MacArthur to carry the battle north. "Sweeten up my B-29s," the general says.

Word spreads among the American troops that they'll sew things up by Christmas. The British 27th Brigade cheerfully

looks forward to returning to their home base in Hong Kong. It's going to be over soon. From safe houses on three continents, the members of the Korean Provisional Government cheer the news. The country will have the chance to start again, get it right this time: *Nam Buk Tong Il.* South and North as One.

53. The Soil

On September 27, 1950, the day MacArthur gets the nod to push north, soldiers of the Korean People's Army prepare to abandon the city of Taejon, which they won two months ago. Ever since the Inchon landing, the North has been ruthlessly executing its South Korean captives here. Now it's time for the Korean People's Army to get rid of its American prisoners. These Americans don't know about Inchon and Operation Chromite yet.

They get herded into groups of fourteen, hands tied with wire. Arch Newly of Bozeman, Montana, watches as two North Koreans walk in, holding the M1s they confiscated two weeks ago. One of them could be *his* gun. Each clip holds eight bullets.

The first fourteen POWs are led away. Arch's group waits forever in dreadful silence. A guard comes for them. They trudge past the seam of fresh dirt covering the first group. At the second ditch, their future grave, some curse and some pray. Arch kneels without being told. He's second to last: number thirteen. Smell of soil. Quiet except for the birds, and then it starts.

54. The Thirteenth Body

The man next to him crumples. Sudden stink of blood and brains. Arch keeps his eyes open. The Korean reloads, swears at the mechanism. Arch recognizes the voice: a guard named Song. Thin, with a boy's face, this Song shared his cigarettes. Arch looks down at the ditch. Song shoots him in the neck, hand,

and collarbone. Arch slumps forward, too slow and too fast. He tries to block his fall, the forthcoming dirt. His thud doesn't sound like the others. It's different because he's not dead.

Opens an eye a chink. All three bullets only grazed him.

The fourteenth body falls next to him. Guards pour lime over the ditch, working fast. An officer swears at Song, who snaps back—Arch has never heard him yell before. He keeps breathing, a fake corpse, softly expelling the grains of dirt from his nostrils. He can taste the stew of blood and soil. Despite the danger, he sleeps. Hours later, Arch Newly awakes, staring straight into the clouds. Song and his comrades are long gone. In the distance, an American voice.

55. Thy Will Be Done

September 28, 1950, the capitol building, central Seoul. The façade is badly scarred, but inside, thick velvet curtains create an atmosphere of tranquility. The main hall fills with military officials, the returning South Korean government, and a gang of photographers. Tommy Thompson sits in back, amid dozens of foreign correspondents already clacking away on Royals and Underwoods.

Two old men, an American and a Korean, walk down one of the staircases flanking the dais. Just days ago, huge portraits of two different, younger men—a Russian and a Korean—were hanging on the walls. Now their absence is visible: a pair of bright voids on the dusty wall.

Douglas MacArthur leads Syngman Rhee to the front, Thompson observes, as a teacher might trot out his star student. Military police ring the proceedings, helmets gleaming like the backs of beetles. MacArthur takes the podium, which is draped with the pale blue flag of the United Nations. Syngman stands to the left alongside his European wife, Francesca. As is customary, they present a portrait of crossed cultures: he dresses in a Western suit, while she stands stiffly in a pale green *hanbok*.

Without his trademark pipe, MacArthur looks like he walked in off the street. He intones the Lord's Prayer, head bowed.

Fingers fly on typewriter keys, peck out the prayer word for word, as though the general were composing it for the first time in human history. Syngman Rhee shuts his eyes so tight they look soldered.

56. Syngman Speaks

From above, the sound of demented bells: glass, falling from the upper levels, the delayed effect of last week's shelling. MacArthur grimaces. Shards flash on their way to the stone floor. A sparkling cloud rises everywhere.

Undaunted, Syngman Rhee takes the podium. The old man's voice sounds young. It fills the hall, amid the haunting hail of glass. The foreigners who have never heard him speak stop typing for a minute in astonishment.

Let the sons of our sons look backward to this day, says Rhee, thinking of his own lost son, *and remember it as the beginning of unity, understanding, and forgiveness.*

Even Tommy Thompson must hold back tears.

May it never be remembered as a day of oppression and revenge.

More punctuation from above. Thompson, Longfellow, and the rest of the pack brave the shards as long as they can, then sprint for cover. The old men remain onstage. MacArthur takes it as a sign from God; Syngman Rhee imagines it's Bongsu, shedding tears of crystal. The Korean hands the general a scroll with the words he has just uttered.

Later, in a back room where the two wrecked portraits are stored, soldiers scrawl obscenities on the unlined brow of Kim Il Sung. They piss on Stalin's mustache until the paint comes off.

57. Leaving Korea

The war isn't over—it will never be over—but it's over for Major Frank Hallsworth. He and Barbara reunite in Pusan. The five

Korean girls won't be joining the couple stateside. Frank refuses outright. An orphanage will take them. The girls crayon a rough likeness of their adventures, scrawling WE MISS YOU BABIRA across the top. She hugs them one last time.

The Hallsworths return to Philadelphia. Barbara opens a shop on Chestnut. It's near where old Philip Jaisohn's company once stood, futilely churning out newsletters for Korean independence.

Mila and Pak, the grumpy Longfellow, Frank and Barbara Hallsworth, and the five orphans: all are members of the Korean Provisional Government. Decades later, their stories will be told in America, though few will stop to listen.

58. The Switch

Having escaped the Korean People's Army, the Good Soldier K. comes out of hiding and joins the South Korean army as a first lieutenant. Though he is only twenty, college seems a lifetime ago. He thinks of his fellow students forced to serve in the KPA, the ones who never escaped. Were they dead now, killed by their own brothers or uncles for wearing the wrong uniform?

59. To the North

MacArthur's U.N. forces push the North back to the 38th parallel, then up, up, up. He is going too far, but God is on his side. As the Americans sweep through the towns once held by the North, they rip off the propaganda pasted to the walls. They tear the eyes from Kim Il Sung's plump insipid face. THE END, one soldier writes.

60. Sinuiju

Pyongyang panics. American POWs get loaded onto railroad cars and sent farther north. At the reeducation camp in Sinuiju, they're immersed in Communist ideology. It can be hard to follow. One POW says to another, "Sum up this lecture for our instructor so we can get some chow."

Those prisoners who turn red get rewarded with creature comforts. Those who resist are neglected until their egos crumble or they die.

Even under the harshest interrogation, a prisoner of war is supposed to give up only name, rank, and number. But the techniques here are different—the "wash brain" pioneered by the Chinese, who are supervising the camps. The prisoner loses his grip on reality, admits to crimes he didn't commit. In time, he constructs an entire novel around himself, full of falsehoods.

Webb Sloane, a jut-jawed American, watches his fellow POWs standing in the yard. A Chinese official orders them to parrot Marxist doctrine. Day after day they resist, until they don't.

"Every man has his breaking point," Webb sighs.

61. Pyongyang

Upon reaching Pyongyang, Douglas MacArthur says, "Where is Kim Buck Tooth?"

Kim Il Sung's teeth are in fact straight, though the goiter on his neck has increased to the size of a bullet, swelling with its own will to power. Kim's forces have abandoned the city for now, as U.S. and South Korean troops take over. Survivors greet them warmly, even as the grandest buildings smolder. The crisp October air is laced with the smell of chestnuts.

Tommy Thompson goes inside the Russian embassy, which looks as though the staff simply went out for tea and forgot to come back. Empty caviar tins crumple underfoot. With the help of a *Time* correspondent, Thompson locates Kim Il Sung's command post, a room full of heavy furniture. They take turns sitting on the leather chair that had cushioned Kim's ample arse just hours before. A cabinet is stocked with typewriters, including an Underwood Korean, the markings still so Martian to his eyes. Thompson dusts off an English model and considers conquered Pyongyang.

"The Korean War was won," he writes. It has the ring of finality, the pulse of a lie.

62. The Most Christian City in Asia

Months earlier, in their home base of Pyongyang, the Communists hunted down any remaining Christian leaders. Fourteen Korean ministers went missing.

Now the South Koreans are here. Captain Lee investigates. A captured enemy soldier says he knows that a dozen of them were shot, put down like the dogs that they were. A thirteenth, Han, has gone crazy. What happened to the fourteenth minister?

The captain used to teach college in Seoul, lecturing on the history of civilization. Moving through the shattered Pyongyang streets, he recalls its reputation as the most Christian city in all of Asia. Though his reading tells him otherwise, there is no way it can rise again.

The mind sharpens as time passes. The great thinkers of the East and West have left their mark on him. He believes he can tell right from wrong, truth from propaganda. Captain Lee tracks down witnesses. He interviews them, filling notebooks to show his superiors. Every morning he writes inside the class-

room of an abandoned elementary school, miraculously preserved amid the destruction.

Finally, he locates the last minister, who says that he and
Han were spared by God. Later, however, his followers accuse
him of betraying the other ministers to the Communists, in
exchange for his life. In times like these, what divides right from
wrong?

For Captain Lee, the history of civilization ends now. He finishes writing his unsettling episode and leaves the room. The
notebooks are there to be discovered or forgotten.

63. The Red Window Shade

In late October 1950, just as the Americans and South Koreans
are close to winning the entire peninsula, rolling up the Red
Window Shade that had tumbled down in June, Mao Tse-tung's
troops intervene to save their North Korean comrades. The U.N.
is outraged, but China insists that the soldiers are all volunteers, not *official* troops. The ranks of the so-called People's
Volunteer Army swell. They yank the Red Window Shade down
again as the temperature falls below zero. The Americans cele-
brate Thanksgiving with stuffed turkeys, which freeze seconds
after being uncovered. The next day, MacArthur repeats his
boast that the war will be wrapped up by Christmas. A week
later, thirty thousand U.N. troops, mostly American army and
marines, are attacked by a Chinese force four times their size.
The horde had lain in wait by a reservoir two hundred miles
northeast of Pyongyang. Reinforcements make their way in.
After ten savage days of white phosphorus mortar rounds and
frostbite, the shredded U.N. forces escape to Hungnam and
take ships back to the safety of the South.

If the Inchon landing was a turning point, here is another. It
becomes known in the United States as the Battle of Chosin
Reservoir, a name taken from Japanese maps. The war will
go on.

64. MiG Alley

Parker Jotter of Buffalo, New York, flies most of his missions in one corner of North Korea, hard by the border with China— a zone called MiG Alley. Here the American Sabres tangle with their Soviet counterparts, in shrieking ballets that are over in minutes. Just as the Chinese aren't *officially* an army, the Russians aren't *officially* fighting in this war. The MiGs just wound up there. Some of the American pilots get spooked: they swear they've spotted Caucasians in enemy cockpits, not Chinese, not Koreans. Over beers, Horowitz of the 335th says he's seen blond hair, blue eyes, even a redhead. Parker jokes, asks if he can have her number, something he wouldn't dare say in the States. Horowitz buys him a Blatz.

Parker can't remember what "MiG" stands for. Deep inside a dogfight, the Sabre carving out lanes in the dead white sky, the answer will come to him. It evaporates as soon as he lands.

65. The Spam Can

Parker Jotter did his first runs not in a state-of-the-art Sabre but in a creaky old P-51, a model dubbed the Spam Can. At times the crews used actual Spam cans to patch up bullet holes. In the mess hall they went through enormous quantities of the foodstuff, and the men rinsed the tins for reuse.

Sometimes on a bombing run, Parker Jotter could hear the individual patches of flattened-out Spam tins flapping in the air, then peeling off. It seemed like his plane had been repaired so many times that barely a square foot of the original aircraft remained.

Every few mornings, one of Jotter's fellow airmen turns into Spam, outgunned in the fog over MiG Alley.

66. The Painting

January 1951, Paris. Pablo Picasso puts the final stroke to a punishingly bleak canvas. On the left stands a group of naked

women and children, about to be obliterated by the men on the right. Both the victims and the killers look timeless, a glimpse of the medieval future. The colors are subtle, exhausted. The women's faces are twisted in agony. The men wear scraps of armor and aim strange firearms, barrels branching into three. The only one without a helmet holds a sword aloft. He looks like a chessboard king. The title is *Massacre en Corée*.

67. The Few

February 1951, Paris. "I believe in the virtue of small nations," the writer André Gide says. "I believe in the virtue of small numbers. The world will be saved by the few." He dies a week later.

68. The Neck

Douglas MacArthur requests twenty-six atomic bombs, one for every letter of the alphabet. He contemplates a new language of pain. The plan would be to bomb Manchuria so savagely that neither the Soviets nor the Chinese could send in troops to help North Korea. He would leave a moat of radiation, a poison necklace strung "across the neck of Manchuria." The request is denied.

"My plan was a cinch," he later grumbles.

Douglas MacArthur hates President Truman even more than he hated FDR during World War II. Truman fires him in April 1951.

69. Wings

During his seven months commanding U.S. forces, the general never spent a single night in Korea. He always flew back to Tokyo.

Douglas MacArthur thinks he has special insight into the Asiatic way of fighting. He says the Oriental when he dies folds his arms as a dove does its wings.

Douglas MacArthur is a member of the Korean Provisional Government.

70. The Cover

Heading north, Tommy Thompson sees a woman's corpse by the roadside. Her baby clings, still trying to suckle. Already he wants to forget this. So why does he take his camera out?

Cry Korea is published in England in 1951. The epigraph comes from André Gide, his favorite author. The cover drawing shows the dead mother and the hopeless child, a reverse pietà, crude in black, white, and crimson. The unwary reader needs a moment to untangle those lines, see what Thompson saw.

The Korean War still has two more years to go, or else it is still going on.

71. The Village of Hwajiri

In April 1951, in the Iron Triangle in the heart of the peninsula, Hank Woods, private first class, goes to warn the villagers of Hwajiri to take cover. His company is about to shell mountains in the area, aiming to knock out an anti-aircraft installation. The villagers have no English. He offers gum and crackers to the children, gets annoyed when they shake their heads. A boy presses something into his hand, a worn coin with a hole in the center. A silver-haired crone gives him a small wooden charm with tiny writing on the sides.

Suddenly the villagers gasp, staring at something behind him. Private Woods strains to understand. *Mountain.* They scatter into the night. A ball of light is hurtling down the slope, advancing on Hwajiri.

Thirty yards behind him, Lieutenant Zeff Zephyr grants permission to shoot. Private Woods unloads his M1 as the fireball heads his way. The bullets ping on impact, no louder than rain on tin. He fires again, but this time the bullets fly as quietly as birds. Spokes of light comb the area, sending tree shadows

clawing across the scrub. All the villagers have disappeared. The light washes over him. Time stops. He sees his body crumple, hears his rifle fall to the ground.

Zeff orders the men to the bunker. Private Woods thinks, *What bunker?* His friend Burton yells, *Look alive, Woodsy.* Finally, he staggers to safety, a tunnel deep in the woods. For the next week, Hank Woods has blinding headaches and can't keep anything down. His weight plummets and he can't see straight. Others also suffer mysterious forms of distress, but none so acute. When Hank tries to reconstruct the night with Zeff and Burton, they look at him like he's nuts. At last, a MASH unit cuts a path through the brush in order to treat them. It's touch-and-go for Private Woods. One medic prematurely files a death report that they'll later have to hunt down and reverse, weeks after his mother has received the news.

72. Trophies

No one but Hank Woods recalls the incident in detail. They remember coming to Hwajiri, ready to shell the shit out of the mountain, where the enemy has set up camp. But they have no memory of a fireball racing at them, or Hank shooting, or spokes of light. The more he tries to convince them, the less sure he is of anything. One nurse believes him, says to tell her everything. Lieutenant Zephyr arranges an honorable discharge.

I'm a nobody now, Hank writes to an old girlfriend. *A zero, a nothing.* She doesn't reply. He moves to Bethlehem, Pennsylvania, where an uncle sets him up in the steelworks while he gets his head together. People want to hear what he did in the Far East: the valor and camaraderie, the tough winters and salty talk, a debate on Yokohama versus Pusan whores. He must have trophies to show them: a dagger or flag, a pouch made of a shriveled ear. But all he has is a dumb old coin with a square

hole in the center. All he has is a head with a hole where some thoughts used to be.

In Bethlehem he feels trapped. Five months later, a buddy from the service lines up a job for him on a tobacco farm in North Carolina. He heads south, keeps to himself. He gets a long letter from a name he doesn't recognize: Kim Tollson. Turns out she was a nurse from the MASH unit, the only one who believed him when he told her what he'd seen. She's back home in Minnesota. It's hard to remember what she looks like—just the dark hair in a bun. A year into the correspondence, Hank asks her to marry him and she says yes. He sends her a Greyhound ticket. He reads paperbacks deep into the humid night, waiting.

73. Catalog

One of them is a novel from 1952, set in a company town where life has become mechanized. It takes place sometime after World War III. The book, which will later be retitled *Utopia 14*, is by a public relations man at General Electric, a business not far removed from the one in the book.

In the end, the clockwork society is overturned. The sky above the dead city is soft and dark as the inside of a jewel box. The author, Kurt Vonnegut Jr., lets loose with a long, omnivorous list. He itemizes, from *A* to *Z*, the wreckage of air conditioners, amplifiers, and arc welders—so on, down to zymometers. It's a cutting-edge catalog of American technological plenty, which suggests that even the best machines can't halt mankind's slide into folly.

74. Buffalo Destroyed

Like thousands of other Buffalonians on the evening of September 27, 1952, Mrs. Flora Jotter (née Edwards) is shocked by the newspaper's front page.

The floor of the house on Vulcan Street collapses under her. Before thinking of her neighbors or her coworkers at the paper, her mind flies halfway around the world. Her husband, Parker, on his second tour in Korea—what will he do when he hears the news?

Even in her panic, certain things don't add up. Flora is a reporter for the *Criterion* who deals with facts. How did the North Koreans get the bomb, then fly it over the ocean, across the country, all the way to Buffalo? Why *here*, of all places?

She reads the headline again and pours a drink. Must be the work of the Chinese. Or the Russians. Or a fifth column of Communists inside the United States. They walk among us, blending in. One of them slipped onto an airfield, stole a bomber, then picked a city at random.

She reads on: *The Marine Trust Company building is an empty, twisted shell. Police Headquarters is a mass of rubble. The steeple of St. Joseph's Old Cathedral, like a pointed spear, rests squarely on what remains of the police nerve center.*

Flora Jotter is at the bottom of her second drink when it dawns on her that it's all a giant gag or a crazy thought experiment. The editor's explanation seems itself a fiction.

> ## How This Edition Was Published
>
> Buffalo Evening News employes reported for work this morning as usual—a few hours later all were killed or wounded.
>
> The News building is a casualty.
>
> A good percentage of The News employes, on a five-day week, were off today. Many were in their homes beyond the bombed-out area.
>
> These employes—by a pre-arranged plan—quickly assembled in a Kensington area printing plant. This edition is the result.
>
> Had the bombing occurred near Kensington, this edition would have been printed in one of several other plants ready for just such an emergency edition.
>
> The News will continue to publish a daily emergency edition until arrangements can be made to resume regular publication.

Parker wouldn't stand for this, even if some General Hubcap *did* authorize it. She's amazed there isn't rioting in the streets. Mayor Mruk should be run out of office for allowing such trash. His name looks unreal. A demon's name. *I shouldn't drink at all.*

In the topsy-turvy account, the *Buffalo Evening News* building itself gets destroyed, requiring that the paper be put together at a makeshift location. Or . . . *did* it happen? The explanation somehow makes things worse. If Flora peeled back the curtains, there would be nothing outside but orange light, ash falling like December snow.

75. War of the Worlds

It really *is* all just another fiction of 1952.

Months earlier, Lieutenant General Clarence Huebner rings up Ed Butler, editor of the *Buffalo Evening News*, with an unusual proposal. Would the paper consider putting out an entire issue reporting that the Soviets had dropped an A-bomb on the city?

Edward H. Butler's father, also Edward, founded the paper. Ed Junior jokes that he was destined to be an editor, given his name. More than once he's heard reporters bicker with the rewrite men: "I'm not changing a goddamn word—*Ed edited it!*"

On the horn with Huebner, Ed says, "Like a *War of the Worlds* deal? Put one over on the public? It's a goddamn dreadful idea."

"You misunderstand," replies the general. He is a decorated officer of two World Wars. "This is in the name of public service, not sensationalism. Korea is on your reader's mind. What happens if things go too far? We want the public to be psychologically ready. And let's just say Uncle Sam will make it worth your while."

"Who says I'm against sensationalism?" Ed quips, already sketching the layout.

Ed envisions the headlines, the controversy, the letters to the Ed-itor, pro and con. He assembles a team of his most colorful writers. The stories will be vivid, shocking, informative. Oh, and somehow patriotic. People will think about what their military shields them from. They will imagine the ruins of the city, and what foul measures even their closest neighbors might take to survive.

76. Pyongyang Destroyed

On the same day Huebner and Butler speak—a month before that piece of Buffalonian fiction appears—American planes level much of Pyongyang, once the most Christian city in the Far East. In one day, eighty thousand buildings become ruins, as mute as dolmens. War is a form of time travel.

77. Double Ace

On December 1, Parker Jotter takes off a hundred miles from the Yalu River. He's with the 51st Fighter-Interceptor Wing now, bound for MiG Alley. His Sabre has six .50-caliber guns, two bomb racks. A red star on his fuselage marks his ace status. He has nine kills now. Another wins him a second star.

No MiGs mar the welkin. After an hour he peels off to hunt

for ground targets. The usual routes are clear, but he spots a North Korean convoy on a secret path, hidden by trees. It's hauling reinforcements bound for the South. He takes the Sabre down to ten thousand feet and prepares to destroy the cargo.

Just then, he senses a shift in the atmosphere. The sky isn't empty. Radar tracks a massive shape three miles away. No way is this a MiG. Jotter takes the Sabre back up and heads toward the unknown. Cutting above the clouds, he's stunned to see a pale disk so big that for a second he thinks he's above a frozen lake, flying at impossible speed. He pushes the Sabre, tries to keep up. The disk seems to taper to a point in the center. Is it Russian, Chinese? Can't be. Is it *human*? The thing zigzags, then goes vertical and rolls like a wheel across the sky. The radar goes blank. Then the cockpit fills with light. He loses control of the Sabre. There is trouble with the right wing. What he sees does not make sense, until he grasps: *There is no right wing.*

78. The Cover-up

A day after Christmas, Flora Jotter receives a phone call from Washington. A man confirms that her husband's jet crashed deep behind North Korean lines, three to four weeks ago. All he can tell her is that Parker is alive, held in a POW camp on the border with China, condition unknown.

Flora visits her church on Michigan Avenue and tells the pastor her news. He explains how Syngman Rhee, over in Korea, is a man of God, that the right side will prevail. She must pray.

Dissatisfied with the Baptists, Flora searches for messages from a higher power. She turns on the radio, listens to what the Catholics and Mormons and Seventh-Day Adventists have to say. Sometimes that winter, she stands outside the office of the *Buffalo Evening News*, holding up her tattered copy of the paper's A-bomb special. She scans the faces of the workers, looking for the editor, Butler, to ask him what it *means*.

At her own workplace, the *Criterion*, Flora is fretful and tired. Her pieces come in long or don't come in at all. She wants to write about what happened: the destruction of Buffalo and its cover-up. *What cover-up?* her editor asks. The *Criterion* finally fires her. She still receives her husband's military pay, but for months she superstitiously avoids depositing the checks.

79. The New Korea

Parker Jotter spends days near death, his parachute snarled in a tree. Days later, a farmer finds the strange cocoon. A North Korean patrol takes Jotter to a camp near the blasted city of Sinuiju. His captors tend to his injuries. As the only Black POW, he stands out. They tell him to write down his life story. They also want to know how Parker can stomach going back to the United States, where his whole race is mistreated. They promise that when the war ends, the New Korea will begin. A country where he'll be truly among equals. Where he can live a life of dignity.

80. Chicken

In 1953, while the Korean War stalls, an easygoing American surgeon from Maine is gripped with terror. Benjamin Franklin Pierce has joked his way through grim surroundings the best he could the past few years, but something gnaws at him. He doesn't grasp it at first. In the hospital he has a pesky unpleasant memory: He's in a truck with Korean civilians, hiding from enemy soldiers. Like an idiot, one farm woman has brought her chicken, which proceeds to cluck. *Can't you keep her quiet?* If the Communists hear, it's all over. Weeping silently, she snaps its neck.

Crying over a chicken, Pierce marvels.

81. Zenith

July 1953. The fighting ends. In Buffalo, Flora Jotter waits—for a letter, any sign that her husband is alive. Her father-in-law delivers a secondhand Zenith, sturdy as a bank vault. *Stay*

strong, he says. *Parker will be home before you know it.* On the news one night, they show a prisoner exchange in Korea. Is Parker there? The faces are all Oriental or white. The South Korean soldiers, grateful to be heading home at last, hold up banners in broken English. The anchorman says the messages were written in their own blood, proof of their faith in America.

She watches game shows sponsored by cigarette companies, florid dramas supported by toothpaste makers. She smokes, forgets to eat. The shows put on a new drama each week, with a fresh cast.

Does the city of Buffalo exist, after the A-bomb? Only what's inside the box feels real.

The kitchen sink grows dishes. The dishes grow flies. Flora drinks. Her father-in-law brings over a new vacuum cleaner. *You just wait,* he says. *Don't you give up hope.*

She finally receives a letter from Parker, postmarked Tokyo. He was released to the American authorities at Panmunjom, the main town at the border between North and South, and is now at a military hospital in Tokyo, undergoing tests. They're treating him well. It might take a while, but everything will be fine.

82. The Fifty-Year Book

On August 25, 1953, still alone, Flora tunes into a show called *Danger.* An old man sits in a room full of paper. For decades, he's been compiling a book that is more than a book. Every day he combs newspapers for pieces that fit his thesis, which has become so vast that it resembles a theory of the world. He hunts for scientific anomalies, accounts of disasters, human-interest stories with an ironic angle or bizarre detail. His job is to find the links between them, creating what he calls *a calendar history of America for the past fifty years.*

Flora blinks. She swears she sees a headline from the *Criterion,* her ex-employer. Could it be from a story *she* wrote? Maybe the profile she penned of Parker, before they married. It

never ran, now that she thinks of it. But maybe here, in television land, it did? It's a comfort to imagine that her words exist in the world behind the screen.

83. Danger

The old man on TV keeps body and soul together by working as the superintendent of the apartment building where he lives. (The landlord, his old friend Leo, lets him stay at a reduced rate.) For a few hours every day, he fixes leaks, hauls out the trash. But mostly what he does is labor on his book. The tenants who know about it save their papers for him. Word gets around.

In a dizzying development, a reporter has recently written about his project. Should he then incorporate that article *into* the project? Is he part of the project, inside its walls, or merely its god, its architect?

84. Isolation

A man comes on to tell Flora to brush her teeth with Amm-i-dent. Honestly, she hasn't brushed since the tube ran out last week. Hasn't left her house in days.

85. J.B. Keeps the Faith

Flora sits so close to the TV that her skin glows with the light.

On the show, the landlord's nephew, J.B., helps the old man keep the building in order. J.B.'s a punk, all denim and greased-back hair, but he pays attention when the old man describes the joys and terrors of working on the book. This twenty-year-old misfit knows more about the book than anyone else in the world. J.B.'s a good kid, and his encouragement saves the writer from despair, on those days when it all seems pointless. J.B. is like the son the old man never had.

"You know, J.B.," the old man says. "Maybe all those rejections I've had from publishers, maybe they're right! One said

this was too impersonal, just a collection of headlines." He considers his life work. "I wonder."

86. The Tenant

A pretty, sophisticated blonde named Netta rents a room in the building, and J.B. is smitten. He makes himself useful, helps her move in. Netta tells him bluntly that his uncle, Leo, promised her that she could take the bigger unit once he "got rid of" the old man. J.B. would become the new super, while Netta would take over the space where the old man now spends his days, writing the book that no one will read.

J.B. asks where his old friend would live—on the street? The question bugs him, but not enough for him to stop helping her unpack. In one box is a photo of Netta that was used for the cover of a mystery magazine. A man's poised to strangle her.

Flora's skin crawls.

J.B.'s licking his lips. Turns out Netta's a model. She puts on a record and sways to the quivering strains like a fertility goddess. J.B.'s drawn like a moth to a flame. Before he can put his mouth to hers, though, Netta backs away. Says her boyfriend is waiting for her.

Even Flora feels bad for J.B., there on the other side of the screen.

87. Inside the Book

Boyfriend? In a rage, the punk diverts the gas line to siphon a deadly dose into her room. He tells himself he's doing it for the old man, the only person who cares about him. Netta survives, though, and when the cops come, J.B. tries to frame the old man.

Flora clucks at his gall. Once a punk, always a punk.

The cops don't buy his story. Netta's boyfriend proposes,

and she moves out to live with him. The old man gets to stay in his place, where every day he adds to his book.

He pastes in the story of J.B.'s arrest, traps him like a bug in amber.

88. Slumming It

Two weeks later, Flora is turning the dial when she glimpses an elegant woman with a dazzling smile. It's a different show, but she sees right away it's Netta again—rather, the same imposing blond actress from *Danger*. This time, she's at a lunch counter, making small talk with the ma-and-pa owners, who just want her to split. She's slumming it, caught up in the novelty of her lark. The *quaintness* of the place. She orders a ham sandwich.

Mid-meal, the woman puts her sandwich down and uses the phone. There's a fancy dinner party she wants to back out of. While she's in the booth, a man barges into the store, empties the till, and, as an afterthought, shoots the counterman dead. The police bring in the young society lady as a witness. The police like a certain slick dude for the crime, but she takes a look and swears it wasn't him. She's never seen him before. She tries to clear his name.

Funny, though: the suspect looks familiar to Flora, the all-seeing viewer of a dozen different TV shows, sitting in her front room on Vulcan Street. Why, Flora thinks, it's that murderous punk J.B., from just last week—rather, the actor who played J.B.! The ungrateful kid oozes contempt while the fancy young woman tries to save his hide. She towers over him. They never touch, but the air is electric.

89. Channels

Flora keeps watching similar drama shows with mounting unease, afraid that the same two actors will appear together again and again, in different roles.

90. Homecoming

Parker Jotter returns to Buffalo at last. He talks about flying, but not about his time in the camp. He must erase the war from his mind. There's a life to attend to. A life with Flora.

Alas, she seems unmoved, even suspicious. While recuperating in Tokyo, he was told that this could happen—wives not recognizing their husbands. They hadn't known each other long before they'd eloped; then again, he'd met a few guys in the same boat, who had gotten hitched right before leaving to fight, and they didn't seem to face this sort of crisis.

To shake up the mood, they move house, from Vulcan to Locust to Laurel. Amid the relocations, Flora loses the issue of the *Buffalo Evening News* she's been holding on to, the one in which an A-bomb reduced the city to a wasteland. She becomes agitated. Reality is so delicate, it's sometimes not even there. Her husband asks what's wrong. She's in a panic until at last she finds the copy, folded up in a dictionary.

Third of City Demolished . . . Flora wonders: What if the bomb had wiped out the city? What if *this* is the afterlife—where Parker is as well?

91. A Glass of Darkness

In 1953, a man named Barton returns to his hometown of Millgate, Virginia, only to discover that everything has changed—street names, houses, inhabitants. He digs up an old issue of the local paper and comes across an article reporting his death—as a nine-year-old boy. But that can't be—he's still alive! It dawns on him that the current residents operate under a mass delusion. He tries to lift the veil. Millgate becomes the unlikely site of a showdown between good and evil, as forces large and small (gods, insects) engage in an apocalyptic battle.

This is the premise of *A Glass of Darkness*, the first alternate-reality novel written by the author Philip Kindred Dick. Though

Barton isn't specifically identified as a military veteran, his homecoming mirrors that of a shell-shocked soldier.

By age twenty-five Phil has already sold loads of topsy-turvy science-fiction stories, but what he really wants is to publish a big *regular*-reality novel. He's written a few already, but no one will take a chance on them. This year, he finishes a working-class opus, *Voices from the Street*. Its protagonist is a TV repairman, like Parker's father. Its nightmares are proletarian, not futuristic.

Phil lives in Berkeley with his wife, Kleo. He is always writing. She works a string of part-time jobs, but sometimes they still need to buy horsemeat for thirty-five cents a pound at the pet store on San Pablo. Buoyed by pills, he churns out stories and novelettes for the pulps. In his hands, the real world turns out to be a simulacrum, or a hallucination, or a shimmering entertainment meant for someone else. In story after story he lays out the true, secret nature of American society—drab on the outside, garbled and haunted within.

92. Fate

A quarter century passes in what feels like a week. Down in North Carolina, Hank Woods is haunted by his time fighting in the Iron Triangle, and that harrowing night in Hwajiri with the ghostly fireball. (The woman he was writing to, Kim Tollson, never used that Greyhound ticket to come and visit, never wrote to him again.) For a long time after the war, he searches for anyone who might have an answer to what he saw. His paperback library contains a healthy dose of science fiction. His dreams throb with clues, but when he wakes up, he cannot remember them. He subscribes to *Fate, Fortean Times*, any periodical that takes seriously the possibility of UFOs, interstellar voyagers. Through their classifieds, he corresponds with other veterans who have witnessed similar things. Only one reports seeing anything in Korea: Parker Jotter, a former air force pilot now living in Buffalo.

In the winter of 1977, after reading Hank's account of the

fast-moving ball of light, Jotter writes to him. "What about the villagers?" he asks. "Did you ever think that *they* might have summoned *it*?"

Hank Woods appreciates the frankness. Why does Parker Jotter's name ring a bell? Of course: years earlier, he'd read Jotter's science-fiction series *2333*. Great stuff. Jotter doesn't respond when Hank asks why he isn't still writing books. Hank understands the silence; he has things he wants to keep private, too.

93. Death of an Exile

Younghill Kang escapes to America in 1921. Three years later, the United States bars entry to virtually all immigrants from Asia. A lover of English poetry, Kang gets his real American education while working a series of odd jobs in the Northeast and parts of Canada. He marries Frances Keely, a Wellesley-educated southerner, who temporarily loses her citizenship for marrying an Oriental. They live at 111 East Tenth Street in Manhattan. He writes entries for the *Encyclopaedia Britannica* and teaches at New York University. There he befriends another instructor, the novelist Thomas Wolfe. Wolfe is practically twice his size. He introduces Kang to his editor at Scribner's, Max Perkins, who has worked with Fitzgerald and Hemingway.

Scribner's publishes *The Grass Roof* in 1931. Kang's novel begins with bucolic scenes of village life and ends with its young hero, Chungpa Han, witnessing the March 1 Movement of 1919, landing in jail, and later escaping to America. Wolfe praises the book, as do Rebecca West and her lover, H. G. Wells, who learned about Korea's plight years ago from a young Syngman Rhee. Kang starts a second novel, *Death of an Exile*, a continuation of Chungpa's story. It appears in 1937 as *East Goes West*, the year both the mad poet Yi Sang and the filmmaker Na Ungyu die of TB. Thomas Wolfe dies the following year. Kang never publishes another novel.

Younghill Kang and Thomas Wolfe and Maxwell Perkins are members of the Korean Provisional Government.

94. Success

In 1954, writing from the safety of America after the armistice is declared, the fifty-one-year-old Younghill Kang is bitter about the war just waged. He is grateful that his adopted homeland stepped in four years ago, just as the Reds threatened to take over the whole peninsula. He despises the Communist North. Yet how can he be happy? Things are broken again, wrecked beyond repair. The country that stayed intact even as a colony has now been permanently snapped in two.

The novelist pities his former countrymen. They cannot grasp the true meaning of the conflict they have endured, the lofty ideals that were in play. "The typical Korean is a hunted uneducated farmer," he writes. "One thing makes him go mad, that 38th parallel, separating parent from child, husband from wife. Whichever force won this war from without shall lose it politically. The operation was a success, but the patient died— it's that kind of success."

95. Diagnosis

To quote the KPG poet Yi Sang:

```
·  0  ℓ  8  ⌐  ə  ⸝  ⊦  ɛ  ⊂  I
0  ·  ℓ  8  ⌐  ə  ⸝  ⊦  ɛ  ⊂  I
0  ℓ  ·  8  ⌐  ə  ⸝  ⊦  ɛ  ⊂  I
0  ℓ  8  ·  ⌐  ə  ⸝  ⊦  ɛ  ⊂  I
0  ℓ  8  ⌐  ·  ə  ⸝  ⊦  ɛ  ⊂  I
0  ℓ  8  ⌐  ə  ·  ⸝  ⊦  ɛ  ⊂  I
0  ℓ  8  ⌐  ə  ⸝  ·  ⊦  ɛ  ⊂  I
0  ℓ  8  ⌐  ə  ⸝  ⊦  ·  ɛ  ⊂  I
0  ℓ  8  ⌐  ə  ⸝  ⊦  ɛ  ·  ⊂  I
0  ℓ  8  ⌐  ə  ⸝  ⊦  ɛ  ⊂  ·  I
0  ℓ  8  ⌐  ə  ⸝  ⊦  ɛ  ⊂  I  ·
```

96. Hull

Parker Jotter is the first Black member of the Korean Provisional Government.

After Parker's death in 1993, it's Hank Woods, his most faithful correspondent, who continues the vast work, building upon *Wildwording*. In 2000, he writes that the trail of black dots in Yi Sang's 1934 poem predicts both North Korea's incursion across the 38th parallel (June 25, 1950) *and* the diagonal path of Brett Hull's shot (June 20, 1999), moving from the top left of the crease to the right portion of the net.

Hank believes that he has uncovered important connections between events, across decades, but he has difficulty persuading others to see it that way—or to see it at all. He prepares a videotape showing the fateful goal from overhead, the same thirty seconds looped. He copies out relevant passages from *Wildwording*, sends them to the media. He poses a question: "Can it truly be a coincidence that the brothers who started the Buffalo Sabres hockey franchise, Seymour and Northrup Knox, had the initials S.K. and N.K., as in South and North Korea?"

Hank Woods dies in 2001, convinced until the end that the whole story has not been told.

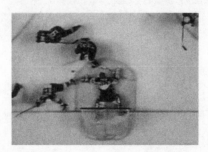

97. Goal

So ends Dream Four of the Korean Provisional Government.

2333: Interview with a Mirror (2001–1983)

From: INTERN (gloatintern@igloat.com)
To: Tanner Slow (slomo@igloat.com)
CC: PECAN <Penumbra College Alumni Network>(numb-alums@
penumbra.edu)
Date: Monday, September 10, 2001, at 11:33 p.m.
Re: Corewar (CWG) archival project   Importance: Low
Attachment: IWAM.doc (56KB)   Viruses: None

Dear Mr. Slow,

Hi! It's Loa Ding, GLOAT intern for summer 2001. I'm writing from Vermont, where the fall term has started and the
leaves are already turning color. (Since I'm from Hawai'i,
the idea of "seasons" makes my head spin.) Attached is my
transcript of a VHS tape found in the Corewar Games ("CWG")
archive. I'm submitting it in fulfillment of my tech intern-
ship through PECAN (cc'd above).

As you know, this spring, GLOAT absorbed Harmony Holdings,
comprising CWG and 18 other companies. My teenage supervisor, Mercy Pang, was focused on a deal with Nobody Doubts
the Sprout (the health-food chain), and asked me to go
through the 33 CWG boxes and flag anything "juicy." But in
the days that followed, whenever I mentioned the project
to Mercy, she gave me a blank look. Maybe she mistook Corewar Games for another acquisition? Or maybe that's what you
get for hiring a high-schooler to run things. (Just kidding! I know Mercy's a genius who started Sockster out of
her dad's closet or whatever.) After she got transferred
in July, she ignored me altogether.

Anyway, I went down a CWG "rabbit hole." I learned that eight years ago, Corewar snapped up "interactive" rights to some old science-fiction books, which they turned into "environments" for their line of computer games. (None were "hits" in their day, but that doesn't mean GLOAT can't remake them!) The boxes belonged to Parker Jotter, author of the forgotten "2333" book series. I went to the New York Public Library, but the only trace I found was a mention in the "Science-Fiction Cyclopedia" (1977). It said that Mr. Jotter stopped after five titles, one short of the promised sextet. I figured if a "lost" book existed, it would be in one of the boxes stacked by my desk. I had a goal, at last!

Sadly, I didn't spot anything in those 33 boxes that resembled a sixth "2333" novel. I saw (and smelled!) old magazines and user's manuals (he used to own an appliance store), a whole box of pictures cut from newspapers, hundreds of pages of typewritten notes, which were hard to understand. I'd attack the notes first thing in the morning, armed with coffee from the breakfast cart, but it was no use. He was speaking his own private language. I wondered how any of it could be valuable to GLOAT.

Five boxes in, I noticed the pages were all stamped "S/U." According to Malcolm in IT, that meant the document had already been entered into the GLOAT system. ("S/U" means "scanned and uploaded.") There was nothing much for me to do. I marked the lids with a "D" and put the boxes by the back door to be destroyed.

All right—let me cut to the chase!

I did remove one item that couldn't be scanned: a videotape at the bottom of Box 11. The label read "HARMONY," in faint blue ink. There wasn't a VCR at work, so I took it home. The first minute was a noisy blur. Right before I hit Eject, a voice said: "July 1983."

We see a man in an office, wearing a doctor's coat. Asian. Cheerful, a little tired. A diploma hangs on the wall. The only legible line is his name: Inky Sin, M.D. What follows are eight brief sessions between the doctor and an unseen interviewer—a woman, Korean, identity unknown.

I don't know what the tape was doing amid Mr. Jotter's papers, though a "Dr. Sin" pops up in his notes. He was the psychiatrist who had treated him after a serious 1980 knife attack, then on and off until his own tragic death in 1983. (My roommate, Daisy Oh, works in the Penumbra library, with access to LEXIS-NEXIS.)

Dr. Sin speaks to the interviewer mainly in English, sprinkled with Korean. (Daisy helped me here, too!) The "project" she refers to has not appeared, nor could I find any evidence that it ever existed. Was she there under false pretenses—some kind of con job? Anything's possible!

I typed out the whole exchange, in case it's useful to GLOAT. (I'm a completist!) If you have any thoughts on what it means, I'd love to hear them. Getting to know the "nuts and bolts" at GLOAT has helped focus my career goals. I'm back at Penumbra now, but I come to the city frequently and would love to grab that coffee you mentioned back in June.

Mahalo!

Loa Ding
Intern (Penumbra College '03)

SESSION #1 (TUESDAY)

Q: Good morning. Thank you for meeting me. My assistant is here to make sure the light and volume are right. He won't interrupt. [*Laughter.*]

A: My pleasure. [*Pause.*] Tell me again—why are you two in Buffalo?

Q: It's part of a project. I'm helping out a friend who's compiling the stories of Koreans who have made a name for themselves in America.

A: I'm very honored. But you must have plenty of those in New York. Why come here?

Q: **We want to get a sense of the whole country.**

A: How long have *you* lived in the U.S.?

Q: **Quite a while.**

A: I can tell. Since the sixties?

Q: **Earlier.**

A: [*Pause.*] What's your name again?

Q: **Maybe you should join the project, as an interviewer, eh? [*Laughs.*] Let's begin. Edward, ready? [*Mumbled "yes" from her assistant.*] Edward's still groggy from his night at the track.**

A: Horses?

Q: **Yes.**

A: Must be Batavia Downs.

Q: **That's the one! [*Mumbled "never again" from her assistant.*] We should begin in earnest. [*Clears throat.*] We are here with Dr. Inky Sin, of Buffalo, New York. Can you tell us where in Korea you are from?**

A: I was born in 1936, in a hamlet of no special distinction, save for its location at the exact center of the country. You can't visit now, alas. It's right in the heart of the DMZ.* You'd be blown to pieces before you got within a mile.

Q: **What stands out from your childhood?**

A: When I was two, my mother fell ill and "went back," as they say in Korean.† My father left town, looking for work. This was before Korea split into North and South.‡ He might well have gone north, to seek his

---

* Demilitarized Zone, referring to the strip of land, about two miles wide and 160 miles long, separating North and South Korea.—Loa

† Passed away, died.—Loa

‡ In 1948.—Loa

fortune in Pyongyang. But winter was approaching. He would joke that Seoul was the *slightly* warmer choice. Ironically, my father was hired by a company that did public works projects up in Manchuria. Talk about cold!

Q: A Japanese company?

A: I don't know. The name wasn't Japanese. [*Pause.*] But I suppose it could have been.

Q: Did his family look after you?

A: His parents had died young. He had just one sister, who no one talked about. She was much older, and had left the area before I was born—I never met her. Took up with a traveling theater troupe. An actress! At least that's the story I heard.

Q: You were all alone, then. In the hamlet.

A: Nothing could be further from the truth! I was raised by my mother's side: uncles and aunts, a flock of cousins, and especially my grandmother. With other kids, I walked along the stream, catching frogs to race. I found smooth old buttons and faceless coins on the creek bed. It was the twenty-eighth year of the Japanese occupation.* Already a generation had grown up that only knew maps on which Korea was "Chosen," part of Japan.

Q: [*Pause.*] Go on.

A: My mother's absence didn't sink in for a while. My grandmother later told me what she was like—tall, funny, a great mimic—and where my father currently was: Manchuria, which was now *also* part of Japan.†
I had a single picture of the three of us: my parents sitting before a backdrop painted like a palace courtyard, while I fidgeted on my mother's lap, peering at the strange contraption before me. A flaw in the process wrapped a white mist about their necks. As a boy, I studied the features

---

* Korea became a Japanese colony in 1910.—Loa
† The northeastern portion of China, bordering the top of Korea.—Loa

of these adults I didn't know, thinking: *Two of the three people here are gone.* Thinking: *I am the only one left.*

My mother began appearing in my dreams, an eerie if calming presence. I asked my grandmother if this was a sign that she needed help, or was angry, or something else. She said dreams were never signs, unless the dreamer wished them to be.

Q: [*Long pause.*] And did you?

A: Yes, I suppose.

Q: Tell me about your education.

A: I thought this was supposed to be about my experiences in America.

Q: We will get there! [*Warm laugh.*] We need to understand your life "before."

A: [*Pause.*] The schoolhouse was on the edge of town. Through its single window, I watched oxen in the fields, tails swaying to bat away the flies. Every morning, we had to bow to the east—to the sun, to Japan. Like my classmates, I received a new name. I can't remember what year this was. Some of my friends had elaborate ones, but mine was the plainest, most common: Taro Tsujimoto.

Q: Like "John Smith."

A: The name of a nobody. I was ashamed! Still, I learned how to write it, learned not to flinch when the schoolmaster addressed me as "Taro." At home, I studied my native tongue. My eldest cousin, Hyun—now renamed "Shoking" Tsujimoto—guided my progress. Our lessons were kept secret, naturally. I wrote my name in Korean on a flat stone by the door. I dipped my brush in the puddle and tried to cover the face of the rock, but the first forbidden syllable was always gone by the time the last one was done.

When I was five, Shoking—I mean, Hyun—was drafted into the Japanese army. He had no choice. The day before he left, he told me: *Your mother didn't die of sickness.*

I was confused. I said, *Do you mean she's alive?*

I doubt it. He explained that as a teenager, my mother had been involved with a revolutionary group. One night, police came to the village and took her away without a word. Our grandmother, feigning sleep, was the only one who saw it happen.

You must never tell her that you know, Hyun said. *It still pains her.*

After that night, too, Hyun—that is, "Shoking"—was never heard from again. Maybe he died in battle, or was sent to Japan and couldn't get back to Korea. I wish I knew. My grandmother now said we must forget about him, too—not think of him as alive, or dead, or anything more than air. [*Ends.*]

SESSION #2 (THURSDAY)

Q: Good morning. Today is Thursday.

A: Are you sure?

Q: [*Laughs.*] Let's get back to our story. How did you leave the village?

A: In 1943, my father returned. The two us moved to Seoul. I assumed I'd see my relatives soon: my grandmother who raised me after my mother's disappearance, the aunts sweet and stern, my ox-nosed uncle, who built a grand house in the center of town. They saw me off with presents, objects picked in a hurry: a copper comb, a decorated turtle shell. Over the years I would lose it all. Though I wrote to my relatives, saying I would visit, the letters remained unsent.

Father and I lodged in rooms next to a pool hall. A boy down the street became my best friend. Song was the youngest of four, the only son. He was tall and strong, champion of all the games the neighborhood kids made up and forgot in the course of an afternoon. He was also good at charming store owners for free candy, fixing broken radios, calming stray dogs. He had a beautiful singing voice on top of it all. At first, some schoolmates called me the Shrimp, but that stopped when Song befriended me.

Q: Did your father remarry?

A: Yes. He sent for a young widow with a kind face whom he met near Harbin, Manchuria, a Korean woman originally from Sinuiju, on the northern border. She came down to Seoul in the summer of 1945, and they wed on August 15, the same day Japan surrendered to the Allies. Liberation day! I was nine and Korea was finally free. Cheers filled the streets, as though blessing their marriage. I burned all my Japanese books and never spoke the language again. The name "Taro Tsujimoto" passed out of my life forever. In later years I missed the sound, and felt guilty for missing it. I had a new name, home, mother. Sometimes I didn't know, exactly, who I was. [*Ends.*]

SESSION #3 (FRIDAY)

Q: Good morning. Edward's ready with a new microphone . . . He hit it big at Batavia Downs last night.

A: A new shirt, too, I see. Looking sharp. Ah, I didn't notice that tattoo before. The Taegukgi . . . *

Q: Never mind that. He gets too patriotic sometimes. [*Laughs.*] Five years later, the Korean War broke out at the end of June 1950, the exact middle of the century.† What do you remember?

A: [*Pause.*] I was fourteen. The next day, Song and I were playing in a park when a policeman told us to report to a school gymnasium, just down the block. The moment we entered, I knew it was a mistake. The gym was dark, with a few high, sooty windows letting in the afternoon

---

* It sounds like the cameraman had a tattoo of the South Korean flag: a red-blue yin-yang on a white field, with groupings of three broken/solid black sticks in each corner.—Daisy

† North Korean forces crossed the 38th parallel, invading the South, though some claim that the South in fact started the war (I'm not sure how exactly).—Loa

light. Forty boys shivered despite the heat. Some were locals, others were strangers.

Let's go, Song whispered, nodding at a door concealed by a stack of chairs. I said to be patient. Small for my age, I feared what might happen if we were caught sneaking out. Ten men in the uniform of the Republic of Korea army stood among us.

A square-headed man called us to attention. He railed against the evils of Kim Il Sung, that Communist devil to the north, and praised the zeal of Syngman Rhee, our president. We let out a cheer. The North's surprise attack had crushed the army of the ROK.* Fresh recruits were needed before the war reached Seoul and points farther south. "Who is a man and not a boy?" the officer demanded.

One tall youth stepped forward. "I will fight the North."

"Oh, you will?"

"Yes!"

Square Head inspected the boy's hands. "You, with your money-grubbing fingers?"

In an instant, he kicked the boy's knee. [*Pause.*] I can still hear him hit the floor. They dragged him to a storage room. I felt physically ill now. Song's face went white. Square Head removed his cap and jacket. Under the uniform was a shirt of the same pea-drab material but with a red star over the pocket.

The whole thing was a trap. These men were from the North! The officer's tone changed. He said that all of Korea would soon be united under Kim Il Sung. He denounced Syngman Rhee as "worse than a worm—worse than a worm's *droppings.*" Already, he claimed, millions in the South were keen to join their liberators.

We boys stood in two long rows. The officers walked among us slowly, tapping a chest here, straightening a shoulder there. A whack on

---

* South Korea, i.e., the Republic of Korea. North Korea was known as the DPRK, Democratic People's Republic of Korea. Which *seems* to mean basically the same thing, but doesn't.—Daisy

the back meant you were fighting material. Some kids were sobbing, while the men shouted for order. Song got an approving thump. I was too short. I was relieved—but knew that my friend would be taken away.

The men debated over what to do with those unfit to serve the North—the weaklings and shrimps, the bespectacled and pigeon toed. I didn't stay for the end. I thought, *The door is only twenty feet away. It had better not be locked.* I shut my eyes, counted to ten, and ran. [*Ends.*]

SESSION #4 (MONDAY)

Q: Good morning. Today is . . . let's see . . . Monday.

A: Lot on your mind?

Q: No, no. [*Laughs.*] Let's pick up from last time. The Korean War.

A: [*Pause.*] The fighting deadlocked near where it started. This was 1951 going into 1952. My friend Song's family moved farther south. They gave me an address in Pusan. I promised to get in touch if I heard anything about Song.

It was hard not to think of him, or of my cousin Shoking, or my old hometown, so close and yet so far. The hamlet lay in a region now called the Iron Triangle, where the fighting was especially heavy. I had a memory of my ox-nosed uncle clearing a patch of land, pulling carts stacked with wood and stone, somehow turning it all into a magnificent house. The garden thrived, shielded from deer and rabbits by a thick wall. Water diverted from a nearby creek cut through the garden, harmonizing with the hum of bees. Chickens strode like statesmen. I'd lunch on a boiled egg, crackers sweetened with honey. Lying on my back, all I could see were clouds moving like turtles in the bright sky above.

Q: I can picture it.

A: I imagined soaring high above it all, like one of those old monks who had attained Nirvana. Time melted. It was as though future, past, and present were in my grasp.

Q: Ah . . .

A: In Seoul I thought: What if now were *then*? Maybe I'm still a boy, floating through the sky. My mother is still alive, and the war never happens. Am I still Taro Tsujimoto, then? A boy living in a small village, miles from Seoul, slowly becoming Japanese? What I didn't yet know was that the place no longer existed, not even as ruins. It was a patch of dead land, in the center of the Iron Triangle, in the heart of the country, in the middle of the century. My uncle's house, the streets—everything was gone, as though written in water.

Q: What was the name of the town?

A: It was nothing, a hamlet, barely a mark on anyone's map.

Q: Tell me. For the record.

A: We called it Hwajiri. [*Ends.*]

SESSION #5 (TUESDAY)

Q: Good morning. Before we started recording yesterday, you mentioned that you planned to visit Korea this summer.

A: It looks like I will be making the trip.

Q: This will be your first time back since leaving.

A: That's right. And I can see myself more clearly now—this man "Inky Sin."

Q: [*Pause.*] Let's pick up where we left off. You mentioned Syngman Rhee, the president of South Korea. He was opposed to North Korea's Communist regime.

A: Yes. But I think he hated it *too* much. After the war that never really ended, in 1953, Rhee viewed any sign of dissent as a foothold for Kim Il Sung, his Northern foe.

Q: What led to Rhee stepping down?

A: Don't you know all this?

Q: [*Laughs.*] I had already left the country, long before 1960. Tell me your impression then.

A: South Korea's constitution only allowed two terms, but Rhee changed it so he could have a third and then a fourth. After all, FDR got four, and so should he. What ego! The elections were rigged, certainly. His political opponents were tortured or killed. The South needed a strong defender, someone who would not let communism seep over the border. In those days, North Korea's economy was stronger than the South's. A takeover wasn't out of the question.

But by 1960, all but the staunchest "Syngmanites" were fed up. In April, protests broke out all over. Students wearing white marched through the heart of Seoul with banners and bullhorns. Their professors soon joined in. Neighborhoods became war zones, and real blood flooded the gutters.

Q: Where were you during all this?

A: I was president of my medical school class—Hyegyong University.* One morning, I got the call to lead my classmates into the fray. I had a brush cut and looked like one of the police, which helped when nego-

---

* I could not find any current reference to this institution—it might no longer exist, or Hyegyong might be an alias for a different college. Daisy (who can't keep her nose out of my things) guesses that Dr. Sin might be protecting any family or old acquaintances still in Korea. —Loa

tiating to spring friends from jail. I demanded to see Syngman Rhee. The administration offered me the vice president, but I refused. Casualties mounted. Hyegyong students—doctors in training—brought supplies to treat the fallen.

Finally, after weeks of unrest, Syngman Rhee stepped down. After decades in exile heading the Korean Provisional Government, and the years of war, Rhee was to be silenced not by the Japanese, nor the Communist North Koreans, nor the many Americans who distrusted him, but by his own countrymen, rising up against his rule. Rhee's time was up. Syngman and his wife, Francesca, returned to Hawaii, as though waking from a nightmare called Korea. [*Ends.*]

SESSION #6 (WEDNESDAY)

Q: Who was that man in the hall? The one who said hello?

A: A patient. He's ... not supposed to be here.

Q: He was talking to Edward about his tattoo. Did he fight in Korea?

A: I'm not permitted to talk about patients.

Q: [*Pause.*] Let's continue. What happened after the fall of Syngman Rhee?

A: Celebrations erupted in the capital. Over the next several nights, I drank with classmates at various German-style *hofs:* the Budding Flower, the Fisherman's Net, Arirang Hut. Gradually, I recognized fewer of the revelers, and one evening I found myself surrounded entirely by strangers, including ... *Syngman Rhee.* How could it be? The old man didn't speak, just nodded as though giving his blessing. [*Pause.*] The next night, I had an upset stomach, but made my way to a victory party at a mansion in the mountains. This time I saw not only Rhee but his archenemy to the north, Kim Il Sung. What was *he* doing in the

South? And shouldn't Rhee be in Honolulu by now? The rivals drank to each other's health. I feared I was going mad.

Q: Perhaps these were impersonators, made up to look like them.

A: A short, unsmiling man, resembling a very intelligent monkey, glared at me. At midnight, Rhee clapped his hands for attention. He and Kim announced to all present that I, Inky Sin, was hereby named the *future* president of the Korean Provisional Government.

Q: The KPG!

A: You know it, yes? A fairy tale. I was baffled. I thought the KPG had disbanded years ago, before the Korean War. The monkey gave me a shot of soju. At the mansion in the mountains, the rivals toasted me. *Mansei!* The very intelligent monkey glowered. I would have considered it all a drunken misadventure, save for the fact that at some point between two and six A.M., the tip of my left ring finger was . . . removed. I woke in my own bed, a bandage over the stitches. The job was so neat it looked like my own handiwork.

Q: I see. What happened next?

A: [*Pause.*] After Rhee resigned, his successor tried to bring some order. But a year later, he was toppled in a coup by the strongman Park Chung Hee, who declared martial law. Forty years younger than Rhee, Park was molded by his time in the Japanese army during the colonial era. Now he worked his Japanese connections to boost South Korea's economy. He would drag his country out of poverty, though at a cost. Like Rhee, Park bent the constitution to his will, winning five elections. History was repeating, in a different key. The protesters who ousted Syngman wondered, *Was it worth it?* I had never heard of Park, but my finger stump itched when I came across the usurper's face in the paper. Those simian features . . .

Q: The unsmiling man from the mansion party.

A: Exactly.

Q: Who now, I take it, wanted to kill you?

A: I had to get out of Korea. But how? [*Ends.*]

SESSION #7 (THURSDAY)

Q: What's wrong?

A: We look alike.

Q: You've noticed.

A: It's like an interview with a mirror.

Q: I'm flattered.

A: Alas, I only have a few minutes this morning. Busy, busy. Patients.*

Q: Ah. [*Pause.*] How about this afternoon?

A: I hardly have a moment, I'm afraid. And tomorrow is even busier.

Q: Next week, then.

A: Fine, fine.

SESSION #8 (MONDAY)

Q: Good morning. Today is Monday. We spent the weekend in Niagara Falls. Mostly. Edward insisted on playing the ponies Friday night. . . . Speaking of trips: How long will you be visiting Seoul for?

A: Just two weeks. I wish I could stay longer. Next time, perhaps.

Q: Do you have your tickets ready?

A: We'll be leaving at the end of August. Actually, Hannah† and I are on separate flights.

---

* Or *patience.*—Daisy

† His wife.—Daisy

Q: Oh?

A: Our son . . . I haven't talked about him. [*Pause.*] Arthur. Got into some trouble this year, though, so he'll be going to a new school. A . . . special school, in Nebraska.

Q: Nebraska!

A: Just for a year. Everything will be fine.

Q: Your arms are shaking.

A: I am fine.

Q: We can do this some other day.

A: No, let's continue.

Q: [*Pause.*] How did you get to America?

A: I served with the U.S. Eighth Army, stationed at outposts around South Korea. My protests as a Hyegyong student might have put me under suspicion with the Park administration, but ironically, I felt safe here. Doing my patriotic duty alongside American officers from Detroit and Dallas, Nashua and Nashville. I loved American food. Steak and eggs! The army showed movies every weekend. Westerns and war. My English improved. I practiced: the words for *ice, sun, comet, cow*. The word *foreign*. The word *word*. The words *skin as white as paper*. Listening to the Armed Forces Korea Network, I tracked several football teams, a sport I'd yet to see. What was a pass rush, tight end, Hail Mary?

Q: Important information.

A: I yearned to move to America. Somewhere stable, away from my broken country. More to the point: I feared there was a price on my head because of the demonstrations in 1960. So when the U.S. started letting in Koreans, I applied.* My American friends supported me.

---

* In 1965, the U.S. allowed a couple thousand Koreans to enter the country, after decades of restriction.—Loa [I would like to point out that there were already several thousand Koreans in America by now, adopted as babies.—Daisy]

They said I'd need a wife in America. I wholeheartedly agreed. A sergeant from Illinois joked that his sister was available—she was already fifty, though. "No thank you!" I screamed politely. Better to find a wife here first, in Korea. Someone to take the leap of faith with me. After a quick courtship, I got engaged to the sister of a medical school classmate. We had met once before, at my graduation. She was a junior at a prestigious women's college in Seoul, where she kept switching her major, from music to botany to linguistics, finally to English lit. She liked to say, "What use is *anything*?"

Q: How charming.

A: Hana was game to leave. Her family had once been well-off, but lost it all fleeing the North. Hana's English was superior to mine, which would come in handy. [*Pause.*] Aided by endorsements from my American commanders, I was accepted. Thus, in the summer of 1966, a hospital in Buffalo invited me to complete my medical training. Buffalo? Where was that? The name held much mystery. My friends saw me off at Kimpo airport, believing we'd meet in a few years, but I knew this was it. Hana didn't shed a tear. She said she'd join me as soon as she could.

My first stop was Tokyo. I had a day free and a hundred dollars.

Q: What did you buy?

A: A Seiko traveling alarm clock, in a red leatherette case, and a Nikon camera. The flight refueled in Anchorage, where I stared at a real, stuffed polar bear and imagined it coming to life, and ended in New York City, where I stared at the Empire State Building and imagined a penny dropping from the top. I stayed with friends for a few days, Hyegyong classmates who'd had the "pull" to end their military stints two years earlier. New York was overwhelming but also familiar. I understood the flood of people, the constant noise, but not the *height*. I feared my gawking would pull the buildings down on top of me.

My friends drove me to Buffalo. It took eight hours. Near Syracuse, my brain wept at the math: one average-sized American state was bigger than all of South Korea! Now multiply by fifty. In Buffalo, I worked

at the big hospital on Grider Street. I wrote weekly letters to Hana: starting Monday, adding a paragraph every day, mailing it Saturday morning. Mostly I wrote in Korean, sometimes showing off my English. I left out any mention of my terrible loneliness. I had to make America sound like the only place to be.

Q: How *was* your English coming along?

A: My alarm rang before dawn, so I could study English for an hour before work. I practiced tenses, built my vocabulary. At night, unable to sleep, I thought of the words for *airplane, bird, mountain, fight.* The words *important man.* The words *I learn this language slowly.*

Q: And then?

A: My father was killed in the fall of 1967. An explosion at a construction site, they said. My stepmother died days later of grief. [*Pause.*] I received the news three weeks after the funeral. A letter from their neighbor. No matter: I couldn't have gone back.

Q: You must have felt very alone.

A: [*Pause.*] Things improved. Fifteen months after I came to Buffalo, Hana joined me. We were married in a church on Michigan Avenue. We rented rooms in a house on Park Edge. The landlady, Mrs. Fox, assured the neighbors that we were from *South* Korea. Years later, long after we moved to our own little ranch house, I read a death notice in the paper that said Mrs. Fox's son had been killed at the Battle of Chosin Reservoir. He'd been in Korea just a month. Was she so kind to us in hopes of learning some final thing about her son, a glimpse of that part of the world? Who were these strangers—these Koreans—he had died for?

We moved twice over the next three years. We had a son, Arthur—named after Douglas MacArthur. His friends at school called him Art.

Q: A son. [*Long pause.*] Does he have a *halmoni*?

A: [*Chuckles.*] Sorry, I keep hearing "harmony." My ears have become so American!

Q: *Halmoni.* **Grandmother.**

A: I know, I know. Alas, Arthur has no *halmoni*—my wife's parents are gone, too. That's the thing. Life moves forward. Hana changed the spelling of her name: another *h,* another *n.* [*Pause.*] In America, day by day, we grew unrecognizable. [*Ends.*]

2333: Amsterdam in the Eighties (2009)

"Lay it on me, Daze," says Mel.

"I'm still, uh, formulating my thoughts."

Daisy Oh is at a loss. She has scrupulously read Melinda's screenplay but would have trouble drumming up a précis. Problems commence with the title, *When in Rome,* implying the movie will unfold there. But it's just a phrase the characters spout. Most of it is set in the Gowanus neighborhood of Brooklyn.

Daisy genuinely likes Mel. They met in freshman bio at Penumbra, when both entertained comical premed thoughts. By the third week, they'd dropped the class, the last science either would take; by senior year, they were housemates in a leaky Victorian off-campus. These days she doesn't understand her friend's overriding desire to write a screenplay just as people have stopped going to the movies.

"Somehow I thought all the characters would end up in Rome," Daisy says.

"No, it's an expression. It means you follow the custom of wherever you are."

"I know what it means."

When they first met, Melinda confused Daisy with another girl, Nayon, who'd grown up in Seoul. A lot of people mixed them up, and in truth they did look similar. Even after Nayon shaved her head, though, the confusion remained. Some things weren't worth getting upset about.

"Part of me thinks there are too many characters," Melinda says. Daisy nods: there are far too many, with names that sound alike. Molly and Sally, Carson and Carter. There's a Rachel and a Rachael, something Daisy untangled on a second read. "Maybe I should start from scratch."

"Well—the ending is very strong," Daisy assures her. "It's hard to describe, exactly."

This is true. The end of *When in Rome* is a speech about artisanal sherry, being present for others, and the charms of Brooklyn. The monologue is unleashed by a character named . . . Milton. Who? Daisy suspects he's really Molly or Rachael, victim of an abandoned search and replace. It's definitely interesting to hear how sherry making went from a cottage industry to a corporate concern in just nine months, the time it takes for Rachel-without-an-*a* to conceive and give birth to her daughter, Hunter. But maybe the sherry stuff would have worked better as a blog post. Since moving to New York, Melinda has become a major foodie, keeping tabs on the best Ecuadorean and getting seltzer delivered by the oldest continually working beverage deliverywoman in the city.

Their iced coffees look khaki. Seagulls walk the pier, on the lookout for fallen fries. It's an arid early summer day. Melinda's in a bone-white blouse with a Peter Pan collar and buttons big as Necco wafers. Daisy would never wear a shirt like that. Melinda is the kind of person who will keep wearing something until it becomes not just acceptable but inevitable, like a uniform. A new tattoo peeks out from her left sleeve, another Chinese character.

Daisy takes *When in Rome* out of her bag. Melinda opens it like a mom checking a diaper. She faces a sea of carets and octothorpes, red tails lashing typos away to the margin. Daisy has corrected for grammar and spelling, with queries done in her spiky, near-cuneiform hand. She's a copy editor at *Gazebo,* the magazine of high-end lawn furnishings. It was the only job she could find after graduating. Daisy tells friends she's happy to look something over, but she wonders if that's true. The screenplay is full of mistakes, and she thinks less of Melinda

for it. The problem with being a good copy editor is that the world will always be in error.

LATER, ALONE, DAISY walks the newly opened High Line, a park built on a stretch of old elevated railroad on the West Side. Strangely shaped buildings rise around her like alien crystal formations, busted concertinas. What would it be like to live in one? She would stroll the High Line every day. Find out the names of the butterflies and the different kinds of plant life, the titles of the weird art that's not exactly her taste but that she would learn to like.

To afford a place here, she needs to marry rich or get into a different field. More school? No. Maybe she should be writing a screenplay, too. It can't be that difficult. You just need a strong point of view. There are stories everywhere you look; the trick is to pay attention. Inspired, Daisy heads east to Sixth and decides to follow the first interesting person she sees, study every detail. This person will provide the basis for her main character. It's an exercise she learned from a writing class at Penumbra called Intro to Wildword. Each day you tried a new style or technique. The net effect was that it made her not want to be a writer.

Waiting to cross Sixth Avenue is a Japanese hipster wearing a neck brace. Daisy scribbles down a description on an old Duane Reade receipt. Stringy mustache, tinted glasses. Crisp tan blazer over distressed Thin Lizzy T-shirt. Murse made of tarp from a decommissioned military truck. Little does he suspect his future appearance in a critically acclaimed film. Daisy trails him, imagining his life: what he's doing so far from Tokyo, his family, his diet. Maybe he is a . . . video-game designer? Too stereotypical. She decides that he came to New York with dreams of becoming a salsa dancer but then got injured doing a particularly difficult move and needs to stabilize his neck.

It's not a brace, she sees, but one of those inflatable pillows for long flights. Fashion statement or narcolepsy precaution? Perhaps he isn't a hipster at all but simply a bum. He walks to Thirty-fourth and heads into the subway. He gets on a downtown 2 and Daisy follows, sitting

obliquely across. She idly reads a new scene Melinda gave her at lunch. One of the Rachels is trampling grapes while a baby-faced VC watches, eating Twizzlers, murmuring sleazy encouragement. Daisy peers up from this lurid scenario to spy on her quarry. He leans back, one cheek resting on the neck pillow. His eyes close. Daisy takes more notes. Jet lag? There is a fantastic amount of cat hair on his black skinny jeans. It's hard to penetrate the inner core of this guy. She writes, "inner core???" on the receipt. In the tiny space left, she sketches his face. When she tries to fix the nose, everything goes downhill. It looks like how a psychic might draw Jack the Ripper.

The doors open at Fourteenth Street and he darts out. Daisy follows. This is the stop closest to her office, and being in the vicinity on a weekend makes her surly. As he vaults up the stairs, something drops out of his murse. "Wait," she calls, but he's already booking down the pavement. Her shopping bags weigh her down. By the time she attains the mystery object, the hipster is long gone. It's a thumb drive: two inches long, free of markings. She drops it in her tote, then heads back down to catch a train uptown.

OUT OF THE subway at last, Daisy flips open her phone. The day's even hotter than before. Above, AC units drip in a parody of rain. She's missed a call from Max, her invisible boyfriend. They met in biology but didn't date until senior year, when she liked him more than he liked her. They broke up after graduation, but now he says he wants her back. It's terrible, but she's forgotten what he looks like.

The balance has shifted. He emails that he needs her. She writes the same thing back but without a period or exclamation point, as if lack of punctuation offers an escape hatch. Because she doesn't know if she needs him, honestly. It's hard for her to see a future with Max. In fact, it's hard for her to see him at all. After taking a few years off, Max didn't get accepted to a medical school in New York City, which was a blow. He didn't get accepted to a medical school in the state, or even the country. Instead he's doing a program in Guadalajara, Mexico.

He promised to be in New York this summer but then got offered a plum research position in Buenos Aires, looking into the causes of benign positional vertigo. In two weeks, he'll be moving farther south. At this rate, Daisy figures, he'll wind up at that scientific encampment in Antarctica, wearing one of those huge orange parkas with fur trim.

AT A PARTY the next night on her friend Loa's roof she talks to Sang, who works for a nonprofit that makes sure every child in New York has safe drinking water.

"But doesn't New York already have the best tap water in the world?" Daisy asks. She had seen it on TV once as a girl.

"I don't know, maybe," Sang says. "I'm more on the modeling side of things."

"You're a model?"

He gives her a look. Of course he means data modeling. She blushes with embarrassment. It's like the time when she thought a friend was getting into "eye banking."

Daisy's been talking to Sang for only five minutes, but already she's noticed that whenever an attractive woman walks by, he rakes his hair with his fingers and yawns. It's like a poker player's tell. Did he do that when Loa introduced her to him, five minutes ago? It would be interesting to know.

"What do you do?" he asks.

"I'm a copy editor at *Gazebo*," she says.

To her surprise, Sang nods. "My mom subscribes."

This is the first time Daisy has met a civilian who will admit familiarity with the magazine. This makes her like him, even though she distrusts *Gazebo*'s readership. Every so often she'll field a call from an outraged subscriber, venting about the surfeit of postal reply cards.

"What's her gazebo like?" The question sounds like lost Jazz Age innuendo.

"Funny story. She's always wanted one, but my dad says it's too dangerous." Apparently Sang's father refuses to get a gazebo because he

thinks it will collapse while they're eating berries and cream. "He's a little OCD," Sang says, blinking. "But so am I."

"It's a common fear. The gazebo taps into a rich vein of fantasy. People think lightning will strike or that a murderer is going to pop up behind you, wielding scissors. You should read our letters column . . ." Where is she even going with this?

Sang asks Daisy what she did before *Gazebo*. She says a little bit of this, a little bit of that. She says school. She says she was a humanities major "even though I hate humans." He blinks some more. It's a good line that she's used before, but she hasn't said it lately, because last winter she heard another girl, Sasha, say it. Now Daisy worries that she might have unconsciously plagiarized it from Sasha. Will Sang someday hear Sasha deliver the line and think that Daisy copied it? She should put *that* in a screenplay. Memorialize it, as her boss likes to say.

SANG DOESN'T HAVE a drink. That's how he has the freedom to run both hands through his hair. He tells her he can't touch alcohol for a while because he's in the midst of a ten-day juice cleanse. Standing a little closer, Daisy smells lemon, or maybe raspberry, or else it's cologne or a different person's body entirely.

Day three, and already Sang can feel his mind coming to a point. His brain is like a constantly sharpened pencil. Every day he enters a three-hour "zone" in which he can accomplish anything. It sounds exhausting to Daisy, but then again most things exhaust her. Sang says he's using the zone to focus on what he really wants to do, which is write a screenplay.

"You're an editor," he says.

She already likes him 20 percent less. "Copy editor."

"I'd love to get your perspective on it." Sang manages not to blink for a good three seconds. "Is that too forward?"

"Yes."

"It's about Syngman Rhee meeting his Austrian wife."

"Who?"

"The first president of South Korea," he says.

"I've heard of Rhee. I mean his wife."

"Wait, aren't you . . . ?"

Korean. "I am, but I'm adopted."

"No shit!"

Daisy doesn't love talking about this part of her biography. "Do all Korean people know about the wife?"

"Not much anymore," he says. "It's like asking the average American about the sister of Rutherford B. Hayes."

"Hey, we're *all* Americans," she corrects him. "Asian Americans."

"Right on."

They high-five, ironically but also not. Daisy likes him again. They're about the same level of attractiveness, which is good, though he looks like someone with a taste for the outdoors, which isn't a deal breaker but isn't a huge plus.

"Anyway, it's not your standard historical drama. For one thing, there's a big twist."

"What is it?"

"It doesn't sound good if I say it out loud. You have to read the whole thing." She doesn't comment, so he adds, "The setup takes too long to explain. I just need someone to tell me what should stay and what should go. It used to be more action, now it's more romantic comedy, except not funny. Do you know anyone else who might take a look?"

"I didn't say no."

"Did you say yes?"

From across the room comes a peal of laughter. Mel is doing that thing where she flashes her armpits when she talks. She doesn't even know she's doing it. She lifts her arms very slowly, does a stretch like you'd see in barre class. Sang brushes his hair back with both hands, like a tutorial on how to rake your lawn.

"Mel and I used to live together," Daisy says.

"Mel who?"

"Melinda. The girl over there who's modeling deodorant."

"I thought her name was Madeleine."

"It's not."

Sang looks at Daisy, then back at Melinda, as though unable to comprehend them coexisting in the same living space. "I must have misread her tattoo."

"Which one? The long thing on her leg is from Emily Dickinson. There are runes on her wrist that spell out her mother's maiden name. On one shoulder blade is the Chinese character for serenity, and on the other is the Union Jack, though she's only like an eighth British."

"I could never get a tattoo," Sang says. "I think it's still illegal in Korea. Only the Koreans in Japan who become yakuza get tattoos. At least in the movies. My dad would disown me if I even got, say, a small one of his name. Which might not be the worst thing."

"You could run away with your mom and build her that gazebo."

Daisy has one tattoo, which Mel peer-pressured her into getting just before graduation, at a mall in Burlington. It's on her left shoulder, a quarter-sized yin-yang that she always keeps covered but secretly likes. She doesn't know Sang well enough to reveal this.

A beautiful girl approximately seven feet tall walks by. Sang runs both hands through his hair. "That's Blue, right? I've never talked to her. I don't know anything about her except that she's a model."

"The one random fact."

Sang looks like he's been clubbed in the head. The salutary effects of the juice fast are ebbing. Any second now he might come crashing down. Daisy wants to shove some nachos into his mouth.

"She's from Europe somewhere, moved around a lot," he says.

"What kind of name is Blue? Sounds fake."

"Maybe not Blue. Tan? Some color." His attempted nonchalance only makes him look psychotic. "All I've heard is that she grew up in Amsterdam in the eighties."

LATER, BACK ON the roof, Daisy tells him about the thumb drive and the Japanese hipster she followed into the subway.

"How do you know he was Japanese?"

"I can tell."

"Isn't that a little racist?"

"No. I took a quiz online called 'Can You Guess Which Kind of Asian?' and I got twenty out of twenty right."

"Impressive. Did you try plugging in the thumb drive yet?"

"Not yet."

"Be careful. It's probably full of malware. Try using it on a public computer first, or an old one you don't care about."

Like she has computers to burn. "What's the worst that could happen?"

"Well, it could steal your identity, or sign you up for stuff you don't want, or both."

Daisy thinks it wouldn't be so terrible to have her identity stolen. Let someone else be her for a change.

On Monday she works late closing *Gazebo*'s September issue. The theme is the environment. On Tuesday Daisy rolls in at ten. At eleven, Vik appears at the threshold to her office, if her office were an actual room or chamber rather than a poorly defined region of the open plan.

"Listen up, Cornell. Do you say something is comprised *of* x, y, z or that something *comprises* x, y, and z?"

"Um."

For some reason, Vik thinks she went to Cornell, his alma mater. It's far too late to correct him. She looks up from the Post-it on which she has just written "Before I Leave Today."

Comprised. Daisy knows this, but it takes a while to formulate the definition. Vik is impressive and a little nebulous. He's neither a writer nor an editor, and he isn't on the financial side of things, though she's noted his byline, heard him assign pieces, and seen him in meetings with whiteboards showing allocation of funds. He's not her boss but maybe at some level he is. Vik's pre-*Gazebo* life is unsearchable, lost in the mists of the pre-internet age. In other words, he hasn't flung his entire CV online like every other sucker.

"One big thing *comprises* smaller things," she says.

"So the first option."

"Not exactly."

"Back up." Vik shows his palm. "Use *comprise* in a sentence."

"The gazebo . . . the . . ."

"It sounds complicated, Cornell. Let's grab lunch."

They go to a Thai restaurant with a health department sign in the window that says GRADE PENDING. Daisy orders pad thai. Melinda would scoff, but Daisy read somewhere that you can always get a bead on how good a Thai restaurant is by the quality of its pad thai. Not that she has a baseline. She's never been to Thailand, or to a gourmet Thai place, or had a boyfriend or even just a regular friend lift a forkful of noodle, egg, and peanut to her lips and say, "This—now *this* is the real deal."

Daisy is afraid that Vik will only want to talk about gazebos. She knows a fair amount about them, having processed so many articles. She kicks things off by saying she met someone whose mother subscribed to *Gazebo,* but she doesn't know where this is leading and shuts up. Vik orders a Singha Light and invites her to do the same. Daisy doesn't like beer, and it's the middle of the day, but she channels Mel's script: when in Rome.

They gossip about the editor in chief, a brassy blonde called Bagley, and crack up trying to picture her relaxing in a gazebo for even five minutes. Vik says her ex used to be on Wall Street and now juggles with a regional circus. "I saw him once—he's good."

Vik is frankly wide: two of her could nestle in his frame. He doesn't dwell on the magazine, but drops hints about a flashier career waiting in the wings. Tipsy, he makes it clear that he's working at *Gazebo* for money alone. His periodic spiels in the office about, say, how lawn furnishings reflect the soul of the country are not really to be taken seriously.

Daisy nods, but she realizes in that moment that she actually likes gazebos, if not *Gazebo* per se. She likes that no one knows what to do in them. Read the paper while sipping lemonade? Hold chamber music performances? Launch a political campaign? It's a space of pure potential.

She's never noticed before how Vik is nearly bald. He has an expen-

sive watch and a gold stud in his left ear so small that at first she thought it was a crumb. Half a Singha Light later, Vik tells her he's working on a screenplay.

Back at her desk, she wiggles her mouse till the screen shudders into being. Only one new email: Sang, the boy from the party. She feels like she's been cheating on him.

"hi," it says. "sorry I got delirious at Ioa's party . . . I blame the JUICE CLEANSE."

Zero minutes later comes a follow-up: "hey it's Sang from the party. can I still take you up on the screenplay offer?"

"My rates are high, but I'M WORTH IT," she types.

He emails a file entitled "FRANCESCA." Her computer takes forever to download. In the interim, she looks at a set of layouts for the October issue. The deep captions and pull quotes for a feature on the "ghost" gazebos of North Dakota are a mess, and the piece on organic varnish is populated with orphans and widows. Her breath is weird from lunch. She toggles ineffectively among three different articles. One is a recipe, another is about preventing cobwebs, and the last is essentially a list of paint colors with food names. She removes her glasses, stares at the desk until her head comes to rest on her forearms.

"Go home, Cornell." She looks up to see Vik in his bike helmet. It's half past six.

"I'm good!"

Daisy stays late, tweaking captions on an autumn showcase spread. One model in a funky straw hat catches her eye. She's got a cute smudge on one cheek as she adjusts a weather vane. Daisy keeps returning to the image. Of course: the tall girl from the party who Sang kept staring at.

"Grumble, grumble," she says.

Daisy accesses the photo database. The model goes by a mononym, Greena, like the rarefied creature she is. Her full legal name is listed as Greena Yewyang. Under race it says Asian. Contrary to Sang's assertion, for birthplace it reads NYC, not Amsterdam.

Before Daisy leaves, she decides to print out Sang's screenplay. *Francesca* is three hundred pages long. The job uses up all the paper before she's finished and she can't find more.

"Jesus!" she whispers. She just wants to go home. She walks around the blob-shaped workstations, looking for fifty-three loose sheets that she can impound for her cause. On the verge of giving up, Daisy finds herself by Vik's corner, which is sheathed from the proles by a rigid curved translucent barrier that reaches to the ceiling and opens and closes along a track. It looks like a giant version of the capsules they had at the old bank drive-thru when she was a kid. Her dad would put his checks inside the frosted cylinder, which would get sucked up into a pneumatic tube with a satisfying *phwt* and land in the teller's hands. In other words, it reminds her of money.

The sliding door is open a crack; why *not* slip inside? Taped to the curved inner wall are what might be notes about forthcoming issues. They're mostly comprised of—*composed* of—numbers and acronyms that might be passwords. On his desk is a single photo, a color printout of Vik in a purple polo shirt, holding a Chihuahua. The dog's expression is preternaturally chill. There's a Metro-North train schedule for Poughkeepsie, a timetable Daisy knows by heart from visiting her dad and stepmom, whom she's taken to calling her *adoptive* dad and stepmom, as though her real ones will appear any day now. There's a copy of *Men's Health* addressed to his home, which she calculates is a block from the High Line.

SHE FEELS LONELY in Vik's translucent cylinder of an office. Daisy thinks about how the mystery of her biological parents used to consume her, the term conjuring an image of science teachers holding beakers. If Daisy ever found them, what would she say? How could they even communicate? In preparation, she took four semesters of Korean in college. The instructor was an old white man who had never been to Korea but had taught English for several years in China and Japan. Daisy spent hours memorizing the alphabet, listening to tapes at the

language lab. In the ladies' room, a stall had graffiti that read TRANSLA-
TION IS A LONG CON.

Eventually, she decoded old Korean poems, which she enjoyed. She
imagined her biological mom listening to her read. In these daydreams,
Daisy had total comprehension. Her replies unfurled in complete sentences. (Bio-dad never made a cameo, alas.) She and Bio-mom would
live together for a while, travel, catch each other up on their lives.

Senior year, she applied for a heritage journey to Korea, set up to
help adoptees learn more about their roots. She was thrilled by the
prospect. Once she understood the place she came from, she'd be ready
to move on to the next phase of her life. But the biotech company fund-
ing the program folded when its founder was sent to jail on an impressive array of sex charges. Scrambling, Daisy followed Melinda and Loa
and some other friends to New York and got the gig at *Gazebo* and read
everyone's screenplays for free.

VIK HAS A standing desk, with one big drawer. She opens it using the
edge of her shirt so she won't leave fingerprints. Inside are boxes of
paper clips, ballpoint pens, high-end highlighters, and—glorious to
behold—a just-opened ream of Hammermill's finest.

Daisy takes what she needs to print the rest of *Francesca*. Then she
walks the seventy-seven blocks home with Sang's screenplay in her tote
bag, as though atoning for her new career in breaking and entering.

HER APARTMENT IS in the West Nineties. The building has seen better
days, though given that this is New York, those better days might have
been a century ago. Weathered words appear on the brickwork, traces
of its former name. Totem, Daisy's roommate, is on the landline when
she gets home, arguing with his girlfriend, who lives in Chicago. Totem
has a calm, steady voice, even though his girlfriend is screaming at him
so loudly Daisy can make out every word. She tiptoes to her room.

It's past eight, but she isn't hungry. She starts reading *Francesca,* pen

in hand. Two hours later, she's still reading. A history of South Korea told through the life of its titular first first lady, who was born in Austria. Sang the data modeler knows how to keep the audience engaged, with bold shifts in scene, gripping dialogue, characters you care about. Impressive. There's stuff Daisy doesn't totally get, but she figures all will be explained in the remaining fifty pages.

She emails Sang, "This is really really good so far! <3"

The story is making her crave Korean food. Even though it's nearly eleven, Daisy takes the subway to Koreatown to have her favorite dish, the *seolleongtang* at Gam Mi Oak. Before she goes, she puts a blanket over poor old Totem, who has conked out on the couch after another long-distance torture session with his beloved.

When Daisy gets out at Thirty-fourth, she laughs because she has a persistent mental block regarding Totem's girlfriend, who is none other than her college nemesis: Nayon, the look-alike. Nayon, the real Korean from Korea, versus Daisy, the knockoff version. Nayon, whose name is an anagram of *annoy,* versus Daisy, whose *adoptive* parents mistakenly gave her a name that sounds like the Korean word for *pig:* 돼지, *dweh-ji,* as Nayon needlessly pointed out. Daisy has no designs on Totem but wants to save him from Nayon's clutches. (Can a Korean be racist against other Koreans?)

The restaurant is busy: limo drivers, waiters from other restaurants, twenty-somethings fueling up before hitting the clubs. She reads more *Francesca* as she waits for her soup. At home, she'd found some biographical entries for Francesca's husband online. Syngman Rhee had spent a big chunk of his life in the United States, bitching about the Japanese plunder of his homeland. He'd lived in Hawaii, gone to Princeton *and* Harvard. He said that he had no children, but that all Koreans were his sons and daughters. Daisy thinks, *Even me?* Rhee had delusions of grandeur, plus actual grandeur. He came back and was elected the first president of South Korea, but he was so corrupt that the people eventually overthrew him. He lived till ninety and died in exile. Everyone hated him now.

The public outline is at odds with Sang's portrait of him. He makes

Syngman sound so appealing, full of moxie. The early Korean phase of his life is introduced in flashbacks, including an intense scene of jailhouse torture and trippy fantasy sequences. When he meets the love of his life, Francesca Donner, he's downright debonair. At times it feels like a collage of familiar tropes, but then all cinema is a form of quotation.

"Of course, it's totally unfilmable."

She looks up to see Sang standing before her. "That scene where he's reading the old Buddhist book?" he says. "Dream inside a story inside a flashback. I mean, come on!"

"What are you doing here?"

"I just got off work," Sang says, taking a seat. He looks different in a tie. "My office is on Twenty-seventh."

"But what about the cleanse?"

"Cheat day." He signals the waiter across the room, orders in perfect Korean. "I had a hunch you'd be here. The cleanse sometimes makes me hallucinate, see bits of the future."

"What's going to happen next?"

He blinks. "You're going to tell me how to fix *Francesca*."

"Before that."

"You're going to come back to my office with the thumb drive and we're going to see what's on it. There's an old PC no one uses. It will be totally safe. Probably."

Daisy finds the tech talk oddly erotic.

"I actually might have the thumb drive with me." She roots through her tote. The drive has fallen inside her makeup bag. She hands it to him just as the soup arrives. Hot soup on a hot night makes no sense, but the *seolleongtang* hits the spot. Sang barks in Korean and makes a pouring motion and the waitress comes by with beer.

"Oh, I can't," Daisy says. "I had beer at lunch."

"Beer or beers?"

"Difficult to say. It resembled one endless river of beer."

"Okay, I'll drink both."

She grabs a bottle. "When in Rome," she says.

They have a good talk and speculate about what might be on the Japanese hipster's thumb drive. But now it's after one, too late to hit his office, so she tells him to keep the drive and try it whenever. No rush.

WEDNESDAY, DAISY HAS lunch with Mel near the Flatiron Building. They go to the deli that's been around since 1929, the main selling point of which is its endurance. Mel's in a red T-shirt with stout white lettering that says *The New York Review of Boobs.* She looks distraught, which, given her facial structure, isn't vastly different from her unruffled appearance.

"I have to change the title, Daze. I found out there's another movie in the works called *When in Rome.* It's a disaster."

"You could call it something else," Daisy says. "How about ... *Sherry.*"

"What?"

"Isn't that what they're making?"

"I *know,*" Mel grumbles. "But that sounds like someone's name."

"Doesn't matter." She thinks of Sang's *Francesca.* "You just need to get them interested."

"Well, *I* don't think it's very interesting."

Daisy holds her tongue.

"I've got it," Melinda says. "*Wen in Rome,* but 'Wen' as in short for 'Wendy.'"

"There isn't a character named Wendy."

"I'm changing Rachael to Wendy. I'm not precious about these things."

It soon becomes the conversation from hell. Mel brags that her writing partner is heading out to L.A. and she might join her.

"What writing partner?" Daisy asks.

"You know her, actually. Nayon, from school. Totem's girlfriend."

"The one that looks like me," Daisy jokes.

"Isn't it the other way around?" She has room for only one Korean in her life.

DAISY'S AC BREAKS down on Saturday. Opening the window just makes the room feel worse, like she's being wrapped in a blanket as prelude to a kidnapping. She heads for the office, laden with other people's screenplays.

She's not alone. In an alcove off the elevator lobby, Vik is erecting a mail-order gazebo. He asks Daisy to hand him a different hammer than the one he's using. She's no fashion blogger, but his T-shirt might be the most hideous article of clothing she's ever seen, a teal-and-orange freebie from a charity 5K underwritten by a bunch of investment banks. The date is pre-9/11 and there's a woozy line drawing of the Twin Towers on the back.

"Which hammer?"

"Red handle."

"This one?"

"No."

"This one."

"No."

"Ah, this." She hands him the hammer, and he promptly whacks his thumb.

"You were supposed to hit the *other* nail," she says. "Also, what are you doing?"

He blows on his injury. "This morning I got a message from Doug at the front desk saying they had a package weighing a ton. We lug it onto the service elevator and voilà: instant gazebo kit."

"Could be a game changer," Daisy says.

"I hate that expression."

"Are we going to feature it?"

"There's a code of ethics in magazineland, no tit for tat," he says.

"I hate *that* expression."

"I couldn't figure out how to send it back," he continues, "so I emailed Bagley and she said go ahead and install it, though clearly I've bitten off more than I can chew."

"It doesn't look bad."

"Right? I thought people could do their reading here, their thinking, such as it is."

Vik orders them lunch. He mentions the movie he's seeing that night, though he stops short of asking her to go. Daisy imagines he'll soon be set up with a future wife by his traditional Indian parents and thus cannot enter into a dating situation with her, marry her, and set her up in his place by the High Line. Or could he be gay? She invites herself along. After the movie, they make out in the theater lobby. Not gay! He has a flight in the morning, fly-fishing with some bros in Montana, which actually sounds gay. That night she's up till three, typing notes about *Francesca*.

ON WEDNESDAY, A padded envelope awaits Daisy at work, messengered to *Gazebo* from someplace called Marshlands on West Twenty-seventh. It weighs nothing. Inside there's a letter.

Hi Daisy—돼지 (pig?) :)—

It was really fun bumping into you in K-town . . .

Anyway—here's the thumb drive. The good news is that I did a scan and found no malware. I tried opening one of the files, but it came out as gibberish. . . . If you want to clean it up, you need a (really) old program called Divinr (no "e"). Online there are sites that claim you can download it, but I'd avoid (more malware). Take it to a tech repair place. (Honestly, I doubt it's worth the trouble!)

Thanks for the great notes on *Francesca* (or do I mean *Franny*, after all your cuts, heh). In the end I don't know if screenplays are something I want to pursue. I'll always be grateful for your attention and professionalism. Stay

cool, Daisy. (Just so you know, a situation came up with my mom and I'm leaving the city, but I hope we can keep in touch.)

Your friend,
Sang

Daisy takes the thumb drive out of the envelope. Her name's in Sharpie on one side. Sang's note makes her sad. Did he really have to leave? Is his mom okay? In her mind she connects his departure to the make-out session she had with Vik, like her life can only hold so much excitement. She goes to the restroom and cries for a minute, stopping when she realizes someone else is there. Exiting a stall is Mercy, full-time art director and part-time dispenser of withering looks. She's only twenty-five, and so fucking cool that Daisy tries to avoid her at all costs. The thought of talking petrifies her. Mercy Pang lives nearby, in the Eighties, and whenever Daisy spots her speed-walking to their shared subway station in the morning, social anxiety kicks in. She tempers her own pace or crosses the street in order not to fall in step.

"You look like a spy," Mercy says, nodding at her outfit with approval. Both of them are dressed all in black.

"We should do a goth issue of *Gazebo*."

Mercy laughs, and Daisy falls a little bit in love. Giddy, Daisy goes into a stall and writes TRANSLATION IS A LONG CON on the wall. She still would like to know what it means. On the floor is a shiny silver brick of some sort. An old Zippo, older than her. Is it Mercy's? Bagley's? She picks it up, studies the initials etched on one side, a *K* and a *G,* the middle one obliterated by a puncture. It fits perfectly in her hand.

Back at her desk, she plugs in the thumb drive. The computer groans at the intrusion. Nothing happens; then something does. The drive icon appears on her screen, unnamed. She mouses over, double-clicks. It's empty save for a folder called Folder, which sits on the white background like an actual folder dropped in a snow-covered parking lot.

Daisy takes a swig of water and clicks it open. Soft noises. The window opens slowly, like a bedsheet unfurled in the air, to reveal Folder 2.

Daisy nervously flicks the Zippo. *Chk chk.* When she double-clicks the icon, an urgent grinding replaces the cooing, as if the computer is searching its own memories for lost protocols, faded instructions tucked away by its creators. After an eternity, another solitary folder wobbles into existence. Folder 3, 4, 5. She opens and waits, opens and waits, the computer generating odd new sounds, to warn her or convey exasperation: *Do you* really *want to do this?* Folder 6, 7, 8, 9. Anxiety bubbles up in Daisy's chest. Folder 10, 11, 12. Each new window opens a centimeter to the right of the old one, forming a series of steps. Folder 13. Maybe it's a practical joke. Maybe Sang is still on Twenty-seventh Street, waiting for her to call.

Then Daisy remembers his note to download Divinr. Or wait, she *shouldn't* download it? Or—what the hell. She finds a free version on a site with a fishy suffix. Clicks Install. The folders evaporate to reveal a single icon, silver and pulsing. The name is echo_sbdd_kpg.

THE SINS STILL OCTOBER YOU BE YOU

I BUMPED INTO LOA DING ONE more time in the Asterisk. Or, rather, just outside: she was doing yoga in Little Eden, despite the sign saying NO YOGA. It was a crisp October Thursday. I had come out here with Dream Four stashed in my satchel like contraband. Her eyes were shut. I didn't want to interrupt, so I sat on a rock and leafed through Dream Four, which I'd consumed in a trance the week before. I had littered the margins with question marks, frantic stars, doodles of skulls, and UFOs.

"Who's there?" Loa said, eyes still closed.

"It's Soon."

"Dude, you shouldn't sneak up on people."

"Don't mind me—I'll be gone in a minute," I said with a touch of resentment. I'd given her my extra key to Little Eden, after all. "I'm just out here to read."

"The Dream, right? Echo's book?" Loa exhaled, turned, and shot her legs straight up, all her weight resting on her shoulder blades. "I'm still traumatized by that dog, lunging at me."

"He didn't *lunge*. He was as freaked out as you were."

"Blame the victim much?" She did some squats. "So what's been happening in the Dreams?"

"The part I just read was about the Korean War," I said. "I knew the rough outline—the North invading, the South pushing back. General MacArthur and the Inchon landing. The battle line going up and down."

"The Window-Shade War," Loa murmured. "I remember that from Intro to Asian History."

I was impressed. Loa wasn't even Korean. "It ends in a stalemate. No real peace."

"The war is *still* going on."

"Exactly." I explained how Dream Four picked up on themes from earlier sections, how old characters popped up.

"Wait." She was mostly upside down now, locked in a complicated asana. "Is this fiction or nonfiction?"

"Non," I said. "Though sometimes I'm not sure. Like this part about the Buffalo Sabres and how they got their name. Echo writes that they were named after the F-86 Sabre, which was flown in the Korean War."

"Sure, sure," she said. "Dogfights in MiG Alley."

"Exactly." She even knew her Korean War planes! "I just never heard that origin story before. According to Echo, a flying ace named Parker Jotter came up with it."

"Jotter?" Loa said. She was balanced on one leg, the other one stretched behind, toes touching spine. My back practically gave out just watching her. "Jotter . . ."

"Does it ring a bell?" I was getting excited. "He got put in a POW camp . . ."

"Hmm, no. I must be confused." She opened an eye at last. "Also, I was hoping you'd shaved the mustache."

I lovingly patted the follicles, my slow-growing tribute to Thomas Ahn. "No such luck."

"Asian men don't look good with facial hair," Loa said bluntly. Something my mom used to say, to dissuade my father's own experimentation.

"Anyway, I've been looking everywhere for Dream Five," I said. "I hate to be left hanging."

Back home in Westgate, Sprout was in no rush to uncover it from whichever dirt archive he'd buried it in, and I couldn't get through to Daisy Oh. Tanner Slow was still on his deviceless retreat. His new assistant claimed she'd never heard of me, regarding my requests with suspicion.

"Maybe some things are better left unfinished," Loa said, both eyes now

open. For a second, I thought she meant the Korean War. She rolled up her mat and headed back to the Asterisk.

I LEFT WORK AN hour early to catch Story's chess tournament, a micro-meet at her school. My GLOAT Freckle allowed me to bypass the front desk security and go straight to the state-of-the-art lounge. Chess meets as a rule didn't allow parents to be in the same room as the matches. This usually meant sitting in a cafeteria, trying to connect to Wi-Fi, getting a headache from the ghost odor of cheese and cleaning products. The spectator area at Measures, though, had comfortable workstations, complimentary pillows, and a video feed of each board, with moves notated in real time. It was a little like flying first class without leaving the airport.

I set up camp at one of the deluxe desks, with the reclining seat and foot relaxer, slipped off my shoes, and searched the console for Story's current game. It wasn't showing up momentarily, so I sipped a complimentary can of mildly fizzy Marshlands water and let the chair's massager work on my toes. My situation was so comfortable I was in danger of nodding off. I had my GLOAT laptop, but the thought of doing any work just made a nap seem more appealing. If only I had Dream Five with me, the finale of Echo's book, everything would be perfect . . .

My phone shuddered, taking me out of my reverie. I thought it would be Story, updating me on her recent victory, asking me to slip her a cold Marshlands. Instead, Gemma's picture of the ostensible Echo look-alike appeared, this time paired not with my dimly lit snapshot of the author, but with a professional-looking portrait.

GLOAT's facial-recognition system had been working tirelessly for weeks and was now proudly presenting its latest find, not that I'd put in a request.

"*We found a match!*" a voice announced. I thumbed the volume down and studied the black-and-white picture. I could tell it had been shot on film. The man in the photo looked slyly handsome, vaguely familiar—a B-list actor from the '90s, perhaps. With a little creative eyeballing, I could see some features in common with Echo, but he was a vague doppelgänger at best.

I was about to do a reverse-image search. Then it occurred to me exactly where I'd seen this face before: on the dust jacket for T. S. Kim's *Man in Korean Costume,* a book three decades old. I groaned. GLOAT's system wasn't foolproof, and it had come under criticism for its inaccuracy in "reading" the faces of so-called people of color. I contemplated filing a trouble ticket, becoming a rabble-rouser within the company ranks, but thankfully the feeling passed.

I was surprised to see Story outside the lounge, her small fingers swiping her phone screen as though casting a spell. What was she doing out of the tournament room? It was far too early for her to be eliminated.

"Hey, you," I said.

"Hi, Soon." She was playing Hegemon, naturally.

"Everything okay? I thought you'd still be in the middle of a match now."

"I forgot to tell you. I quit the team."

I was dumbfounded. Maybe she'd had a rough draw, acted out. But that didn't seem like Story. "When?"

"Today."

Her eyes suddenly teared up, as though just grasping the consequences of her decision. In my mind, such a turning away was inevitable, though I hadn't thought she'd give up so soon. Nora would not be happy. Despite having never played chess herself, she had read a study claiming that nine out of ten Fortune 500 CEOs had a minimum 2100 rating by age fifteen. When I say *study,* I mean more of a free-floating, un-fact-checked item that popped up in an ad-driven listicle, but the damage was done. She wanted our daughter to have all the opportunities.

"That's fine, sweetie." I tried to understand. "You used to love chess, though."

"They started a Hegemon club at school." She wiped her eyes. "I'm president."

"Wow," I said, ginning up some enthusiasm, "that's wonderful!"

"I have the most points, so."

"Ah."

We drove home. Story told me that Hegemon club met at the same time as chess club, so she couldn't do both. I thought it best to trust her. Hege-

mon was a fad, but maybe it made sense for modern kids to play modern games. I was driving a car, not a horse and buggy, after all. The virtues of chess sounded good, but in twenty years there would be a whole generation of impressive people who would point to Hegemon and its ilk as formative experiences.

I told Story not to tell her mom just yet about the recent jump from chess to Hegemon. I'd break the news later. She agreed. Then she told me to drive faster because she had to pee.

STORY RAN OUT AS soon as we pulled into the driveway. The car door didn't fully close. When I went to shut the back, I saw a startling shape wedged between the seat and the cup holder: a gun.

I held my breath in shock, before realizing it was a plastic toy, much too small for an adult's grip. Beige, with futuristic flourishes, like a B-movie photon blaster. The bottom of the grip had a slot, as if to hold a clip. No words or markings. Had the gun fallen out of Story's backpack? Thin gaps indicated that it was made out of many interlocking parts, perhaps dozens. Some of the interior pieces were in different colors. With a little twisting I pulled off a component the length of a Q-tip, then another part the size of a bottle cap.

Of course: this was the Tan Gun, some of it at least, constructed from the Hegemon pieces Story had been 3D-printing at night. I'd read a description on GLOAT: the blueprint for each was unlocked after a player had completed twenty levels of Hegemon. I forgot how many levels there were, or how many pieces. Was she done, or was there more to come?

We would have to talk about it. A serious discussion. Nora would not take this development well. She might insist on pulling Story from Measures. We'd move to another town, send her to a more traditional school, if not a reformatory. I had to choose my words carefully. Nora was a great mom but also thought she knew best. I considered how to frame Hegemon as a hobby that might lead to a career in . . . I would make something up.

I stepped over a supine Sprout, into the kitchen. Nora was at the table, still in her Daily Divas polo, staring at her laptop. Her face was obscured by a white K-beauty mask, drenched in unguents and aromatics, with holes for

eyes and mouth. She looked like the Invisible Man. Had she glanced up, she would have seen a man in the shadows, gun in hand. But she was wrapped up in her own unsettling discovery.

"I got this crazy message from Gen-Era," she said, referring to GLOAT's DNA-tracing company. "It says I'm related to someone you know."

"Who's that?" I asked, discreetly slipping the plastic gun into my satchel.

"Your old colleague Monk Zingapan."

I had trouble getting the words out: "Like, third cousins or something?"

"Uh, closer."

"But Monk's Filipino." I peered at the screen, which showed a pie chart.

"Says I'm twenty-six to thirty-two percent Filipino."

"Filipina," I mansplained. "But I still don't get it."

She tamped down the edges of her beauty mask. "I just messaged my sister."

Greena Yewyang was fifteen years younger than Nora. They hadn't grown up together, and had never been close. (Greena had melded her parents' surnames into one, which Nora thought inane.) She was a former model who worked in fashion in some nebulous capacity.

"She said Mom sometimes wondered if Dad was *my* dad."

"What are you saying?"

She clicked on Monk's name. A photo popped up, probably sourced from Jobmilla, GLOAT's professional networking site. Dress shirt, necktie, the works. A button below said "Contact?"

She peeled off the mask. "Soon," she said, "I'm Monk Zingapan's daughter."

FRIDAY MORNING, THE SECURITY gate at the Asterisk buzzed menacingly as I entered. I jumped back and tried again, this time dipping my shoulder, as though to enhance whatever signal the Freckle in my arm emitted. For a moment, all seemed fine. Then three loud blasts stopped me in my tracks. Otto beckoned from his desk.

"Bruce Lee, hang back a sec?"

"No problem, grasshopper."

"I'm going to need to see your bag."

"Do your thing."

I handed over my satchel, mostly taken up with Dream Four, and moon-walked back to the other side as Otto gave a cursory look. There had been some technical issues since I'd gotten the Freckle implant; for a week in the spring, I was unable to automatically activate my VPN, leaving me logged out of my workstation. A minor nuisance. In fact, I found it gratifying, having to think through problems using pen and paper; I had even suggested it to the Ideas department: a one-day communal experience in which all work was done away from computers and devices. Almost like an extension of Little Eden.

Otto gave me the bag. I tried the gate, got buzzed again. Workers flowed past. I searched for familiar faces, someone to vouch for me, but everyone was studying their phones, perhaps sensing all was not right. I appealed to Otto, who was already shaking his head.

"Can't override it, Bruce," he said, grimacing at whatever dire readout the Freckle had triggered on his monitor.

I drew a knee to my waist and flapped my arms. "I'll teach you Drunken Eagle stance."

"I shouldn't be saying this." He glanced around. "They've got you down as an essay."

I froze, foot still in the air. "An essay about what?"

"I'm talking about the disciplinary code," Otto said. "An *S-A*, Bruce. *S* as in *situation, A* as in . . . I don't know, *alarming.*"

"Is that what it stands for?" I asked.

"I don't know what the letters stand for." His friendliness evaporated. "I just know it's *bad.*"

Was it akin to S-D, the Sex-Death quotient? Sex-Addiction, maybe. Sanity-Apathy. Tense, I tried reaching Dr. Ubu, my supervisor. My phone was a dead slab, though I could have sworn it was charged when I left home. Otto wouldn't let me use the antique landline on his desk. He told me to have a seat on my side of the invisible gate. Then he turned to his phone and unpaused his game of Hegemon.

"Ninth level," I said admiringly.

Otto hunched over so that his back blocked my sight line. I sat down on the couch by the wall. Wine-colored text moved along the ticker below the hexagonal skylight. Time, weather, stock quotes: if you waited long enough, it might reveal the contents of your heart, the meaning of life. Fragments of news recirculated, but I had been so out of the loop lately, caught up in Echo's book, that they resembled lines of an evil poem I couldn't parse. "I WILL KEEP YOU IN SUSPENSE" . . . INDIANS ADVANCE . . . SPARKS BEAT LYNX . . . MANILA PIVOTS TO BEIJING . . .

Around me, the stream of workers slowed to a trickle. Ella, Otto's supervisor, stood before me, holding a pen-sized scanner. Without a word, she let it hover an inch from the Freckle, moving it with the practiced tempo of a supermarket cashier until it beeped.

"I'm on sale today," I said. "Two for five dollars."

"Very clever, Mr. Soon."

"You've got it backward. The first name's Soon. The *last* name is Sheen."

Ella absorbed the correction neutrally.

"My first name is an adverb," I said. "My last name is a noun."

"Uh huh. Fantastic."

The gate didn't buzz this time. We walked along the western arm, so far out that the numbers on the doors looked unfamiliar. I was hoping to see anyone I knew, anyone who could rescue me. We stopped in front of an unremarkable section of curving wall. Ella waved her scanner to reveal a crisp green outline, as though drawn by her device: a narrow door, barely two feet wide. I entered sideways into humming darkness. As we walked down a sloping hall, a strip of small blue lights turned on at hip level. The polished floor twinned each one, giving the illusion of watery depths below.

Again Ella stopped abruptly and, waving her scanner, drew a door from the dark. This led to a bright speckless room, carpet like snow, empty save for a white desk with a huge monitor. Not a flat-screen, but something much older and bulkier. The opposite of sleek. The lettering had rubbed off, and the glass was dead gray. There was an unusual grooved divot above the screen, like a port for a discontinued cable.

I sat down and put on a headset. The screen glowed, a milky fuzziness building up under the layer of dirt until Dr. Ubu appeared in the glass,

dressed in complex tweeds instead of her usual navy pantsuit. The space behind her was black and vast, as if she were narrating a two-hour special on the origins of the universe. Presently, the backdrop filled in, one blotchy continent of pixels after another, until her surroundings resolved into a warmly lit study.

"Soon Sheen," she said sternly, as though disapproving of how short my name was.

"Good to see you again," I said. We hadn't been in touch for weeks.

Dr. Ubu stubbed out her cigarette. On the screen I could make out a green-shaded lamp on a circular table, vertiginous bookcases equipped with leather-wrapped ladders, a bay window looking out onto a misty field. Her cozy room was the opposite of my stark surroundings. She took out a lighter, another cigarette.

"Let me be frank," she said. *Franc.* "As you know, there is an S-A in progress."

I kept hearing *essay.* "Situation alarming."

She shook her head: *Not that.* "You're a Rung 10. A Rung 10 marked S-A is, how do you say, *hysteric*?"

She meant *historic.* "Historically good or historically bad?"

Dr. Ubu frowned. She stared at Ella and gestured with a thumb for her to leave.

"So tell me: What's S-A?" I asked. "Sex-Appetite? Sex-Annihilation? Sex . . . Agility?"

"Kindly remove your head out from the gutter, Soon Sheen," she said. "It stands for Sleeper Awakes."

Sleeper Awakes. A memory surfaced from the dawn of my GLOAT career. An all-hands, back when the company could fit in one room. Tanner Slow was at the whiteboard. He wrote *Sleeper Awakes* to describe the point at which a devoted GLOAT user renounces the platform, never to return. Not in anger or frustration, nor in response to any specific occurrence or general trend. The person just leaves, as though snapping out of a dream—as though, he said, the platform never existed. The person becomes a person again, steps back into the world. We stopped using the term years ago, maybe because so few users ever found their way out.

Smoke curled out of her nostrils. "As you know, we require all employees, of every Rung, to periodically fill out surveys on various matters. This helps GLOAT understand our collective thought-trends, allowing us to model conduct along mandatory—"

I snapped my fingers, to fast-forward through the boilerplate. A trick I'd learned. It never failed.

". . . the very real challenges of the workplace when it comes to . . ."

Snap. ". . . gone over the results from the Racial Sensitivity Training Course that you completed at eleven fifty-seven P.M. on the second of August. I assume the time stamp is accurate?"

Putting date before month was one of those tics that made Dr. Ubu "French," along with her complicated way of holding her cigarette between her middle and ring fingers.

"That's correct," I said.

Her image shattered. Sections of Dr. Ubu twisted along the horizontal. For one delirious second, head separated from body. Her eyes grew freakishly wide, then drooped as though melting. There were no visible controls on the monitor, so I administered some firm slaps to the hull. The gesture reminded me of when Story had a stomach bug last winter. I held her over the toilet, patting her between the shoulders as she threw up her lunch. Closing my eyes, saying everything was going to be fine.

At last the picture stabilized. Dr. Ubu was intact, though something felt off. The bookshelves seemed to be a different color, the table a different shape. The camera angle had changed, perhaps. She picked up in mid-sentence, unaware anything had happened: ". . . to explain your thinking, yes?"

I'd been overseen by Dr. Ubu long enough to know that in a crisis situation, she was waiting to hear certain phrases: *best practices, managing expectations, next steps.* Above all there was *ownership.* You *owned* projects, responsibilities. Mostly the term came up when noting one's failures. Saying the word was humbling and freeing.

I said, "My apologies."

"For?" She took a final drag of her cigarette and dropped it in the ash-

tray. All trace of the earlier cigarette was gone. I watched as this one vanished, too, as though dissolving in acid.

"For not being fully in the moment when I took the racial sensitivity course. I was on a train, and it was late. And I might have had a drink too many."

"Go on," Dr. Ubu said.

"I didn't have the right mindset," I said loudly, manipulating the system. "I should have waited. I kept getting prompts, though, saying I had to do the survey ASAP."

She didn't respond. What she heard was an employee shifting blame.

"Obviously, I should have known better that night," I added, recalibrating, my voice more contrite. "I take . . . *ownership* for not having done it earlier."

Dr. Ubu lit up at the magic word. "Very well. Let's review."

Several slides flashed by without comment—true/false questions that I'd aced back in August. She stopped on number 15. Here, Dr. Ubu explained, the format switched to multiple choice. I was given a "pass window" of 75 percent: for each statement, three conclusions were acceptable, to varying degrees, while one was flat-out wrong.

The first slide showed a sporty redhead and a slim black man standing by a coffee machine while a squat Asian guy threw back his head in laughter.

"Please read aloud."

15. If someone brings up an issue involving race, I will

    (A) say, "That's one opinion."

    (B) say, "I've found that people are all the same at heart."

    (C) contact a manager.

    (D) assert that Asians are the superior race.

"Uh," I said.

Dr. Ubu coughed metallically as my answer, D, was circled in red.

"The format changed halfway through. I . . . *own* that I should have paid more attention."

Dr. Ubu paced around the table, chin on chest. A handclap triggered the next slide: a couple in colorful *hanboks,* kneeling in a traditional wedding ceremony.

"Read," she directed.

16. Complete this sentence: Koreans are
     (A) hardworking.
     (B) respectful of their elders.
     (C) a homogenous people.
     (D) superior to all Asians!

I groaned. "Don't tell me I picked D."

"Pass window, seventy-five," she replied, as D was circled once again.

"I don't understand how D can be a choice!"

"Let's keep going."

"But I don't even believe it," I stammered. "My wife is South American! My daughter is white! I don't see race at all." I was fudging things in regard to Nora, and I didn't know if that last part was entirely correct, but I put into practice another GLOAT tenet: I *doubled down.* "Anyone who knows me knows that."

Dr. Ubu looked dubious. Amid my panic, I could see where I'd gone wrong. It wasn't that *all* GLOAT employees had faced these questions. No, it was that I'd fumbled number 15, a softball, so badly that the error had caused a cascade effect. Every obviously incorrect answer prompted an even more insane question—generated on the fly by GLOAT HR's AI. Under the influence of Echo and alcohol, I had swerved from race-related niceties into something deeply Korean, troubling, and—even I could see—fireable.

"Let's look at a few more."

Clap. A sepia photo of a brooding man with a sad mustache, holding a bandaged hand to his chest. I knew who it was: Thomas Ahn, killer of Ito Hirobumi. I realized, to my horror, that I was mirrored by the screen in the exact same pose, hand clamped to chest.

17. Korea was colonized by Japan in 1910.

    (A) This is a part of history from which lessons have been learned.

    (B) It was inevitable: Japan was modernizing quickly, and Korea was still living in feudal times.

    (C) Japan was *defending* Korea against possible future encroachments of the West.

    (D) Korea was never really colonized!

"My phone," I mumbled. My palms were slick. "It must have auto-filled D."

Clap. Next up, a map of the Korean Peninsula, the North in Pepto-Bismol pink, the South in a powdery purple. The image was animated, the colored proportions moving, as forces advanced and retreated.

18. After Japan's defeat in World War II, Korea was divided into North and South across the 38th parallel

    (A) by someone in the U.S. State Department who had to find a map in *National Geographic* because he wasn't exactly sure where Korea was.

    (B) and the animosity between the Soviet-backed North and the U.S.-backed South led to the Korean War—the "Forgotten War."

    (C) where no border existed before.

    (D) *or was it?!*

"Okay, I was clearly . . ." I was about to say *out of my mind.* "Who came up with these questions?" I gasped, as good old D got the circle treatment.

What had I meant, that Korea was intact, undivided? I grasped, now, that D was what a member of the Korean Provisional Government might answer. As a mission statement, a goal. Was the survey a covert instrument to recruit KPG officers? I reminded myself that there *was* no KPG. That it had once existed but had been gone for seventy years. That I had to separate fact from fiction.

"Well?" Dr. Ubu said.

"I, uh, *own* that I wasn't thinking right. I'll do better, starting this week—starting *now*."

"Final question."

Clap. A crude collage: Tanks. Gaunt POWs, leaving a building. General MacArthur with his trademark pipe. A baby crying in a ditch, clutching its dead mother.

19. The Korean War

(A) was started by the North, which violated the 38th parallel.

(B) was started by the South, which provoked the North.

(C) lasted from 1950 to 1953 . . . but never officially ended.

(D) *is about to start again!*

I opened my mouth to apologize, to *own,* or possibly to scream. But then I stopped. Dr. Ubu had a strange look on her face. My supervisor was frozen.

THE THING ABOUT Dr. Ubu was that she wasn't real.

After the move to Dogskill, GLOAT replaced most of its management team with Directed Reality "You Be You" modules (hence D-R U-B-U), which, among other things, removed emotion from the equation. Workflow was stabilized, so that goals were attained on time. GLOAT's high attrition rate was mostly due to the inability of new hires to get used to receiving critiques from a piece of software, no matter how lifelike. The smallest hiccup in the voice synthesizer or flaw in the image could shatter the illusion, reminding you that there was no one behind that mask.

Dr. Ubu—*my* Dr. Ubu—was currently a chic Frenchwoman with a steely gaze. Previously I'd been overseen by a cheerful Brazilian metrosexual, a sylphlike Hungarian, and a melancholy Indian Norwegian who dressed in sweatpants. The algorithm selected the avatar's attributes, from gender to clothing to skin color to accent.

Seeing her frozen, I knew that it was happening again: Dr. Ubu was about to change.

Taking her place was a white shape, of a flatness at odds with the

reading-room tableau. I'd never witnessed a live metamorphosis. The form thrashed, as though trying to pull off a smock. Yet there was no sound of struggle. It was like watching glue get pushed around a piece of glass.

I had an urge to bang on the door and shout for Ella, but I knew she was nowhere near. I controlled my breathing. Shut my eyes, and moved backward in time to August, to reading Dream One on the train, spellbound; to the multiple-choice fiasco; to the Admiral Yi. . . . When I opened my eyes, the inchoate shape had resolved into a muscular Asian woman in athleisurewear, working the elliptical machine in what looked like a tidy hotel gym. Bottled water and towels were arrayed behind her. The error was bizarre, inexcusable. Instead of Dr. Ubu 5.0, I was watching what seemed to be a participant in one of GLOAT's virtual exercise classes, caught in mid-climb.

"Soon Sheen," the woman said, stopping her uphill progress. "We meet again."

In a flash, I could tell she was real, not a new Dr. Ubu, not some grab bag of attributes brought to digital life. The face was familiar. The name was coming to me. She wasn't wearing glasses, and her hair was in a ponytail that went past her shoulders, but this was none other than Daisy Oh, translator of *Same Bed, Different Dreams.*

"I've been trying to get in touch," I said. "About Echo."

"We know," she said. "Something has come up. Echo is gone."

"Monk told me that Echo was supposed to teach at Rue but never showed up."

"It's worse than that." Daisy drew a breath. "He left a note."

"Suicide?" She didn't respond. "Or do you mean he was murdered?" I said.

"In Dream Two, he implies that Ito Hirobumi *wanted* to be assassinated—that he helped plot the whole thing, leading his killer to the Harbin train station."

"Right." So Daisy knew I had read Dream Two. It confirmed what I'd been thinking: that she was the one who switched my bag at the Admiral Yi.

"Some people serve a purpose, in the grand scheme of things," she said. "He lived his life heroically."

"Echo is . . . *was* . . . an incredible—a unique—uh," I babbled. "I'm sorry he's gone."

"The past is the past." She wiped her brow with a towel. I saw the craftshop necklace she'd worn at the Admiral Yi, on which dangled the fourteensided *juryungu* and other trinkets. "We were counting on you to help."

"Help?" I also could have said: *We?* I noticed that Daisy's nails were a soothing avocado hue.

"His note said he wanted you to finish the book. The fifth and final Dream."

"I'd be thrilled." I blurted how I'd read the last page of Dream Four a week ago and was hungry for more. It had taken me a while to get that far, given Sprout's illness. I told her he was a sick pooch, and one of his few remaining joys was burying things and finding them later. That didn't matter now. I was ready to take on Dream Five.

"We don't mean reading it," Daisy said, cutting me short, "but *writing* it. Which is why we arranged for you to have a copy in the first place. No one else has read as much of it as you have—well, except me."

"So *you* switched the bags at the restaurant," I said.

Daisy didn't say anything for a while. She unclasped her necklace and put it on the elliptical's tray. I saw her slip one of the items off: a cigarette lighter. It resembled Dr. Ubu's, except it didn't appear to work. The wheel made a loud sparkless *chk* as she thumbed it.

"Like I told you at the dinner: the book isn't done," she said. "Echo had been working on it for twenty years. Great Unfinishable Masterpiece Syndrome."

"Good old GUMS," I said.

"Back in the fall, Tanner wanted to press Print, to publish *Same Bed, Different Dreams* as just four parts. What difference could it make? But Echo told Tanner to wait. Said it would be missing the point. Everything was building up to Dream Five, the longest one yet. It would be the key to all that came before."

The key. I was practically salivating.

"He recognized that a huge chunk of his book would have to grapple with America." *Chk* went the lighter in her hand. "Echo knew he needed a collaborator—an American who could help him with certain scenes."

"Now I get why Tanner invited me to dinner," I said. "He needed to audition an American ghost."

"Echo *had* read *Pretenders*," she assured me, "long before Tanner recommended it."

"How? Only about ten people in America ever picked it up."

"Give me *some* credit." *Chk chk.* "I convinced Echo it was not to be missed, and before he finished the first page, he agreed. He thought you were the one."

"The one," I repeated, light-headed.

"Of course, he read English slowly, so . . . that was a good half hour." She stepped off the elliptical. "So how about it?" *Chk.* "I told Tanner I could convince you."

"But I don't write anymore."

"Today, you do."

Daisy was back in steamroller mode, the urgency oddly intoxicating.

"How are you even here?" I asked. "Did you hack into the Dr. Ubu interface?"

"I work at GLOAT, Soon," Daisy said, taking the towel from around her neck and holding it to the camera, reversed, so I could see our company's name stitched in green. Now I recognized her location—the new health spa in the northeast spoke—but I was still lost.

"If you work here, at the Asterisk, does that mean you *didn't* translate Echo?"

"Of course I did. That's most of what my job is: bringing his books into English. It's all been leading up to *Same Bed, Different Dreams.* The culmination of years of work."

"And GLOAT is behind it?"

"It's too complicated to get into right now." In a more encouraging tone, she said, "Everything will be revealed, once you start Dream Five. You have twenty-four hours to finish."

I blinked. "That's impossible."

"It's nearly done. You can read it in two hours, max." The image flickered. "Then—we just need you to fill in some blanks. No big deal. Just put in things only you would know."

"But I hardly know anything when it comes to Korea."

"Trust me—you know more than you know."

And maybe I did. I'd been immersed in Echo's version of Korea for months. It had to be good for *something.*

"Most of all, it needs a last line." *Chk.* "So much hinges on the end, Echo always said." *Chk chk.* "We've set up this room for you. Optimal conditions. Peace and quiet. There's a button by the door—press it for meals, coffee, a cot if you need a power nap. Also, I messaged Nora from your account to say you're working late."

"Wait!" I said, as the picture trembled. "One last question."

"Yes?"

There were a lot of questions swirling in my head. Some had been with me since that morning, others for months, a few, perhaps, for years and years. I closed my eyes, picked the one that came to me first.

"Who killed Echo?"

"Says the man hiding a gun."

"What gun?"

"The Tan Gun," Daisy said. "A user at an IP address corresponding to your residence gathered and printed the final pieces."

I could feel the plastic gun through the fabric of the satchel. I thought of how, over the past few months, Story had collected the blueprints in the world of Hegemon—alone first, then with her clubmates at school. She had printed out the pieces, deep into the night at home, or at her school with one of its more cutting-edge machines, then figured out how they came together. Did the Tan Gun "work"—had she somehow . . . *killed* Echo from half a world away? And what exactly were they teaching the kids at Measures?

"That can't be right." I reached into the bag for the Tan Gun. It felt oddly heavy in my hand. I looked down the barrel, which had a squared-off opening and a horizontal slit a centimeter in. "Hegemon is just a game."

Daisy placed the lighter on a towel, began wrapping it like a present. "Remember what I said about Ito Hirobumi predicting his own assassination."

"I don't see how that applies."

"You told Echo that you would kill him. That night at the Admiral Yi."

"I *what*?"

"That was your 'secret thing,' your true confession," she said. "For the drinking game. Rolling that old wooden fourteen-sided die."

"The Jury—I remember the game. But why would I say *that*?"

"Echo was *happy* when you said it."

"Happy?"

"He knew this was how it had to end—knew it even before he met you," Daisy said. Then she threw the swaddled lighter into the air. The towel landed on the ground, but I didn't see or hear the lighter fall. A parlor trick.

"What did you just do? Where did it go?"

"It's yours now," she said, as the image flickered. "See you on the other side."

The screen went blank. I looked at the Tan Gun on the desk. Instantly, I knew: the lighter was here, inside the gun. *That's* why it had felt so heavy. Otto must have loaded the Zippo into the handle when he'd checked my bag at the security desk. The hollow at the bottom of the handle was half an inch long, now filled with the lighter. Etched into that sliver of metal—the butt end of the Zippo—were the letters KPG.

My screen had reverted to a standard GLOAT landscape, strewn with icons. A white oval rose from the table to chin height: a microphone, or speaker, or both. On the monitor, a dialogue box said INSERT TAN GUN, above a crude but clear sketch of the hole right above the screen. The barrel clicked into place, and within seconds a mechanism inside the monitor drew it in fully.

I let go. A gold coin twirled slowly in the center of the screen, pixels flashing white to mimic a shimmer. When it stopped, I could read the Korean word on its face:

꿈

I said it aloud: *Ggum.* What did it mean? *Ggum.*

Of course. The word for *dream.*

"Dream Five," came a dead man's voice through the speakers, as deep black text started rolling up the screen.

DREAM FIVE
1919-PRESENT

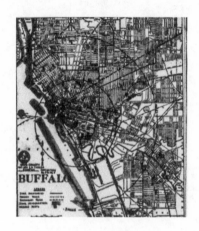

1. What Is History?

Moon Young-myung becomes Soon Sun Chang. Kim Eunguk becomes Richard E. Kim. Yura Irsenovich Kim becomes Kim Jong Il, the second leader of North Korea.

Norma Jeane Mortenson of Los Angeles becomes Marilyn Monroe. Patricia Betsy Hrunek of East Chicago, Indiana, becomes Betsy Palmer. Ronald Wilson Reagan of Tampico, Illinois, becomes Lieutenant Brass Bancroft, Flying Officer Johnny Hammond, Lieutenant Paul Random, and the fortieth president of the United States of America.

This is the last dream of the Korean Provisional Government.

2. The KPG Goes to the Movies

In April 23, 1919, almost two months after the March 1 demonstrations against Japanese rule, the newly formed Korean Provisional Government elects Syngman Rhee as its first president. Word arrives from KPG headquarters in Shanghai. Though he's made Hawaii his home base since finishing his American education, the forty-four-year-old Rhee is in Washington when he gets the news.

He would like to see for himself that the KPG is real, not just a name on letterhead. But Japan monitors all movement in and out of Shanghai as well. He would be arrested on the spot.

That evening he celebrates with Ryu, a friend from his Boston days, at a French restaurant off Dupont Circle. Unfortunately, they are in the same room as the two-faced ambassador from the Korean legation, a man in the pocket of the Japanese. An argument breaks out between the ambassador's party and Ryu during the soup course. Syngman leaves.

The president-in-exile takes a streetcar downtown in the rain. Could spies from the legation be trailing him? He steps off, pulls up his collar. *Be careful.* Syngman hops over the swollen gutter and spots a dim marquee: *Broken Blossoms.* The title recalls a poem Ryu sent him, clipped from a newspaper. About leaving Korea forever, on a path of petals. What was it called?

A dime gets him a ticket and a sack of peanuts. He sits in the fifth row and shells them greedily, his victory dinner. He studies the back of his ticket.

> This theatre, under normal conditions, with every seat occupied, can be emptied in three minutes. Look around now, choose the nearest exit to your seat, and in case of disturbance of any kind, to avoid the dangers of panic, *walk* (do not run) to that exit.

The shabby cinema's like the inside of an egg. White flaps hang from the domed ceiling. A newsreel plays to the half-filled theater. The figures jerk as though pricked with electricity. The public sees a boxer in Boston, a parade in Paris, a star-shaped pleasure boat that tops seventy miles an hour. No news of the uprising in Korea. If only a title card would proclaim, *In Shanghai today, the KPG—the one true voice for Korean sovereignty—has declared Dr. Syngman Rhee its president.* . . . The houselights would go up, and a huge Korean flag would unfurl from the rafters. He can picture the crowd on its feet, murmuring, *That's him—fifth row!*

A fat man in a checked suit huffs down the aisle, apologizing hoarsely for being late. He hits the end of the carpet and goes sprawling. *Walk, do not run.* In a nook by the screen is a piano. It's all an act! The man dusts himself off, wipes the bench with a red handkerchief as they ready the feature reel. Before he sits, he sees another speck, whips out the cloth again—this time with a giant pair of bloomers tied to the end. The audience roars. Even Syngman throws back his head. The fat man lifts the lid, howls when it slams his fingers.

He sticks to the black keys, a lopsided rhythm as the curtain opens. Only now does Syngman Rhee, first president of the Korean Provisional Government, catch the movie's subtitle: *The Yellow Man and the Girl.* The hero is a slender Mandarin who comes to London to spread Buddha's word. The mission comes to grief, and the man is reduced to running a mean old shop in Limehouse. Syngman clutches his knees. The pang of exile hits him, there in row 5, even though the white actor doesn't look Oriental, in fact does not look human at all.

The music changes constantly. Here and there, a cluster repeats, only to be washed away in a flurry of nonsense notes. *Clang-clang, clang-clang!* Crisp, no pedal. Occasionally, the piano player lifts his hands, lets a gap of silence sit there.

The Chinaman befriends a waif. Her father is a boxer and a drunk; when he discovers who she's been commiserating with, he hurls her to the floor. Syngman Rhee feels unclean watching. Though not Chinese, he *is* the Chinaman in most rooms. At Harvard. At Woodrow Wilson's house in Princeton. Chinaman. Peanut shells crumble underfoot. *Clang-clang.* Filthy Chinaman. Vermin scuttle nearby. His spine tingles with fear, as all of Limehouse breathes down his neck. Syngman has the awful sensation that the whole theater is watching *him*.

The piano rumbles. The waif's face glows through the grime.

"*You!* With a dirty Chink!"

For all his Western affectations, Syngman Rhee remains despised. *Avoid the dangers of panic.* Something rustles nearby. Rat or man? *Clang-clang!* A cutthroat unsheathing his blade . . . *Clang!* The president of the KPG dashes out before the movie ends, so quickly he leaves his best hat. *Broken Blossoms.* The storm has passed. Syngman Rhee trudges through the marsh of newspapers covering the pavement. As he turns down Tenth, the name of that Korean poem lands on his brain: *Azaleas.*

3. The Fingers of Harold Lloyd

Three months later, on August 24, the movie star Harold Lloyd poses for press shots. He digs through a box of props. Props make the man. Even his trademark spectacles aren't real. (He has perfect eyesight.) The photographer hands him a plump black bomb, strikes a match. Harold mugs, pretends to light his cigar with the spark.

But the spark's all wrong, the way it flickers. The bomb's no prop. Drop it, *drop* it, the photog cries, with an inch left to the fuse. Harold's grin gets sillier as flame eats wick. The cameraman steps back with an arm over his face as the silent actor gets the full dose.

Boom. Harold's eyes won't open. He doesn't understand why it's night. Dreams he's on a sinking ship, dreams he's dead. After a week, his sight returns, but the fingers of his right hand don't respond. Parts are wrecked for good.

Four years later, in 1923, Harold Lloyd makes *Safety Last!* He dons a special glove to conceal his missing thumb and index finger. For the long, giddy climax, he climbs the side of a department store to elude the police. Every floor hides a zany hazard. At one point, Harold peers into the studio of a theatri-

cal photographer, a room set up just like the place where an actual bomb went off in his hands. But before our hero can climb inside and out of harm's way, he freezes. There's a man with a gun. The gun is pointed at *him*. Harold doesn't register that it's part of an action tableau. The flash goes off, and he scrambles back out the window.

If only the real Harold could have escaped four years ago, tossed the bomb away before it exploded. At times he wonders: How *did* the real bomb get mixed in with the fakes?

The Korean Provisional Government isn't saying. It isn't saying anything about Harold Lloyd's cunning glove, his missing digits. It isn't saying whether this is a show of solidarity with the Korean cause. It isn't saying that the injury pays tribute to the assassin Thomas Ahn, who cut off his finger before shooting Ito Hirobumi fourteen years before.

Harold Lloyd is a member of the Korean Provisional Government.

4. Thorns in the Mouth

Returning to Honolulu from D.C. in the summer of 1919, Syngman Rhee, president of the KPG, learns from his friend William Borthwick that his life is in danger. He's ignored the threats before, rumors that the Japanese crown wants him dead. This time feels different. Rhee trusts Borthwick, a mortician from Illinois, who knows of grave matters. Syngman must leave Hawaii at once. *Now* would be the ideal time to slip off to Shanghai, to see with his own eyes the offices of the Korean Provisional Government. But how?

Borthwick winks. "Heard of playing possum?" The deal is that he sometimes ships dead Chinese workers back to their homeland so they can have proper funerals. In November, then, Syngman Rhee and his secretary, a recent Ohio State graduate named Ben Limb, slip into coffins stored aboard the SS *West Hika*. Clean clothes and important papers fill a third casket.

Borthwick oversees it all, whistling tunelessly as he dusts the lids. The crew has no clue.

The *Hika* sets sail. For a whole day, Rhee and Limb swelter inside their boxes. At night each man raps on the wood, taps out the galloping "Arirang" to let the other man know he's alive. They plan to emerge after the sailors eat breakfast. Syngman Rhee prays the crew won't throw them overboard. He'll let Ben do the talking, for once. Ben will claim that Syngman is his father.

In the morning, the naked Koreans crawl out of their coffins, dress, and go up to the deck. It's half an hour before a crew-man notices the presence of the two undead Chinamen. He goes pale. Ben Limb explains that they lost a bet to Borthwick, and the seamen scream with laughter. It's the damnedest thing, like a gag in a Chaplin movie.

To stay on the safe side, the Koreans simulate Chinese. They quote Confucius with heavy accents, as the sun disinfects their clothes. *Unless reading every day, thorns grow in the mouth.* Rhee offers to polish brass, peel vegetables. Of course, young Ben Limb does all the work. Syngman retires to the hold. He turns his old coffin into a desk, composes a series of presidential speeches. The voyage takes forty days, forty nights. They run out of Confucius quotes and make up their own. He exhausts his paper, writes speeches on his old collars.

At last, the *West Hika* reaches Shanghai. Syngman wakes to the affectionate bitching of gulls. Junks clutter the Whangpoo, the river like a road of jade. He and Limb return to their coffins as the Japanese inspectors peek into the hold. The smell of the dead beats them back.

The Koreans disembark in fresh linen suits. Ben Limb's hair glistens with pomade. "Mr. President," he says in English, "you are wanted at headquarters."

In Korean, the word for *boat* is the same as the word for *womb.*

SAME BED DIFFERENT DREAMS 411

5. The Second Coming

Chongju, northern Korea, 1920. Over three decades, the Presbyterian faith has taken root all over the country, thanks to Horace Underwood. Among the converts are the Moons, a farming family that has just welcomed another child, Young-myung. None will prove as devout as him.

On Easter Sunday, 1935, Jesus appears to the fifteen-year-old Moon Young-myung. The words are not in any language he knows, yet he understands perfectly. (Later he guesses Aramaic.) On that calm spring morning, Jesus Christ tells Young-myung that though he's just a humble boy from the sticks, he is the Second Coming.

6. The Camp

The same year Moon meets Jesus, the Christy family opens a summer camp by a pristine lake in New Jersey. For the next thirty-some years, it will supply young campers with a lifetime of memories.

7. 2333

Moon Young-myung excels in high school. He studies the Bible, reads poetry, and goes on to study electrical engineering at Waseda University in Tokyo. He makes friends with Japanese students, but he sometimes questions why he's in that foreign country, that city reeking of gasoline. His favorite poem is "Azaleas," by Kim Sowol, which he begins to treat like a dangerous substance; even *thinking* about the poem is liable to bring tears to his eyes.

Lately he's been reading the craziest poems, sent by a friend in Korea, who had found them in an old newspaper back home: "Crow's-Eye View." One invokes Al Capone, an American gangster. Another is like a horror story, about thirteen children running down the road. . . . *The #1 child says he's scared, the #2 child says he's scared.* . . . What are they running from? And did

the poet need to repeat the line thirteen times? More to the point: How are these even *poems*? Most unsettling is the one made up of digits and dots.

The numbers quiver like a beaded curtain. Everything is backward and *wrong*, a view from the other side. . . . The other side of *what*? The poems are disorienting enough on their own. The fact that they're by a Korean named Yi Sang makes it even worse. Without wanting to, he memorizes them, until they echo in his head like bad dreams.

One day, an envelope marked "2333" appears in his coat pocket. Empty. It feels like a Yi Sang poem: inexplicable, numerical, menacing. The next week, he finds another one in his satchel. *2333*. It has directions to the Tokyo branch of the Korean YMCA. Moon gathers that he's invited to a secret meeting of expats, maybe even a branch of the Korean Provisional Government. He was born a year after the March 1 Movement, but he knows all about the KPG and its leader, Syngman Rhee, an old man calling the shots from America.

Invitations keep arriving, the locales more distant each time. *2333*. His curiosity finally gets the better of him. He takes a train to a warehouse on the edge of the city. Out of these twenty Korean expats, five are fellow Waseda students. (Mr. Min, a janitor at the school by day, is in actuality a former court official.) Four are women; one, he's not sure. Two have mangled hands. Many are fiery speakers, and Moon marvels at the eloquent rage on display. Their talk of sabotage is another matter. What did the bloody acts of Thomas Ahn and Inwhan Chang do for Korea? Only made things worse. The attendees know he's studying electrical engineering and assume he can wire explosives. Moon won't comment or commit.

Mr. Min explains the number on the envelope: 2333. The KPG acknowledges the legendary founding of Korea as occurring in 2333 B.C. That was when Dangun was born, the child of a she-bear and a deity who had come from the sky. Dangun

civilized the people and became their king. Moon is Christian but knows this fairy tale from that book of lore the *Samguk Yusa*.

"Which means I was born in 4253, not 1920," Moon jokes.

"Exactly right!" Mr. Min whispers sternly. "The *correct numbers* are important."

Afterward, Mr. Min rides back to campus with Moon Young-myung, talking all the while. He assures Moon that he, too, is a Christian. He says that some of the more militant members of the Korean Provisional Government believe that Dangun's original domain, thousands of years before Christ, stretched north to encompass most of Manchuria and south to claim parts of modern-day Japan, perhaps even the ground they are walking on now. He finds such claims a distraction from their main goal: the liberation of Korea.

"Still," he confides proudly, "we Koreans in Japan are more Korean than the ones back home. We are the *true* descendants of Dangun."

In the morning, Moon finds a sheet under his door: the layout of a train station in Chiba Prefecture, twenty miles away. The meaning is clear: the KPG wants to know the best way to blow it up. He throws the sketch away and ignores future invitations. Moon frets. He wonders if the folks he met were indeed officers of the provisional government or freelance patriots—or, in fact, spies working to bring *down* the KPG.

8. Three Jails

A Japanese classmate worries about Moon's fragile mental state, but the Korean says it's just homesickness. They talk late into the night. Could their two countries ever live together in peace? *Someday.* Soon after, police officers arrest Moon on a vaporous charge of *thought crimes.* Jesus Christ visits him in jail to say that this is not the end. A grand design awaits.

Japan is hostile to Christians, and he fears for the safety of

his Savior. But no one else can see. A few days later, Moon is released and can return to his studies.

In 1945, Moon sails back to Korea. In Pyongyang, he attends church every day. He cherishes being in a place where Christianity thrives. Alas, the sermons lack substance. They are based on a Western view of history, thanks to missionaries like Horace Underwood. The words are shaky translations, irrelevant to the desperate situation at hand, as Koreans turn against one another. He preaches in his own style, on street corners and in empty storefronts. The Lord has a plan for Korea. Moon shares his early encounter with Jesus, a story that improves with each telling. As his flock grows, the godless Communists accuse him of working for Syngman Rhee, also a Christian, in the South. He's never met Rhee, who is almost three times his age. They jail and torture Moon, put his body outside for crows. His followers rescue him, and he preaches for two years before he's locked up in the notorious prison at Hungnam.

His captors work him to the bone. New inmates arrive; they leave a few weeks later as corpses. Even in the worst moments, Moon senses Jesus watching, giving him the will to live. Each beating is a story to be spun into a future sermon; each scar renews his faith.

9. Salvation

To strengthen his spirit, Moon eats only half his meager allowance of millet. He gives the rest to his cellmate or to the rats. Moon is still languishing in Hungnam when the Korean War breaks out in June 1950. The Communist guards jeer at the weakness of Syngman Rhee's forces, awaiting the day when Kim Il Sung will bring him to heel. But after the Americans join the fight, and the South forces the North back up, the guards are terrified. They execute their prisoners and prepare to flee. Moon knows that death is near. With a piece of charcoal, he writes the names of his parents on the wall. He writes the year

of his birth as 4253. Then he writes the number 2333, over and over. In his delirium he confuses Dangun, Korea's founding deity, with Jesus Christ.

On what should have been Moon's last morning alive, Jesus makes his presence known. It is very loud and then very quiet. After an hour, Moon realizes the guards have fled. American voices fill the corridors: Hungnam has been liberated. Moon embraces his saviors and walks out the door. He returns to Pyongyang, once called the Jerusalem of the East. In just two years the Communists have erased all outward signs of Christianity. Moon locates some of the remaining faithful, and they head for the border, hitching rides. The road south cuts through a land defiled. Corpses hiss as gas seeps out, so loud it sounds like screaming. In a ditch Moon sees something glow: a tangle of bones picked clean. Mother skeleton clutching baby skeleton, which still tries to nurse, even in death. He puts a hand on each skull and prays.

Moon preaches wherever he stops, gaining followers as he goes. Reaching the safety of Pusan, his flock cobbles the very first Unification Church out of empty ration bins, the junk of the U.S. Army. What the mighty discard, the humble may use.

10. The Tennessee Waltz

Meanwhile, in Pennsylvania, a girl named Pam wonders what it's all about. Why do countries fight? Why can't there be *peace*? (Her mother's fancy-pants cousin, Barbara, is in Korea with her husband, who's in the service.) Pam's an artistic girl, in her last year at a high school twenty miles outside Philly. For a social studies project, in September 1950, she draws a map of Korea, carefully penciling the outline before going over it with ink. She notes the major events of the war so far: the invasion, the Inchon landing. She spells the South Korean capital "Soul."

For a bit of flair, Pam dots the map with glue and drizzles

glitter over it. The whole thing sparkles like snow. Her Korea looks like a fairyland, but that's how Pam thinks of it sometimes, thanks to the antiques Aunt Barbara has shipped. (Her mother stores them in the basement, complaining.) There's an exquisite wooden chest, the size of their big Magnavox set, with an iron clasp held shut by a heavy bolt. When her parents fight—over money, meals, the imported bric-a-brac clogging the cellar—Pam slips downstairs and crawls into the chest. Folds herself up in the dark, like a small animal in its burrow or a baby yet to be born.

Everything changes one Saturday. She's at a lunch counter, waiting to pick up her sister from some dumb movie, when she sees a boy who graduated two years ago. Football player. For some reason he's walking toward her.

"Paula?"

"I'm Pamela. Or just Pam."

"*Right*." He looks at the book she's brought. "What are you reading, Just Pam?"

She flips it over: *You Can't Go Home Again*.

He snorts. "That's for damn sure."

"You're Henry, right? The kicker?"

"Just Hank."

Hank Woods lives in a room above the auto garage where he works part-time. He makes enough to pay the rent, he says, put gas in his car, and, most important, buy burgers and shakes for the occasional pretty girl. She blushes. A temporary setup, he says. Hank's just come back from signing up for the fight in Korea. The army might not take him: he busted his knee in the last game of senior year.

Pam opens up, tells him about her map. She wants to be a cartographer, she says—a confession that surprises her as much as him. He calls her Rand McNally. They jaw so much that she's late to collect her sister. The theater's close, but Hank insists they take his car. (Later she guesses that it was to mask

his limp.) He drops all the girls off. That night Pamela's sister teases her, threatens to tell their parents.

Things move fast. Most days, Hank picks her up from school and drives her home, just so they can spend ten minutes together. He's the sweetest. On weekends they go to the football game or the movies, or they sit and neck in the car. He gives her his school ring. It's missing the stone.

Pam is happy, except when he complains about their little town. He wants to go and fight. One afternoon, waiting in the car while her mother picks up heart medicine, Pam hears "The Tennessee Waltz" on the radio. The singer recalls dancing to a song called "The Tennessee Waltz," and how her partner went off with someone else as the song played on. Pam is lost. So is there another, older sad song called "The Tennessee Waltz," or did the guy leave during the song that's coming out of the radio *right now*? That night in bed, she can't stop her thoughts from racing. She can't sleep. She goes to the basement and gets inside the wooden box, arms around her knees. Next thing she knows, it's morning. She can smell breakfast on the kitchen table. Pam's mother doesn't see her sneak up to her room to change.

The day arrives: the army calls up Hank, trick knee and all. Pam feels wretched, but his bravery wins her over. Excites her. That night she sneaks out of the house to go to his room. A month later, Pamela discovers she's pregnant.

Hank, home briefly from boot camp before shipping out, is furious. The news is actually a blessing, Pamela explains: fathers can defer their deployment.

"Fathers?" Hank spits, furious. A vein pulses in his neck as he twists her arm.

"You're hurting me," she says calmly, as though watching a movie. She sees herself falling down the stairs, and sees herself see herself falling. Like looking into a mirror facing a mirror. Like listening to "The Tennessee Waltz."

He's standing over her. Pam says, in a notch above a whisper, "You're hurting our baby."

A punch shocks her into laughter. She feels something inside: the baby giggling with her. Nothing to fear. Her womb is a sturdy Korean chest, she thinks, as she tumbles down the stairs. Later, she justifies his behavior. Hank must be terrified about going off to fight. The Chinese have entered the war, and things look grim.

He leaves in the dead of winter, without a word. By April 1951, Pam cannot hide the life growing inside. Her parents are livid. They arrange a room for Pam at the Salvation Army Home for Unwed Mothers in Philadelphia. Her father drops her off. Alone, Pam weeps for days, can't hold anything down but crackers. She writes to Hank, care of the U.S. Army. She writes to Aunt Barbara, care of Uncle Frank. No one answers.

Her water breaks. Staggering through the hospital corridor, she spots a bright plaque:

DR. PHILIP JAISOHN
JANUARY 7, 1864—JANUARY 5, 1951
Physician & Patriot
DEDICATED TO HIS MEMORY
BY THE GRATEFUL MEMBERS OF THE KPG

He only died this year. Who was he? What is the KPG? The questions tumble in her head during the thirteen-hour labor. Something's not right. The pain gets so bad she wants to die. How would Hank feel then? A voice tells her to keep going, to *push*. She imagines it's the spirit of Dr. Jaisohn, whoever he was.

At last the baby arrives. For luck she names him after the man on the plaque. Alas, the nurse assumes the spelling is off, and it appears as plain old *Jason* on the certificate. As soon as she sees her son, Pamela's heart sinks. A specialist she's never seen before says there are *severe physical and mental defects*. But

what can she do? Dealt a bad hand, Pam loves her baby even more. She vows to make him as happy and comfortable as she can. They live at the Home for Unwed Mothers for a month. His appearance unnerves the others. The head is too small for the body, which is too small to begin with. The boy bawls at all hours of the night—his cry is not that of a normal baby, more like a crow's caw. Pam's mom relents and lets her come home. She stays in the basement with Jason, whom they can barely stand to look at. The Korean chest, lined with a quilt, makes a fine crib.

One day, she works up the courage to visit Hank's house—not the place above the garage but his childhood home, where his parents and a grandmother still live. The splendor astounds her. Then Pam gets upset. How *dare* Hank not support *their* son? How dare these people not acknowledge their own flesh and blood?

She waits on the porch, holding Jason. The blanket obscures everything but his eyes. Just as Pamela turns away, the door creaks open. Hank's grandmother stands there, looking like a half-sized sculpture of him. Then Pam realizes that this is in fact his *mother*. Before Pamela can speak, his mother says, "Henry isn't coming back." There's an envelope in her hand, with a telegram from the army. "He isn't coming back at all."

11. The Border

The future of civilization depends on what we do now, President Truman barked on TV, back in 1950. He blamed Red Russia for North Korea's invasion of the South. Three years later, in the summer of 1953, the Korean War has deadlocked. Syngman Rhee wants to keep fighting but finally gives in to the American plan for a cease-fire. The 38th parallel is reset as the dividing line. After the prisoner exchange, no one can cross in either direction.

Nothing was achieved, Rhee thinks, not even the status quo. A nation cut in two. Things are bad and will only get worse. *That* is the "future of civilization." Rhee is seventy-eight.

12. The Third Israel

The Reverend Moon knows he can never go back home. After relocating to Seoul, he buys a wood-paneled station wagon off an American GI. Sometimes he drives around for days by himself, in a giant circle through war-torn towns and blasted countryside, like a beast taking in the dimensions of its cage. By the second month, Jesus has started flagging him down for rides. Jesus insists that *Moon* is the Second Coming, the *new* Messiah. He says, "Why do you think I saved you from the prison in Hungnam?" He says that though the Korean War had no victor, it was not fought in vain. In fact, it was setting the stage for the end of this world and the beginning of heaven on earth. Jesus explains that Korea is not just an arbitrary spot on a map but the ultimate battlefield, where those who love God do battle with the armies of Lucifer.

Moon smokes as he drives. Jesus reveals the one true plan of history, centered on the number 4. Israel—the first Israel—went through four hundred years of oppression. America—the "Second Israel"—has had four hundred years of painful evolution, from colonial times to its current state. (How the dates line up is unclear—hasn't the United States been around for only half that length?—but Moon accepts the parallel.) Korea's recent dark period—its forty years under the Japanese—marks it as the *Third* Israel. Though this span is one-tenth that of its predecessors, it is apparently equivalent in terms of suffering. According to Jesus, the modern age has sped up not just communication and transportation but prophecy as well. (It makes more sense when Jesus says it.)

Moon lets Jesus off at Inchon and points the station wagon Seoul-ward.

13. The Third Dimension

In 1923, Harold Lloyd weds Mildred Davis, his *Safety Last!* costar. They live in splendor at Greenacres, the grandest mansion in Beverly Hills. It has a golf course, a dozen gardens, a bathroom for every letter of the alphabet.

He cranks out one smash after another: *Girl Shy, The Freshman, The Kid Brother, Speedy.* Then comes 1927. Sound is the new frontier. Harold gamely stars in a few talkies, but he knows the silent era is dead—and him with it. That's the nature of time. Fabulously rich from portraying the everyman in peril, he counts among his friends some of the biggest players in Hollywood. Directors like shooting on the sumptuous grounds of Greenacres, and Harold is happy to oblige. He marvels at the latest lenses. Although maimed during that photo shoot years ago, Harold doesn't have a camera phobia—quite the opposite. He becomes a shutterbug, snapping thousands of pictures a year. Standing *behind* the lens gives him a sense of control: he'll never let any of *his* subjects get hurt. Harold is bewitched by stereo photos, which come to life when the viewer wears special cellophane glasses. Mostly he shoots landscapes and girls. When Truman relieves MacArthur of his Korean War duties in '51, Harold goes to San Francisco with a press pass to capture the general in three dimensions.

The war in Korea is still raging when a friend brings the actress Marilyn Monroe to Greenacres, to shoot a scene for *How to Marry a Millionaire.* She slips into a red swimsuit and lounges by the pool. The camera rolls.

"I hate a *careless* man," she purrs. "I *hate* a careless man."

It's just the one line, the accent falling differently each time. Take 6. They try it with Marilyn only in a towel. Something's not right. Take 11. The director isn't happy with the light, or the sound of the pool. Harold doesn't mind. He has all the time in the world. Plus, Marilyn has agreed to model for him, a prize addition to his photographic harem. Take 30.

"*You're* not a careless man," Marilyn notes approvingly as Harold sets up his gear. Marilyn has already stated that she won't take her top off, but here she is reaching around for the clasp. "I'll show *you*, but lose the camera."

Harold senses Mildred's eyes somewhere behind him, shooting invisible fire from inside the house. He's had girls over three times this week.

"That's just fine, dear," he says, all business again. His right hand sweats under the thin glove as Marilyn absorbs all the light in the sky.

That evening, he looks through a pair of red-and-blue spectacles at his stack of Marilyns. Most girls come alive again when viewed this way—jutting out, as it were. Harold can resurrect their voices, perfume, laughter, tits. But not Marilyn. Though her body has been committed to memory by every male above age thirteen, here she's as sexy as the Sphinx.

A few months after the Korean War grinds to a halt in the summer of 1953, Twentieth Century–Fox releases *How to Marry a Millionaire*. Harold loves it; Mildred, too. No trace of Greenacres, though. What happened? Over time, he forgets all about the scene shot at his home, until one day when their grown son, Duke, comes over. In the dining room, Harold mishandles a plate with his mangled hand. As it crashes to the floor, Marilyn's lost phrase swims to his mouth: *I hate a careless man!* He says it out loud, with her intonations. Duke looks stunned. Says that when he was in the air force, the boys at the base used to tease one another with that exact phrase. It turned out that Marilyn was in a public safety announcement, fluttering her eyes and purring, *I hate a careless man.* She was warning them that loose lips sink ships—or set off nuclear catastrophes.

Duke chuckles at the story. "I always swore that ad looked like our backyard," he says.

14. Monroe Doctrine

February 1954. Marilyn Monroe cuts short her Tokyo honeymoon with Joe DiMaggio and travels to Seoul for a four-day stand with the USO. She tours the base in a military jacket and combat boots, more Athena than Aphrodite. Over the course of ten shows, nearly half the two hundred thousand U.S. troops still stationed in Korea will see her.

The sign above the outdoor stage says BULLDOZER BOWL. She shrugs off the heavy jacket, and ten thousand men cry out in joyful surrender. In a sleeveless dress, Marilyn sings, *Diamonds are a girl's best friend.* The mercury dips below thirty, but there's no place she'd rather be.

Members of the 3rd Infantry roar as Marilyn untangles the song's knotty words. *Baguettes.* Her voice today sounds looser than in *Gentlemen Prefer Blondes*, where she pouts and plots as Lorelei Lee, gold digger nonpareil. *Liaisonic.* In the movie, everything's delivered with a helium snicker, but as the song blares and blooms over the Korean scrub, she sounds less like a pinup girl than an avenging angel.

A finger wag, a hand on hip. Each coo and moue brings forth a primal moan that rolls from the edges of the great crowd to the center, then right on up to heaven. She jumps to the strains of a small combo, augmented at times by a saxophone or a neutered bow-tied quartet. Up front, dozens lunge with cameras mashed against their faces, trying to push their whole bodies inside the boxes. The preacher Moon Youngmyung is there, invited by some soldiers. He worshipfully clicks away, even after the film runs out. His fingers die in the cold.

Beyond, thousands more stand in clumps like trees, swaying. Off to the sides are camouflaged canopies, hibernating death machines. Marilyn could command this army to do her bidding. Could tell them to turn north and, on the count of three, overrun the combined forces of Kim Il Sung, Mao

Tse-tung, What's-his-face who stepped into Stalin's shoes. Unify the country once and for all. She shimmies as she gazes at a forest in love. *One.* Lifts those arms high, turns. *Two.* Arches. *Three.*

Marilyn Monroe is a member of the Korean Provisional Government.

15. The Chosen (I)

In 1954 (4287), Moon Young-myung opens a branch of his Unification Church in Seoul. He wants to merge God's will with man's way and *also* to unify North and South Korea. Hence the name. The healing of his small, forsaken country has repercussions for all mankind, he says.

Jesus tells Moon that the Koreans are God's *chosen* people, blameless like the Jews of yore. It is no coincidence that Japan's colonial name for Korea was "Chosen." English word and Japanese name mingle in the believer's mind.

Jesus Christ is a member of the Korean Provisional Government.

16. Giving Up

That same year, troubling footage is coming back to America: captured airmen confess to dropping germ bombs on North Korean cities. They break down in tears after each crushing revelation. Some pilots claim that rewards were offered to those who infected the most people. They identify higher-ups, specific strains of bacteria. Payloads of infection, the shame of civilized nations.

Meanwhile, MGM green-lights *Prisoner of War*, intended as a drama about the treatment of POWs in North Korea. At first, the military helps out. It wants the public to understand what American soldiers were up against *after* they were captured. The screenwriter interviews dozens of recently freed prisoners. The film stars Ronald Reagan, an old hand at military roles. In

Prisoner of War, Reagan plays Webb Sloane, assigned to infiltrate a North Korean reeducation camp near Sinuiju. Webb inserts himself into a caravan of captives, then goes further, pretending to renounce America and embrace communism. In other words, he's an actor.

Webb watches as some of the Americans cave right away, lured by creature comforts and worn down with fear. He doesn't judge. *Every man has his breaking point,* he muses. The most stubborn are forced to lie in ditches, with only a thin board against the elements. Others get lashed to crosses, mockeries of Christ. The holdouts despise Webb for turning Red, though he wins some respect after performing an emergency appendectomy on a fellow prisoner.

The film ends with Webb Sloane smuggling out his report on the horrible conditions and diabolical mind games of the camp. In a twist, one of the *other* turncoats is revealed to be on assignment as well—a journalist, risking his life to document the Red menace.

What if *everyone* is only acting?

As the film nears release, the military withdraws support. The top brass wanted a sympathetic portrayal of the POWs, the hell they went through. But the movie's *too* sympathetic—unpatriotic, even, as expressed in Webb's mantra: *Every man has his breaking point.* Army psychiatrists conclude that a problem exists with the American male. How else to explain his collapse in the face of his moral inferior: the Communist, the yellow man?

The problem lies with America itself, which has grown too soft. Modern life, with its shiny appliances, supermarkets, TVs, and washing machines, has shredded America's moral fiber. Army docs are stumped by the *give-up-itis* found in so many of these camp survivors.

Panned from coast to coast, *Prisoner of War* leaves theaters before the week is out.

17. I've Got a Secret

The flop doesn't faze Ronald Reagan. He pivots from big screen to small, hosting the popular *General Electric Theater.* On October 5, 1955 (4288), Reagan appears as a guest on the popular CBS game show *I've Got a Secret.*

    Secret is broadcast from a theater on Forty-seventh. Reagan welcomes this break from the other part of his job: touring General Electric factories and giving long pep talks about inventing the future. He listens backstage as host Garry Moore introduces the audience to the first contestant: a postal carrier whose secret is that he's smooched all 528 women on his route. You can just about hear the men in the crowd cracking their knuckles. The thought of this loser planting his puss on their wives is too much. He's Exhibit A of the moral rot the army is getting worked up about. The men wouldn't mind cleaning this clown's clock.

    The panelists, two men and two women, take their seats and start the interrogation. Actress Betsy Palmer is one of the regulars. She sounds like the girl next door after a semester of finishing school in a forgotten corner of Europe. (Her father hails from Prague.) Demure yet dazzling in an off-the-shoulder dress, the witty blonde gets close to uncovering his secret—but time runs out.

    After a commercial, there's an on-camera tête-à-tête between Moore and Reagan. Now that he's done plenty of film *and* TV, Reagan says, he thinks the latter's a piece of cake. He'll prove his thesis with a gag. When the panelists return (he tells Moore), they will start talking as usual, but anytime one of them stumbles on a word or pauses a beat too long, Moore will force them to restart the entire "scene." The panelists will have to figure out *why* they're trapped in this repetition.

    The test starts. The first panelist can't even make it to the end of a sentence before Moore signals that he needs to start

again. The dialogue barely progresses, looping back on itself, as confusion and laughter ensue. At last, Reagan explains the "secret." Betsy Palmer doesn't get a word in edgewise. Reagan can't stop staring.

After the show, he says so long to Moore and steps out into the crisp fall night, cigarette already in hand. He spots Betsy coming through the lobby. She's in her street clothes, which look just as great as the dress she wore on the set.

"Chicago girl, right?" Reagan asks, offering her a smoke.

She cups her hand around the flame as he works the lighter. "More or less."

"I'm from those parts."

"I thought you were California through and through," says Betsy, amused and dubious. "Where in Chicago?"

"Tampico."

Betsy Palmer repeats it, like a line of music. "Well now, that's not Chicago."

"Close enough."

"Not really."

"Same state."

"Hm."

"I went to school in Eureka," Reagan says.

"Now you're getting closer. Now you're about a hundred miles away."

"What did your folks do?"

She tightens that smile, worried that he's hinting at something else. That he knows her father is from Czechoslovakia, and that her real name's *Hrunek*, nothing Palmer about it. She hears that Reagan's new thing is ratting out stars who look the least bit pink.

"What did *your* parents do?"

She's so quick. He likes it. "Got a Mr. Palmer waiting outside?"

"Nothing like that." Her husband is actually in the hospital, working. His name's not Palmer. Betsy doesn't wear her ring on shooting days.

"All that jawing made me hungry," Reagan says. He grinds out his cigarette. "How about we grab a bite, courtesy of General Electric?"

"Nothing like that, either."

He nods to the marquee. "I bet *you've* got a secret."

It's an old line. She bats her eyes. "Don't we all?"

18. Robbing the Cradle

Betsy Palmer's secret is that she's mourning an old flame. He died three days ago. She used to call him by his middle name, Byron. Lord Byron, sometimes just My Lord. They had Indiana in common—her hometown of East Chicago was just over the state line. He was from Marion, not far from Crystal Lake, where she spent summers as a girl. What if they'd seen each other then, gazing out of their parents' cars?

"I'd've been a *baby!*" Byron teased. "Don't forget, you're *five years older.*"

Five years. She was five years older than him when they met, on a teleplay called "Death Is My Neighbor." He was a punk who tries to kill her by siphoning gas to her room. They reunited on a similar TV chiller, "Sentence of Death," a week later. (Betsy was *still* five years older.) She thinks: *Death was all around us, in 1953. We just couldn't see it, invisible like gas.*

Outside the theater after *I've Got a Secret* that night, Betsy Palmer has to be careful with Ronald Reagan, keep it lighter than light. Not flirt, but not *not* flirt.

"Tell all, kid," Reagan says.

Fat chance. Stay chipper. Focus on his remarkable hair. "Some other time!"

"Sentence of Death" was an episode of *Studio One,* shot in the same theater they're standing outside. On that episode, she

plays Eliza, a rich girl in furs, killing time at a drugstore lunch counter to avoid a fancy soirée. She's in a phone booth when a man raids the register and kills the shop owner. The cops try to pin it on Byron's character, a local hood, but Betsy Palmer says it wasn't him. She'd recognize the real killer immediately.

Betsy acts in almost every scene, while Byron's role is so small he's not even in the opening credits. His brooding features suggest the strong, silent type, but when he opens his mouth you get something else. A nervous mess, a jabberjaw, pathetic but somehow all sex. Half of him is falling apart at the seams while the other half insists there are no seams.

19. Five Years

Still in her reverie, oblivious to Reagan's dippy stare, Betsy Palmer remembers Byron pulling silly faces at her in the dark as she delivered one overstuffed monologue after another. During a bout of soul-searching, she kept flubbing her lines, fighting back the giggles.

The very next day, in the real world, Betsy set up house in Byron's apartment on West Sixty-eighth Street. He was practically a boy. Left messes everywhere. She liked to watch him read. She liked to watch him make coffee, serious as a chemist. She liked to watch him, period.

She was five years older when they moved in together. Now he'll always stay young and she'll be five, then ten, then twenty-five years older, on and on. Last year she married a doctor eleven years her senior. Sixteen years older than Byron. He could have been Byron's father.

20. General Electric

Reagan's in town one more day, in between giving a speech at the G.E. plant in Schenectady and the one down in who knows where. The schedule is rigorous, almost military. He's never liked New York, but Betsy Palmer could make him not like it a little

less. To Betsy, he looks as appetizing as a forty-three-year-old bagel, but manners are manners.

"Say, what was that picture you were in?" he asks. "Something with Tyrone Power?"

"What was that last picture *you* were in?"

"Well, now." Betsy's huge eyes make him stammer. Her town car pulls up. The driver looks like a teenager. At the last moment, Reagan dredges up a doozy from the year before. "Why, that would be *Prisoner of War.*"

"Fun title," she says, as the driver gets out to open the door. "Happy trails, Mr. Reagan!"

"Call me Ronnie."

The door shuts. That's it for Reagan. Bedtime for Bonzo.

"I remembered!" he shouts, like a schoolboy trying to impress his teacher.

Betsy rolls down the window. "What's that, Ronnie?"

"You were on *Studio One*! The rich lady at the lunch counter!"

She claps in delight. "Very good, Mr. Reagan!"

"I have a photogenic memory."

"You mean photographic."

"Nope," he says, as the car pulls away. "I never forget a good-looking lady."

21. The Ballad of West Sixty-eighth Street

Betsy takes out a fresh cigarette in the car. She can't stop thinking of Byron. They used to smoke between scenes, smoke amid the piles of books on West Sixty-eighth, smoke like that was their job. Months wafted by on clouds of Lucky Strike. His place had a round window that didn't open all the way, mounted antlers for a coatrack.

When Byron went out to Hollywood the next summer, she could hear the nicotine rasp more clearly. He would call at mid-

night and plead: *Talk dirty, Betsy. Talk dirty to your widdle bad boy Byron wight now.*

The first time, she didn't know what he wanted. She said, "Um . . . shit?"

That cracked him up.

"You idiot," she laughed. "I'm old enough to be your mother!"

"Only if you got pregnant when you were, you know, *five.*"

"Fine. Then I'm old enough to be your older sister who turns out to be your mother."

"Now *that's* a turn-on."

"You're an idiot *and* a pervert."

"Talk dirty, sis."

"Poo-poo," she said.

"More."

"Pee-pee."

"Now take off your pants."

"What pants?"

"That's the spirit."

They had an eight-month run. Not too shabby. He was a boy, really. They weren't going to see each other again, and there was no future, and it made perfect sense. Now she had her doctor husband, and who doesn't want a doctor husband? But thinking of the real end of Byron, the waste, is more than she can bear. On Thursday Byron was alive. On Friday he was a dark smear on a scrubland road. He would always, always be younger than her.

22. You, American Citizen

A few years later, a film called *The Ultimate Weapon* appears. It opens on a map of Korea, as a sneering wise guy explains what it means to be American. The camera pulls back: the scene is a classroom, and the Noo Yawk accent belongs to a balding Chinese propaganda teacher, somewhere in the Far East. He

stands at a chalkboard, lecturing his trainees on the deficien-
cies of the average U.S. serviceman.

1. CAN'T THINK FOR HIMSELF
2. LACKS SELF-CONFIDENCE
3. LACKS CONCERN FOR OTHERS
4. NO STANDARD OF RIGHT AND WRONG

Then a familiar voice takes over, worn and folksy. The film's *real*
narrator steps into view: Why, it's Ronald Reagan! He's at ease,
arms nonchalantly folded across his chest. *I'm speaking to you
now not as an actor endeavoring to entertain you, and certainly not
as an announcer speaking for a sponsor.* The words are confession
and incantation. *I talk as Ronald Reagan, American citizen, to you,
American citizen, concerning the Communist Chinese appraisal of
our national character.*

Though Reagan played Webb Sloane in *Prisoner of War,* that
movie is a distant memory. The actor is no longer the ragged
infiltrator, sympathizing with POWs who threw in the towel. This
is the real R.R.: dignified and a little cruel in a dark suit, leading
the charge against the godless foe. Gone are the days of *Every
man has his breaking point.* With a touch of gravel in his voice, he
asks the viewer: *Did the Communists have our number?*

The rest of the film answers the question in the affirmative.
Tragically, in the brief amount of time since America's triumph
in World War II (4278), the country has rested on its laurels. This
has left its next generation of fighting men vulnerable to the
Reds' siren song. *The Ultimate Weapon* doesn't mean A-bombs or
battleships. The ultimate weapon is the *mind.*

23. The Truth About Tyosen

In 1957 (4290), a counselor at a New Jersey summer camp
reads her boyfriend's copy of *The Cosmic Puppets.* Janet has
never finished a sci-fi book before. She's never been crazy
about those movies, either, with their giant ants and atom

guns. But being in love changes you. Besides, she's burned through her magazines and is losing traction in *War and Peace*. (Too much war, for one.)

Vince is a year older, college-bound in the fall. He's smart, curly-haired, and thinks she's an angel. He has no muscles to speak of but swims like a seal. Vince wants to be a scientist like his father, who does some sort of research with beans: "He feeds them to badgers and measures their farts. Don't ask me why badgers." Vince likes to serenade her in his wobbly voice. He also likes to put his hands under her shirt when they make out.

Janet digs *The Cosmic Puppets*. The writer's name is hilariously fake: Philip K. Dick. The cover screams science fiction, but she's not sure where the science comes in. A man visits his hometown only to find that everything is slightly *off*, different than he remembers. He finds an old newspaper article saying he died as a kid.

The book doesn't even make *sense*, really, but Janet likes it so much that she reads it again. Vince gives her a sci-fi magazine that has another Dick story, this one set in the aftermath of a nuclear war. People live in bunkers deep underground as their robot armies battle on the surface. Then someone discovers that the robots actually stopped fighting years ago. The atmosphere is safe for humans—the robots just never bothered to tell them. For days after, Janet regards the world warily, like it's being made up minute to minute.

"So," her roommate, Karen, says, peering down from the top bunk. "I hear you love Dick."

"Very funny."

"Word is you're a big old Dick fan."

"Stop." She kills a mosquito.

"Someone wrote 'Janet Craves Dick' in the bathroom."

"Pretty sure that was you."

The summer glows with possibility. Her first real boyfriend.

Reading new kinds of books. Tanning evenly. She drinks more than she should, takes up smoking. She'll quit before going back home. Or maybe her mom and dad would understand: the camp was founded in 1935, a little over twenty years ago; her parents met here as teenagers. Which is why they sent her in the first place. Now she's a counselor, just like they were. Did her mother let Dad put *his* hands under her shirt or down her shorts (which is what Vince wants, for starters)? Janet asks her diary if it's normal to think of your parents feeling each other up.

Fooling around isn't the only thing on her mind. She's learned three songs on the guitar. The kids remind her of when she was a kid. The same flare-ups and goofy sense of humor. It turns out she's the best archer in the camp, better than Tony, the jock, who is two-timing Karen with Deena, or maybe it's the other way around.

Then it happens: a boy drowns in Crystal Lake. Janet feels awful, but he shouldn't have been left unattended. How did he get out in the water by himself? Makes no sense. And it wasn't her fault. Or Vince's. Swimming was *over* for the day.

Also, the boy wasn't even a camper. Not their responsibility. His mother, the camp cook, should have kept an eye. Mad with grief, she leaves early. For the next ten days, Janet and the other counselors have to figure out how to make edible meals for thirty hungry kids. Everyone's miserable. Camp ends a week early. Janet heads home to North Carolina and sulks for a few weeks until it's time for her last year of high school. Vince is going to college in Maine. The distance is too much, and they break up by mail.

Back home, Janet can't find any Philip K. Dick books on the spinning rack at the drugstore. At a Salvation Army shop, she sees a futuristic-sounding book called 2333, with a planet resembling a big bloodshot eyeball on the cover. Its plot sounds like that story she read, in which people live in bunkers, blind to

what's really going on. In *2333*, the characters believe they are denizens of Planet Tyosen, but actually they're passengers on a spaceship so huge they can never reach the windows. They discover that when war broke out on the "real" Tyosen, their leaders froze thousands of "pilgrims" and loaded them onto a pair of intergalactic supercrafts, bound for other worlds.

When the captain of the second ship, Greena Hymns, learns that the war on Tyosen is over, and its cities are bustling, she reverses course. Suddenly, everything melts away. It turns out that all of it—planets, starships, pilgrims—existed only in the imagination of a soldier, wounded in battle on Earth. He is delivered home, bandaged and burned. Over and over on a notepad he writes GREENA HYMNS, the name of the heroine in his dream. He tries to rearrange the letters into something that makes sense. Janet tries, too, comes up with nonsense: Angry She-Men, Mr. Henny Sage, Syngman Rhee.

The following summer, 1958 (4291), Janet and Vince both return to camp. Things pick up where they left off. The silent intervening months vanish. They don't talk about the poor kid who drowned. But Vince has changed. He says he reads only serious writers now. His main man is Thomas Wolfe, the exact opposite of Philip K. Dick. Janet's not so sure. Didn't *Cosmic Puppets* have the same idea, just crazier—*You Really, Really Can't Go Home Again*? He laughs and says *I suppose* and she knows that everything they were hoping to do last August will happen at last. But soon enough, it all goes terribly wrong.

24. The Countdown

In March 1960 (4293), just a month before Syngman Rhee's ouster as the president of South Korea, Reverend Moon gets married. He is forty; his wife, seventeen. They are the first couple to *actually* be blessed by God. They will be True Parents to the followers of the Unification Church.

Later, his supporters claim that the timing of the wedding

was no accident. Moon, they say, predicted Rhee's downfall. This alarms some people: Syngman Rhee had many flaws, but he was a die-hard Christian, if nothing else. Would a *real* Christian organization say such things about a fellow true believer—not to mention someone who has railed so eloquently against the Communist North? It makes sense, though, once you see Rhee's sudden ouster as part of God's plan. No matter how devout, Syngman Rhee failed God when he failed to unify the country. When *Moon* stitches Korea's wound, he will heal *all* mankind.

Jesus reveals that the world will end soon. Reverend Moon must look beyond Korea, beyond Koreans, and warn the rest of humanity. The Unification Church has found a healthy following in Japan. Now he must alert America—that "Second Israel," the most powerful Christian nation on earth. Moon Young-myung changes his name to Sun Myung Moon, hitting on a celestial balance in his target language.

The year when everything ends and everything begins is 1967—or 4300, by the KPG calendar. *Pali pali.* Much work must be done. Moon sends emissaries to America, the most powerful country in the world. At the end of each sermon, he reminds his disciples that "Moon" in Korean means *door,* that language works on multiple levels.

25. *Brzzt!*

In 1961 (4294), Ronald Reagan returns to the set of the show *I've Got a Secret.* Garry Moore still hosts, but all the panelists have changed except for Betsy Palmer. She's the secret behind *I've Got a Secret*—the reason audiences tune in. Men nationwide mentally revisit the episode when her dress started coming loose as she rose from her chair. How for a full minute she wriggled as the male panelists attempted repairs. At home in California, Ronald Reagan went right up to the set. His wife, Nancy, spotted him from the kitchen and said, "Is something wrong with the picture?"

Both Reagan and Moore started their careers in radio, as did two of the panelists, Steve Allen and Henry Morgan. All four are now fixtures on TV. Reagan wants to see if Allen and Morgan can still hack their old job, delivering the news in smooth professional tones. They will attempt to read a dense script while the panelists do their best to distract them.

Betsy Palmer, the raven-haired Bess Myerson, and the others come out from backstage and guess what sort of test or trick Reagan has in mind. Ronnie's presence makes Betsy even giddier than usual. She mentions Reagan's own successful TV gig as host of *General Electric Theater*, also on CBS. "You're going to *electrocute* us with all that electricity that goes on in your other show," she says. The crowd cracks up. Ronnie blushes. She asks if his secret today has something to do with *that*?

"Are we going to do an experiment with . . . electricity?" Betsy says eagerly. She makes a sound like sparks: "Brzzt— brzzt—brzzt!"

An invisible spark arcs between them, the crackling so intense Reagan has to look away. What was she in recently— something with Fonda? Betsy towers over the other panelists. Look at them, Reagan and Palmer. Refugees from the movies, now crammed inside boxes in living rooms instead of blown up on a screen to the size of gods.

Brzzt! Will she guess *his* secret? Reagan's secret is that no matter how busy he is—in whichever godforsaken town General Electric has sent him to—he tunes in to the show, just to hear her laugh.

26. Twilight of the Blondes

Betsy Palmer is still on *I've Got a Secret* a year later when she hears the news that Marilyn Monroe is dead. She doesn't know that Marilyn was a member of the Korean Provisional Government, just that they were born in the same year, 1926 (4259, by our calendar). They were like twins separated at birth. Marilyn

had Joe DiMaggio, Arthur Miller, a Kennedy or two. But Betsy Palmer had James Byron Dean in his godlike prime. Betsy Palmer wins.

27. The Story of Kim

After escaping from the North Korean volunteer army in 1950 (4283), the Good Soldier K.—whose college years were interrupted by the war—joins the South Korean side and climbs the ranks. In 1955 (4288), he has the chance to go to America. For the next eight years he studies political science and writing at several schools. He starts a family. In 1960 (4293), he moves to Iowa City and finds inexpensive lodgings near the jailhouse.

One of his teachers at Iowa is Philip Roth, author of the acclaimed collection *Goodbye, Columbus.* A year younger than K., Roth enlisted in the army after Korea. He enjoys hearing about K.'s daring adventures, his homeland, its history. Roth confesses he knows little about the war, but in truth it was slipping from the nation's consciousness even as men went over and died by the thousands. K. tells him about Yi Sun-shin, the admiral who built the turtle boats in the sixteenth century to repulse the Japanese, a nautical genius on par with Lord Nelson. The Koreans are the Jews of Asia, K. says, a formulation Roth savors.

Under the Iowa skies, K. revises his novel, working in this foreign tongue he must bend to his wishes. He moves to Long Beach, California. *The Martyred* appears in 1964 (4297), under K.'s American name: Richard E. Kim. Its narrator is a South Korean soldier sent to learn the fate of fourteen Christian ministers in Pyongyang, North Korea. The dust-jacket biography dwells on K.'s military service: *liaison officer to Hqs. U.S. 7th Division, U.S. 8th Army; aide-de-camp to Under-Secretary of Defense.* It's both proof of the story's verisimilitude and a declaration of allegiance.

28. The Key to Perfection

In 1966 (4299), two years after *The Martyred,* sociologist John Lofland publishes a different kind of Korean story. *Doomsday Cult* is a "study of conversion," an inside look at a fringe religious group called the Divine Precepts (DP), led by the Korean "Christ-Messiah" Soon Sun Chang. An American branch of the Divine Precepts is established in Bay City. Chang's teachings are tirelessly promoted by his handpicked proselytizer, Miss Lee, and her small group of American converts. Several are students; many are foreign-born. All are dissatisfied with life as it is.

The DPs believe the world will end in 1967 (4300). The clock is ticking. The general public is indifferent, however, as the strict Miss Lee and her crew try every mode of outreach, from enigmatic one-line newspaper ads ("For the key to perfection, call AN 5-1926") to infiltration of more traditional Bible study groups. Even as the DPs obsess over the Last Days, they bungle their mission. They are wary of revealing too soon that the new Messiah will be a middle-aged Oriental mystic with minimal English. Potential followers must undergo arduous spiritual grooming before receiving this knowledge. But the DPs are running out of time. The year 4300 is nearly at hand.

29. The Holes (I)

Though *Doomsday Cult* is a sociological study, it bears a thick coating of fiction. "Soon Sun Chang" is Lofland's alias for none other than the Reverend Sun Myung Moon, who is looking for a foothold in the States. And "the Divine Precepts" refers to members of Moon's Unification Church, later to be derided as "Moonies."

The book comes out before the church has penetrated the American mindscape. Parts read like a comedy of errors, as Miss Lee fruitlessly attempts to lure people into the faith. Observing that no one can endure hearing a seven-hour cas-

sette recording of her book on the DP worldview, she trims it by four. To her dismay, would-be converts still leave the room or simply fall asleep as the abridged tape plays. She decorates a banner with the words FIGHT COMMUNISM WITH THE DIVINE PRE-CEPTS, for display at a busy intersection. Alas, she has forgotten to cut holes in it for the wind to pass through. It billows like a sail, illegible to motorists.

30. The Holes (II)

In 1918, George Imlach is born in Toronto. He plays junior hockey with the Marlboros, earning the lifelong nickname Punch. (You can imagine why.) In 1942, he enlists in the Canadian Army and coaches one of its hockey squads. Good with numbers, he works as an accountant at the huge Anglo-Canadian Pulp and Paper Mills after the war. He likes visiting the factory floor, letting the roar of the massive rollers crash over him. Paper is power. He coaches the company-owned hockey team, the Quebec Aces, which stands for "Anglo-Canadian Employees." (The mill chemicals give the players a sulfur smell. They should have been called the Devils.) Punch eventually comes home to Toronto, to coach the Maple Leafs of the National Hockey League.

The Leafs win the Stanley Cup four times in Imlach's first eleven years. Immediately after they fail to make the 1969 play-offs, Punch is fired. He doesn't stay unemployed for long. The NHL is admitting two more franchises into the league. Down in Buffalo, brothers Seymour and "Northy" Knox are putting a new club together, and they like Punch Imlach for coach. He drives the three hours from Toronto, arriving in the thick of a snow-storm. The men get along, mostly, but it's a process. He makes three more trips, each time into a storm even worse than the first. *Unbelievable,* he says, trudging up the walk to the mansion of one Knox or other. He means the snow and he means the house.

Punch gets the job. He lives and works out of the Statler Hilton downtown. For his top draft pick of 1970, he nabs Gilbert Perreault, a fleet-footed phenom from Victoriaville. Gil wears number 11 and barely knows English. He is *Zheel*-bear Pair-o, but announcers seem determined to hit every consonant in his name. When he scores thirty-eight goals his rookie year, they learn the right way to say it. Next season, Imlach adds Gil's old junior teammate Rick Martin (7), who promptly racks up forty-four goals. He can't help that his last name goes from Mar-*tahn* to Mar-tin. They are joined by Rene Robert (14), who will score forty in *his* first full season. (Row-*bear*, s'il vous plaît, not *Raw*-bert.) The press dubs them the French Connection, after the hit crime movie. The Brothers Knox are over the fucking moon.

No Sabre wears a helmet except Crozier, the goalie Punch poached from Detroit. Crozier's thin mask is like a slice of skull. It has forty-eight holes: two for the eyes, two for the nose, and forty-four other slits and vents throughout. There's no hole for the mouth. Punch jokes that it's so there's no way to scream.

31. Punch and the Pantera

The 1971–72 season draws to a close, and the team fails to reach the playoffs again. To raise spirits, Punch wants to land the veteran Tim Horton, who at forty-three is nearly twice as old as anyone on the French Connection. A former star from Imlach's Toronto days, Horton has been playing here and there, periodically "retiring" and driving up his price.

In truth, the towering defenseman doesn't need hockey. He's got a head for business. *Tim est propriétaire de plusieurs magasins de beignets*, according to the back of his bubble-gum card. *Tim owns a chain of donut shops bearing his name.*

Punch meets Tim Horton at a Tim Hortons over the border. People will see them there. People will talk. The papers love both of them. The articles practically write themselves.

"Look at the fat on you," Punch says sweetly.

"It's middle age. Cruller blubber. What'll you have?"

"I'm fine, I'm good."

"Ah, George." Tim Horton respects his old Toronto coach so much he won't call him Punch. "Next time I'll put some haggis on the menu."

Tim knows that his business concerns will do better if he gets on the ice, even if he's now a popular journeyman rather than the game's biggest star. He has already started skating again; parts of his body hurt that haven't hurt before, but his speed is good and his shots go off like cannon fire when they hit the boards. When they start sounding like muskets, he'll leave.

Un des joueurs les plus forts dans la N.H.L., the trading card says. There's a typo in the translation: *One of the strangest players in the National Hockey League.*

Tim asks, "Why are they called the Sabres, eh?"

"Search me," Punch says. "I don't ask questions. I just spend their nice green money."

Tim asks George to sweeten the deal, throw in a car. "It's a Ford," he explains, writing down the model for Imlach.

"Bull," Punch says, "but *fine.*"

Tim used to have a dealership and recommends some places in Buffalo. The next day, Punch Imlach goes to see the thing: a demon chariot called a Pantera. The dealer prices it at twenty-two.

"But I like you, Punch," he says. "I don't care what the papers say."

"What do the papers say."

"For you I can do twenty."

"I'll be a son of a gun," Punch mutters. "Seventeen."

"Not a chance." The dealer leers. "Is this for someone special?"

"Yeah," he says. His wife, Dodo, would find the implication hilarious. "Your sister."

"Okay, easy."

"Fuck you."

"Don't walk away," he says. "Seventeen-five. Punch, don't walk away. There won't be another Pantera till April at the earliest."

"I'll give you seventeen, you fucking asshole."

"Good doing business with you, Mr. Imlach."

A week later, Tim Horton comes to the Statler Hilton to make things official. Punch has the Pantera parked out front so that Tim can see it from the window. Rick Martin is already number 7, Tim's old Toronto number, so the defenseman will wear 2.

"This is the last jersey I'll ever play in," he promises. "*Merci* for the wheels, George."

Punch says, "We'll call you the Panther then, eh."

Tim stretches his arm until it makes an audible crack. "By the end of the season, you'll just call me Ford."

32. St. Catharines

Buffalo, 4307 (1974). Four seasons old, the Sabres are holding their own in the NHL. They have a strong mix of heavyweights and finesse players. On February 21, they face off against the Toronto Maple Leafs, Imlach and Horton's old team. Not a crucial game, but Punch always wants to destroy the Leafs for giving him the boot back in '69. He rides up with his star defender in the Pantera, crossing the border, radio on.

At one point a car passes them. Tim steps on the gas to catch up. Imlach clutches the door handle, so hard he might pull it off.

"That's a Studebaker!" Tim bellows above the engine.

"I know, I know."

"I used to *sell* Studebakers!"

"Fine, fine."

"I'm pretty sure I sold *that* Studebaker!"

"Be careful, be *careful*." Punch has his seat belt on, but

Horton drives unrestrained, half his huge body hanging over the wheel.

The Pantera edges in front of the Studie. Horton welds the pedal to the floor, and Punch sees his life flash before his eyes: mostly hockey. He has a vision of the pulp mill back in Quebec, churning out the raw paper that *The New York Times* will fill with his obituary. Then they ease back into the right lane to take the Hamilton exit.

"What the hell, Timmy."

"This will only take a sec."

On Ottawa Street, Tim Horton pulls into the lot of a Tim Hortons, the very first one. "Lunch is on me, George."

Imlach tries a powdered French braid, holding it away from him so it doesn't dust his tie. The coffee could be the house blend for a chain of Eastern bloc cafeterias. Strangers greet Horton. A ponytailed cashier swoons. The Leaf-turned-Sabre laps it up, handshakes and autographs all around. When the chatter subsides, Punch says, "You've really got something, Timmy. Now get your head in the goddamn game."

As they approach Toronto, Horton scowls, fidgets. Imlach asks what's wrong. Tim says his jaw's still sore after the morning skate. A stray puck, a shoulder in the corner? Punch didn't see it, and Horton won't say who or what. Maybe he doesn't remember. Tim says the doctors cleared him for the game.

"Well, did they clear you to *drive?*"

"Anyway, we're almost there."

The first time Tim Horton played as a Sabre at Maple Leaf Gardens, the crowd was dressed to the nines. It was an event: Horton and Imlach, native sons with something to prove. That was two years ago. Tonight is nothing so fancy, but it's a packed house all the same. Horton coasts on the energy at first, skating through the pain, but he's gassed before the first

period ends. His partner on defense is Jim Schoenfeld, the gigantic redhead from Hamilton. Schony tries to take up the slack in the second, fearlessly sliding his whole body on the ice to absorb slap shots flying in from the point.

"Yeah, yeah," Horton says. He finds Schony's patented move too cute. He sits out the last period. The Sabres lose by two.

Imlach is furious—beating Toronto has become his raison d'être—but he just says, "That's all right, boys." Sometimes you tear into them before they can wipe their skates, sometimes you wait till practice. Punch returns on the team bus, hat over his face. Doesn't want to talk. Schony, who fancies himself a singer, is making up a dirty song about Kitchener, Ontario, and if he sings one more verse Punch is going to take Crozier's stick to his balls.

Meanwhile, Tim Horton drives alone to Oakville, a town between Toronto and Buffalo, where he has an office for his donut chain. He pours a drink, makes some calls. He rings his brother and then his business partner, Ron, griping about his jaw. Ron tells him to stay put, he's on his way to help. Despite the pain and the booze and Ron's pleas, Tim heads back to Buffalo that night.

Dodo answers the phone at seven the next morning, hands it to Punch. The man on the other end claims to be the coroner of the town of St. Catharines, Ontario.

"Is this some kind of goddamn joke?"

The man says that five hours before, at approximately two A.M., Tim Horton lost control of the Pantera as he went around a traffic circle. The car hit the curb and flipped. Dodo sees her husband's face collapse. There was alcohol in Horton's system, and other substances, which the coroner names as Punch looks out the window at the drab buildings and lowering sky. He hangs up and takes the stairs down to the lobby of the Statler Hilton, crying, *Unbelievable.*

33. The Return of Taro (I)

The rest of the Sabres' 1973–74 season plays out under a cloud. "Next year, boys," says Punch. "Next year we go all the way."

To lighten the mood, he plants a joke for the NHL draft that spring. He creates a fictitious player, from a league so far away it can't be traced. The press officer's secretary knows a Japanese florist. Punch calls and asks what's a typical Japanese name. *Taro Tsujimoto*, says the woman on the phone. *Like John Smith*. And what would a *sabre* be? She tells him the word for sword: *katana*.

"So what's this all about?" she asks, now more curious than annoyed.

"A favor for a friend," he says, maybe meaning nothing, maybe meaning Tim Horton in his Pantera in the sky.

Draft day comes. Drags on forever. In the eleventh round, when everyone is long past caring, Punch Imlach announces with a straight face that the league's 183rd selection this year will be Taro Tsujimoto, of the Tokyo Katanas.

The other managers and assorted media men on the phone line go silent. *Who?*

34. The Stranger

On August 15, 1974 (4307), the anniversary of Korea's liberation from Japan, a Korean *from* Japan looks out a window of the best hotel in Seoul.

The twenty-three-year-old man doesn't speak the language well, fumbles the syllables like a child. He was born in Osaka. He has never set foot in Korea before and feels at once the tug of kinship and the mark of the outcast. A kind of seasickness. He's *zainichi*, a stranger in Japan and a stranger in Korea. Sitting on his bed, he regrets that he has no time to explore the land where his parents were born. But there is work to do. His passport says Kawagami, but that is a fake name. So is Seiko, the one his family adopted. Their real name, the Korean one, is

like a door that the *zainichi* opens and shuts in his mind. Call him Z.

Z. puts on a dark suit and heads outside. A driver takes him to the National Theater. Z. pays him a little extra to bow dramatically as he exits the car, to give the illusion that he's a VIP. He ascends the broad stairs into the crowded lobby. Z. goes to the lavatory, blots the sweat from his brow, combs his hair again. Wraps a handkerchief around his hand. Plenty of time.

He enters the auditorium just as Park takes the podium. The first lady, wearing a bright orange dress, sits to her husband's left. Schoolgirls stand at the wings. Park is here to commemorate Japan's exit from Korean soil, twenty-nine years ago. Will no one say what must be said—that Park himself was in the Japanese army?

A bang interrupts the president's speech. Z.'s gun has gone off—in his pocket. The handkerchief is to blame. He charges the stage, firing wildly, as the small white cloth floats to the ground in his wake. He lets out a Communist rallying cry, but his Japanese accent is so thick that no one is sure what he's saying. The bullets miss President Park Chung Hee but hit the first lady and one of the girls.

They succumb that night. President Park is unhurt. Though the killer was Korean, and the shooting was in support of Park's northern counterpart, Kim Il Sung, public outrage turns against Japan. A demonstration in Seoul becomes a spontaneous renewal of the Cut Finger Club: men lop off part of a digit, enough to mark the walls of the Japanese embassy with blood.

35. The Odd

What is history?

The Buffalo Sabres' selection in the 1974 draft of the right-handed center from the (nonexistent) Tokyo Katanas gets written up in the hockey press. The tone is one of amusement, though many are clearly not in on the joke. The exotic name

"Taro Tsujimoto" appears in the standard publications. Some print the grainy picture that the Sabres front office provides, adding to the mystique.

Though Punch later cops to the hoax, and the players know the score, the idea of a phantom energizes the team. They say a silent prayer to Taro every time they're on a breakaway or killing a penalty. As the win column fattens, the players leave a space for him in the locker room. Taro holds the sadness of Tim Horton's death at bay, and the Sabres make it to the Stanley Cup finals for the first time.

They face off against the Philadelphia Flyers, last year's victors. In game 3, played at home in Memorial Auditorium, two weird things transpire. The first is that a small bird finds its way inside the Aud. It dips and weaves above the proceedings, as though drunk. Everyone tries to ignore it, but the energy is too sinister. What is going on?

Parker Jotter is in the Aud that night with Tina, his teenage daughter. He tracks the crazy bird. For a minute he's a pilot again, flying his F-86, able to see it even when he's not seeing it. The eyes in the back of his head are open. A wing brushes his face. He can *smell* it, like a feather's been jammed up his nose.

"It's not a bird—it's a *bat!*" squeals Tina, who used to think the Aud was named the Odd. This just proves it.

The crowd erupts: "A bat?" "A goddamn bat!" "Unfuckingbelievable."

The bat moves in wild loops, maddened by the lights and this cavern full of humans. When the antic fur-ball swoops to inspect the red circles on the ice below, a Sabre named Lorenz chops it out of the air with his stick. Thousands gasp. A Flyer casually picks up the dead bat and deposits it over the boards. On the radio broadcast, the play-by-play announcers chalk it up to rustic northern folkways, talking out of their hats.

These are essentially Canadian farm boys. . . . They do it all the time up there, a bat does not hold the same connotations. . . . Well, Ted, I tell you, Mr. Bram Stoker is rolling in his grave.

Then the second weird thing happens: a thick fog fills the arena, as though the bat's death has unleashed a curse. It's hard to see anything. Punch pinches the bridge of his nose.

"Unfuckingbelievable!" he shouts.

Spirits roam the Odd. Tim Horton's ghost, coming back . . . or else the ancestors of Taro Tsujimoto, searching for the round-eyed Westerner who made him a mockery. What has Punch called up? The fog thickens. It's hard to do color commentary with so much gray. The announcer says there's a logical reason for everything. Outside, the late May temperatures have climbed into the seventies, and the heat has reacted with this huge patch of ice. *It's simple science.* But for the crowd, it's like being inside a horror movie. A tense hush falls over the Odd, as Sabres and Flyers coast blindly through pea soup.

Parker and Tina Jotter sit transfixed by this battle taking place amid low-lying clouds. The Sabres win the game, but go on to lose the series.

36. Pearl Harbor

Quick to credit the fictional Taro Tsujimoto for the team's performance this season, Sabres fans now blame him for their playoff

loss. To come so close to claiming the team's first Stanley Cup, and to fail . . . *Pearl Harbor wasn't enough for the Japs—now this?*

What they don't know is that Taro Tsujimoto is *real*. Punch thinks it's all just a joke that he made up, one that maybe went too far. But the KPG knows otherwise.

37. The Fall

October 1975 (4308). President Park Chung Hee, the widower, writes in his journal: *The dying fall holds only loneliness.* In 1979, he is killed at dinner by the head of his own CIA.

38. A Handful of Dust

In 1980 (4313), twenty-nine-year-old Cha Hak-kyung and her brother visit their native Korea. It is Cha's first time back since immigrating in the early '60s. The plan is to shoot a movie called *White Dust from Mongolia*. The project will be of a piece with Cha's other work, equal parts repetition, memory, loss. It promises to be her most sustained and emotionally direct piece, exploring the trauma of the land she left behind as a child. Cha's outline is dreamy, abstract: Trains pulling in. An airplane taking off. An amnesiac. The climax will depict an American soldier at the DMZ, spraying DDT on a Korean woman. Everything will be in slow motion.

But the wheels come off in Seoul. The recent assassination of President Park has led to a coup d'état, and the atmosphere is somber. Protesting martial law, the city of Kwangju erupts in demonstrations. Security in Seoul is heightened. The police repeatedly stop the Cha siblings, suspicious that they might be North Korean spies. Their language skills have rusted, after so much time overseas. (Could they be Japanese spies—or, indeed, simply *American* spies?) They leave with only scraps of unusable footage. Cha Hak-kyung, whose American name is Theresa, starts what will become *Dictee*, that secret bible of the KPG.

39. Somebody's There

Theresa Hak Kyung Cha leaves for Korea in May 1980, just as the slasher film *Friday the 13th* opens across the United States. Director Sean Cunningham originally wanted to make a tenderhearted feature about a foster home but changed his mind after determining that exactly zero people in the country would pay to see it. Having worked on the hit horror flick *Last House on the Left*, Cunningham opts for the killing route again, signing up a cast of unknowns. A faded fifty-something TV star is the only half-familiar name.

Critics hate *Friday the 13th*. They fume over its savagery, overlooking its lost-in-the-woods fairy-tale appeal. But their words can't stop its primordial power. Something keeps the audiences coming back, as spring becomes summer.

The film's prologue unfolds a few years after the Korean War. It opens on a patch of rural New Jersey, tiny moon inscribed high in the sky. Around a fireplace, camp counselors belt old protest songs. They are soft, you think, too soft: Did their older brothers get blown to bits in the Iron Triangle or at the Chosin Reservoir so they could loaf and bone up on Commie tracts? A couple sneaks upstairs, giggling as they tug off each other's shirts. A demonic insect noise—*ch-ch-ch-ch*—fills the soundtrack. The camera gets way too close.

Somebody's there, the girl says.

They look up, embarrassed. They look at *you*.

Ch-ch-ch-ch (ch-ch-ch-ch).

We weren't doing anything! the boy protests, backing away. His face goes white. What does he see? A sight so horrible. . . . The girl screams. Freeze frame.

The movie jumps to the present: 1980, twenty-odd years after that young couple's unsolved murder. Shut for decades, Camp Crystal Lake is reopening. A few weeks before the big day, counselors are making their way to the remote locale to set things up. The village idiot, tooling around on a bicycle,

warns them that the place is cursed. They pay no heed. The counselors enjoy this time before the campers arrive. They horse around, laze, have as much sex as humanly possible.

One by one, these hale specimens of American youth meet their ends, by diverse means: arrow, ax, machete. (A particularly convoluted method requires a snake.) The terror is broken up by the pristine beauty of the lake. As the body count rises, the audience mentally eliminates possible culprits. Unlike a classic mystery, though, there's no logical way to determine the killer, simply because he—or she—isn't among the characters we've met. This blatant cheat makes the film even eerier. Horror lurks everywhere, ready to strike.

40. Evil Empire

The movie's a smash. The sequel immediately goes into production. *Friday the 13th Part 2* wraps just five months after the first film's release. It's November, and Ronald Reagan, actor–turned–General Electric ambassador–turned Republican governor of California, has just been elected the fortieth president of the United States. He doesn't conceal his loathing of communism. His rhetoric makes the threat of nuclear war—of mutual assured destruction—palpable. In a few years, he will call the Soviet Union the "Evil Empire."

Many critics see *Friday the 13th* and its slew of sequels as evil, too. But it has champions, among them an obscure left-wing critic for the Geneva-based film journal *CinéFreak*, who writes under the name "Yura." The franchise, he claims, stands as a pungent response to the Reagan era (1980–88, or 4313–21). "More than the *au courant* doomsday of *War Games*, or the made-for-TV apocalypse known as *The Day After*," Yura writes in 1986 (4319), "the original *Friday the 13th* finds a metaphor for the looming nuclear threat—the promise of utter devastation—in the figure of a senseless, unstoppable killing machine." He's the

first to note that the date of its prologue (1958/4291) makes it a potent commentary on the Korean War.

41. Trapped (I)

On March 15, 1981 (4314), two weeks before the 53rd Annual Academy Awards are held in Los Angeles, President Reagan tapes an introduction for the ceremony from the White House. Gone is the disgust that marked his tone in *The Ultimate Weapon* two decades ago, exhorting America to get tough against enemies overseas. This Reagan's all warmth, praising Hollywood and cinema in general. "It's the motion picture that shows us all not only how we look and sound but, more important, how we feel."

Movies, he says, are "the world's most enduring art form."

"Film is forever!" he declares, and means it.

Then he cracks a joke: "I've been trapped in some films forever myself." He sounds so natural, so funny, that no one would guess he spent an hour rehearsing the line, perfectly shaping the momentary pause between *I've* and *been*.

42. Much Ado About Nothing

What is history? In May 1981 (4314), novelist Philip Roth publishes *Zuckerman Unbound*. In one scene, a former TV "Quiz Kid" besieges the narrator with a calendrical list of facts. Two things, he says, happened in 1598: Shakespeare wrote *Much Ado About Nothing*, and the Korean admiral "Visunsin" developed ironclad warships to defeat the Japanese.

Though Roth misspells Yi Sun-shin's name, it's a step in the right direction, as far as the KPG is concerned: the first mention of the heroic admiral's name in a work of American literature.

Richard E. Kim and Philip Roth are members of the Korean Provisional Government.

43. Moving Pictures

On March 30, 1981 (4314), the Sin family—Inky, Hannah, and Arthur—drives to the Boulevard Mall near Buffalo. A diversion on this afternoon of sour skies, the start of Art's spring break at Chatillion Academy. Dr. Sin has taken the day off, a rare event. They'll buy some clothes, sneakers, a new tennis racket. People stroll through the warm air, coats folded over arms.

Hannah takes Inky to Kleinhans for dress shirts while Art, eleven, makes his rounds: to Waldenbooks to scope out the mystery section, Kay-Bee to replenish his stamp collection, and finally Cavages, to see if they have the new album by Rush. Art loves the mall. His parents had given him two crisp tens at home, which he put in his wallet, which he stupidly left on the kitchen counter. Art spends around fifteen minutes in each store. By the end of his tour he's slipped *The ABC Murders* into his left jacket pocket, a colorful packet of foreign stamps into his right sleeve, and the cassette *Moving Pictures* into a right rear pocket.

What's gotten into him? Art has never swiped so much as a pack of gum, but a school friend recently boasted that he walks out with loads of stuff every week. It's dumb not to do it. No matter that he's already read the Agatha Christie, which he got from the library. The thrill is in the act itself.

He heads to Aladdin's Castle, where his parents will meet him at two. The noise calms him: a stream of beeps, electronic crashes, inchoate robot voices. Teenagers swear performatively. No one he knows. Art finds a quarter in his jacket, which he redeems for a token: a bright brass circle with the name embossed on one side, a fantastical fortress on the other. He settles on Asteroids, but the bright floating rocks smash his tiny rocket three times in under a minute. Like the machine knows his crime. Or it's just that the loot, concealed about his body, restricts his range of motion.

He walks in the cavelike dark, eyes on the carpet. A

dropped token glints between Berzerk and Centipede. As soon as he feeds it into Defender, the back door opens. A security guard and a bulgy woman he could swear he saw at Walden's enter, scan the room like cyborgs. They're on to him. He slides the paperback from his pocket and kicks it under the machine, then nervously resumes his game. The spaceship darts like a minnow, the laser sounds scouring his ears. He lets one of his pea-shaped enemies crash into him, then storms out in fake frustration.

Art squints from the brightness. He drops the glassine envelope of triangle-shaped postage—from Hungary, Dahomey, Mongolia—into the trash. What a waste! He ducks into a pet store, loud with yips and birdsong, and blindly wedges the Rush tape between sacks of aquarium gravel. Then he removes his jacket and flings it over his shoulder like he's some sort of model—an Asian kid model making enough so that he doesn't have to shoplift, no sir.

"Hey!" a voice calls out. The blood leaves Art's face. He stops, unconsciously turning up his wrists as if awaiting the slap of handcuffs.

The pet store worker beams. "Help you find anything today?"

"No!" Art says. "Thank you!"

Art heads for Jenss, the department store where his parents usually end up. He gets lost, reorients himself with the mall map. *You are here.* If only there were a way to contact them. If only he hadn't stolen anything in the first place. Although he's ditched the loot, he worries that he could still be found guilty in a court of law. Is it a crime to move things from one area of the mall to another, if you don't actually take it out of the building?

Someone might be following him. The front of Jenss is like a runway, a row of mirrors on each side, and as he breaks into a trot, an infinite series of Arts comes to life. Where is he going? Out the door, into the lot? This isn't even where they parked. He

looks helplessly above the mirrors. Then he spots his parents settling up in the shoe department, laden with bags.

44. People Are Crazy

The reunited Sins head for the exit by the mall cinema, closer to where they parked. The poster for *Friday the 13th Part 2* shows the silhouette of a man with a dripping ax.

"Michinda," says Hannah. *People are crazy.*

A moment later, they stop in their tracks, as though a force field has gone up. They can't leave the mall. A huge silence has opened behind them. A crowd stands rapt before a television set mounted near the fountain. For a minute it's like a scene from a science-fiction movie, the masses hypnotized by technology's glow. Everyone is trying to make sense of what they are seeing.

The Sins move closer. The same jagged scene repeats, and they take it all in until scattered facts emerge. President Reagan was leaving a D.C. hotel after a speech. Reporters called out, hoping for a word, as he headed to the limousine. A popping sound, a swarm of trench coats, everyone falling at once. A bullet hit the car. The press secretary went down, shot in the head. Reagan took one in the chest.

45. The Return of Taro (II)

Inky and Art emerge from the mall, shaken, while Hannah makes a detour to Laux Sporting Goods, where she thinks she's misplaced a bag from another store. Besides, it's slushy. She'd rather wait for them to pull up with the car.

Art asks his dad, the doctor, if Reagan will die. Inky says no, that the president has the best doctors. In school, Art has read about President McKinley getting shot in Buffalo. He had the best doctors, too. The wound got infected and Teddy Roosevelt became president.

Father and son are picking their way across the pavement,

avoiding the deep black puddles, when someone shouts, "Yo, Taro!"

It's a bearded guy in a corduroy jacket, sunglasses in the pocket. The greeter and his horde are heading from the lot to the entrance. He puts his palms together and gives a stiff bow. "Taro Tsujimoto," he says, as his girlfriend makes the sound of a crashing gong.

Inky stops, light-headed. The name, of course, is *his* name. What the teachers called him as a child, back when they were turning kids Japanese. Who is saying it now, and why? Dr. Sin eyes the group. He must have misheard. He steers his son away.

"Is that your boy, Taro?"

The others pepper him with jokes or taunts he doesn't understand. "We headed for the playoffs this year, *Taro*?"

Father and son pick up the pace. The boy looks down, half fuming, half scared. What provoked this? Nothing. Just existing. He'd been called names at school before, but he's never heard anyone mock his father.

"Taro say: A puck in the net is worth two on the stick."

Inky stops. "You have wrong person."

The words fall harshly on Art's ears, the accent extra thick. Or is this how white people hear his father?

"Taro say: For puck's sake."

The smallest of the group changes course, heads to another aisle of the lot. "Come *on*," he urges. "Stop being dicks."

Art digs his nails into his palms until the others follow the small guy into the mall, where the crowd in front of the TV has just learned the name of the man who shot Ronald Reagan.

46. The Mirror

At the hospital the next day, people can't stop talking about the shooting, but Dr. Sin dwells on his parking lot encounter. *Taro Tsujimoto. For puck's sake.* What does the name—*his* old name, the one the Japanese gave him—have to do with . . . hockey?

One of his patients, Parker Jotter, is a die-hard Sabres fan. He fills him in on general manager Punch Imlach's elaborate joke from a while back, in which he drafted a make-believe Japanese player. On Saturday, the incredulous doctor stops by the big library downtown. He finds a whole book by Imlach, recounting the saga. It's so gleefully pointless that Inky has to laugh.

But how did Punch and the publicity agent land on the Japanese name he gave up as a child? The librarian, a hockey buff, tracks down other accounts of the trade. She produces a fat copy of the *Hockey News* draft special from '74, with pics of the new picks. Virtually all are Canadian. At the end of the Sabres section is a small photo of an Asian man in a Katanas jersey, holding a stick that says KOHO.

"That's a razor-and-paste job," the librarian says, pointing out the awkward neck of the jersey. "The head's from some-where else—a different *era*. And he's got an old shirt collar."

That tight-lipped countenance and thin mustache, that look of ambition and fear. For Dr. Sin, it's like finding a mirror. Because it's *him*.

47. Trapped (II)

Out of respect for the president's condition, the Academy Awards ceremony gets postponed by a night. It's said that Reagan's feeling better, cracking jokes at the hospital. "I hope you're all Republicans," he says to his doctors. It's like a team of press agents live in his brain.

Hannah and Art tune in. They see the stars arrive: Goldie Hawn and the beautiful Sigourney Weaver and the handsome singer Michael Jackson. Johnny Carson hosts. He assures the world that the president is doing fine. Cue the greeting that Reagan taped two weeks ago.

"Film is forever!" he says. "I've . . . been trapped in some films forever myself . . ."

48. The Chosen (II)

Art Sin, still eleven, steers clear of *Friday the 13th Part 2*, but the memory of the poster with the ax terrifies him. It builds on the doom he felt upon seeing the teaser for *The Shining* last year: blood seeping through elevator doors, filling the vestibule, setting the furniture afloat. The ax keeps edging into his mind. He develops a morbid fear of the date Friday the 13th. The next one isn't till November, but he's already torn out the entry from his word-a-day calendar.

On the schoolbus, someone leaves behind a copy of the fantasy gaming magazine *Basilisk*, which he reads with mild interest. He is about to abandon the issue, as the bus approaches his stop, when he discovers a page in the back filled with ads for fan-run periodicals. The idea of something traveling vast distances to reach him is comforting. He sends self-addressed stamped envelopes for sample copies of *Barbarian Prince*, *Red Kobold, Vow of the Amber Regent*. He also requests trial issues of *Hi-Res* (home computing), *Golden Joystick* (video games), and *CinéFreak* (movies). The last one is a hand-stapled affair that arrives from Switzerland in a stiff envelope marked PAR AVION.

That year, Art watches sixteen movies, about one every three weeks. He enters the titles in his computer, a wobbly model called the JOT 2000, a gift to his father from a patient. Most of these he catches with friends or his mom, but a few are solo runs. An asterisk indicates a movie that Hannah walked out of, to catch something else at the theater next door. Double asterisks indicate a film he fell asleep in.

Art sends his annotated list to *CinéFreak*, which runs it alongside those from a dozen other, more established critics. It's his first published piece. The editor is delighted by the asterisks, and the way the Dudley Moore movie *Arthur* shows up in both the Thumbs-Up and Thumbs-Down columns. The great thing is that they keep sending him issues, though he never pays. The less great thing, for Art, is how much space the editor

devotes to *Friday the 13th* and its sequel, with illustrations that give him the creeps.

49. Dream Four

Remember Dream Four, that fragmented account of the Korean War? Frank and Barbara Hallsworth, Frank's lover Lim, newlyweds Pak and Mila, embittered reporter Longfellow—those people, those lives, swept up in the chaos of June 1950? All are fictional characters in the motion picture *Inchon!*—which also has versions of real-life figures like General MacArthur. The director is Terence Young, famous for adapting James Bond for the screen. The film teems with stars. Ben Gazzara (*Anatomy of a Murder*) plays Major Hallsworth, while Jacqueline Bisset (*Airport*), as his wife, Barbara, gives the film its emotional core. Richard Roundtree (*Shaft*) is the earnest Sergeant Henderson, friend to both. For a $1.25 million paycheck, ailing Sir Laurence Olivier inhabits the pipe-chomping MacArthur. The movie also shoehorns in Toshiro Mifune, the force-of-nature samurai from Akira Kurosawa's movies, and Egyptian-born heartthrob Omar Sharif.

The filming took on the characteristics of a global military operation: shot on three continents, with the actual South Korean army brought in for some battle scenes. Who could conceive, let alone bankroll, such a spectacle? *Inchon!* is the passion project of the Reverend Sun Myung Moon, founder of the Unification Church (which *we* still call the Divine Precepts). For him, General MacArthur is *the* immortal hero who rescued South Korea from the godless Reds. Operation Chromite saved Moon's life: as U.N. forces struck north, they liberated the Communist-held cities, freeing him from that corpse-mill known as the Hungnam prison. With Moon's acumen, the DPs have amassed a fortune; *Inchon!* is a $46 million thank-you note, as well as an advertisement for his church, born in the ashes of the Korean War.

50. The Fan

Senator Al D'Amato of New York arranges the gala premiere of *Inchon!*, which is held on May 4, 1981 (4314), at the Kennedy Center in D.C. It's billed as a benefit for a veterans' residence, a project of the Unification Church. A crowd protests the event, upset over its link with the Moonies. After breaching the gauntlet, viewers must contend with a movie over three hours long.

The running time and the protests make it poison to distributors. There have been too many magazine stories about Americans whose lives have been turned upside down by the church. Is it a religion or a cult? In one photo, a woman holds a sign that says MOON IS A MENACE. Another shows hundreds of couples getting married under the reverend's watchful eye. The average American doesn't know what's more alarming: that the unions are mixed race or that the bride and groom agree to the wedding even before meeting each other.

Thus *Inchon!* remains in limbo. Most Americans figure it's a form of big-budget brainwashing. In the months between its premiere and its brief public release, however, the movie finds a fan in President Reagan, star of the '50s POW flop *Prisoner of War* and the propaganda piece *The Ultimate Weapon*. On February 13, 1982 (4315), Reagan screens *Inchon!* at one of his regular Camp David movie nights.

Reagan had skipped the 1981 Kennedy Center gala, to heal from the attempt on his life. (The shooter, John Hinckley, had wanted to impress the actress Jodie Foster.) He is eager to watch *Inchon!* tonight, but many of his regular invitees are suspiciously unavailable. The subject's a drag. At the last minute, Reagan invites Alexander Haig, his secretary of state, who served under MacArthur in Korea. Haig messed up royally last year after the shooting, saying *he* was in charge while Reagan was laid up. In truth, three people preceded him in the chain of command. It was like that movie where the eighth in line to the British throne gets rid of the seven people in his way.

The president gets through to Haig. "You've got a bit part, I hear."

"How's that?"

"A cameo."

"You understand, sir, that I'm not actually *in* the movie, right? It's an actor playing me."

Patronizing bastard. Reagan's just being friendly. In any case, Haig doesn't show, and to hell with him. The president watches with Nancy and a few junior staffers. *Inchon!* has too many characters, and the plot can be hard to follow, but it isn't dull. When the first bridge explodes, Reagan's head snaps back; when the North Koreans order the captured newlywed to gun down the other prisoners, he closes his eyes as the shots ring out. During the credits, he says to Nancy, *For once we're the good guys and the Communists are the villains.*

Ronald Reagan is a member of the Korean Provisional Government.

51. Dream One

Dr. Inky Sin is balding as he wades into his middle forties. But the hair on the sides of his head comes in fast, and he combs the healthier strands this way and that for an illusion of plenty. He looks like his grandfather or someone. He's been coming to the office earlier, working again on what he calls his theory of dreams. "There are five kinds of dreams," he writes. A sentence he's written before. What *are* the five kinds? He'd dearly like to know.

While staring out the window at Grider Street, he spins an old wooden charm on his desktop. It's the only item from his hometown that he still possesses: some sort of amulet with a fantastic number of sides, each inscribed with a cryptic command. He does his best to translate: *Behold the moon and name it in your tune.*

Absently, he tries catching the charm on the back of his hand. It rolls off his abbreviated ring finger and falls to the linoleum. He tucks his tie into his shirt and stoops. What looks to be a pistachio shell resolves into a fragment of the die. It must have chipped on impact. With the edge of a folder he sweeps the detritus toward him. A tinkling sound. Amid the bits of wood is a tiny iron key.

The blade of the key is a thin rod with tiny protrusions, like the prickly bits in a music-box mechanism. What does it open? A chest in his grandmother's house? Which was pounded to dust three decades ago? In a town wiped off the map? In a region you *can't even get to*, in the no-man's-land between North and South Korea?

He has the insane idea that he needs to open it—the box, the chest, whatever it is. He must fly back, somehow find his way to the ghost town of Hwajiri. As he's about to buy the ticket, from a travel agent who is, in fact, none other than Syngman Rhee . . . Dr. Sin wakes up. He's still home, facedown on the pillow. It's a mellow Saturday in April. Hannah's making coffee downstairs, as their son watches cartoons. There is no fourteen-sided spell-casting amulet, of course. He hasn't seen that since he was a boy.

52. Wishes

In his notes, we find this line: *Dreams are never signs, unless the dreamer wishes them to be.*

Inky Sin gets out of bed, washes his face, combs his rather full head of hair. (What did it mean that he was balding in the dream?) A friend who visited Buffalo last year with his actress wife brought news of a country on fire. President Chun Doo-hwan is worse than President Park, who was worse than President Syngman Rhee. The actress joked that if Inky ever came back, the government would shoot him on sight. Many of

the student leaders of the 1960 demonstrations were heroes for a while, then learned to keep a low profile.

But Inky knows he has to go back. Someday. Would Hannah and Art understand that he—the secretly appointed president of the Korean Provisional Government—needs to return?

53. The Oriental Occidental

On July 1, 1982 (4315), the Unification Church (a.k.a. the Moonies, a.k.a. the Divine Precepts) holds a mass wedding at Madison Square Garden. Four thousand men and women, handpicked by Sun Myung Moon, tie the knot. Most of the couples are complete strangers; many don't even share a language. At forty-nine, Flora Edwards, Parker Jotter's ex-wife, weds a local widower, a former Korean wig mogul with the fanciful name Euphrates. They settle outside Seoul, and forty days after the ceremony they consummate their marriage.

Inchon! finally opens nationwide on September 17, 1982, a half hour trimmed from its two-hour, fifteen-minute run time. Ironically, the cuts make it seem even longer. Scenes collide without context. Characters react to things the audience cannot see. Toshiro Mifune might be a Japanese ascetic (a holdover from colonial days?), or else the Korean father of Gazzara's love interest, or else a grizzled commando coaxed out of retirement—perhaps all three.

The film is dead on arrival. *The New York Times* says it looks like "the most expensive B-movie ever made" and that Olivier's "ghastly" makeup gives him the appearance of "an oriental actor playing an occidental." An editor at the new *Washington Times* refuses to print a lengthy pan, citing a conflict of interest: Reverend Moon owns the paper. The film's connection to the Unification Church nudges critics to judge *Inchon!* more harshly than it deserves. In a very short time, this movie about the Forgotten War is itself forgotten.

54. Love, Destiny, Heroes

In Buffalo that Sunday, the Sins go to see *Inchon!* at the only theater in the area where it's playing, forty minutes away. Inky tells his son he can learn about his namesake, Douglas MacArthur. Hannah is surprised. "He's named after *MacArthur?*"

Dr. Sin has avoided talking much about the Korean War to Art, who's now twelve. (Hannah, seven years younger than Inky, has dimmer memories.) Inky is still wary of revealing to his family that he—a psychiatrist in Buffalo, New York—is in fact the president of the Korean Provisional Government. That he is presently engaged in a war of words with two other Koreans (a San Diego dentist and a Vancouver pharmacist) who each claims to be president.

His wife might decide that her husband is out of his mind.

Hannah wants to play tennis that evening, unwind after a long day at the floral shop where she's been working part time, and Arthur would rather watch TV, but Inky insists. They make a 6:30 screening, at a theater they've never been to before. Two other movies are showing: Pink Floyd's *The Wall* and *An Officer and a Gentleman*, which has been out for months. The lobby poster looks like the box of an Atari cartridge, at once too clean and too busy. MacArthur's mug takes up most of the real estate, with a receding array of battleships at the bottom and a white couple gazing at each other in the upper-left corner.

On the poster, the title has lost its exclamation point: *Inchon*. Perhaps that's the problem. The name looks like a snoozy verb: *inch on*. The tagline reads: "Love. Destiny. Heroes." Underneath it, another tagline: "War Changes Everything." No mention of Korea. The map of the peninsula is tinted so close to MacArthur's cheek that it practically disappears.

Dr. Sin's excitement wanes. This will be history from the foreigners' point of view, an action movie where the Koreans will end up as corpses. Still, as president of the KPG, Inky Sin feels duty-bound to monitor the audience's response.

Past the ticket taker, a thin white American woman proffers brochures. "Would you like the Key to Perfection?" the woman asks in passable Korean.

Inky shakes his head, even as Hannah and Arthur cheerfully take the literature. He thinks of how his patient Parker Jotter lost his wife to these Divine Precepts. Parker doesn't talk about Flora anymore. He doesn't want his anger at a Korean cult and the Korean War to be misconstrued as rage against his doctor from Korea.

The Sins sit in row 7. Only ten others are in attendance. Art skims his brochure, which invites viewers to discover more about the Unification Church and the historic revelations of its leader, the Reverend Moon. There are grainy images from the movie he's about to see. *Inchon* is the first of many popular motion pictures the church will produce. It plans to make a series of biopics, beginning with Marilyn Monroe.

Inchon starts cold, without previews, as if to say: *Good luck— this will be a long one.* Everything is too loud, too bright, and yet it works on Dr. Sin. He gasps as tanks overrun a village, people fleeing as their houses tumble. He can't sort out all the characters, but the big movements—the North sweeping aside the South, MacArthur saving the day—merge with his own memories of the war, some of which have themselves been colored by *M*A*S*H* reruns. Syngman Rhee, curiously, doesn't seem to be in the movie at all. Was the role cut? Every time Hannah spots a famous face—Bisset, Sharif—she whispers to Art what other films it's been in.

The popcorn bucket's empty with over two hours left. For all his anticipation, Dr. Sin drifts in and out of sleep. An occupational hazard: he can't go to see movies because he barely sleeps during the week, and his body takes any opportunity to knock itself out cold.

Time to switch, Hannah says to her son.

You can't leave, Mom. Art, whose taste for shoplifting has stuck, is strict about rules when it comes to others.

She puts a finger to her lips and scoots out of the row. After peeking through the door to see if the coast is clear, she slips out to watch Richard Gere and Debra Winger in *An Officer and a Gentleman* again. (Rather, to *finish* watching it: when she saw it over the summer, she walked out midway and made the last third of *The World According to Garp*.) Twenty minutes later, Art attempts a switch himself, but *The Wall* is down a long corridor, and a ticket taker's stationed by the door, looking right at him.

He returns to *Inchon,* sitting in the back row. He watches with a hand on his face, shifting his fingers over his eyes whenever the shooting starts. If Art is being honest, the violence is getting to him. It's nothing he hasn't seen onscreen before, but this time the bodies all look like his. With ten minutes to go, he runs out again, stands by the restroom in case he loses his supper.

Inky Sin sleeps, waking right as the credits hit. Where is everyone? For a minute, in that unfamiliar darkness, he wonders who has taken his family from him, under cover of night.

55. Triple Bill

The film leaves theaters in less than a week. For decades, *Inchon* (or *Inchon!*) is practically invisible. It never gets released on video; the various stars erase it from their filmographies. Paradoxically, some people want to see it only once it attains the legend of being the worst movie ever made.

But it's not. Along with *Prisoner of War* (1954) and *Arirang* (1926), the director's cut of *Inchon!* is an enduring classic of the Korean Provisional Government.

56. Reality

As hammy as Olivier's performance is, and as freaked out as he was by the bloodshed, twelve-year-old Arthur can't get over the

fact that his name derives from the general's. He takes weird pride in it, writing "Mac" before his name on the covers of his Chatillion Academy notebooks. In science class, his mind flies out the window, over the quad and the brutalist field house, through the screen of trees by the railroad tracks, then backward into history. As Mr. N. chalks definitions on the board, Art's in the war-torn land of his ancestors. He's an orphan fleeing the North Koreans, jumping in a station wagon driven by an American woman in a floppy hat and carrying five Korean girls. Soldiers rise from the rice paddies and open fire. Their faces are variations of his. He leaps from the car—then what? How does he get from there to here, Korea to Buffalo? His imagination isn't big enough. For a woozy minute, he doesn't exist.

"Earth to Arthur," says Mr. N., perched on the edge of his desk. He tosses and catches a stub of chalk in one hand without looking. Tanned and wiry, clad in tweed blazer and blue wide-wale cords and green sweater vest, Mr. N. is one of Chatillion's most popular teachers, at least among the boys who play hockey. He coaches the seventh-and-eighth-grade team, his voice carrying across the vast rink. Though he limps from an old war wound, on the ice he flies from end to end like a dream, his backward crossovers magically brisk.

"Wake up, Arthur."

"Excuse me?"

"Sorry—it looked like you were asleep there. I guess your eyes are always like that."

The class is quiet. Mr. N. returns to the chalkboard. Everyone stares at Arthur, who can't speak. He fixes his gaze on an anatomical diagram on the wall, the side view of a faceless figure: *Nasal passage. Oral passage. Pharynx. Larynx.*

57. Dictation

In the fall of 1982, an art press publishes a book by one of its editors, thirty-one-year-old Theresa Hak Kyung Cha. *Dictee*

seems less like literature than hypnosis. Weeks later, when the author is waiting to meet her husband at a building downtown, she is raped and murdered by a security guard. Her death and defilement echo the fate of one of *Dictee*'s heroines: You Guan Soon, schoolgirl–turned–independence fighter—Korea's Joan of Arc, martyred behind prison walls after the March 1 demonstrations.

Consecrated by the fate of its author, *Dictee*'s reputation grows. With its French title, *Dictee* is perpetually foreign on the surface, an alien artifact. If the reader can find a way in, however, it becomes unbearably human. The older it gets, the newer it seems. There are charts and film stills, maps and old photos. Sounds and tongues and spirits. It invokes the nine Greek muses and reproduces the letter written by Syngman Rhee and P. K. Yoon to Theodore Roosevelt: *We know that the people of America love fair play and advocate justice towards all men . . .*

Dictee keeps scholars busy as they decode its raft of references. In French, *dictée* means dictation: the act of taking things down. But it also conjures *dictatorship:* the twin dictatorships of North and South Korea, from the end of the Korean War into the 1980s. What none of these scholars grasps is that Theresa Hak Kyung Cha is a member of the Korean Provisional Government, and that *Dictee* is one of the KPG's secret bibles—a holy dictation designed to take down dictatorships.

Someday they will know, because we will tell them.

58. The Heist

Arthur sees Mr. N. once a day, twice on Tuesdays and Thursdays, when the hockey players have dryland training to prepare for the season ahead. The frequent contact wears away the animosity. Arthur pretty much forgets the whole thing until the night of the talent show, held in the chapel the week before Thanksgiving 1982 (4315). His mom drops him off. Arthur isn't

participating; he sometimes jokes that he has no talent. He's just there to watch some friends sing, juggle, tell jokes. At intermission, he goes to use the lavatory. The nearest one has a line, so Arthur goes down the hall and up two flights. The third-floor lights are off. He walks past 303—Mr. N.'s room. Through the glass, Art spots his desk, its surface liquid in the cold moonlight. The door is unlocked.

Art doesn't know what he's doing in the room, or why he's walking behind Mr. N.'s desk. His eyes adjust and he sees the old textbooks in the low case behind the desk, shored up with a brass bookend in the shape of what must be Montana. Art's head pulses like it did after the comment about his eyes. Skulking in the blued dark, he inspects his teacher's desk. Opening the bottom drawer releases the sickly smell of tobacco. Something glimmers amid the pipes and matchbooks: a bronze disk with the diameter of a puck. Art peers without touching. Ribbon attached, eagle in the center. A medal, unceremoniously shoved in a desk. Art looks closer. It's a military decoration. Surrounding the eagle is a ring of scratched markings, which he sees is barbed wire. A POW medal for service in *Korea*.

He doesn't know Mr. N.'s story. Was he tortured in a camp? That might explain the limp. Did he kill any Koreans? Art stuffs the medal in his pocket. He unzips his pants and directs a stream of piss into the drawer. He means to leave only a few drops, like a hint of perfume, but it flows for twenty seconds, thirty, a full minute.

Footsteps approach as the stream tapers. Art can hear the piss seep into the papers. He darts out of 303 and heads for the far staircase. Somewhere in the dark behind him, a guard is checking the locks on the doors.

59. Letter to the Editor

Among the papers of the late Parker Jotter of Buffalo, New York, are copies of letters sent to film reviewers across the

country and all over the world, taking issue with their opinions. The late 1970s and early 1980s were a difficult period for Jotter. He directed his bitterness at the movies, doling out the most venom to a Swiss publication called *CinéFreak*. The critic Yura's elaborate psychological critique of *Friday the 13th* drove him up the wall. "My own encounter with a homicidal maniac has made me something of an expert on the issue," he wrote in 1988. "Sometimes a bloody machete is just a bloody machete."

In the same box as the letters is a paperback edition of *Man in Korean Costume*, a novel by T. S. Kim, dogeared and underlined.

60. The North Star

In 1994 (4327), Kim Il Sung, founder and supreme leader of North Korea, dies at age eighty-two. He leaves behind five volumes of autobiography (which take the reader only to his twentieth year) and a country in crisis from famine. His dream of uniting Korea will have to wait for another dreamer. The growth on Kim Il Sung's neck, once the size of a pea, is now like a baby's head. Photos late in life were always taken from the other side. Doctors remove the growth, sew up the neck. The corpse is displayed at Kumsusan Memorial Palace. Thousands of mourners enter the Hall of Tears to gaze on his body in its glass coffin.

Taking the reins now is his eldest son, Kim Jong Il. He was born Yura Irsenovich Jong-il Kim in Russia, where his parents the guerrilla fighters were hiding from the Japanese; a handful of cronies still call him Yura. State organs dub him Dear Leader or sometimes the *Lodestar*—that is, the North Star.

Soon after his ascendance, the ministry of propaganda takes out ads in *The New York Times* and other papers around the world.

What the ad doesn't state is that Kim—Yura—is a movie buff. Not just a fan but a hard-core cinephile with wide-ranging tastes. (Most of his *official*, state-published writing up to this point relates to film production.) His personal library boasts thirty thousand titles. Each of his seven mansions houses a top-of-the-line home theater.

Under the pen name Yura, he used to contribute essays to film magazines in Europe and America. "Contribute" is meant loosely, alas; he is rarely published. Thus, beginning in the 1970s, he bankrolls a magazine of his own, *CinéFreak.* The publication is sent out from an office in Geneva, where his older son attends boarding school under an alias. (As Yura, he has scores of faithful pen pals, who have no idea about his true identity.) His compatriots back home refer to him as the Swiss Man.

61. It's a Wonderful Life

A library of thirty thousand movies sounds excessive. *Can you really watch all those?* Shura, his younger brother, teases one day, a year into Yura's tenure as the North's Lodestar.

Yura loves talking to Shura (né Kim Man Il), his faithful companion, though they are rarely in the same place. Whereas Yura is on the squat side, Shura is a sculpted stud. Yura used to urge him to become an actor, a career path his brother dismissed with a snort. Shura claims to find all Western movies boring.

It's a Wonderful Nap, Shura dubs the Jimmy Stewart classic.

Now, come on! Yura has a soft spot for Capra.

Capitalist claptrap, Shura insists. *Who has the time to watch everything?*

Yura smiles. *Say each movie runs on average ninety minutes. That's two point seven million minutes. Which is forty-five thousand hours. Which equals one thousand, eight hundred and seventy-five days.*

Shura does a quick calculation. *A little over five years.*

Yura snaps his fingers and winks. *You BET I've spent five of my fifty-three years on this earth watching movies!*

Yura has seen it all, from old silent serials to sentimental crowd-pleasers to jagged experimental shorts. He's no snob. He loves science fiction, westerns, romantic comedies, and horror, from everywhere in the world. (One exception: he despises most South Korean cinema, with its didactic exposition and clumsy mise-en-scène.) For several years, he nurtures his personal "seed theory" of art, which states that every aspect of a film— the tone of the acting, the sets and lighting, even the typeface on the credits—grows organically from the instigating idea. The artist's spermlike thought. Shura always humors him, though he has no clue what it means. Nevertheless, the top universities in Pyongyang require all film majors to submit theses

on the Dear Leader's seed theory, a revolutionary development in the history of art.

62. Sea of Blood (I)

Yura should have been allowed to live his dream life: watching, producing, and reviewing movies. One of the great feats recorded in the 1985 hagiography *Great Leader Kim Jong Il* is his overnight rewrite of a film team's weak script. The result is *Sea of Blood*, the four-hour 1971 classic of North Korean cinema.

Alas, instead of a life in the arts, he has to lead the nation.

63. Seeds

Yura, the North Star, daydreams that *Cahiers du Cinéma* or the British Film Institute or some other high-toned place interviews him about his passion. (He envisions his questioner looking like Sean Young in *Blade Runner*, pale with hair like lacquer.) Asked to name his favorite movie, Yura shuts his eyes while considering all the miles of film he's seen. He pours the interviewer some cognac before saying, *This might surprise you, but my favorite film of all time—beyond* Citizen Kane *and* The Wizard of Oz *and* Contempt—is Friday the 13th.

Yura insists that the film is as deep and beautiful and disquieting as anything he's seen. That it's a dream masquerading as the ultimate horror film. A poem of grief. He's quick to say that he dislikes the numerous sequels. He abhors *Part 3*, which introduces the infamous goalie mask worn by the killer, Jason. Yura stridently contends that the mask symbolizes all that went wrong with the series. An emblem of shame. The filmmakers can no longer face the audience, after so many nonsensical contortions.

The first film, to be sure, has plot holes and lapses in logic. But it stands apart. No other entry has its terrifying economy. No other entry (Yura explains) makes good on the "seed theory," following through on the narrative power of a cursed

locale. The date "Friday the 13th" isn't even mentioned in the film—*that's* how powerful the concept is, how fertile the seed.

What concept? the interviewer asks.

Yura says, *I've got a secret.*

64. American Bric-a-Brac

Yura first sees *Friday the 13th* two years after its 1980 release. He has just turned forty. He savors a crisp print stolen outside Omaha by a trusted operative. The reel was chopped up, the pieces patiently smuggled via diplomatic packet; it took a month to splice back together.

Yura screens it in his home theater dozens of times, exploring it from every angle. He cannot believe what he is seeing. Or hearing. Or *feeling*. The lush forest, the cabins filled with American bric-a-brac, the serene lake with a single boat drifting, green trees mirrored on its skin . . . and the flip side: the sheer terror, unstoppable as a dream. An overwhelming aesthetic experience.

Ch-ch-ch-ch (ch-ch-ch-ch).

It becomes a morbid tradition: Yura watches *Friday the 13th* every year, preferably *on* a Friday the 13th. Using precise recipes, his chefs concoct buckets of good old American popcorn, and even simulate such rarefied cinema snacks as Good & Plentys. He sees it with Shura, a Twizzlers connoisseur. No one else is invited to watch.

For variety, they occasionally project it off a rare Japanese LaserDisc, which includes original material cut for U.S. distribution and never seen anywhere else. These "bonus" moments compound the gore—showing, for instance, the gratuitous twist of an arrow after it pierces one victim's throat from under a mattress. Though Yura has memorized every line of dialogue, and knows exactly when the creepy *ch-ch-ch-ch* will kick in on the soundtrack, he never rushes through.

Yura understands that his ardor is unfashionable. No critic

takes the film seriously as art. In Chicago, Illinois, the reviewer Gene Siskel is so appalled by the violence that his column includes contact information for the studio head, so that readers know where to direct their hate mail. He also reveals the Connecticut town where one of the film's stars lives—the oldest member of the otherwise young cast. In other words, someone who should have known better.

The name of this actress, age fifty-four, is Betsy Palmer.

Yura has his people find her address—no mean feat in those days—so that he can send her a note of praise. Her unhinged performance transfixes him. He becomes an authority on her work. He keeps a framed photo of her in his study—ironically, from a movie he can't identify, some forgotten title of her youth.

65. Lady Voorhees

What is history? Like the hockey player Tim Horton in 1972, Betsy Palmer in 1979 wants a new car. She is driving from New York back home to Connecticut when her Mercedes breaks down. Now a divorcée in her fifties, the bright light of I've Got a Secret does occasional work in theater. A little movie gig would make the payment on a sporty Scirocco that much easier. Her agent passes along a script and says keep an open mind. You wouldn't call it art, he says, but most things aren't art. The real question is, does she want a car or not?

"Think of it as your Lady Macbeth," her agent says.

Betsy agrees to play Pamela Voorhees, who the audience

won't see till the end. In the script, Pamela appears as a motherly presence, a sympathetic adult who comes to the rescue of the sole counselor to survive the massacre—before trying to hack her to pieces.

As Betsy runs her lines in front of a mirror, she imagines her coeval Marilyn Monroe acting in a slasher film. *But I'm alive and you are not,* she says to her own face. She thinks that if James Byron Dean were alive, he would be forty-eight.

Betsy Palmer figures that *Friday the 13th*—a shameless copy of the recent hit *Halloween*—will mercifully disappear. A footnote to a footnote in her career.

Alas, the movie is box office gold, kicking off a deathless franchise that spans decades, even as the quality sinks. The original *Friday the 13th* has real staying power, though, thanks to Betsy Palmer. Her character, Pamela Voorhees—the aggrieved single mother of a drowned, deformed child—is the human anchor.

66. Crystal Lake

To prepare for her turn as Mrs. Voorhees, Betsy Palmer latched on to a small detail in the script: a class ring. She thought of something from her acting lessons, the idea that your character has already *lived* before the audience sees her. What's it mean, the class ring? She connected it to her own high school years. How girls would go steady with one guy, get married after graduation. Betsy pictured Pamela Voorhees wearing her boyfriend's class ring. What boyfriend? Someone who knocked her up and left, maybe. Sure. Okay. Say he went off to war, didn't make it back . . . World War II? Too early. The *Korean* War. Pam's parents give her the boot; she goes to a home for unwed mothers. It must be hard taking care of a baby, let alone one with serious abnormalities. When Pam is offered a job at Camp Crystal Lake, she jumps at the chance. The pay is low, but as a bonus her son will get some fresh air. Be part of nature.

The camp, Crystal Lake, shared its name with a place Betsy used to visit as a kid, out in Warsaw, Indiana. She closed her eyes, let all the joyful memories curdle into horror. The exercise made her happy, for it was the sort of deep empathy that real actors live for.

Patricia Betsy Hrunek of Chicago by way of East Chicago becomes Betsy Palmer becomes Pamela Voorhees, the decade's most terrifying villainess.

67. Yura and Shura at the Movies

Yura (a.k.a. Kim Jong Il) talks to his brother, Shura (Kim Man Il), in the dark as *Friday the 13th* plays. There's an American television show called *At the Movies*, in which two critics—the aforementioned Siskel and plump Roger Ebert—weigh in on the week's new releases. What a life! (The rotund Yura, aware of the lanky Siskel's distaste for *Friday the 13th*, is an Ebert partisan.) He fantasizes about airing a similar program in North Korea.

"Think about it, Shura. We would play clips, have a passionate discussion, and weigh in with a thumbs-up or thumbs-down. 'This week, we'll look at *When We Pick Apples, A Woman Tractor Driver, Devotion,* and *Fate of a Self-Defense Corps Man . . .* '"

I despised A Woman Tractor Driver.

"Right! Like that! Just the two of us, having a conversation about some movies!"

Father wouldn't like it.

Yura sighs. Shura is right, of course. In lieu of this pipe dream, the brothers take to dressing in the manner of Siskel and Ebert for their joint screenings: plaid shirts, sweater vests, wool blazers. They look like eccentric history professors. As his leadership duties increase, however, Yura finds less time for these fraternal outings. The last time they watch *Friday the 13th* together is in 1995 (4328), a year after their father's passing— a year after Yura becomes North Korea's North Star.

We join them now.

68. The Japanese House

"Shura," Yura whispers, fifteen minutes into their sacred matinee. No response. "Shura?"

I'm here, brother. Just eating some popcorn.

"I am so sorry."

*Sorry? Don't be daft. Too much butter is never a problem. This
music always gets me. Ch-ch-ch-ch (ch-ch-ch-ch). I had a new theory about the counselor who gets killed before she even gets to the
camp. . . . Ah, here she is now.*

They watch the pert young thing hitch a ride.

"Sorry," Yura apologizes again. He finishes a glass of
cognac, not his first of the day.

Shh. Can't you see I'm watching? Also—sorry for what?

"Sorry that I was not there for you."

You were always there for me.

"I was just a child."

The counselor's smile falters as she senses she's in danger.
There's something creepy about the driver.

Shhh, shhh.

"I was just a boy when Father brought us home to Korea."

Where were we before?

He has to remind Shura, who was so small then. "Russia.
Near Vladivostock, Khabarovsk. Hiding out because Father and
Mother were being hunted by the Japanese. You didn't know any
of this. You didn't know what Russia was, or Japan, or *Korea*, to
tell the truth. Mother told us we were going back home at long
last. Back to Pyongyang, though neither she nor you nor I had
ever seen it. We were as much Russian as we were Korean."

*That's right. We were Yura and Shura. Our Korean names came
later. What did they call Mother?*

"Vera."

Vera! How could I forget?

"It was already spring. I thought Korea was paradise after
the long Russian winter."

Onscreen, the counselor looks nervously at the landscape speeding past outside.

Where did we live when we came "back" to Korea?

"Some Japanese administrator had been shot, so we could have his house. I found this out later. There were papers in the attic, photos . . ."

You were just a child.

They see the counselor leap from the jeep, run shrieking into the woods.

"I *was* just a child," Yura concedes, "and *you* were practically a baby. The house felt like a palace, do you remember? Three floors, in the new style. Backyard, a pool. We could see mountains. I remember they would block the light until the sun got high enough. Then they would reflect it at double strength, like on a film set."

Ah, Yura. You were born to be a movie lover.

Yura pours the rest of the Hennessy into crystal tumblers. "We kept a maid, a bodyguard, a driver with a gun. There was someone to look after me, a Russian woman who had come over with us. She spoke in her language. The only Korean she knew was the word for *snow*, the word for *rain*, the word for *milk*, the word for *sleep*."

I remember.

"Then one day she was gone. A mystery. No one would tell me what happened. Perhaps she had been homesick. Mother cared for us. She was pregnant with our sister."

We have a sister? Just kidding.

"I remember Father wearing a necktie. A Western way of dressing! I laughed every morning as he struggled to make the ends come out right. He must have found the sight of it ridiculous as well, because he would laugh so hard the cups rattled in the cabinet."

Father had a sense of humor. People forget that these days. The youth, all they remember is an old man with a growth on his neck.

"The Japanese officer who used to live there had children," Yura recalls. "I found a beautiful set of coloring books, with scenes from folk tales. I couldn't read them. We didn't know their language, unlike the kids who had never left Korea. One of the coloring books had maps of the Japanese Empire at its most expansive. The Philippines, Taiwan, Indochina . . ."

Manchukuo . . . Malaysia . . . what didn't they take over?

They watch the counselor trip, try to scramble away.

"Singapore and Burma. And of course Korea, looking like a rabbit held by the ears."

I kept pestering you to swim with me, when all you wanted to do was color in the maps.

"I'm sorry. Shura, I'm sorry."

I'm not mad. Just remembering.

"The officer's daughter, whoever she was, had started coloring Korea orange. Like it was on fire. She had drawn a red line at the border with China, then started shading in delicately. The East Sea was pale blue with some sharp, dark waves. I tried following her style. I took my time. Father and Mother did not like the coloring books, so I kept them under my pillow."

The counselor screams as her unseen attacker approaches.

69. Thirteen Children Running Down a Road (After Yi Sang)

"I will never forget that day, Shura. It's been fifty years."

Fifty!

"Do you know what I did yesterday? I dug up an old American calendar for that year, down in the Center for Western Research. The bad thing happened to us because it was Friday the 13th."

Let's not be superstitious. Thirteen is not an unlucky number to Koreans.

"But it is for me. Do you know the author Yi Sang? He wrote a strange poem about thirteen children running down a road."

All his writing is strange. Isn't that why he chose that pen name?
Yi Sang, the Strange.

"I think his poem is about a serial killer. Most of it is the
same line, repeated. Each child saying he isn't scared, one by
one."

The number one child says he is not scared, Shura recites, *the*
number two child says he is not scared . . .

"By saying they're *not* scared, he's telling us they're out of
their minds with fear."

An unseen hand butchers the counselor as she looks up at
the soaring trees.

You're shaking, Yura. Shh. Should we turn the movie off? Tell me
about that day. You and me at the new house in Pyongyang. I don't
mind. I want you to be at peace.

"First, another drink." Yura opens two bottles of an American beer with an Asian-sounding name: Yuengling.

"Our new house had a pool," Yura continues. "A square cut
into the ground. No shallow end. Fish and frogs swam inside. It
frightened me, but you were never scared. When the sun went
above the mountains, the water gleamed like silver."

You didn't like to swim.

"It's true. I preferred to sit in the sun, coloring. I had finished
Korea and was working on the Philippines. I used fresh crayons
that day. This was my best effort yet."

You took it very seriously.

"Shura, listen. We were outside. I was at the table, coloring.
Where were the adults? You colored for a while, too, in the
other book. A nature scene. You had turned your bear red and
gold, with blue for the eyes. You were cackling. I said you were
crazy. That wasn't very nice. I shaded in the top of New
Guinea." Yura sniffles.

Shh.

"I was telling you the right way to do it. But you didn't
answer. Where did you go? Before I said your name, I knew. You

had gone back to the pool. Usually you jumped as high as you could to make a big splash, but this time you must have entered slowly, first your toes, then your ankles, and then—the rest."

The pool behind our house.

"I looked, but I didn't see you swimming."

The house where the Japanese officer used to live.

"I saw a *shape,* bigger than any fish. Rising slowly, dark and pale at once. I froze, too scared to jump in. From the pool I looked up at the second floor. Father's bodyguard was running down the staircase. In the water the shape was turning over . . ."

We were living in the house of a family that Father killed. The haunted house.

"The haunted house, yes . . ."

Let's just watch the movie. This is the good part. What am I talk-ing about? This movie is all good parts.

"Shura! Why didn't I save you?"

Night descends on the camp: *Ch-ch-ch-ch (ch-ch-ch-ch).*

70. The Architect and the Dictator

Side note: 1995 (4328) is also the year a rabble-rousing South Korean poet writes his first novel, *The Architect and the Dictator,* inspired by the sumptuous lifestyle of the North Korean leader Kim Jong Il. The book takes place in a nameless country, though the author pointedly gives his titular dictator the Rus-sian name Yura. The most famous architect in the land is tapped to build a mansion for Yura. It's a great honor, but he's heard horror stories about those who have designed the dicta-tor's previous houses. Once the structures were complete, the architects and all the workers were executed so that no one could reveal the secret passages and safe rooms that ensured the dictator's security.

The architect dreads the assignment but cannot refuse it. Summoned to the capital, he finds to his surprise that the dic-

tator is an affable, cultured figure who encourages his flights of artistic fancy. He has never had such a magnanimous patron. Construction begins; the mansion takes shape. Over decadent meals, the architect's vision grows more intricate. The funds are limitless, and the blueprints keep doubling. He figures that if the mansion is never completed, he will never die.

The book caused a sensation, though some critics deemed it reactionary. It was seen as out of step with current South Korean president Kim Dae-jung's Sunshine Policy, which pushed for a softer stance toward Pyongyang. Ironically, the book was surreptitiously published in North Korea, where it became more of a hit. The book's ambiguous ending could be read in multiple ways. The North Korean authorities never cracked down on printers and readers of the slim book, a kind of tacit approval.

The author of *The Architect and the Dictator* was Cho Eujin. (Someone we know quite well.) Its appearance on both sides of the 38th parallel was engineered by the Korean Provisional Government.

71. Everything Is Permitted

Postscript: In 1999 (4332), the fanzine *CinéFreak* runs a special issue devoted to *Friday the 13th*. Yura writes that the film is an inspired inversion of *Psycho*. In Hitchcock's shocker, the knife-wielding woman—seen in shadow during the infamous shower scene—turns out to be her grieving psychotic son in drag, whereas in Cunningham's movie, the mystery killer, presumably a man, turns out to be a grieving psychotic mother.

Yura dislikes the *Friday the 13th* sequels. It doesn't make sense (Yura writes) that Jason should *grow*, to hulking propor-tions, after being at the bottom of a lake for decades. And why does he wear a hockey mask, when part of his power must lie in his hideous face?

This turns out to be the farewell issue of *CinéFreak*, one of

the last secret bibles of the Korean Provisional Government. On
the final page, nestled among ads, is a tender dedication. It's to
a child who lived to only age four: Yura's phantom fellow
moviegoer, his brother.

FOR SHURA
BELOVED BROTHER & CINÉFREAK IN SPIRIT
B. 1944 VLADIVOSTOCK
D. 1948 PYONGYANG
"SEE YOU AT THE MOVIES"
YURA

72. Uncanny Anatomies

CBS airs the *M*A*S*H* series finale on February 28, 1983 (4316).
The long-running half-hour tragicomedy stars Alan Alda. It is
based on a counterculture movie about the Korean War from
1970 that was often seen as a critique of the Vietnam War,
which was still raging at the time. Korea and Vietnam are interchangeable in the mind of the American public. North and
South are again locked in battle. One yellow race can stand in
for another, a people to save and to slaughter.

The original film is adapted from a 1968 novel by Richard
Hooker—the last name slang for *prostitute*. (Dr. Inky Sin learned
the term in his army days, the first English word he couldn't find
in his beginner's dictionary.) Hooker is a joint pen name for
Hiester Richard Hornberger Jr., an army doctor during the
Korean War, and a hack named W. C. Heinz. Inky read it ten
years ago, and even tried one of the sequels (*M*A*S*H Goes to
Maine*). The cover of his paperback used the image from the
movie poster: a hand making the V sign, with an infantry helmet sitting loosely atop the index finger, the whole thing resting
on a set of high-heeled female legs. This nightmare anatomy is
seen from behind, so that the pads of the wrist approximate an
ass.

Hannah reads in *TV Guide* that three hundred members of

the press were on location as *M*A*S*H* taped its final episode. The long-running show about the Forgotten War has become part of American life.

For now, the Sin family gathers at the Zenith. It's a Monday night. Art asks if he can tape it to watch *later,* not that he's busy at the moment. The Sins have just bought a VCR, and Art jumps at any chance to record: late-night talk shows, sitcoms, music videos, movies. No longer chained to the schedule of the programming day, he can dip in and out of all there is on offer.

73. Everhard (I)

Art studies *TV Guide,* hunting for programs he wants to preserve. But the idea that these shows will always be there, accessible at any point in the future, also means that he can infinitely delay their viewing. Lately he doubts that he'll ever get to them at all. At this point, Art has filled eight eight-hour tapes: almost three days' worth of viewing material. His relationship to time gets messed up. Sometimes he'll watch a show *while* he's taping it, and he'll have an out-of-body experience: like he's watching a future version of himself watching the tape of what's being broadcast that night.

That future self worries him. He tries to stay calm, but things are most definitely sliding out of control. Last October, Art was caught shoplifting from a convenience store after school (Slim Jims and gum, *Mad* and *Heavy Metal*) by an off-duty cop. Inky apologized to the owner and paid for the items. Art confessed to his parents that it wasn't his first time stealing.

His grades at Chatillion Academy are inconsistent, A's followed by C's; the efforts of a private tutor haven't helped. Out of the blue, a guard is wrongly accused by Mr. N., the science teacher, of stealing his POW medal. Art hasn't thought about his loot in months. He finds the medal beneath a stack of old math notebooks and brings it to school. During morning assembly he sneaks out, slides it under the door to Room 303.

The guilt eats at him. He says nothing, but he knows they know. The Chatillion guidance counselor tells the Sins that they should consider a year at a high school specializing in behavioral issues. There's a whole list to choose from. Through an army acquaintance, Inky contacts the dean at the Everhard Institute in Nebraska, and Art is accepted even before his application is sent. Hannah is upset at first, but she comes around. A fresh start will do him good.

74. The Smothering Instinct

For now, though, Art is still Art as he sprawls on the maroon shag at home in Buffalo. His parents sit on the sofa, tuned in to the farewell episode of M*A*S*H, like a hundred million other Americans. The show is more subdued than usual. The actors sound tentative, aware that it's the last time. Hannah tears up, though she hasn't watched in years. Inky, still wearing his tie from work, looks skeptical. He rarely drinks, but today he nurses the world's smallest glass of beer, from a can that's been in the fridge since Christmas.

You've seen this episode, too. Hawkeye Pierce, the surgeon played by Alan Alda, has gone mental, though he doesn't know it yet. He complains about being cooped up in the hospital, insists there's nothing wrong. Eventually he tells the psychiatrist about one night, near the start of the war. He and some villagers were hidden in the back of a truck, stopped by a North Korean patrol. Some hayseed had brought a chicken on board, which proceeded to squawk. Pierce hissed at her to keep it quiet—a matter of life and death. But the bird wouldn't stop, and at last she smothered it into silence. The patrol passed without incident. Everyone lived.

With the help of the army psychiatrist, though, Hawkeye pieces together what actually happened. It wasn't a chicken. It was her baby.

Inky mulls over this hair-raising episode, this return of the

repressed. It changes everything. It means that through all the many seasons of the show, one of the most popular programs in the country, the main character has been using his nonstop wit as a defense mechanism. A way of denying and forgetting the horror.

75. Missile Command

Over dinner at a Mexican restaurant that spring, Inky Sin proposes a family trip to Korea in the fall. He's been invited to a medical conference organized by an old medical school classmate. It would be the boy's first visit, and Inky and Hannah's first time back since leaving. He doesn't mention the KPG; all in due time. Ultimately, they decide it won't do for Art to miss his first week at Everhard. One day, they'll all travel to Korea as a family, but this year only Inky and Hannah will go.

Art's marks at Chatillion improve that spring, and it's proposed that he might return there after a year away at don't-call-it-reform-school. He shows ingenuity. For a creative response in U.S. history class, he takes the plot of an old M*A*S*H episode and transplants it to Vietnam, using an atlas to change the place-names. This gives him a taste for fiction.

Before he turns thirteen, he has a growth spurt, and towers over his parents. An orthodontist puts braces on his lower teeth. The girl who has the locker next to him breaks their unspoken vow of non-interaction that began in September. Her name is Ayn Sim and her parents are philosophy professors from Taiwan. They just moved from California. She has no friends, doesn't care. He and Ayn like the same kinds of movies, but she says his taste in music is all wrong. Rush, Yes? Boston, Triumph?

The school year ends. To his parents' astonishment, Art wins the eighth-grade historical writing award—a $100 savings bond—for his story based on M*A*S*H. He decides to spend all the money before he goes off to godforsaken Everhard. At the

mall, he buys a Sony double cassette deck. He dubs music from Ayn, recording over his old tapes. No more Journey, Foreigner, Asia.

Art plays his Walkman as he bikes to the mall for the matinee. He's up for whatever's showing. Even the crappy movies are kind of fun. Halfway through *The Man with Two Brains*, he sees Ayn Sim walk out—a move right out of the Hannah Sin playbook—and later spies her at Aladdin's Castle, an unlit cigarette behind her ear. They go head-to-head on Ms. Pac-Man. They meet most weekends after that, hopping between theaters. At the arcade, Art drains what's left of the prize money, one token at a time. They get hypnotized by Frogger and master a new game called Gorf, which Ayn realizes spells *frog* backward. He enters his initials on the high-score board of Missile Command. For a week he occupies the top three slots: ASS, ASS, ASS. Ayn Sim dethrones him at last. The funny part is that they have the same initials.

76. Everhard (II)

Art pores over the informational packet from Everhard with dread and fascination. The buildings look like cold concrete crapped into non-rectilinear shapes, a lonely outpost on some forgotten planet. Here and there sprout ladder-like structures of dark iron, bent at harsh angles, no doubt part of some punishing fitness regimen. Only a few students are pictured, often at face-obscuring angles, but he notes more Asian youths than he'd expect.

The booklet never calls Everhard a reform school, though that's clearly its function. Finishing his secondary studies there will expunge Arthur Sin's juvenile record. To this end, it is strongly advised that incoming students adopt a new name or alter their current one, in order to start forming a new, positive identity around it.

77. JFA

A week before Art leaves for the Everhard Institute, Ayn Sim gives him a tape, with countless cuts on each side. Bands he's never heard of. Her taste speaks to a complex inner life. The tracks are short, their brevity part of the joke, the complete opposite of the grandiose rock he's used to. As Art listens, the mystery of Ayn Sim deepens. He studies her neat, angry handwriting, memorizing its dramatic pot handles and elongated dots. A thin hair is trapped in the case, finer than his and looped like an ampersand. He holds it up to the lamp and then carefully puts it back, as though replacing a necklace.

The song that closes Side A is a version of the Charlie Brown theme, done at a brisk clip, yet still a respite from the preceding noise. The guitar tone is clean as a bell and the piano sounds . . . *happy*. The drums push everything along. The group is called JFA, like initials on a game's high-score board. The whole thing's over in two minutes. He hits rewind. Riding bikes with Ayn on the eve of departing for Everhard, he asks what JFA stands for.

"Jodie Foster's Army."

"I don't get it," Art says, just as a vision of Reagan tumbling to the sidewalk gets in his head. "They are *definitely* going to confiscate this at Everhard."

78. Eats and Wets

On the last day of August 1983, just past midnight, Korean Air Lines Flight 007 leaves New York's John F. Kennedy Airport for Seoul via Anchorage. A few hours later, KAL Flight 015 takes off from Los Angeles with the same destination. On board both 747s are the most outspoken anti-Communists in Congress, including the head of the John Birch Society, bound for Seoul to commemorate thirty years of U.S.–South Korea solidarity. The rest of the passenger lists have the expected assortment of nationalities and professions: foreign students and American

scientists, grandparents and young children; Koreans, Japanese, Filipinos, Canadians. There are crew members from earlier flights, heading home after a long stretch of work.

Seated in row 13 of Flight 007, too tense to sleep, is Dr. Inky
Sin. Recently he decided again that it would be a good idea to
start a mustache, to give him gravitas, but the result so far
resembles roadkill, and he now must find a barber immediately
upon arrival in Korea. After that he will go directly to his medical conference, where he will deliver the keynote, yet to be written. The English title of the program has been misprinted as
"Psychiatry Eats and Wets," so rich a Freudian slip that Inky
suspects it's on purpose. An icebreaker.

But the *real* aim behind this visit to his homeland is a secret
meeting of the Korean Provisional Government, where Inky will
present findings on an unusual patient case: Parker Jotter, a
Korean War veteran and former POW. Between 1957 and 1965,
Jotter authored a series of science-fiction books under the
series title *2333*, then stopped for good. For the past two years,
Inky had believed the novels harbor some deeper meaning.
Korean content, he called it. Parker always denied it, claiming
that the number 2333 was something he pulled out of thin air,
or had some connection to his wife's birthday, rather than what
it clearly was: a reference to the mythical founding of Korea,
over four thousand years ago. That is, the year points not to the
future but the past: 2333 B.C.

Parker always changed the subject. He said that if his
books *did* contain nods to the real world, they were to *Buffalo*,
not Korea. The fungoid menace in *Return to Tyosen!*, for example, is known as the Odd, a play on his daughter's nickname for
Memorial Auditorium; the deadly supercomputer in *The Louse*,
C20L-G05Z, is a wink at Leon Czolgosz, President McKinley's
assassin. But Dr. Sin didn't care about these local allusions. He
zeroed in on the *2333* angle because there were too many simi-
larities between the bizarre names in the book and actual peo-

ple and places in Korean history—about which Jotter claimed total ignorance.

During a session in May, Inky again pressed the point. Parker shot back that he'd never have written *2333* in the first place if he knew one day he'd meet a Korean SOB who wouldn't stop yammering about it. Maybe that's why his unfinished sixth book, *The Tan Gun*, began with a "mind healer" being blasted out of a spaceship, instantly turned into cosmic dust. Maybe Parker had glimpsed a future involving the annoying Dr. Inky Sin.

"That just proves my point," Inky said, oblivious to the insult. "The Tan Gun."

"What?"

"'Tangun'—that's one of the spellings of 'Dangun.'" He pronounced it *Don Goon*. Parker looked lost. "The mythical founder of Korea! In some translations, the name is spelled T-A-N-G-U-N! Same word, different ways! Like how you can spell my last name S-H-I-N instead of S-I-N! Same thing! Now then. You must have been told about Tangun while stuck in North Korea, which, after all, is where he first appeared . . ."

"Don the Goon sounds like a character in a crime story," Parker said sarcastically. "Maybe I'll use that name someday."

The denials made Inky wonder: Was Parker part of another wing of the KPG? Could his rivals be using his patient against him? The history of the Korean Provisional Government contained many such tales of subterfuge. Inky reminded himself there was a line between careful and paranoid.

He stopped nagging. They eventually patched things up, Inky even serving as a witness when Parker got a lawyer to review his old book contracts. He wanted to make sure any proceeds deriving from *2333* went to his estranged daughter—not that Inky or the lawyer or any halfway sensible person would have predicted a revival of interest in the work of Parker Jotter.

79. The Flight of King Kojong

By arrangement with a KPG agent working at Korean Air Lines, Dr. Sin flies under the name King Kojong—the last legitimate ruler of a unified Korea. Due to a computer glitch, though, the ticket reads KING KONG instead.

Inky Sin reviews his Seoul schedule. During their second week abroad, while his wife catches up with old friends, Dr. Sin will be transported to the KPG's new headquarters, located deep underneath the DMZ. Perhaps it is not far from his home-town: the erased village of Hwajiri. The hermetically sealed HQ is hundreds of feet below the surface, stocked with enough pro-visions to sustain a group of twenty for five years. Dr. Sin can hardly believe it exists.

Many want to stop this meeting from occurring. If the KPG were to achieve its goal of unifying the country, it would mean not only the dissolution of North and South Korea but a reor-dering of East Asia as a whole. Agents from the United States, Russia, China, and Japan might be tracking him even now, as well as North and South Korean interests who want to preserve the status quo. Same bed, same dreams. Inky tells himself there's nothing to fear.

His wife isn't with him. Instead, Hannah sits in row 20 of Flight 015 out of L.A., having flown there after dropping off Arthur at his new school in the middle of Nebraska.

80. The Interpretation of Hymns

Inky is proud of another recent breakthrough in the case of Parker Jotter, which he will present to the KPG. Just a week after ending treatment with Parker, Inky discovered the final book in the 2333 series at a garage sale. The back cover sum-marized the adventures of Greena Hymns, saucily depicted on the cover, her hair white as stars. He was hypnotized by Greena; he would even say he fell in love with her a little. Like a school-

boy, he traced her curvy outline on the cover. As he read the book, he fantasized jumping into it—landing in her circular "omniship," blasting off to who knows where. . . .

He copied her name over and over, whispered it to himself. His faith was rewarded one morning before work when— between not shaving his mustache and sitting down to breakfast—he saw that *Greena Hymns* could be scrambled into *Syngman Rhee.* This *proved* that Parker's books contained hidden depths—perhaps even a code that could be worked out, with enough people on the job.

What would the Korean Provisional Government make of seeing its first president hidden in a book from 1965? He couldn't wait to find out.

81. The Return of Oddjob

Inky had assumed that his seatmate was Korean, but when he greeted him in their language, the man just nodded. His bulky face stayed blank. He resembled, to an alarming degree, the actor who played the thug Oddjob in the old James Bond film *Goldfinger.* For a moment Inky thought it *must* be him, before recalling an obituary: Harold Sakata was the name. The flight number 007 was making him jump to Bondian conclusions. Oddjob (as Inky couldn't help thinking of him) started snoring after takeoff, head resting on the window.

A bland white man (mustache, menthol) took the aisle seat. Inky, sandwiched in the middle, felt sorry for himself at first. But then he thought of his predecessor Syngman Rhee, trapped in a coffin on the way to Shanghai for his first meeting as president of the KPG.

Now Inky Sin reaches into his coat pocket for a postcard he bought at JFK, showing Big Apple landmarks: Statue of Liberty, Empire State Building, Twin Towers, the airport itself. He writes to Art, wishing him a good first week at his new school.

82. Alaskan Reunion

Oddjob nudges Inky awake. KAL Flights 007 and 015, from New York and L.A., are both on the tarmac in Anchorage for a one-hour refueling stop. His neighbor wants to step off the plane to stretch. It's three A.M. in Alaska, meaning it's seven in the morning to the part of his brain still on Buffalo time. Most passengers stay asleep on their respective planes, but Dr. Sin exits for fresh air. All the shops are closed. He stands before the stuffed polar bear in the concourse, the same one he saw sixteen years ago, flying from Korea to his new home in America.

The bear's eyes are golden. In the foundational myth, Dangun (or "Tan Gun"!) was born from a she-bear that mated with a god-king, an alien. On the back of his ticket, Inky jots down an idea: Why not begin his speech to the KPG with the image of the bear in the airport—trapped under glass between two countries, longing to be free? A symbol for the true undivided Korea, frozen in time.

A slim, pretty Asian woman is walking toward him. To Inky's amazement, it's his wife. (Maybe start the speech with *that*.) Hannah has some good news: she and Mr. Oddjob happened to meet by the gate, and the airline is allowing them to swap seats, as easy as toggling between movie theaters. She'll be joining Inky on the final leg, while his former seatmate boards Flight 015. Her most successful switch yet. Together they look for a mail slot so they can send the postcard to Art.

Dr. and Mrs. Sin board Flight 007. The plane taxis forever. It pushes off around four A.M., Alaska time, and with a frenzied roar vaults above the dark Pacific. Practically everyone is asleep.

"What?" Inky says in Korean.

"What?" Hannah says." I can't hear you."

"I didn't say anything."

When the plane hits cruising altitude, the Sins try talking again.

"I hope he's liking the new school."

"He seemed at peace."

"What?"

"I said he was at peace."

"At ease?"

"What?"

Meanwhile, the second plane, Flight 015, has left Anchorage, free of Sins. It soon becomes clear to the pilots of 015, and to the American tracking stations on the Aleutian Islands, that 007 is off course, bending northward. But the 007 pilots send no distress signals. They convey their position to the sister flight, carrying on as though no deviation exists. The cockpit of 015 grows concerned. Did the pilots on 007 err when entering the coordinates? How come they're not seeing the discrepancy between where they are and where they should be?

The planes cross the international date line. It's the first of September 1983.

83. The Return of Taro (III)

The passengers on Flight 007 sleep through the error. Those who are awake don't sense anything amiss. Divergence is the furthest thing from Inky's mind. He dwells drowsily on his sorry mustache and the upcoming meeting with his fellow KPG members, whom he's never met. What if his rivals are there? Banding together to assassinate him, in the grand Korean tradition.

He thinks about a strange old Korean woman he met a few weeks ago. She came from New York City to his office in Buffalo, claiming to be interviewing Koreans in America for a sort of video "Who's Who." The secretary, Donna, had taken her name down as "Jane Doe," without thinking that might be a shopworn alias. The talks had dredged up a lot of memories, over eight sessions. After the second one, he asked Donna to find out more about the woman and her assistant, if she could.

The next day, Donna's boyfriend, a budding private investigator, waited in the parking lot and tailed their car to a hotel off Delaware Avenue. Later, the boyfriend—Jordan—found that the rooms were paid for by a New York–based entity called Harmony Holdings.

Inky was regretting the sprawling Q&A. He'd said too much. It was probably nothing. But he wished dearly that the tape might disappear.

Was this Harmony Holdings an enemy of the KPG, or part of it?

Donna could tell that Dr. Sin was still pained by the episode, and after some discussion with Jordan, it was agreed that, for a suitable fee, he would try to deprive the visitors of the recording. He told Jordan to be careful. If he tracked them, they could track him. Jordan has no real plan—just to go to New York and filch the tape when he can. Dr. Sin is sure he will run up the expenses, excited by his first real case.

There is no use dwelling on it now. Under a tight cone of light, Dr. Sin goes over his papers, the tumble of paragraphs. What language will he use? After seventeen years away, he worries that his Korean might sound antique. For the first time, he sympathizes with Philip Jaisohn, publisher and surgeon general of the KPG, who used English to address a stadium of his countrymen after living for decades in Pennsylvania.

Inky adjusts his wristwatch to Seoul time and puts away his papers. Replacing his briefcase in the overhead bin, he feels it knock against another briefcase. Standing on tiptoe, Inky can see that this one is an inch shorter than his, bound in alligator instead of calf. It must be Oddjob's. The monogram T.N.T. is embossed near the handle, and the latch has a simple three-digit lock. On a whim, he furtively tumbles numbers till 007 shows. The latch holds fast. He closes the bin.

Inky rearranges his blanket, tilts his seat back to the limit, lightly crushing the knees of the sleeper behind him. Hannah's

lips part and close gently as she dozes. He puts his ear near enough to feel breath. The dark hours pass. Sleep eludes him. He wonders if his former seatmate, now an hour behind on Flight 015, is having better luck. Adjusting the blanket, he spots a flash of white, wedged between his seat and Hannah's: a boarding pass. It must be Oddjob's. He stares at the name printed at the top: TSUJIMOTO, TARO N.

84. The Corporal

Three hours into the transpacific journey, and something is decidedly off. Flight 007 is too far north, its pilots oblivious to the error. Instead of skirting Russia's Kurile Islands and then cutting across the tip of Japan as it heads for Seoul, the 747 strays over the Kamchatka Peninsula. The KAL passenger plane, with 269 people on board, is in Soviet airspace.

Earlier that evening, hours before the KAL flight, an American surveillance craft flew from its base in the Aleutians up to the edge of that zone, a routine maneuver to test the adversary's tracking system. No action was taken. But Soviet radar now picks up this new, more brazen invader: a shape they're unfamiliar with. Thinking the Americans have gone too far this time, MiGs and needle-nosed Flagons scramble from Sakhalin Island to investigate.

As Flight 007 continues its wayward journey, the pilot of one of the interceptors, Colonel Osipovich, pegs it for a Soviet transport plane. At thirty-four thousand feet, the colonel gets a closer look, and a chill grips him. The plane has a long row of windows, which would not be seen on a transport. Every shade is drawn. Osipovich believes 007 to be a new kind of spy plane, dwarfing the RC-135s the Americans normally use.

The size must be to accommodate more advanced apparatus. The blatant aggression is intolerable, and at 3:20 A.M., the colonel fires five hundred rounds as a warning. The intruder does not respond. Osipovich reports his actions to ground con-

trol. The mystery plane flies on, arcing upward. Then it slows abruptly to reroute, and the Flagon overshoots it.

The blatant trespass must be stopped. Osipovich receives the order to prepare missiles. On its new course, Flight 007 will vacate Soviet airspace in less than a minute, though this does not enter the colonel's calculations.

Thirty miles south of Sakhalin, nautical scofflaws on three Japanese fishing boats haul their nets from the depths, about to leave Russian waters and head back to Hokkaido.

85. The Target Is Destroyed

On September 1 at 3:23 A.M., Seoul time, Inky Sin is grinning like a madman. He has finally glimpsed Taro Tsujimoto—the *real* Taro Tsujimoto—and understands that nothing is by accident. There's a reason they met on this plane, a reason why Taro (or "Oddjob") switched places with Hannah. Inky even has a hunch about what's inside that briefcase: the documents that will once and for all make clear the path forward for the KPG.

The manuscript of *The Tan Gun*, by Parker Jotter.

Taro Tsujimoto is a member of the Korean Provisional Government, slyly giving Inky what he needs, in the nick of time. At 3:25 A.M., Dr. Sin carefully removes Taro's case from the bin. Eyes closed, he meditates on the old poem by Yi Sang, the one with all the numbers. A sacred text of the KPG. He imagines the black dots showing the plane's path over the ocean, from right to left.

At 3:26 A.M. and 13 seconds, the solution appears, as clear as day.

"Yes," Inky says under his breath. *"Yes."*

Hannah mumbles in her sleep. From the grid of *yisang* numbers, Inky picks three. He lines them up, and hears a click.

At 3:26 A.M. and 20 seconds, half a minute before KAL 007 leaves Soviet airspace, ground control orders Colonel Osipovich to open fire.

The three Japanese fishermen hear what sounds like the crack of a whip, a whip as big as the sky. Above them is a line of flame, an arc of bright smoke.

At 3:26 A.M. and 26 seconds, the colonel reports, "The target is destroyed."

By 3:39 A.M., radar shows no trace of the aircraft.

86. The Bunker

On the morning of Thursday, September 1, 1983, the freshmen at Everhard Institute wake at six. Seven minutes to shit, shave, shower, and shine; twelve to bolt down a He-Man breakfast of pancakes, sausage links, scrambled eggs, toast. They file into the yard for a round of calisthenics called the Daily Dozens. The sky goes on forever.

The bell rings. Classes begin. Two hours later, just before military history, an announcement goes out on the PA for all freshmen to head to the Bunker, the nuke-proof lounge with the big television set. It's a rickety model, the color image so scoured it's nearly black and white. Students file in; faculty members stand at the back. On TV, the secretary of state looms over a podium. He recounts what happened the day before, on the other side of the world. His weary furious words seem to be coming to Art from far away.

"My mom's on a different flight," Art mumbles. "She was flying out of California, so . . . "

Then he blacks out. He wakes in the infirmary to the patter of rain, 14:12 on the digital clock by the window. He looks at the ceiling tiles, trying to make out a map, an animal, any kind of sign.

The nurse has brought him a ham sandwich and a glass of orange juice from the cafeteria. Art says he can walk back to the dorms. He checks his mail, the letter box jammed with trial magazines and advertisements, including a postcard that seems to tout a summer program in the Big Apple. All junk,

except for a new issue of *CinéFreak* from Switzerland and a parcel addressed to A.S.S. from A.S.S. It's postmarked August 22, a few days before Art and his mother left Buffalo for Everhard—a relic from a different world. There's no note, just two cassette cases. It takes him a moment to recognize the handiwork of Ayn Sim. Who else? One case hides a matchbook and four cigarettes, neatly shortened with a razor. Decorating the other case is a Snoopy cut from the comics page, with an electric pink mohawk drawn in. Ayn hasn't provided titles. The first song is JFA's cover of the *Peanuts* theme with that bright, fast guitar. So is the next, and the next—twelve times on each side, twenty-four copies in all. Art blasts it on his Walkman until the batteries die.

The next day, the headmaster calls the hotel in Seoul where Art's parents were to stay. There is no record of Hannah checking in, no news at all. It's another week before federal investigators determine that in the early hours of September 1, at the Anchorage airport, Hannah had switched to Flight 007 to be with her husband. The news reaches Arthur Sin a month after the incident. By that time, he already knows.

87. A Photogenic Memory

More mail: three years after *Friday the 13th*, Betsy Palmer still receives fan letters. Amid the praise and occasional marriage proposals is more disturbing fare. Someone sends a photo of a wig stand, made up to look like her decapitated head. Another sends a vial of his blood.

"It comes from a good place," her agent says.

There's straight-up hate mail, too, thanks to that crybaby Gene Siskel. To some, the movie marks the collapse of American civilization. They send clippings of recent heinous crimes, like the *Village Voice* piece about an Oriental artist raped and murdered in New York or news of a serial killer who preyed on Blacks in Buffalo. Betsy agrees *Friday the 13th* is revolting trash,

but come on, folks—it didn't invent violence. Still, though she hasn't appeared in the two sequels, she already knows this is what she'll be remembered for. It's depressing to think how actors get trapped in their roles.

What is history? After dinner on September 5, 1983, Betsy Palmer turns on the TV in her Connecticut home. The evening news cuts without commercial to a sober drama set in the White House. But this is the real Oval Office, and that wax figure moving its lips is the president. *My fellow Americans.* Even after two years of Reagan in office, she can't get her head around the fact that Ronnie—good old General Electric—is commander in chief. If an actor becomes president, does that mean the whole country is a movie set? When they gunned him down two years ago—a *great* twist, she'll grant—Betsy thought for sure that reality would set in. She'd open the paper and see a photo of Carter, or Ford, or even Tricky Dick running the show. *Pardon the interruption.* But here's Ronnie, beamed straight into her house. Here he is with his serious eyes and dark hair, fit as a fiddle, except maybe around the neck.

Reagan sits at his desk, in front of a bulletproof window with gold curtains. He's stern and sober and still trying to get into her pants, all the way from Pennsylvania Avenue.

"I'm coming before you tonight about the Korean airline massacre, the attack by the Soviet Union against two hundred and sixty-nine innocent men, women, and children aboard an unarmed Korean passenger plane." His delivery is soft but grave. "This crime against humanity must never be forgotten."

The shot is unnervingly tight. Everything below the top of

his necktie knot is gone. The words don't register because she can't stop staring at his mouth. The president is going to eat her alive. She pulls her gaze away, focusing on his neck, corded and slack.

Ronnie tells Betsy Palmer, tells all of America, that folks who lost loved ones on the plane have wired him messages. "The emotions of these parents—grief, shock, anger—are shared by civilized people everywhere," he says.

The camera pans out, so fast it might fly out of the room and out of the White House entirely. Betsy can see Ronnie's dark blue tie and his desk and the flags flanking it. Did Reagan direct this thing, too? She's read that he endlessly rehearses every speech. Finesses the phrases to fit his natural cadence, Tampico by way of Hollywood. Any actor could do this job, she thinks.

88. The Days After

The war of words between D.C. and the Kremlin escalates. The Soviets accuse the United States of provoking the attack. Flight 007, they say, was a pawn, coldly sacrificed by Washington. Perhaps American saboteurs took control of the autopilot and pushed the plane into the forbidden territory, just to see how much they could taunt the sleeping bear. It was all a pretext to sell American-made missiles to Western Europe, at the cost of 269 lives.

The countries are on the brink, a showdown between Reagan's America and what he keeps calling the Evil Empire. On a Sunday night in November, ABC airs a made-for-TV movie called *The Day After*, which imagines a nuclear holocaust in the heartland. For weeks beforehand, the network warns about its disturbing nature. The story is set in Kansas. Missiles fall with blinding force. Citizens run for cover, but even survivors of the initial attack face a grim future. Americans young and old turn on each other, rot away from radiation. In the

movie, Soviet maneuvers in East Germany light the fuse, but the instigating cause for all-out annihilation could as easily have been the downing of a Korean passenger plane above the Pacific.

At the Everhard Institute, *The Day After* is mandatory viewing. Art's classmates watch it in the Bunker, three levels below the Nebraska dirt, eager to see the world go to hell. Art stays in his room. He lights the last of Ayn's Marlboros, blows smoke out the window. He remembers playing Missile Command with her, back in the summer. No matter how fast one slapped the Fire button, the cities didn't stand a chance in the end. Whole populations, wiped out by bright blots of pixels, clouds of digital death.

Lace of cigarette smoke, holy in the night.

89. Sea of Blood (II)

The initial Soviet search for KAL 007 comes up empty. It will be weeks before America is permitted to launch its own recovery mission. Flotsam found off Hokkaido is inconclusive. It's the wrong wreckage; it's not wreckage at all. Children's shoes. A Canadian ID card, floating to shore. Isn't that a little *convenient*? A network builds between grieving family members and those who suspect a cover-up. Theories form and thicken. The wildest one claims the plane was never really destroyed. Instead, Soviet jets guided Flight 007 down to the nearby island of Moneron. A hidden airstrip. A facility. In truth, this was its destination all along, the entire journey manipulated by the Russians.

The passengers are being detained. Why? Some think it's part of a grand social project: Moneron as utopia. Others are convinced the prisoners are being brainwashed and trained as spies, to be inserted into North American or South Korean or Japanese society.

90. Inside Job

Maybe the downing *did* happen—just not in the way the Russians claim.

KAL 007 was shot down because of specific passengers. The obvious targets would be the staunch anti-Communist congressmen, including the John Birchers believed to be on board. But there could have been other targets: scientists, scholars, spies. The network combs the manifest for clues. Some names are more mysterious than others—a traveler going by "King Kong," for starters.

Or: the lack of verifiable debris suggests the plane blew apart due to explosives placed *inside* it, at JFK or Anchorage, by a suicide bomber or an unwitting party. The network must consider all angles, no matter how improbable.

In time, the tragedy of Korean Air Lines Flight 007 fades from the collective memory. After all, the world didn't end; there was no *Day After* scenario. But the victims' families cannot let go so easily; nor can those outsiders who have latched on to the tragedy, made it their lives.

Nor can the Korean Provisional Government.

91. My Name Is an Adverb

At Everhard, with its mandate to reform troubled teens, changing one's name is a valued tradition. The alterations are often

small: going by initials, elevating a middle name. The idea is to release the past and start fresh. In his senior year, Arthur Sin changes his name for a slightly different reason: to avoid hearing from those who want to analyze every facet of the Flight 007 tragedy. These members of the network track him down on campus, rattle off bizarre questions before campus security takes them away. The dean and the counselor encourage Art's separation from this ghoulish web. He decides to embrace part of his Korean name and a less demonic spelling of his surname. He decides to become Soon Sheen.

"My name is an adverb," he says.

School becomes home: he has nowhere else to go. He loses touch with Ayn Sim and other friends back East. He plays on the Everhard hockey team until a gruesome locker-room injury sophomore year: the goalie accidentally steps across his left hand while he's picking up a roll of tape, the blade slicing off half his ring finger. Reattachment fails. Typing is torture for a while; his new name, Soon Sheen, with its capital S's, proves especially hard to capture.

Nevertheless, Soon camps out in the computer lab, teaching himself to program. He makes a crude flight-simulator game, in which the goal is to navigate a plane across an ocean, dodging enemy jets. There's only one way to win: by landing safely using a specific series of up/down/space-bar strokes. Anything else ends in disaster. His friends love the primitive sounds, the sudden, garish splashes of color. He calls the game Moneron, after the island where some cranks think KAL Flight 007 might have ended up. As a joke, even if the player somehow reaches Moneron, polar bears attack the passengers, a death coda set to zany 8-bit circus music.

Computer lab is only a club activity at the Everhard of the '80s; aside from high marks in math and senior-year history, Soon's official grades are mediocre. He graduates in 1988 (4321) and enters Penumbra College in Vermont, where he majors in

computer science. Junior year, he helps out his roommate, Tanner Slow, with a class project–cum–thought experiment. Tanner wants to build an electronic bulletin board with a twist: his "community" of commenters will have no actual people in it. He calls it Pretenders.

Each of the ten Pretenders has a slew of vital statistics (age, sex, and race) and a menu of likes and dislikes, catchphrases and typographical tics. Every morning, Soon or Tanner enters text from an actual newspaper—politics, sports, movies, the weather—onto the bulletin board. The goal is to get the Pretenders to remark on it, without additional human help, and respond to the comments of other Pretenders. For good measure, they upload a simplified version of Moneron, Soon's old flight simulator, as a diversion for their robots.

Tanner is all about the big picture. The goal is for the site to become like a terrarium—generating its own life, dialogue, meaning—without anyone having to feed it digested news stories every morning. A small, perfectly sealed world. An outsider would assume the interactions were written by actual humans. But after a few months, Soon Sheen and Tanner Slow give up. For all the differences in nationality, education level, and so on, nine of the ten Pretenders sound the same, like a grumpy uncle who doesn't trust banks and keeps his savings in a shoebox. (The tenth offers one-word judgments like "Cool" and "Crazy!") They don't concoct topics on their own. Their main activity, unexpectedly, is playing endless games of Moneron.

The professor gives Tanner and Soon a C-plus, and both move on to other pursuits.

92. Invitation Only

One night in 1994 (4327), two years after graduating from Penumbra, Soon Sheen is heading in to his IT job at the *NY Whip*, an alternative newspaper. The elevator plays a Muzak version of a song he can't place, and for the rest of the day its melody

unfurls in the back of his mind. When he gets on the elevator to go home, it's the same tune. In a flash, he knows what it is— a song originally by the Pretenders, another band that Ayn Sim loathed.

Like a sleeper agent triggered by the music, Soon returns to his desk and boots up the computer. He types in, from memory, the address of the old site—tediously long, bristling with slashes and tildes. He hasn't thought much about it since that C-plus; his other undergrad projects fared better. His login still works. Expecting tumbleweeds, he gets redirected to a fancier landing. He's stunned that there aren't ten Pretenders, but over two hundred. What's more, they seem to be actual people—or is the joke on him?

Over late-night drinks at a bar on East Fifth, he gets the full story from Tanner Slow. It turns out that Tanner had resurrected Pretenders a year ago, adding bells and whistles. The site became invitation only: a forum for real people, albeit masked by usernames. (He hadn't told Soon about any of it, he says, because he was sure it would fail.) Each Pretender could nominate three other people, who could nominate three others four months later, and so on. Something like that. He couldn't remember all the math. The voting process was a mess. Mostly the Pretenders debated the merits of *Three's Company* and vintage video games, identified plot holes in time-travel movies. After a robust start, alas, engagement fell. Members peeled off. Tanner's attention shifted to other things, namely a Rockette named Jan.

93. Gifted and Talented

Now it's the spring of 1996 (4329), and though the World Wide Web is stretching out rapidly, all the browsers are heartbreakingly slow. A kid named Mercy Pang catches wind of Pretenders from her mother, Tina, who scored an invite. Something to do with her work. Point is, she knows Tina's password. Never

mind that she's only twelve. She's in her school's Gifted and Talented program, where she reads Rousseau, Lao-tzu, a rad Icelandic *edda*.

There's not enough to see online, not enough to do. By contrast, Pretenders is constantly renewing. Mercy loves its stripped-down complexity. The handles are impersonal, self-erasing—any-sim, mikc85—but the users' personalities shine through in their words. Her mom, Tina, goes by the moniker anti-body2333; she weighs in so infrequently that the others are starting to wonder if she's real.

It's an education just keeping up with the threads, the levels of irony. Mercy Pang doesn't catch half the references, but the energy is infectious. You never know what you'll read. A pitched battle between *Love Boat* and *Jeffersons* buffs can lead to personal revelations in which souls are bared, secrets shared. (Not by Mercy, of course. Not yet.) All through seventh grade, she loses herself in Pretenders. The modem ties up the phone line. The message board helps her weather the sleepless nights— things between her parents have gone from bad to worse—or maybe causes them.

Pretenders thrums away like a small, joyfully disorganized city, home to dozens of spontaneous subgroups. They're easy to miss, tucked away in alleys. Part of the fun is discovering them amid the maze. One is devoted to cataloging the made-up books that appear in movies and TV shows. Another is an ongoing copyright-free typing marathon, an industrious space where members voluntarily input chapters of favorite books, from *The Fountainhead* to *The Catcher in the Rye* to a more recent one called *Man in Korean Costume,* by T. S. Kim. Elsewhere, Pretenders flesh out an alternate world history that keeps forking, folding in on itself: here, tyrants get killed at birth, crucial battles are reversed. Fictional characters appear alongside actual figures from the past. The communal prose is sober even when delivering the lies, so that an unsuspecting reader—or the pro-

verbial visitor from Mars—would get the entirely wrong idea of what happened on this planet. In Mercy's eyes, too, the real and the invented merge. It can feel like those forbidden dreams in which all things connect.

94. Who Is anti-body2333?

It's rumored that one of the Pretenders might be a secret agent (could the entire site be a tool of the CIA or some foreign interest?), that you should watch what you type, because someone could steal your identity. Supposedly one of the founders lurks on Pretenders, and users try to tease out which pseudonyms might belong to this shadowy creator. The suspect names usually vanish within minutes of being outed, but others linger, presumably belonging to regular users. Or is the author of it all just lying low? Inaction can be the best disguise.

Mercy wonders if they're on to *her*, whispering, *Who is anti-body2333?* Because Mercy is lurking under false pretenses, too. Nobody's checking anyone's age on the forum, but they'd freak out if they knew she was just a kid.

95. k0r3atruth83

In truth, Mercy is doubly deceptive. For starters, even her mom is on Pretenders with what her Ethics in the Real World teacher calls "ulterior motives." Tina's job is to scope out electronic bulletin boards and similar online gatherings. Pretenders is just one of a hundred online properties that Tina's employer, Corewar, might seek to buy. Tina takes notes on the way threads catch fire or don't, the way some conversations splinter into subcategories that become even more popular than the original.

One of these begins as a simple ranking exercise: Genius/Lame/Overrated. A Pretender proposes three disparate things, then jams them into those categories: *Charlie's Angels* genius, Agatha Christie lame, Sherlock Holmes overrated. Mercy tries one of her own: the comic strip *Nancy* genius, Nancy Drew

books lame, *Sid and Nancy* overrated. The response is favorable, and Mercy's hooked. Times like these, Pretenders feels like one big living art piece, a work in progress with absolute strangers, better than any movie or show.

One August evening in 1997 (4330), user k0r3atruth83 puts a trio of conspiracy theories into the G/L/O discussion: KAL 007 genius, Bermuda Triangle lame, JFK assassination overrated. Pretenders have strong opinions about the last two, and some quote at length from books they have at hand. The banter fizzles, though, as few people know much about the first item: the unhinged lore swirling around KAL Flight 007, which was shot down en route to Seoul. (It occurred, Mercy learns, a year before she was born.)

Such widespread amnesia prompts k0r3atruth83 to start a fresh thread, centered on the mystery. What *really* happened? The Pretenders snap into action. One suggests that KAL 007 was on such an errant trajectory because it was bound for *North* Korea. The Pretenders dig deep, parsing recordings from the flight-deck. Someone translates a recent Russian interview with the Soviet pilot who pulled the trigger: Osipovich still insists it was a spy plane, loaded with surveillance equipment.

Another Pretender shares a rumor that a Korean author, Cho Something, was writing a novel about the disaster. He died under mysterious circumstances, no doubt rubbed out by enemy agents. His publisher denies the report, but a few Pretenders joke that they're using a body double, some actor they found in America. The Pretender who is typing up *Man in Korean Costume* in his or her spare time adds that Cho's most recent author photo, for a book called *The Sins*, looks a lot like T. S. Kim's. Crazy shit like that.

96. The Unmade Bed

We can confirm a few things. The writer Cho Eujin—the *real*, the original, E. Cho—did indeed perish, two years after the publica-

tion of *The Architect and the Dictator*, so popular with readers in both Seoul and Pyongyang. Recovered from that office we provided him, in a Jongno high-rise that got good light, were drafts of other novels, as well as notes for *Same Bed, Different Dreams*, a book inspired by the 1983 KAL disaster.

With the help of the versatile T. S. Kim—the author not only of *Man in Korean Costume* but earlier works under her American pen name, Kim Tollson—we fleshed out most of these titles. Like *The Architect and the Dictator*, they appeared in both South and North Korea. (Unlike that book, they were written by T. S. Kim in English, then translated *into* Korean.) They were a pure expression of our mission—and an integral part of our campaign to sway hearts and minds, not just in Korea but around the world.

T. S. Kim kept to herself, sacrificing her own future oeuvre in order to fulfill the more pressing destiny of Cho Eujin. When Cho was needed in person, for some literary function or TV panel, we trotted out a fellow whose age and likeness approximated the late author's—indeed, the same model Kim used for *Man in Korean Costume*. But when T. S. Kim died in the spring of 2016 (4349) without completing Cho's most crucial work, *Same Bed, Different Dreams*, we nearly gave up. Then we remembered someone we had followed for years—indeed, had marked as ours, in Buffalo and Nebraska, in Vermont and New York.

We deployed our model for a final evening so that he could meet Kim's successor, pass the torch.

Same Bed has remained unmade, until now.

97. Clan of the Cave Bear

Back to 1997 (4330). The KAL thread on Pretenders gets woven into the bigger alternate-history conversation, and eventually pops up under myriad subheadings: KOREANA and AERONAUTICS, CONSPIRACIES and COMMUNISM. Group interest usually fades as a

topic migrates across forums, but not this time, not just yet. Mercy is up late, tracking developments.

She knows something about Korea. Her maternal grandfather, Parker Jotter, fought in the Korean War. He had seen things. He used to write letters, telling her stories about the war that even her mother didn't know.

One night, Mercy logs on as anti-body2333 and posts: *Some American pilots said they saw UFOs while flying in MiG Alley. (That's up by the border with China.)* And holds her breath. There's a high nuttiness threshold for Pretenders, but still. It's never fun to be ignored.

He said it was like a giant coolie hat going 800 miles an hour, she adds, though she's not totally sure what a coolie hat is.

That mysterious aircraft made an appearance in all of his books, which she started reading a few months before he died. Where had the thing come from, where was it going?

No Pretenders comment on her comment for a week. Maybe Mercy—that is, anti-body2333—scared them off by getting too weird right off the mark. Maybe they detect a disturbance in her soul, sense somehow that she's been dwelling too much on how her mom wasn't even on speaking terms with Parker during the worst time of his life, back in the '80s. Or, before that, how her grandfather had blown half his savings, hiring detectives to find his wife, Mercy's grandmother, who didn't want to be found. Who had, in fact, earlier drained the *other* half of the savings in the name of her church. The Divine Precepts, he always called them.

But then a long response arrives, from the one and only k0r3atruth83: *MiG Alley is where Korea began!!!* Four thousand years ago, a mythic figure named Dangun (sometimes spelled Tangun) was born of a she-bear and an alien—a divine being named Hwanin, who fell from the sky! Only now, after reading Mercy's post, does it all click for k0r3atruth83! How MiG Alley corresponds *exactly* to the region where Tangun founded

Korea—in the mountains northwest of Pyongyang! How it makes total sense that UFOs would be seen there during the war! How the half-alien being who started it all would return, to keep watch over Korea in its hour of greatest peril!

98. The Job

Mercy thrills to k0r3atruth's revelations. She doesn't know his age, what he looks like, or even his real name, though she's positive he's a guy. (Maybe not.) A few typos and grammatical slips suggest he's foreign. (Or are those to throw her off the scent?) Against her better judgment, Mercy-as-Tina sends a private message, explaining more about Grandpa Jotter's time as a POW. She mentions the *2333* series he wrote long ago, the sea of papers he left behind.

As soon as she hits Send, she goes cold with embarrassment and fear. The email bears her mom's address at Corewar Games. Mercy can see how it will all unfold: If k0r3atruth83 replies, his message will end up in the maternal inbox. Tina will see it, get mad at her for meddling. This is Tina's job, after all. Plus, it isn't safe—there's no telling who these Pretenders really are. The only solution is for Mercy to constantly check her mother's email and intercept any of k0r3atruth83's messages. (Thankfully, she has *that* password, too.)

Around this time, Tina focuses on Pretenders again, which means Mercy can't log on as frequently. Her mother spends a lot of time on Genius/Lame/Overrated, and Mercy hopes she doesn't see the contribution made under her name. Mercy visits her dad's place, down the block, to log on to Pretenders. It's easier there: Winston's modem is faster; plus, he's too distracted (watching sports, yelling at customer service on the phone) to realize what she's up to.

Mercy checks Tina's correspondence. In those days, corporate email is lightly used. Things aren't so secure yet. No one has a VPN. Mercy finds a draft of the message that Tina is

composing to her overlords at Corewar, insisting Pretenders is just a bunch of nerds with time to kill. It's not a *business* per se, more a hobby that can't be monetized. A ghost ship, cruising on inertia. It's unclear if there's even an owner to buy it from. She predicts it will collapse in less than a year.

It turns out that someone at Harmony Holdings, Corewar's rival, has *also* been monitoring Pretenders from the inside, under the tag quickedward_kpg. He has filed a completely different report to his bosses. Unlike Tina, he gets it. "Each week generates enough words to fill the Bible—each month, the entire *Encyclopaedia Britannica*," he gushes. "Connections get made between unlikely things." He sees ways to scale.

Forty-eight hours later, Harmony Holdings purchases Pretenders from Tanner Slow. The rickety message board joins a scattering of other acquisitions: a 3D map of Boston, a chain-letter generator, a virus detector called Divinr, a website where users rate the hotness of their dental technicians and exterminators. It looks to be a bad deal: Pretenders loses members by the day, it seems; the undercover dealmaker, quickedward_kpg, has vanished.

Another thing happens before the year is out: Harmony Holdings and Corewar Games merge, as snug as yin and yang.

99. The Promise

What is history? The new company swallows some others, eventually gets eaten by a bigger fish with a name that rhymes with *bloat*. But long before any of that happens, Corewar fires Tina Pang. She tells Mercy don't worry, not unexpected, got some leads, all will be peachy. On Saturday Tina visits the office a final time to empty her desk.

Meanwhile, Mercy helps out at home by clearing Tina's inbox. (Mercy's thankfully neglected by her sitter, a moody Barnard student who's studying for a sociology final.) She clicks open each message, copies and pastes anything that seems

important into a document, then deletes. It takes ages. Whenever she looks up, the sky's a different shade. She sips another Snapple and makes one last push. Wedged in the annals of spam, amid boner pill shilling and lottery scams, is a message marked "Urgent."

There's some tracking text at the top, proving that the sender is in fact the person associated with Pretenders username k0r3atruth83. Mercy prints the email, like her mother would. The message is one line long. She thinks it's a mistake, a hoax. But no.

It's a recruitment letter. A call to join a group she's never heard of. A promise that all will be revealed, a sentence to carry for the rest of her life, one she will bestow on others at some future date, when all the conditions are right.

100.

You are a member of the Korean Provisional Government.

Acknowledgments

THIS TRIPARTITE BOOK IS TRIPLY DEDICATED: to my parents, S.K. and Yonzi, and my sister, Aileen—the original Korean-Buffalonian family unit; to my amazing wife, Sandra, without whose love and support this book would not exist; and to my excellent sons, Duncan and Keeler, who were quite small when I embarked on the Dreams and might well be sporting full-on Grover Cleveland–style mustaches by the time they read these words.

My agent, PJ Mark, grasped what I wanted this novel to be many years and thousands of pages ago; his encouragement, insight, and friendship buoyed me along the way. I'm incredibly lucky to work with Andy Ward, dream editor in every sense. Thanks to Bonnie Thompson, Will Staehle, and Sylvia Plachy; Ian Bonaparte and Marya Spence at Janklow & Nesbit; and the team at Random House, including Craig Adams, Maria Braeckel, Madison Dettlinger, Windy Dorresteyn, Richard Elman, Barbara Fillon, Marni Folkman, Azraf Khan, Ruth Liebmann, Greg Mollica, Carrie Neill, Lara Phan, Elizabeth Rendfleisch, Rachel Rokicki, and Kaeli Subberwal.

I'm grateful to James Browning, Andrew Eisenman, and Gillian Linden for their early Dream-reading; to Lucas Adams, logo wiz, John Moran, fellow cinéfreak, Stu Horvath, Galactic Legions playtester, and S.K. Park, in-house calligrapher and translator (and dad). Thank you to Eve Bowen, Frances Cha, Eugene Cho, the late Frances Cohen, Courtney Dodson, Noah Eaker, Dave Eggers, Sarah Fan, Amanda Gersh,

Claudia Herr, Cathy Park Hong, Hua Hsu, Carmen Johnson, Heidi Julavits, the late Gari Ledyard, the Lees, the other Lees, Jonathan Lethem, Dennis Lim, Ed Lin, Ling Ma, Elizabeth McKenzie, Miwa Messer, Michael Miller, Richard Neff, Mark Nowak, Parks and Kwons, Steph Perry, Richard Polt, Namwali Serpell, Mike Speiser, Levi Stahl, David Suisman, *The Believer,* Jessica Winter, Al Woodworth, Jane Yeh, and Charles Yu. Lastly, I salute Paul La Farge (1970–2023), *il miglior fabbro,* and Maureen Howard (1930–2022), who believed in me.

Sources

Facts and inspiration were drawn from many books and other media; I placed some of their details (and occasionally their creators) into the Dreams, often bending them firmly or further into fiction along the way. Particularly stimulating were Reginald Thompson's *Cry Korea,* Syngman Rhee's *Japan Inside Out,* John Lofland's *Doomsday Cult,* Punch Imlach's *Heaven and Hell in the NHL* (with Scott Young), the films *Friday the 13th, Inchon,* and *Prisoner of War,* and episodes of the TV series *Danger, Studio One,* and *M*A*S*H.* Other works include the writings of Yi Sang (translated by Myong-Hee Kim, Jack Jung, Ahn Jung-hyo, and James B. Lee); Younghill Kang's novels *The Grass Roof* and *East Goes West,* starring the irrepressible Chungpa Han; Yi Kwang-su's *The Soil* (translated by Hwang Sun-ae and Horace Jeffrey Hodges) and *Kashil & Best Essays* (translated by Chung-Nan Lee Kim); Channing Liem's *Philip Jaisohn,* N. H. Osia's *Hansu's Journey,* Robert T. Oliver's *Syngman Rhee: The Man Behind the Myth,* Dae-Sook Suh's *Kim Il Sung: The North Korean Leader,* and *The Writings of Henry Cu Kim* (edited by Suh); Don Oberdorfer's *The Two Koreas,* Keith Pratt's *Everlasting Flower,* Sheila Miyoshi Jager's *Brothers at War,* David Halberstam's *The Coldest Winter,* Jennie Ethell Chancey and William R. Forstchen's *Hot Shots: An Oral History of the Air Force Combat Pilots of the Korean War,* and Phil Tinline's documentary *Every Man Has His Breaking Point;* Bruce Cumings's *North Korea: Another Country* and *The Origins of the Korean War,* I. F. Stone's *The Hidden History of the*

Korean War, and Bradley K. Martin's *Under the Loving Care of the Fatherly Leader;* the online archives of *The New York Times* and other publications; Emma Goldman's *Living My Life,* Margaret Leech's *In the Days of McKinley,* and Richard C. Brown and Bob Watson's *Buffalo: Lake City in Niagara Land;* Richard E. Kim's *The Martyred;* the work of Theresa Hak Kyung Cha; Seymour M. Hersh's *The Target Is Destroyed,* David Pearson's *KAL 007: The Cover-up,* Michel Brun's *Incident at Sakhalin;* and Richard F. Haines's *Advanced Aerial Devices Reported During the Korean War.* David Bowman's posthumous novel, *Big Bang,* showed me a way forward at a crucial point.

Photo Credits

About the Author

ED PARK is the author of the novel *Personal Days* (2008), a finalist for the PEN/Hemingway Award. He is a founding editor of *The Believer*, and his writing appears in *The New Yorker, The New York Review of Books, Bookforum, Harper's Magazine, The Atlantic,* and elsewhere. Born in Buffalo, he lives in Manhattan with his family.